THE WRONG OUTFIT

Al Gregg

authorHOUSE®

AuthorHouse™ UK Ltd.
500 Avebury Boulevard
Central Milton Keynes, MK9 2BE
www.authorhouse.co.uk
Phone: 08001974150

First published by AuthorHouse   8/20/2010

ISBN: 978-1-4520-0152-4 (sc)
ISBN: 978-1-4520-0153-1 (hc)

Front Cover - Gregg/Allen

This book is printed on acid-free paper.

FORWARD

There's something about innocence which declines explanation. Its all pervading, sub-conscious slipstream of utilitarian beauty, defies both contingency and contamination. Not to mention time. The latter of which, to varying degrees, we are all running out of.

As such, the trajectory of innocence remains a life sentence without bars. A miraculous twist of fate, as equally potent when you're nine, as when you're forty-nine, or indeed, should you live to be a hundred and nine.

Whether it's keeping your balance on a bicycle for the first time, partaking in your first football match, kissing your first partner, going bonkers at your first gig, or simply feeling like emotional ravioli at someone else's wedding. They all leave their inadvertent/indelible mark(s), which, from time to time, sting with quintessential exuberance.

The manifestation of which is pure joy - by way of ruthless, unquestionable sincerity.

The French poet Charles Peguy once said: "It is innocence that is full and experience that is empty. It is innocence that wins and experience that loses." *The Wrong Outfit* does very little to suggest otherwise. All rampant credulity and wishful thinking, the words contained herein are a (royal blue) celebration of love and life and all things in-between. They know not the cynicism of power and politics; nor the petulance of an increasingly anesthetized (broken) Britain. Instead, they rather sparkle with lust and longing.

And what could be better?

Like the book's protagonist, Adam, I too was (and remain) hopelessly romantic, curious and in love with life. On first hearing the cathartic and amphetamine fueled, seismic surge of such musical/social innocence as 'Do Anything You Wanna Do' by Eddie & The Hot Rods or 'Sheena Is A Punk Rocker' by The Ramones or 'Teenage Kicks' by The Undertones, I too understood that life wasn't utterly dependent upon a stanza of social stasis. Life was about embracing the here and now. Still is.

Regardless of outcome. Regardless of opposition. Regardless of outfit.

David Marx

Brighton 2009

1

KICK OFF

Find yourself a worn paperback A to Z street atlas of London. Open it up at page 75 and locate square reference 7K, which you should find located at the bottom right hand corner of the page. Then, take a good look at the most prominent feature within the square. Yes, quite correct. Stamford Bridge. The home of Chelsea Football Club, right there at the top of the square, just outside the Royal Borough of Kensington and Chelsea, in the London Borough of Hammersmith and Fulham, SW6.

Then if you turn to the next page 76 and shift up one square to reference 6A, you will find yourself looking at the exact location where Adam Nedman was born in the mid 60's, the West London hospital also just a stone's throw from the King's Road running diagonally up the same page. Born so close to Stamford Bridge that only the Brompton Cemetery, an overground railway line and the Fulham Road lie between.

Perhaps because of the proximity of this location, whenever asked where he was born, Adam would always want to say; 'Outside the Bovril Gate entrance to the Shed End', or perhaps, 'Between the scoreboard and the rubble in the North Stand', or even, 'Along the King's Road, not far from the World's End'.

Sometimes he would grin inanely and say 'Chelsea', but that seemed unrealistic and silly to be born in a place that to a kid was best known as a football team. At other times he would say 'Fulham', because that was really near to Chelsea, in fact it seemed almost right within it, but Fulham identified him with those close footballing neighbours at Craven Cottage, so as youngsters do, he would try even more precision; 'Fulham Broadway!' He would reply triumphantly, thinking that he had finally solved the problem. (Fulham Broadway being the nearest Tube station to Chelsea's ground – return to page 75 again and you'll find it on the right hand edge of square 7J).

Adam would try and be really earnest about it and almost like a character from a famous Oscar Wilde play, who was first discovered inside a handbag in the cloakroom at Victoria Station, Adam felt as if he might actually have been born at Fulham Broadway Station with a day return ticket in his pocket. (Turn to the back cover of the A to Z and you'll find on the Tube map that Fulham Broadway is located on the Underground between West Brompton and Parsons Green on the District Line, which for those of you fortunate enough to be unfamiliar with London Transport, is usually coloured green).

FIRST STEPS

Adam's early history is quite hazy, although by the age of one he already had great potential as a dribbler, even though he didn't quite know it. He was also pretty useful at playing with his food and flicking it around instead of swallowing it, and all the other habitual activities were fairly normal.

His parents lived in Roehampton, South West London. The family home was a post war classic suburban semi-detached. Adam was never too sure at the time what his father did exactly, he could have been a bus conductor, an astronaut or a brain surgeon for all it mattered, as it seemed sometimes that even Santa Claus paid a more regular visit to the household. After finishing his National Service, Adam's dad had plodded the beat, but was now a civil servant and 'something in the city', whatever that was, and as a result was a habitual user of public transport. Adam's mother meanwhile had once worked part-time as a hairdresser, but had long since given that up to look after the children, of which there were four, three boys and a girl, Adam being the youngest.

What was apparent to Adam by the age of about three was an unusual manifestation taking place in the house. His two older brothers and even his sister enjoyed kicking a round plastic object around the house, and sometimes inside it. They even had a name which they shouted out at the top of their voices; 'Alton United! Alton United!' Alton was the name of the local estate near where Adam lived, and both his brothers were in the local team. He heard these unusual words repeated many a time, usually accompanied by wild emotion and cackling. This was followed by talk of 'Bobby Moore', 'Bobby Charlton', 'Geoff Hurst' and 'We won the World Cup!' in exalted tones. What was this strange disorder? Was it what Adam would soon find himself taking part in? Once he was a little more steady on his feet. It seemed as if it was something that had to be tried out. Perhaps when he became bigger and stronger - and judging by the amount of food that he had put away already that wouldn't be long.

And it wasn't. Adam had certainly taken to heart his mother's advice to eat all his greens and with lots of older siblings, he had learned to chew at a prodigious rate. His oldest brother Alan was usually the first to finish at meal times, in about five seconds, soon followed by the younger, John, so it was always a struggle for Adam to obtain a place in the queue for a second helping. But manage it he did.

Not only did he obtain seconds but he also built up a host of culinary delights if he felt a little peckish between meals. He would raid the kitchen larder, when no one was around and even though he had to stand on a chair to get to the grub he was never deterred. Chocolate digestive biscuits he ravaged like the plague and anything with the least hint of sugar. The problem was that he hadn't any taste, so he would eat virtually anything: Tomato Ketchup sandwiches with a layer of 'Hundreds and Thousands'; Rice Crispies followed by pickled onions. There was certainly hell to pay later on, once semi digestion had taken place.

Adam particularly enjoyed breakfast cereals. Sugar Puffs he consumed until he was almost physically sick. He loved trying to collect all the special offers on the different cereal boxes, so if that would mean eating a disgusting treacly pulp to obtain a replica plastic flagship 'Mary Rose' or a Batman outfit, then wolf it he would.

Alongside his eating skills he was pretty handy at humming. If it wasn't the odd nursery rhyme picked up from friends, it would be a song his brothers both liked, and one day it would be a Chelsea tune called 'Blue is the Colour' which both of his brothers would sing almost religiously. It would become a valuable ditty and Adam was proud of his melodic ability, repeating it many a time down the years. It had a catchy melody and fine lyrics, even if the Chelsea side that sang it on 'Top of the Pops' in the early 70's had distinctly suspect haircuts. Adam used to hum and sing it over and over again to his parent's dismay. The song had three verses, but Adam found the first one quite sufficient.

After its release, each morning come rain or shine, on his way to school, he would whistle the tune as he went along. When asked what he would like to be when he grew up, he would say, 'Play number nine for Chelsea!' or 'Be a Chelsea Ball Boy!' or 'Be the Chelsea Groundsman!' Adam's friends usually wanted to be Firemen, Policemen, Doctors or Nurses.

What was clear was that he was already a confirmed Chelsea fan. His choice had a lot to do with being born very near the ground and his two brother's persuasive natures, but Chelsea also seemed to be an exciting team and were winning things. Anyway, it was a Chelsea household, so God forbid that Adam would decide to follow The Gunners, Spurs, or the Happy Hammers.

IT'S A KNOCKOUT

Apart from kicking a ball around, Adam used to spend quite a lot of time with his sister, Marie, when he was about six. She was the nearest to him in age and wasn't as tall or imposing as his brothers were, so he could compete on a more level playing field. They both enjoyed watching 'It's a Knockout', a frivolous television game show. They sang the theme tune, 'Jeux sans Frontieres' together at the top of their voices and sometimes they became so excited that Adam's sister would suddenly hurl him over the sofa or knock him off his feet. After watching the programme's closing credits, they would always plan to re-enact what they had seen, in their back garden the following day.

They would find a couple of buckets, a wheelbarrow, some chairs, string (ideal for the finishing tape), bamboo sticks for making hurdles and various bits and pieces and odds and ends. They managed to construct a most unusual track. The Royal Green Berets would have found some of the obstacles a challenge. The penultimate obstacle would usually be the wheelbarrow which they would have to manoeuvre along some planks that sat on a few household bricks. Other tricky obstacles for Adam were the buckets which had to be jumped over and the bamboo sticks that lay across two chairs for them to hurdle. These two obstacles he found particularly difficult to negotiate as he had rather plump, stumpy legs at the time and his school shorts allowed little dexterity. As a result, he spent a lot of his time coming second, which afforded his sister many opportunities to practice her victory laps around the garden. While she celebrated, Adam was busy picking himself up off the ground or tucking his shirt in.

'It's a Knockout' it most certainly was, especially when one afternoon Adam gave it that little extra bit of effort on the third lap, with his sister in his sights and he forgot to jump over the bucket. Instead, he caught his leg in the bucket's handle and flipped himself up into the air to land with his front teeth right on the edge of the wheelbarrow. Adam had never yet been to the dentist for anything major, so he obviously thought it was about time that he did. The dentist wasn't able to do much for him though. He had a large gap where his front incisors used to sit.

BIRTHDAY PRESENT

On his seventh birthday, Adam received a brilliant present. A bow and arrow. The arrows had little red suckers on the end that if you licked before firing would stick to anything. Adam always wanted to try them out on the next door neighbour's bald head, but unfortunately was never allowed the opportunity. Alongside the arrows it had little round coloured targets which could be stuck to objects to use for shooting practice: the fridge door; the pet dog; the television set and so on.

Adam was becoming a pretty accomplished shot and looked particularly convincing when he wore the other half of his present - bright Red Indian head gear. He would roam the garden at the weekends covered in feathers trying to shoot anything that wasn't nailed down. He would warble, yelp and hiss and make pretty much any sound that was appropriate. He thought his sister was intrigued. Adam had decided that 'It's a Knockout' wasn't for him anymore, mainly due to the annoying fact that he was always coming second and he now wanted to have more of a quiet life roaming the prairie searching for prey. He also wanted his missing teeth to grow back as fast as possible. However, his sister, as always, just had to muscle in on the act, so it was decided that they take turns in chasing each other around the place (although a major concession allowed Adam to keep the headgear). One of them would be the hunter with the bow and arrow, while the other would be the prey. Adam found it great fun, and the one that had the bow and arrow felt invincible and yet each of them knew that soon they would be hunted down when it was time to swap around. The rules were like football's Three and In, which Adam played a lot of at school. Three successful 'hits' and then you swapped around.

One day their game became perhaps a little too frenzied. Adam had been denying categorically that he had been hit, even though it was obvious he had been repeatedly miscounting palpable contacts. Marie, despite being a particularly bad shot, became infuriated because winning was something she wanted desperately to be very good at. The next thing that Adam knew, the sucker on the end was off the arrow and his sister had fired it straight at him. He happened to be in the middle of a very loud Sioux Indian war cry, when suddenly he was finding it difficult not to swallow an arrow. On its journey, the arrow managed to proceed through Adam's bottom lip and right into his tongue, and he knew immediately that his carefree days of hunting buffalo were numbered.

Adam then behaved uncharacteristically. He went straight and told his mum. His mouth bleeding profusely;

'She took the sucker off, mum!'

'Sucker?'

'She took it off!'

'Who did?'

'My sister!'

'She did what?'

'She took it off!'

'Took what off?'

'The sucker!'

'Oh, dear....'

'She did! She took it off and fired it right at me!'

Before Adam knew it, he was marched once more off to hospital, his sister sniggering in the background like the dog Mutley from the popular cartoon TV series 'Wacky Races'.

HOBBIES

Despite Adam's injuries he always had the right mental attitude to bounce straight back. It helped a lot that for at least a year, Adam believed that he was Paul Metcalfe, otherwise known as 'Captain Scarlet'. Adam already knew a great tune when he heard one and the theme music to Gerry Anderson's children's television series was memorable. So were the lyrics that stated the fact that you could crash him, burn him, smash him, but he would always return, to live again.

'Fantastic!' Adam thought. 'That's clever. He's indestructible. He can cheat death'.

Captain Scarlet would have made a very tough adversary for Adam's sister and would hardly have even flinched at the dentist. His scarlet kit was the only disappointment, since he looked rather like he might be a 'Koppite' and Liverpool supporter. Adam always used to wait for Captain Blue to turn up, being in the nearest thing to Chelsea colours, but he would usually get 'Mysteroned' or blown up after saying only one or two lines, so Captain Scarlet it had to be.

Alongside Spectrum, and the Mysterons, Adam was obsessed with Virgil Tracy and International Rescue from that other Gerry Anderson puppet production, 'Thunderbirds'. Adam really enjoyed booing at the bald headed baddie 'The Hood', because he was always up to mischief and looked like one of Adam's less favourite teachers at primary school. He would cheer on Parker - Lady Penelope's cockney chauffeur - and could often be heard saying 'Yesh, Mee Lady!' whenever the dapper flunky appeared and again he loved the exciting theme tune and the rousing start to the programme: The Tracy swimming pool moving apart to make way for the take off of the Thunderbird One rocket and the parting of the palm trees to allow the trundling green Thunderbird Two transporter to lift off dramatically, were enjoyed with relish. Adam also used to accompany the introduction of the programme with the loud countdown 'Five, Four, Three, Two, One!' and made wild explosive noises as the music came to a crescendo and all the buildings exploded.

Adam was fortunate to possess a large green plastic toy Thunderbird Two, that a miniature Virgil Tracy reliably piloted, and some accessories, like the different numbered green pods, one of them containing the bright yellow underwater Thunderbird Four inside it, which he played regularly with at bath time. Sometimes, when he was able to go round his best friend Brian's home, situated at the top of a high rise block, right next to school, they would travel up and down in the flat's creaking, metallic lift, imagining that they too were being transported on another dangerous International Rescue mission.

The other children's TV series Adam relished were 'Stingray', probably because he was besotted with the conversationally challenged mermaid, Aqua Maria, and also 'Joe 90', although by then the stories were becoming a bit stale or too farfetched and the toys that accompanied the series were more and more feeble - Joe 90's suitcase with a secret compartment and disguise kit, for a start.

The winner every time had to be the toy doll Action Man. He was a prized possession in Adam's satchel, and he would swap accessories regularly with his friends at school:

'An Action Man Scuba diving kit complete with shark, for a Special Boat Service rubber dinghy with outboard motor!'

That sounded like a steal. Adam used to play with his Action Man all the time and he was a regular at the dinner table. He quickly understood why his Action Man had a scar on his cheek - he had probably been knocked about by Adam's sister. Adam thought the doll's cropped hair looked cool, and sometimes when he pulled a tiny cord at the back, Action Man would speak - in 'command mode' - although he would usually splutter if he was under water.

Action Man could also be just as fashion conscious as a Cindy doll. In fact he was a bit of a natty dresser. Adam used to dress his Action Man up as a Buckingham Palace Guardsman and then sometimes as a Cricketer at Lords. Sometimes he would become bored and transform his loyal recruit into a hybrid of various kits: A cricket playing, amphibious commando, or a flippered, Cuirassier helmeted policeman.

The best thing about Action Man was his irrepressible valour. He would always be willing to go that extra mile for another medal for gallantry, and Adam used to really test him. Once, Adam made a small parachute out of bits of old sheet and string and attached it to his Action Man. The doll had no objections - his vocal cord had broken. Adam then ignited the parachute and chucked him out of his bedroom window. The result was superb. Action Man managed to fall like a dying swan. When he hit the ground with a crunch, the parachute was already engulfed in flames (Adam had thought up a brilliant ploy of soaking the parachute in white spirit, left over from his Airfix model making exploits).

Sometimes, Adam did feel sorry for Action Man. The odds were always stacked against him, but then again, weren't they always in battle. Unfortunately, Action Man was never the same again. His hair was badly singed and one arm was now molten plastic.

One of Adam's favourite other hobbies throughout this time was model making. He loved plastic Airfix kits. He was so obsessive about them that he would do his best to even paint the interiors of the planes and then stick them together. He would spend hours trying to outline the dials in the cockpit and more time would be willingly cashed in, securing tiny German black crosses to the side of a trusty Spitfire.

Adam also enjoyed trying to recreate the feel and ambience of the First World War trenches, which he had seen in many war films and comics. He was also greatly influenced by his Grandad, who although he never knew him, had played his own gallant part, venturing up in a hot air balloon unarmed, to take photographs and spy on the German trenches while the Red Baron tried repeatedly but in vain to shoot him down. For his heroic efforts Adam's Grandad was awarded the French 'Crois De Guerre' with palm and DSO medals and this piece of history was relayed to Adam through the family grapevine.

To create the trenches, Adam collected plenty of mud from the bottom of the garden and placed it on a very large piece of cardboard, and then he positioned his tiny plastic soldiers around it. Sometimes the mud might include a little twig which he would stand up on the board to represent the ravaged landscape. The damp mud was very convincing at first, and it was easy to mould a complex network of trench formations and shell craters, despite the enemy being only a few feet away.

The problem was that after a couple of days the mud became as solid as a rock and if Adam had buried any troops in the thick of it, due to a heavy bombardment, they were now most definitely missing in action. Many in fact would never return, due in part to Adam's mum who would clean his bedroom out on an unfortunately regular basis.

Mud from the garden was optimum for trench warfare, as was long grass for a jungle campaign. Washing powder was terrific for any conflict in a freezing climate, like 'Stalingrad'. Sand taken from a children's playground was totally convincing for the 'Desert Rats'.

'War gaming' was a big hobby of Adam's both at primary school and at home. The former being usually the re-enactment of World War Two both inside and outside the classroom to the teachers consternation and the latter a more considered approach to warfare with his diligently collected miniature toy soldiers.

Any military sphere of operations could be re-enacted, within reason, both against a friend, if one had been allowed round for tea, or alone. Alone was usually more fun because despite horrific casualties, Adam would be assured of ending up on the winning side.

Even though Adam had scant geographical and technical awareness at this stage he would always try to make the war games as believable as possible. So he would try to find out if the trajectory of a pee shooter was equivalent to that of a Napoleonic cannon or a Roman catapult, for example.

1815 and the battle of Waterloo was always popular, with its model farmhouses, highly colourful armies and outrageous uniforms. Boadicea and her loyal hordes trying to defeat the Roman Empire was another top skirmish and good old 'Tommy' versus the 'Jerry' (both World Wars) was always reliably exciting.

If Adam got bored, which was more than likely, he would usually mix up the opposing armies making them totally ridiculous: Colonel Custer at the Battle of Little Bighorn ably assisted by U.S. Marines: 19th century French Foreign Legionnaire's finding themselves surrounded by Cowboys and a German Panzer Division.

Rules were scant, but a role of a dice usually decided the body count. By the end, however, the bloodletting was usually hard to contain and kicking the soldiers over was usually the finale; always referred to as a large bomb exploding or the sudden invention of nuclear war.

If Adam had heard of any of the characters in the battles, for example

Napoleon or Sitting Bull, he would try and be that character or at least represent him by a silly accent, outfit or gait. Yes, play acting was becoming an important social skill, alongside the measured depiction of the adult world.

MR PAINTER'S PLANK

As well as being a bit of a dab hand in the garden, Adam's dad was always keen on bonfires. Every weekend if he was at home he would find something to burn. Like most kids, Adam used to enjoy the ritual too. I suppose they were both confirmed pyromaniacs, although they could never quite admit it to each other. Nothing was too good for a burning. The Sunday newspapers would usually be torched before anybody had even had a chance to glance at them. Adam's father couldn't get out of the house fast enough sometimes to ignite rubbish. He would at times be seen down the garden, in his dressing gown because of his all consuming desire to kindle the weeks refuse.

Adam would stand transfixed watching the flames eat up all in their path. In private, he enjoyed striking matches and tried to hold one as long as humanly possible. He would try to burn one end down and then turn it quickly round and try and hold the other end already burned and watch as the flame engulfed the rest of the match. Most of the time he would scorch a finger or two but it was well worth it.

Once, Adam's parents decided to have some major decorating done around the house. The decorator had brought his favourite wooden plank which he placed across two trestles as his work bench, and he could stand on it whilst wallpapering and painting. After about two days the painter was getting on swimmingly with everybody. He had copious cups of tea taken up to him, with lots of sugar and he whistled very tunefully whilst digesting his biscuits. Adam was in awe of him, especially when the man started to wallpaper his own bedroom. It all looked so fidgety, yet the decorator was always patient and in good cheer. Adam called him, 'Mr Painter', which he thought was really original. When he returned from school, Adam would venture straight upstairs to his room to see how the decorator was getting on.

'Hello, Mr Painter', Adam would say, and the man would be there teetering precariously on his beloved plank wallpapering away.

'Hello there....' Mr Painter would reply.

At the weekend Adam was really bored. For some reason, his brothers were out and only his sister remained to look after him. However, she was preoccupied in her bedroom, busily brushing her hair and playing her Sandie Shaw records. It was a Sunday. The parents had gone out for the afternoon to see friends:

'What to do?' Adam thought. 'I know....why don't I build a really big bonfire, just like Dad? He'll be well pleased with me when he returns and sees that I've burnt all the litter and Sunday papers. I'd be giving him an afternoon off'.

So, off he trotted to search for good igniting material. It was a nice sunny day, so he knew that starting a fire would be easy, and he had his trusty box of matches from his satchel. He walked around the side of the house and rummaged in the bins. So did the pet dog, inquisitively. There were a few pieces of old cardboard and cornflakes packets. 'Perfect', he thought. Adam collected them up and carried them down to the bottom of the garden. It took quite a few trips. There was still a lot of scorched wood and charcoal where a hollowed out tree stump had burnt away, so he put everything inside it and constructed a pyramid shaped bonfire. Eventually, he lit some paper at the bottom and the result was better than expected, the flames soon became so hot that he was in danger of singeing all his hair off.

After a while, the fire began to subside. Adam blew on it, but it was no use. He stared at the flames, but it was definitely petering out. So he decided to have another look for combustible materials. He trotted off again and searched and searched, but there was nothing left. All the rubbish had been burnt, even all the newspapers. Suddenly, he turned round and there, right in front of him was Mr Painter's plank propped up against the wall next to the trestles. He surveyed it;

'I bet that'll look good on fire. It's huge! Besides it's only wood - he's probably got another one'.

The plank turned out to be very heavy, being about six foot long, but Adam grabbed one end and began to drag it with all his little mite down the garden to the bonfire. Every so often the pet dog would try and bite the other end or grab it with his paws pulling the plank back. Perhaps he knew something that Adam didn't ;

'Don't be silly!' Adam said to Sam. He was after all only a dog.

It took Adam a long time and much exertion, but he finally managed to place the plank over the dying embers. He blew underneath it and fanned the flames. Nothing was happening;

'I know, I'll go and fetch that can of liquid that makes the fire bigger'.

So once more, he ran off and after a little detective work, found the half empty, smelly, damp container in its supposedly secret hiding place in the rickety garden shed. A cunning ploy by his dad, placed as it was out of sight and out of mind, but Adam had spied on him one afternoon when he least expected it and he had an accurate idea of where the dragon fluid lay. It lay hidden behind some wood and garden tools. After slowly lifting it out, back he went triumphantly to the site and poured what was left of the paraffin onto the plank and, 'Whoosh!' The result was fantastic. It went up like a firecracker. Right in the middle. Sam started barking and dancing around it as if the plank had suddenly come to life. The flames took to the wood so proficiently that they licked and crackled straight up to a good height, a lot taller even than Adam. It wasn't long before the plank began to blacken in the centre as the fire ate into it. Then he thought;

'What about the wooden stands?'

Before you could say 'The Roadrunner', he had sped off, but just as he reached the trestles, hurtling out of control, he heard the distant sound of a van pulling up. He peered through the fence at the side of the house and saw Mr Painter striding up to the front door. He panicked.

'What do I do if he wants his plank?' Adam thought for a moment, 'I s'pose I better not answer the door'.

So he didn't. And anyway, whenever he had answered the door before he always felt that he had made a fool of himself by doing or saying the wrong thing. On one occasion when a next door neighbour asked Adam whether his mother was about, he replied:

'No, my wife's not in at the moment!'

Adam didn't know quite why he had said it. He very rarely did. Especially at that age. I don't think the friendly neighbour quite knew either. He just grinned and muttered, 'Well if you could let your wife know that I called', and off he went on his way. So, answer the door? Not a chance. I mean you could just picture it:

Adam: (Slowly opening door) Yes...?

Mr P: (surprised) Hello. Are your mum and dad in?

Adam: No....

Mr P: (urgently) Well, d'you know when they'll be back?

Adam: (shaking his head) No....they've gone away..

Mr P: I see - 'cos it's about my plank....

Adam: Yes....

Mr P: I'll be needing it.

Adam: Well....I'm afraid it's on fire now.

Mr P: (After a pause) ON FIRE?!'

Adam: Yes....on fire.

You see? 'Oh, no, but what about my sister?' Adam reasoned, quickly crashing back to earth. 'Let's hope she's still listening to her records'.

Mr Painter rang the door bell more than once in his haste, but Adam just crouched as still as possible, managing also to silence Sam who was doing his best to give him away and prayed for Mr Painter to return to his van. Eventually he did, and as he turned the key and the van spluttered into life Adam suddenly thought about self preservation, so he immediately rushed back up the garden and surveyed Mr Painter's rapidly deteriorating plank. Unfortunately, he was a bit too late, because the plank was now a complete right off. Adam already knew about weight ratios in those days. If Mr Painter was going to stand on the plank when he was at work, it was definitely not going to support him long enough for him to slurp his tea or dunk his biscuits.

Adam quickly stamped out the rest of the flames, which luckily had gone down while he was away and waited for the plank to cool down, it's once solid wooden appearance transformed. In the middle, it now resembled a charred stick. At least it was easier to drag back down the garden. Although this still took a lot of effort.

Just as Adam returned the plank to its rightful place next to the trestles, he heard his parents arrive back. Panic gripped him once more and he noticed himself covered in dirt, charcoal and smelling of smoke. He raced indoors and up to his room, just as they entered.

'Pheuuww. That was lucky!' Adam thought.

He quickly changed his clothes and had a quiet wash. Later in the evening, just before Adam was off to bed, his dad announced;

'Who's been having a bonfire?'

His father looked knowingly at him as Adam just shrugged his shoulders and looked at the ceiling.

The next day Adam returned from school as slowly as possible; 'Mr Painter's bound to know about the plank', he pondered. 'What am I going to do?' He sheepishly entered the house, knowing that soon the axe would fall.

His parents were furious. So was Mr Painter. Adam was made to apologise face to face. While all about was recrimination, Adam thought to himself, 'What's all the fuss?' He felt that he had only been doing his best to be helpful. He had just got a little bit carried away.

As Mr Painter was knocking off work, Adam went reluctantly up to his room to see him. The decorating job had been completed and he was busily clearing up for the final time, his face still red with rage. Adam even thought that Mr Painter might hit him. He certainly seemed to want to, but his anger was enough. As Adam retreated, the decorator towered over him.

'Sorry....'

As Mr Painter stared down, nostrils flaring, Adam tried to avoid his gaze.

'Do you know what you've done? Do you?!'

'Yes, I'm sorry'.

'Your parents have offered to pay for the damage. So you're lucky this time.

Make sure you never do it again'.

Do it again? How could he? Adam was certain he would never again see a plank quite like it, and he was right. Because of its blackened twig-like centre, Mr Painter eventually sawed the plank in half. 'What a shame', Adam reckoned shaking his head.

As you can imagine, it wasn't long before punishment came from Adam's parents and he knew that it was unavoidable. He received a severe telling off, a serious debit on his weekly pocket money and a grounding for the next ten years.

BLUES HISTORY

Because Adam was hearing so much about Chelsea, all around the house, it's probably wise at this stage to give a brief potted history of Chelsea Football Club, as a background to his story.

The Club was born on April 20th, 1905. Their founder, Mr H.A (Gus) Mears, had previously bought Stamford Bridge in order to make it the country's finest stadium. He formed his new club, calling it, 'Chelsea', and signed a squad of experienced players, with such legendary names as Willie Foulke, Chelsea's captain and goalkeeper, who at 31 years, 6 foot 2 inches and 22 and a half stone certainly filled it. His shorts were legendary too, being five sizes bigger than anyone else's.

Chelsea began life in the second division, but had high hopes. A new acquisition, George (Gatling Gun) Hilsdon, helped them on their way and they soon gained promotion to the first Division. There they stayed temporarily until relegation. This was to be the story for the next few years: A celebrated team, huge crowds and not so much as a piece of cheese in the trophy cabinet (Chelsea lost to Sheffield United 0-3 at Old Trafford in the FA cup Final of 1914 -15).

So celebrated in fact had Chelsea become, that their first enduring links with show business began. George Robey, was a renowned Music Hall star and actor at the time. Chelsea signed him as an amateur. He even led the team out at Stamford Bridge in a benefit match. Throughout his career, George Robey was known as 'The Prime Minister of Mirth', and was later knighted for his pains. He could not have picked a football club with more affinity to his stage persona, with his oddly grand manner and paternal way with an audience, whether it be with a broken umbrella, half a walking stick or an absurd hat.

Music Hall might also have had a major effect on the early Chelsea supporters. Another star of the day, Marie Lloyd sang a popular tune called 'My Old Man Said Follow The Van', which was amongst the repertoire sung by many supporters up to the 1980's: 'My old man said be a Chelsea fan, and don't dilly-dally on the way'.

In the following years, Chelsea continued to buy the best. The legendary striker, Hughie Gallacher, all five foot five of him, cost £10,000's. They had a record nine English, Scottish and Irish internationals on their books. They also recorded their highest domestic attendance at Stamford Bridge to date when 73,334 saw them play Arsenal in 1930-31.

Despite having brilliant individualists, extracting consistent perform-ances from them remained unsolved. Manager Les Knighton said,

'I have never handled a more intriguing side than Chelsea'.

Chelsea continued to flirt with the First Division but could never marry it, until after the Second World War, when both Tommy Lawton and Roy Bentley were acquired. The 1950-51 season saw the most remarkable survival act by Chelsea to escape relegation in the history of the Football League, escaping by .044 of a goal.

Ted Drake then became manager and all the previous scarcity of success was to change. Chelsea's image as a foil for Music Hall gags and repetitive japes about their nickname 'Pensioners' (Due to the Clubs hospitality to the war veterans at Chelsea hospital) had not helped to win them trophies. Drake tried to change all that, constructing a well organised team (Drake's Ducklings) with players from lower divisions. As a result, Chelsea finally became League Champions in their Golden Jubilee year, 1955. However, there was a price to pay, as many of the players were now quite old and regrettably had to be replaced with younger blood. This was not too much of a problem though, because the youth policy at the club had been thriving: Both the reserves and the junior teams won their own respective divisions when the first team won the League Championship. The results were almost immediate, with Jimmy Greaves quickly establishing himself as one of England's greatest ever strikers. He also scored a new club record of 41 League goals in the 1960-61 Season. Having achieved 100 goals before the age of 21, he then departed for Italy. Relegation soon followed him, even though Chelsea had managed 25 consecutive years in the top flight.

Tommy Docherty, known as 'The Doc' became the new manager and fresh hope sprang eternal. A youthful swagger graced the team and under his auspicious leadership, a team of mercurial winners evolved. In 1964-65, Chelsea won the League Cup against Leicester City over two legs, and over one million spectators watched the likes of Peter Osgood and Bobby Tambling, over the season.

In 1966-67 Chelsea lost to Tottenham Hotspur 1-2 in the F.A. 'Cockney Cup' Final, Jimmy Greaves unfortunately turning out for the triumphant Lillywhites. After six promising years Docherty resigned and Dave Sexton, took over the baton. In the 1969-70 season, Chelsea finished third in Division One. They won the FA Cup Final, beating the mighty Leeds 2-1 after extra time at Old Trafford in a replay (the first of its kind) following a hard fought 2-2 draw at Wembley. David Webb scored the winner off his cheek. In fact, Webb turned out to be a very handy player. He could play in defence, midfield, would have a go at being a striker and was even seen in goal. Webb's vital FA Cup match winner had been created by a colossal Ian Hutchinson throw-in. His throw was considered the longest in the Football League.

The following year, Chelsea, reached the final of the European Cup Winners Cup and defeated Real Madrid, in another dramatic replay 2-1, two days after drawing 1-1. Clearly, winning would always be a titanic struggle for Chelsea and when eventually achieved, more often than not it would usually be in a most unusual fashion. The Blues were also without doubt accomplished 'never say die' replay merchants.

HOME LIFE

From the age of about seven, Adam became more and more aware of the strong influence that his brothers were having on him. When the Beatles had brought out their first few singles, his two older brothers had stood regularly, tennis rackets in hand strumming away to 'Can't Buy Me Love' or 'Please, Please, Me'. Yes, even the Beatles in the early days could be controversial. Adam's parents were not too keen on the suggestive nature of a few of the lyrics, rather as middle America had been about Elvis Presley's shaking hips. Even 'I Wanna Hold Your Hand' for example, was too much for some sensitive pallets and any outward signs of the disease called rock'n'roll, like dancing badly or wailing in the bath were not welcome or encouraged (although Adam's dad loved a good sing-song in the tub).

It was no surprise when Adam's brothers began to combat their parent's lack of credibility and rebel against all that had gone before, for rebellion's sake. They proceeded to grow their hair as long as possible, so long in fact that they looked completely ridiculous. It was like having two adopted Yeti's from 'Dr Who' in the family. Adam's oldest brother Alan, went for the hipsters, afghan coat and Jim Morrison beads, while his other brother, John, went for the tie-dye shirts, outrageous flares and crusty sandals. They even formed a motley band for a time, with a weird unpronounceable psychedelic name like, 'Intergalactic Starfish', or something similar, and Adam could hear their stomach churning renditions of 'Burt Weedon's Classic Guitar Tunes'; 'How To Play The Bass Guitar Completely Out Of Time In Easy To Follow Steps' and 'Singing Like A Cat That's Being Castrated'. But despite the youthful lack of proficiency, they seemed to enjoy themselves, especially as a line of young groupies never seemed to be far behind.

Around this time of great musical experimentation, Adam's brother, Alan, visited France on a short holiday and was met with wild exclamations of 'It's Rubber Plant!' It's Rubber Plant!' The local Parisians thought that Robert Plant, the lead singer of Led Zeppelin, had suddenly ferried across the Channel and trained it into town, not realizing that it was actually some long haired likely lad from SW15. It was made even more confusing for the locals, as Adam's brother's best friend also on holiday with Alan, looked just like Cat Stevens, with the same dark bushy hair and silly sideburns.

It was clear that Adam's brothers were getting up to all sorts of mischief, while he was missing out. They also had the whole of London as their playground. So, one day, Adam decided to find out more about them and what exactly they were getting up to. Adam's bedroom was near to theirs in the house and in the evenings and weekends he would listen to a wide variety of musical influences around the same time that 'Camberwick Green' and 'Trumpton' were doing the rounds on television. In those days, even children's shows had a lot of musical interludes that were catchy. Adam particularly enjoyed the acoustic guitar on 'Tales along the Riverbank', for example.

Alan and John (as Adam found out years later) played everything from The Doors, Jimi Hendrix, Cream, The Kinks, The Yardbirds, The Animals, The Small Faces (his brothers loved them and Alan had heard that they created their name when the band asked themselves, 'What shall we call the group?' One of them replied; 'How about the little shits?' Then one of them said, 'Cos that's what we are? Small faeces!' To have been addressed perhaps as a 'turd' for evermore would have worn a bit thin, and would have effected commerciality, so the more polite 'Small Faces' it became), and then there was latter Beatles, Santana, King Crimson, Pink Floyd (the extraordinary Syd Barrett was another of his brother's heroes), Frank Zappa, Jefferson Airplane, Captain Beefheart, The Rolling Stones, The Who, Led Zeppelin, Yes, Deep Purple, in fact, you name it they span it. Right veritable DJ's they were becoming. Adam reckoned they must have got through the odd record player stylus or two.

So, Adam would end up spending many a night just lying in bed, listening to his brothers fast expanding record collections, before they would have to turn the volume down later in the evening. He enjoyed the bed time music and it was comforting in the background, especially when tucked in and unable to sleep. Some tunes became so familiar, Adam knew exactly when a guitar solo would break out, or when the drums and bass would take over, or some distortion or effect would encompass everything and the record built to a crescendo. He would hum the tune again and again, until it tailed off into the beat pause before the next track began. Then he would sometimes fall asleep.

One time, when his brothers were away, Adam managed to pluck up the courage to venture inside their room. This was a dramatic moment. What if he got caught? What would be his excuse? He carefully pushed open the door. It creaked as he entered inside. He looked about him. All the walls seemed as though they were painted in a kind of mural effect or scatty montage. Books, records and small bits of paper lay about, a funny odour filled the room (what Adam would later discover to be the scent of incense or Josticks). He looked up. A large poster of the revolutionary hero, Che Guevara, wearing a beret, stared triumphantly from the wall and on another a pretty, naked girl with prominent rounded breasts had been sketched and colourfully painted on a large wooden board. The style of the picture was a sort of impression of the girl, but Adam was not too sure if it was a complete likeness. He blushed as he looked at the image, not knowing exactly why it was there, but something within him was enjoying it all the same.

But Adam felt as if he better leave the room. Maybe he had seen too much. Besides what if he got caught? What would his brothers do? What would his parents say? Alan and John would then know that Adam had seen more than enough and he wouldn't have any secrets. Adam thought it was well worth having secrets. It invested a certain amount of power. Besides, he could now listen to the music and have an inkling of what was happening in the room at the same time, especially when his brothers friends turned up: a chorus line of tennis racket thrashing hippies perhaps, or a smoky room full of vacant looks and infectious laughter.

Both of Adam's brothers girlfriends were attractive, but there was just no way that he could properly come to terms with them. They might as well have been from outer space.

'If kiss chase at school wasn't the whole story, then what the hell was?'

There was a lot more to the picture of the naked girl in their bedroom, that he was sure, and it had nothing to do with Scalextric or Hot Wheels either.

Adam felt himself wanting to grow up magically within a day, so he could find out exactly what all the fuss was about with girls and then after he had discovered, to change quickly back again into being just the little brother and the baby of the family. But left with a rather large grin on his face.

Adam's sister, Marie, would sometimes allow him into her bedroom to fill him in with the up to date events from around the house. She was like a special oracle service for juveniles. Any juicy gossip was quickly relayed to Adam after he returned from a hard day at the office.

'Dad's car's been filled up with water!'

'Filled up with water?' Adam replied, bemused.

'In the petrol tank, silly! Filled up from the hose pipe!'

'Cor! Did it make it go faster?' He chirped.

'It wouldn't start....'

Or,

'Our brothers have been expelled!'

'What's that?' Adam asked confused.

'They've been chucked out of school'.

'Chucked out! Why?'

'They were caught smoking a pot....'

'How do you smoke a pot?' He probed, intelligently.

'They've been very naughty'.

'Cor, does that mean they won't ever come home'.

'Probably'.

And so on.

Adam would also watch a lot of television when he got the chance, that's if his brothers or sister hadn't got in there first. At the weekends, he would try and watch 'The Flashing Blades' which was full of historical swashbuckling daring-do and he would avidly follow the dashing heroes galloping adventures. He loved to 'get on board' with all the kids in the 'Double Deckers' and their comical exploits round his school friend Brian's house some Saturday mornings. They would frequently argue about who they liked the most. Adam wasn't sure if he wanted to be blonde haired Scooper, or Sticks, who was cool on the drums. Brian wanted to be Spring, well that was until one day when the fattest boy in class retaliated when Brian called him Doughnut;

'He called me golliwog....'

'What?' Adam replied.

'He called me golliwog!'

'Now, that's enough!' said Brian's mum, interrupting from the kitchen.

'Why did he call me a golliwog?!'

'I dunno….you called him Doughnut', replied Adam, quietly.

Doughnut was one of the less favourable character's from the TV series, that's if you discounted Brains. The character of Billie was certainly more favourable, if you were a girl, and Tiger too.

'What's a golliwog?'

'You mustn't say that!' replied Brian's mother, pointing at him.

'Well, what's it mean, mum?!'

At that moment Adam decided it was probably wise to make himself scarce, especially when the ensuing debate might touch on Enid Blyton or god forbid, the unforgivable, 'The Black and White Minstrel Show'.

'Banana Splits', with all the characters dressed up in silly cartoon-like costumes, was also brilliant fun: lots of zany car chases, close-ups of 'Bingo' with his goofy teeth and glasses, and Adam didn't have to wait long before he was singing: 'Tra, la, lah! La, la, la, lah! Tra, la, lah! La, la, la, lah! One banana, two banana, three banana, four!'

The two other weekend programme's he really loved were, 'Champion the Wonder Horse', which despite being old, black and white, cheesy and American was always top entertainment and Adam used to annoy his mum and dad for the rest of the day with the theme tune: 'Champion the Wonder Horse!' 'Champion the Won - der Horse!' The other black and white, 50's series, 'The Adventures of Robinson Crusoe' was an absolute must: The wistful theme tune was so memorable Adam could hardly ever seem to get it out of his head and the character of Crusoe was both resourceful and enigmatic by turns.

One morning Adam saw a nifty film that didn't contain any dialogue at all and it was about a lonely young boy chasing after a red balloon through the streets of a foreign city, like Paris. As soon as he got near to the balloon, or was about to grab it, each time it would get away. Eventually, the boy managed to catch the balloon and only then was he content. It was a good film. Adam's only criticism was that because of his love of Chelsea, the balloon should have been blue.

After the Saturday morning television came the important business of the afternoon sports programmes. Adam would avidly watch 'Grandstand', and he would try and keep up with any news about Chelsea. If he became bored he would turn over to BBC 2 and would try and catch the matinee film, which was usually a stuffy old black and white movie or an unfunny comedy with a chirpy chappie trying to play the Ukulele.

One Saturday, Adam was watching the classic feature film 'Moby Dick' which starred Gregory Peck and he knew from the epic music that a real adventure was in store.

'Would the whale be caught and killed? Adam wondered. Or would it escape?'

The scenes of the ship in the storm and Peck trying to catch Moby seemed amazing. Then, just as the film was nearing its climax, the pet dog, Sam, suddenly entered, all hot and bothered. He had sensed something was up. This Scottish terrier seemed to know what side his bread was buttered alright. The day had been close and clammy and there had been a commotion around the house. A storm was brewing. Sam seemed to know that before anyone else. He panted and sweated and then took off up to Adam's room to find sanctuary from the first great crack of thunder.

'How did he know there was going to be a storm? There was one on the television,

but that wasn't real. That was a film crew, on a great big set, throwing buckets of water over each other'.

It seemed perhaps, as if the dog might be able to predict the future. 'But that's impossible', Adam reasoned. Despite his scepticism, he then ran up to his room to question Sam on forthcoming football predictions, like final League placings and FA Cup conquering. He eventually found Sam under the bed, shivering with fear.

'What a strange dog', thought Adam.

After a moment's pause, Adam just shrugged his shoulders and opened one of his 'Valiant' comics.

As the storm outside spent its fury and the rain shimmied, Adam suddenly realised that he had missed the football results service. Another Chelsea win perhaps? Or maybe they had suffered a thrashing? He reckoned there was a good chance that Sam knew exactly what the score was but didn't want him to see it.

FATHER CHRISTMAS

Santa. Did he exist? Who cared? Well Adam certainly did. He reckoned old Santa had a few tricks up his large red sleeve and a few cracking stories and if Adam was good, which wasn't always cut and dried, it might just mean that he ended up with the present that he wanted more than anything (a plastic replica Tyrannosaurus Rex, a submarine or a dodgy biplane - it didn't matter) failing that some other top yuletide offering (a game called 'Mousetrap' or a new chuff-chuff for his train set).

One winter, when the '60's were finally giving up the ghost and the weather was too cold even for brass monkeys to hang about, all was chocolate boxy and the whiter than white snow seemed like it would never go away. Just like kids dreams. In fact it was so white that Sam disappeared for days on end, because his canine coat blended perfectly with the scenery. Then when you least expected it, he would suddenly appear right out of nowhere and Adam would find himself toppling over him into a face full of snow.

Despite Adam's frost bitten hands, he managed to roll a huge round base for a snowman out in the crunchy garden and an equally big round top-half soon appeared and with the help of one of his brother's, he managed to place the latter on top of the former with crushing consequences. The snowman looked as if he had just exploded, especially as he didn't seem to have a head. Eventually, Adam made him one and once he had found a mouldy carrot for a nose and large buttons to represent his eyes, he seemed more than happy to have a half recognisable face. The finishing touch was of course placing Adam's knitted, hand-me-down, blue and white Chelsea scarf around his chubby neck.

Then Adam had to protect him as if his life depended on it, because his sister was always about with thoughts of sabotage, and if it wasn't a snow ball shoved down Adam's neck when he wasn't looking, then it might just be a irrevocable demolition job on Mr Snowy. But for some reason the crumbly totem managed to survive for as much as a few days, and while Adam ritualistically opened the pages of his advent calendar every morning and accompanied it with a 'Thunderbirds' countdown, he would look out of his bedroom window to see the cold soul still standing proudly upright. That meant only one thing. All was well. Santa was coming with interest this Christmas and it was going to be a white one for sure. Yes, people having a little flutter at the bookmakers about whether it would snow or not on the 25th was for once going to be completely unnecessary.

Christmas Eve soon came around and all day Adam spent his time trying to decide what exactly Santa might bring: a gleaming new bike with two little back wheels to stop him crashing about the neighbourhood perhaps, or maybe it would be something that Adam couldn't even imagine, because he liked surprises more than anything else. He was so excited that every five seconds he rushed up to the Christmas tree in the living room to see if any presents had been placed there for him to pick up and shake to try and guess what was inside.

With the onset of another Siberian night approaching, Adam checked outside once more to see if his snowman was still there and sure enough he was exactly where Adam had left him, intact, his sister thankfully having moved on to some other destructive occupation for the moment.

As Adam retired to his bedroom with out-of-tune carols and good tidings jangling from the TV set downstairs, he looked forward to Santa's visit. Only this time he was going to wait up for his arrival. Adam couldn't work out exactly how Santa was going to enter the house, because he reckoned there was no way Santa would be fitting his beer gut down their narrow chimney. 'Still', Adam presumed, 'only he knows best and I'm sure he'll think of a way'.

So he lay in wait for Santa. He was supposed to deliver presents in your stocking in the early hours so Adam would hide under his bed and wait for him to do just that. Then Adam would know for sure that he existed. If he didn't show at all, that meant he would have to do a bit of rethinking on the 'what does Christmas all mean front?'.

At about three in the morning, the television downstairs long since switched off, Adam looked down to the foot of his bed. He could just make out the long colourful sock lying at the bedstead waiting to be filled with Christmas goodies. He was hoping that Santa knew about his sweet tooth, because he was hoping on loads of chocolate to see him through the harsh winter. Failing that a wide variety of sweets would certainly put a silly grin on his face.

In the half light from the full moon peering through the curtains Adam got out of bed and placed his pillow and some cushions under the blanket, bunching it all around so that it looked roughly what it would have done had he still been inside it. In fact it looked so convincing Adam suddenly felt as though he was having an out of body experience and looked at the lifeless corpse in the bed while chuckling to himself. 'Santa will never know that I'm not in bed and I can spy on him from under it as he fills up my stocking'.

He was all ready. Just then he heard a noise from out on the landing. Someone was approaching. He hastily scrambled under the bed, knocking his head on one of the metal springs as he went. Adam tried to muffle the 'ouch!' but it was impossible, and anyway, the noise of the collision was loud enough to wake the dead. 'Shhhh!!' He thought to himself, 'Santa won't come if you make a noise'. 'Don't be daft, he's big, fat and laughs like a drain. And I'll bet HE'S not quiet when he moves about!'

Just as Adam chastised himself, there was a creaking sound from outside and the bedroom door slowly opened. Adam ducked down and held his breath. 'Is it him?' 'Is it him?!' 'Is it?'

After he caught his breath, he bravely peered from under the bed to look for Santa, but there was no sign of him. There was only what seemed like a small shadow in the open doorway. Before Adam could make out exactly what it was, the pet dog licked him excitedly full on the face.

'Urrgh!' Adam moaned. 'Thanks a lot!' he said, as he wiped his nose with the sleeve of his pyjamas. 'Here!' Adam commanded. 'Stay! That's it, good boy!' Eventually Sam settled down and decided that he too was going to wait for Santa. So there the two of them were, hiding under the bed in the dark.

They didn't have to wait long, which was lucky, because it was becoming chilly, but Adam couldn't take the blanket off the bed as that was doing an excellent job of covering up the disguise so he just rubbed his arms and shivered. Just as Adam contemplated giving up the stupid prank and returning to bed and warmth, again there was another sign of movement from outside the room and Sam's ears immediately pricked up. As they both listened intently, Sam turned his head slightly from one side to the other and then began to give out a low growl.

'Shhhh, Sam!' 'Shhh!'

The stupid canine was going to give the game away for certain, so Adam held Sam's jaw closed and instead of a growl there now emanated a sort of comic humming sound.

The next thing Adam realised was a sharp pain in his back and the cold, racing right through him. He had gone to sleep just at the wrong time. Just when Santa was going to be making an appearance. Typical. What an idiot.

There was no sign of Sam. No doubt he had got bored, what with Adam falling into a slumber and had disappeared back downstairs to chew on a bone. Adam lifted up his head to wipe the sleep from his eyes and just as he did so he whacked his head right against the underside of the bed.

'Aaaaarggghhhh!!!'

Another metal spring dug into Adam's head and as the stars whizzed around his head and he cursed himself, it suddenly dawned on him that it was 'Christmas Day!'

He hurried out from under the bed and looked at the bedstead to find a big sock now full to the brim. Before he had time to think, even for a moment, of missing Santa's visit, he was launching in to the chocolate and various goodies that lay stuffed inside the sock.

'This is going to be a brilliant Christmas!' Adam announced as if Sam was still in the room and it wasn't long before he had to take a contented breather from overeating the swag.

Unfortunately, Adam never did fathom out that night whether Santa existed, but he was right about one thing. It was a great Christmas and he managed to receive roughly what he had hoped for, including a 'Captain Scarlet' pistol with holster and a dark blue plastic policeman's helmet, (his brother John took an excellent photograph of Adam proudly wearing them).

The only sad note was concerning the snowman. He had managed to make it right through until Boxing day, only to melt the day after as the Siberian temperatures finally went back to where they had come.

All that was left of him was a nibbled carrot, some buttons and the long, hand knitted Chelsea scarf, which now sat bedraggled on the slushy grass.

WILLY WONKA

It was Adam's eighth birthday and he fancied inviting a few friends from primary school to see the recently released film, 'Willy Wonka and the Chocolate Factory' at the cinema. He would have invited them to Stamford Bridge given half the chance, but he hadn't been there himself yet. Both his brothers were going on a pretty regular basis, but Adam's friends were less prepossessed by Chelsea and as a result would probably have feigned instant nausea, or a rare malignant disease.

No, 'Willy Wonka' it was, and what a fine choice Adam had made. There's nothing like escapism, and if it wasn't cartoons, there had to be as little of reality and as few of anyone older than his age present on screen. Yes, Adam was already becoming a budding Barry Norman in baggy shorts.

The cinema was along the Fulham Road, a good location, it being so close to Stamford Bridge, and this lent a real flavour to the entertainment. In reality, the choice of cinema had been made by Adam's parents, but he liked to think that he had initiated something. He liked to think that he had even contributed to the making of the film, or helped work the projector, anything, even to the point of suggesting that he might have purchased the interval sweets.

The Fulham Road was a great place to be, especially for a film as diverse as 'Willy Wonka'. The sixties had turned the corner by at least a year, but the buoyant swinging mood was still afloat, and everything looked bright and optimistic for the decade ahead. Adam watched the world of the early 70's whiz past from the car window, as his mum drove, and he sat with some of his school friends in the back.

A new decade. What would it bring? Loads more film opportunities like this Adam hoped. It seemed as if the streets were paved with cinema trailers: If you missed an opportunity to see one preview, there would probably be another one just up the road.

The film was fantastic, Gene Wilder, playing Wonka, became Adam's surrogate father, albeit an eccentric one, for an hour and a half and he even had a sense of humour to boot. Adam also ate enough popcorn and chocolate throughout to kill ten horses, but he was still sitting comfortably by the end. His buddies were enjoying themselves too and more importantly so were the few girls that had been invited, including Karen, who Adam was trying not to admit he was rather smitten with. There were about nine of them altogether and their faces were smeared with various impulsive purchases; Toblerone's, Curly Wurly's, strips of liquorice, sticky wrappers and that third tub of chocolate ice cream. By the end, Adam was chewing manically on an ice lolly stick, reviewing the film as the credits rolled:

'That was really good. Nine out of ten!'

It had lost one point only because Adam had wanted to be in it.

'Yeah', said his friend Steve. 'It was brilliant! I liked the beginning bit and the middle bit and I really, really liked the ending bit'.

'Yeah, I liked that bit too, and that little bit before the middle bit, that was good too that was', Adam replied excitedly.

'And when he fell over and got covered in chocolate - that was the best bit', said Karen.

'Yeah, and when they went up in the balloon at the end, that was a brilliant bit, that bit!' said Brian, as Adam smiled.

And so their chatter would continue all the way home. Adam saluted Stamford Bridge as they sped past and told his friends that Chelsea had just won the FA Cup and another Cup in Europe and that his brothers went a lot.

'Do they?' said Steve. 'Cor! My younger brother supports them. It's a big ground isn't it'.

'Yeah....and it's going to get even bigger, now'.

'Bigger even than Arsenal!' admitted Brian, even though he was a Gunner.

Adam grew noticeably in his seat. He was revelling in the warm glow he felt inside himself. 'So this is what it's all about?' Enjoyment without any consequences. He could make a habit of that alright.

They arrived back at the house, and Adam looked forward with his friends to assaulting the large strawberry and chocolate birthday cake in the fridge while continuing the intriguing debate on the merits of Willy Wonka.

When all his friends were sat in a circle, everyone got the turn, one by one, to roll a dice. If a six was rolled the winner could stuff their faces with as much of a large chocolate bar as possible. Even at Adam's tender years, he had considered rigging the dice, but luckily it wasn't long before everyone was covered in chocolate anyway because after a while it didn't matter what number they rolled, they just attacked the bars with everything they had.

Unfortunately though, right at that moment, for some strange reason, Adam's friends had to leave. They had been advised to return home:

'But it's only seven o'clock?'

'I'm afraid they can't stay', said Adam's mum.

'But, why?' he countered, wiping his brown face.

'They just can't. The other parents will be along soon to pick your friends up'.

'But we want to play pass the parcel'.

Adam also thought that a quick game of Sardines would be fun. Unfortunately, Kiss Chase wasn't on the curriculum, which was a shame because Karen had appeared especially coquettish at the cinema.

Here he was, on his birthday, feeling like 'Mr Trousers' and the evening was already about to end. The celebratory novelties were hurried and routinely enacted. Adam blew extra hard at the eight candles on the cake in frustration, knowing that he was probably going to be the only one scoffing it and before you could say 'Wonka', his friends parents arrived.

'Happy Birthday!' his friends called back to him as the front door finally closed. Yes, for Adam it was a birthday of two halves alright.

Not only did Adam enjoy the cinema, (once the lights went down, it was the only place he could eat huge amounts of grub without anybody noticing) he was also a little bit of a theatre critic as well.

His mother tried to take him as much as she could, the Christmas pantomime was always anticipated with great relish. It acted as an early initiation into the world of the greasepaint, and for Adam was also another bloody good excuse for a feast.

The show that topped them all in Adam's formative years was the annual production of 'Treasure Island' at the Mermaid Theatre in the West End. Adam sat spellbound: The expectation, the bustle, the colour, the crescendo of drums, the opening curtain to reveal a picture inside, a variety of pirates, muskets, cutlasses, a parrot, the smell of gunpowder and a boy only a little older than himself who he could identify with, narrating the story. That was it. Adam was hooked. He loved joining in with the audience participation too, even though he had to wait a little time before enough children chipped in, yet he could never quite catch the sweets thrown into the audience by the performers. You couldn't be too sure if he quite understood what it was all about. He just knew it was a brilliant way to spin a yarn and with all that drama taking place on the stage, much better than bedtime stories ever were.

Adam was enthralled. He even wanted to inspect all the fixtures and fittings and have a chat with the parrot at the end of the show, but felt too silly to ask. It didn't matter though, a gem had been planted in his thoughtful head.

'One day', he pondered, 'I might even give it a go. I get to play dead, can come back to life again and if they're chucking sweets at us, then they must have loads and loads in reserve!'

The trip back afterwards in the car was an event in itself, driving through the sparkling West End of London, a picture at night.

'It's lit up just for my visit', or so it felt.

Somewhere a goal had been scored but in the pell-mell of the moment it had slipped his attentions.

Trips to the movies or the odd theatre or pantomime trip were probably Adam's real education. He didn't really learn much at primary school. It wasn't a very efficient place of learning. The teachers weren't the best (there had been an unsuccessful change of Headmistress) and Adam was a slow learner with a short attention span and given to bouts of day dreaming.

In fact he came away from his first school with only four accomplishments, apart from football in his pocket: playing 'War', 'Kiss Chase', stealing golf balls from the nearby Golf course and collecting caterpillars. He didn't realise it at the time, but these so called accomplishments weren't really going to help him along a career path and up the ladder to success. Adam certainly wasn't going to be making much of a living out of them.

He would always compare it to going to watch Chelsea, who in later years would become unsuccessful and underachievers and repetitive in a fashion, yet you felt they still tried to give a lot of people entertainment. That was the most important thing. Why did you have to succeed? What was it exactly? Who was it for? Just for yourself? And so it went on.

FIRST MATCH

It was an unforgettable moment. Adam's first Chelsea football match, in the flesh. Chelsea versus Huddersfield Town, in the First Division, in the spring of 1972.

Okay, so perhaps it should have been against more illustrious company, but Adam wasn't concerned. He knew that he would never forget this particular Saturday afternoon. He had heard a lot of talk about football at home: 'Silky', 'sheer skill', 'class', 'chipped', 'nut-megged', 'blinder', 'left-peg', 'wellied', 'one-two', 'screamer', 'super-sub', 'dummied', and it wasn't just on the telly.

Adam's brother John, felt the time was right to take Adam to Stamford Bridge, and Adam wasn't going to disappoint him. The two of them, and a friend of John's, sat expectantly on benches in the West Stand enclosure, anticipating the entrance of the home team from the tunnel.

They had arrived early, so they found they had a lot of time to kill.

The entrance to the Stadium had been one of the day's great rituals; queuing up at the turnstiles amongst mostly smiling, happy supporters full of anticipation. Adam's brother purchased a match day programme for 5p and once they entered, and Adam had taken a sharp intake of breath at the size of the place, he was escorted through the enormous terracing and down some steps to the side stand, where you had to pay a little extra to sit. As it was Adam's first match, John wanted to fill him in on all the details of the game and answer any questions he might have, and that was much easier to do sitting down.

Music seemed very important in the pre-match build up. Both from the loudspeakers and from the terraces, all in anticipation of the main event. The speakers blared out 'Blue is the Colour', probably one of the first airings of it with Adam recognizing the song immediately as it was moving rapidly up the Pop chart and also a funky type of tune which he would later come to know as the 'Liquidator', a Ska record by Harry J and the All Stars (this would become a cult tune pre-match at Stamford Bridge and it was at this time a popular tune with early 70's Skinhead culture).

The terraces were filling up quick as were the seated areas. The Chelsea fans were in good voice and they echoed the musical choices of the resident DJ and his 'pre match spin'. The Huddersfield supporters were gathered in the North Stand, the vast expanse of terracing away to the left. They seemed to be cooped in, with Chelsea supporters close by, and both sets of supporters bantered with each other.

Adam felt right in the thick of it. From the bustle coming off the tube train at Fulham Broadway station, and the short trek along the Fulham Road. While the three of them scuttled between supporters belching as they left pubs and sidestepped the odd Policeman on horseback, Adam helped devour his brother's ketchup strewn Hotdog. The day was taking shape. And he loved it. He loved the event. Like that first cigarette in later years, always a bit risky, but once Adam had done it and survived to tell the tale, he knew he was hooked.

This was a defining moment. Adam was about to find himself another home from home and there wasn't going to be much need for the return ticket. He was already addicted. He wasn't aware of it completely yet, but he was probably going to spend the rest of his life, paying a lot of money into the Chelsea fund, but unfortunately, early on he wasn't likely to see much return for his expenditure. He was going to have to put up with a lot of barren years. He was going to have to put up with a lot of Oldham 1 Chelsea 0.

The first thing Adam noticed was the Chelsea kit. Royal blue, except for the socks, which were white. As the players warmed up, it looked so good set against the green grass that was its canvas. It was almost as if some famous painter supported Chelsea and had fashioned a work of art. There was no doubt. Thing is, he may have also supported West Ham, Tottenham - Leyton Orient.

In the mid 60's and in much later years, white socks were an important issue at the Club. Because for some reason, Chelsea didn't have them. They had blue ones instead. From what Adam could see, that was like wearing Armani boxer shorts with a string vest.

But here he was, about to watch the recent FA Cup holders, the European Cup Winners Cup Winners, and about to be finalists in the League Cup against Stoke. Yes, Adam's brother had kindly taken him along to see many people's 'proverbials', but little did Adam know that they were soon going to return to being legendary underachievers.

Hearing the tannoy announcement, Adam's brother frowned at his match day programme, in disappointment:

'No Charlie Cooke!' He said, in a tone of voice that smacked of 'I want my money back'.

Charlie Cooke was someone else Adam had heard a lot about. He felt almost like a fourth brother. He was all things Chelsea. One minute incredible. He would do things with a ball that even Einstein would have had trouble explaining. He would tear up the pitch, the ball tied to his toes, trick ten players for fun, spend some time dribbling around the corner flag, then return triumphantly and pass the ball back to the goalkeeper. So when his brother said, 'No Cooke', Adam knew that he was going to be missing something. Cooke was a master chef with the ball. He'd nearly always dish up something memorable. It would be one of Adam's few regrets. Not seeing Cooke.

However, he did see Peter Bonetti in goal, nicknamed the 'Cat' for his feline elasticity, who dived about as if he'd been shot out of a cannon

(He was a brilliant goalkeeper who Adam's brothers felt was unfairly blamed for England's defeat by West Germany in the semi-final of the 1970 World Cup. It was certainly a tough call to be held responsible for a Nation's disappointment, when in the end it was a team game. It was always overlooked that Bobby Charlton had been substituted at a crucial moment in the match and all Chelsea fans agreed that it certainly wasn't all Bonetti's fault. If anything, they probably supported him all the more because of it).

Adam also saw the tough Scottish left back, Eddie McCreadie (nicknamed 'Clarence' because he was cross-eyed) who would never back out of a tackle: the stalwart defender John Dempsey who had scored a rare goal to help Chelsea triumph in the European Cup Winners Cup: the ever dependable midfield motivator John Hollins who had a cracking long range shot: the versatile swaggerer David Webb who would never admit defeat, even if that meant playing in every position on the pitch: the unassuming and underrated winger Peter Houseman who was crucial to the 1970 FA Cup success: and the Captain, Ron Harris, known as 'Chopper' to all of his opponents, because if they were lucky enough he would give them a damn good kick about for free all Saturday afternoon. As a defender, he was considered as hard as nails, as if he himself had coined the phrase (George Best's favourite goal was scored against Chelsea, not surprisingly, because he had managed to somehow ride a crunching tackle from the great maestro, Chopper, himself, before chipping Bonetti). Harris had a very distinctive playing style, all 'short back and sides and up and at 'em'.

Then of course there was the icing on the cake. Osgood. Adam's brothers even knew a song about him; 'Osgooooood, Osgood, Osgood, Osgood! Born is the King of Stamford Bridge!'

Now Adam knew why. Osgood oozed class. He oozed an extra dimension. Even his sideburns could score goals. On television, his goalscoring celebrations were always memorable: Right arm pointing straight up to the heavens, and smiling at the opposition, as if he knew all along that he was going to score. It was just a case of how many.

Another important part of the afternoon ritual was the match day programme. This enabled the supporter to find out who exactly would be playing. It was also useful to idle the fifteen minutes away at half time, with news pertaining to the Chelsea situation. There would also be a small section dedicated to the away team, who were far from unknown, with both Trevor Cherry (Captain) and Frank Worthington gracing the Huddersfield side.

After dabbling with the Chelsea crossword, John made some diligent changes when he heard there would be no Charlie Cooke. He made further disgruntled biro marks when it was announced that there would be no Alan Hudson, due to injury. Adam had heard and seen a lot about Hudson too on TV's 'The Big Match' and 'Match of the Day'. The young prodigy. The Chelsea midfield dynamo with supreme skill and tantalising vision. What's more, he was born and brought up near Stamford Bridge, so he had Chelsea blood in his veins.

Another thing that caught John's eye in the programme was an article about Bill Oddie, the writer/actor from BBC's popular 'Goodies' comedy series, in a section called 'Stars in the Stand'. His brothers loved the 'Goodies' on TV and even though Adam couldn't fully appreciate their depth of humour at the time, he enjoyed the hilarious theme tune, 'Goodie, Goodie, Yum, Yum!', and their madcap antics, with oversized caps and black puddings. 'Well, if one of the 'Goodies' is a supporter, Chelsea must be popular', he thought. Or at least it showed he had good taste (little did he know that around this time the likes of Paul Newman, Steve McQueen, Raquel Welch and Laurence Olivier had all watched matches at Stamford Bridge, due probably to the hospitality of the actor Sir Richard Attenborough, who was on the board of directors. All of these famous actors certainly gave Chelsea a glamorous appearance and attested to Chelsea's long links with show business).

Bill Oddie had some valid things to say in the programme about being no lover of the physical stuff that was taking over the game. He had come to be entertained, to enjoy the superb skills of players like Peter Osgood, Charlie Cooke, Alan Hudson - especially him that season. He certainly hadn't paid to see the stars chopped down, and he reckoned the referee's revolution hadn't come a day too soon.

This was certainly true of Chelsea versus Leeds fixtures around this time, where the respective hard men: Harris and McCreadie; Bremner and Hunter, took turns to kick lumps out of everyone (Adam's brothers both acknowledged that Chopper Harris had helped to win the FA Cup against Leeds in the replay, by deliberately fouling the prodigious talent Eddie Gray early in the match, leaving Gray a sad and sorry 'walking wounded' for the rest of the game. Unfortunately, the Leeds team and supporters also thought that and had been out for some sort of revenge ever since).

Oddie continued, citing Chelsea versus Manchester United as his favourite match as the Blues always had great games with them. The play flowed and so did the entertainment. That's really what it was all about for Oddie, if only more managers and coaches would try to see things from the spectator's view. It saddened him, though, that a lot of fans seemed to get more of a kick out of the bad, sometimes rough play than out of the game's great skills.

For Adam, it was sad, and true. It seemed a big cheer always followed Harris wherever he roamed on the pitch. Whether he was putting an opponent into local intensive care or launching them into row Z. One thing that you couldn't question though was his commitment. Sometimes rough? Harris was always rough, as Adam's brothers used to testify. Thing is, it was clear he wanted to win at any cost, and so he did. At least, alongside the likes of Hudson and Cooke, their superb skill looked even greater, making Harris a sort of litmus test of a footballers 'bottle' and craft. Without doubt 'Chopper' and his ilk at other clubs received a ton of respect.

Then there was the Chelsea supporters home end, 'The Shed'. Adam's brothers had talked about it many a time. It became this mythical thing.

'Did you go in the Shed?'

'Yeah, did you?'

'No, but I wanted to'.

The Shed was the Chelsea home terrace away to their right and it was foreboding. It was all concrete and corrugated iron, like a building site. Part of the terrace was covered by what looked like the roof of a cattle shed. The rest was a vast curved swathe of open terrace, littered with vintage crush barriers, and if you stood there long enough, you were in for a good soaking.

Another thing Adam noticed about the Shed, was that this area of the ground was where most of the atmosphere was coming from. Also, as the fans chanted (mostly in the middle and towards the top of the stand), the supporters held their arms above their heads and clapped in unison to a particular rhythm. From a distance this looked and sounded like some tribal ritual. A mass rally.

Deciding to sit on the West stand benches turned out to be an ideal position to see all the players coming out of the tunnel from the East stand, on the other side of the pitch. As they ran on, Adam could hear the home supporters getting behind the team. He could certainly hear the Shed. Everyone stood up and made their presence felt, with a deafening roar and thousands of blue and white scarves held aloft. (Adam's brothers still had an old wooden rattle that they had taken to matches in the mid to late 60's. Adam suggested bringing it along to the game to make a din, but John thought that was unnecessary).

John was right. The noise was deafening. Supporters raised the roof and pledged their undying loyalty; 'We'll support you, we'll support you, we'll support you ever more!' Adam was amazed at how animated everyone had become. Supporters weren't acting their customary 'stiff upper lip' selves.

'This is going to be brilliant', he concluded.

As soon as the pleasantries were done, and coin tossed, at last the game kicked off, the supporters eagerly maintaining a running commentary on the fortunes of the match. If any Chelsea player managed to encroach within sniffing distance of the Huddersfield net, everyone would stand up or surge further forward in anticipation of a goal. Eventually, Adam found this ridiculous, as he spent his whole time springing up and down like a yoyo. Sometimes he got his timing wrong so that when all the supporters were standing up, Adam was busy sitting down and vice versa. Sometimes because of his size, when the supporters stood up he had to stand on the bench seat and crick his neck up and around between people's heads just to see the odd moment of play.

'You'll get used to it', John's shorter haired friend wagered .

Alongside the physical roller coaster, loud 'Oohs' and 'Aarghs' broke out, especially if the ball ended up whizzing past the goal. If likewise, Huddersfield threatened the Chelsea goalmouth, which was noticeably less common, then the home supporters became pensive and everyone bit their nails and looked at their watches. The away supporters would then become more cocky and would begin to perform their own vocal repertoire. Loud chants of, "Uddersfield!' "Uddersfield!'

When the visitors scored, due to a defensive mix up, most of the ground went deathly silent. It was like a bereavement had just been announced or some thoughtless person had let off a very bad smell. The moment of despair was then punctured by recriminations. Chelsea supporters all around the stadium vented their pent up emotions, words like 'donkey' and 'carthorse' were preceded by a rich use of swear words which made Adam blush (some expletive's were already familiar but he found his vocabulary growing rapidly). Meanwhile, the travellers from Yorkshire just jumped around wildly and swung their scarves about.

'This is amazing', Adam said to his brother, even though he was disappointed because Huddersfield had scored, but John and his friend were too caught up in the moment to respond. In fact, the Chelsea supporters had become more determined now and were following their heroes with even more devotion. Willing them to score. Willing them on to victory. Not one instant missed their attentions. They commented on every moment. The boring bits: 'For we are sailing, please give us a goal!' Any questionable decisions by the main official: 'The referee's a wanker! (Another word that made Adam blush at the time).

And then finally, what the devoted had long waited for, a classic Osgood goal. There was a moment of suspense, as if to double check that the ball had gone in the net. Then Stamford Bridge went off its head. Adam was suddenly involved in what reminded him of a very ludicrous TV episode of 'Monty Python' (another show that his brothers loved), Chelsea fans were jumping up and down ecstatically all over the place as if they were on trampolines. Complete strangers hugged each other while they bounced across the terraces, pledging again their fervent loyalty to the team. While the supporters celebrated with wide eyed expressions and ample swearing, John was busy shaking Adam senseless.

'What a shot! What a goal!'

The vocal energy now was quite awe inspiring. Lots of people were soon going to have to be visiting the doctor for a sore throat. The

Huddersfield fans now took their turn to sit in the dumps, while King Ossie completed his irrepressible celebrations. As he did so, the crowd rang out, 'Ossie! Ossie!' once more.

'This is incredible', Adam thought. 'All these people, thinking exactly the same things at the same time. They must have some sort of leader to give them their song cues'.

But it was difficult to tell. Perhaps there was one supporter who had a very loud voice and liked one song in particular, because the supporters had a habit of repeating their material. But either way, the level of vocal passion brought a lump to the throat.

After the two goals, the game settled down again and then the match repeated itself with two more goals. Huddersfield were playing well and managed to match a tired Chelsea team for 90 minutes, which was still recovering from a titanic midweek victory against Tottenham Hotspur, in the semi-final second leg of the League Cup.

Eventually, the final whistle blew. The match finishing all square at 2-2.

It didn't matter that Chelsea hadn't won. Or that it hadn't been the greatest of games. Adam had seen Peter Osgood play and he had scored. In years to come that was definitely going to be something to cherish.

As they left the ground reluctantly, John was soon grinning at Adam, knowing that his brother, despite seeing a less than classic fixture, would always remember this match. As the three made their way home, Adam now knew one thing for sure. He had begun his apprentice-ship.

2

NEW SCHOOL

The day after his first match, Adam was packed off to school, in the west of England. It was an all boys school of the boarding variety. Adam would have preferred to have stayed at his primary school, so he could continue to watch Chelsea on a more regular basis, but he had no choice in the matter. For certain family reasons he was not allowed to stay at home. This was unfortunate because he was now fairly settled in at his primary school, even though the teaching was clearly not the best. In fact they had so many supply teachers you could have assembled the equivalent of about five football teams from them. Also, Adam had some close friends like Brian and Steve and more importantly it meant that he possibly wouldn't ever see Karen again, who he had to admit, privately, he did have a bit of a crush on. Especially after the Willy Wonka cinema trip, anyway. Adam's last image of her on his final day at the school was of her dashing out of the classroom, up the bank and across the grass past Brian's house to go home. Adam waved to her but she just carried on running into the distance.

After a long journey, Adam arrived at his new school, which was all boys, a term late because of a different syllabus, so he was the only new boy (something that would be repeated throughout his school career). His parents drove him silently to his new picturesque surroundings, all hilly fields and rusty tractors. Adam felt so empty, so homesick and he knew that it would be a long, long time before he was at Stamford Bridge again.

It was a strange world, and the people seemed somehow different, detached. Adam's friends up to that point had mainly lived on the sprawling Roehampton estate, where his primary school was. The boys at his new school certainly weren't from an estate. They were mostly from leafy middle England. Yes, now it was clear. Adam was having to come to terms with a whole new concept. Class. Was he supposed to be part of what was called the middle of it, or part of the lower part of it, or had he been just the upper part of the lowest bit and back just around the middle bit. Whatever it was, he really didn't feel a member of any of it. In fact, he couldn't remember ever having purchased a ticket.

But here he was in what can only be described as Tom Brown's schooldays. The school's red brick Victorian outbuildings were exactly as you would imagine. The establishment even had a Latin 'motto' on their crest, which it advertised proudly, similar to that of some Football clubs, like Tottenham Hotspur, who maintained their clubs heritage with a worthy saying: 'Audere est Facere'; 'To dare is to do'. Adam's new school's motto loosely translated meant, 'It must be built' or 'It must be erected'.

Later that first day, Adam was eventually left by his parents in a decrepit pottery shed with his fellow pupils, all of whom already knew each other well. Everyone was required to make something useful out of clay and the most ingenious pupils would have theirs glazed in the kiln. Most made mugs or pots or misshapen blobs. Adam managed to make a miniature replica League Cup trophy, although the handles were a bit floppy, so when it came out of the kiln it looked decidedly drunk. It was then that he realised that egg chasing was one of his fellow pupils main interests:

'Do you like Rugger? I hope so. I say, we're also wizard at marbles!'

And cricket. Adam already knew that Football was the sport for him. Rugby he would have to play a lot of, not being optional, but he could never see it shrug off its 'toff' image:

'Come on chaps, all hands to the pump! And you lot in the scrum, let's give it some Wellingtons! Oranges at the half.'

As for hitting hard balls with a length of willow, Adam was crap at it. He used to make sure he was always an outfielder because he had a long throw and it meant that he could spend a lot of time just hanging about which he was very good at. Sometimes Adam was used as a secret weapon. Being a left hander was a very useful ploy to annoy the opposition. They would spend their entire time swapping from one side of the field to the other and back again. The only problem was he didn't ever stay at the crease long enough to really make a good go of it. Shame, because had he had more ability it would have made a nice relaxing way to spend the summer afternoons. The post match sandwiches and squash were usually tasty too.

Just like the brochure advertising, there were some very unusual eccentrics at Adam's new school. To call it Dickensian would be an understatement. They had their 'Mr Chips', they even had their 'Fatty Arbuckle', and there was a surfeit of 'Mad Professors'. There seemed to be a lot of unusual looking people, both pupils and staff. It was as if an exploratory mission had been made to Mars and a weird set of aliens had been brought back and set up in a little known village near Worcester. Either that or there was some serious inbreeding going on.

One unfortunate boy in Adam's class seemed to be suffering from some sort of precocious puberty, because when they had their statutory early morning cold showers, it was quite clear that he was a lot further along the physical conveyor belt than the rest of them. Adam felt especially sorry for him as he had already been labelled with the nickname 'Pubey' and he was certainly not happy with it.

Another boy, in the year above Adam's had a well documented unusual fixation. It was as if he believed that one of his hands was in reality a butterfly and it was fluttering around him wherever he went. He even gave his creation a name, which no one could decipher and made loud noises, squeaks and confided in it religiously. At meal times he could even be seen sharing his food with his pet insect, to the accompaniment of sniggers from his class mates. Adam wondered why the 'Butterfly Boy' as he was known, was at the school at all, because he certainly wasn't getting the sort of attention he needed, and doing his studies with the interference of his companion must have been impossible. Luckily for him, inhabiting his complex, autistic world he never noticed the constant ribbings and mimicry from his fellows, which after a period of time seemed to grow amazingly into a peculiar form of affection.

Adam also found it odd having two flaky nannies and a pompous matron to look after them. Adam reckoned that no matter what, he could hopefully look after himself, but in this institution it was clear there were young boys who most definitely needed a helping hand.

Matron reminded Adam of a chirpy concentration camp commandant: All sugar, spice and a great big clip round the ear'ole. In contrast, the part time Nannies could be friendly and as luck would have it, sometimes attractive. Although this could become awkward because after washing, the boys had to line up and present themselves in their birthday suits, for the nannies to inspect. It was quite a ritual. The boys had to smile, stick out their tongues, present both sides of their hands, proffer their elbows, lift up their knees and then spin their bodies right round. If they were sufficiently scrubbed they could then continue. If not, then they had to wash once more, return to the back of the queue and go through this humiliating Haka all over again. 'Butterfly Boy', Adam found out, used to show the Nannies his freshly washed friend and they would play act along as if the insect was for real.

The very first evening while on his way to his new sleeping quarters, Matron passed Adam a plastic sheet.

'Go to your dormitory. Make sure you put it on your bed'.

Talk about pisser. First day at school and already the 'prefects' (the oldest boys in the school) would know that Adam has a little psychological problem with the waterworks, due to some stressful experiences at home. He wasn't sure if his parents had informed the school already of his difficulty but he was sure to be teased just the same by the 'older and wiser' prefects. His fellow pupils were more understanding though. Some of them were pissers as well.

The prefects were a mixed bag. Some could be quite friendly.

'You support Chelsea?'

'Yes'.

'Good team they are'.

Others weren't quite so nice.

'So….did you piss the bed, Rag?'

'Rag', that was Adam's name. Each form had a name. The new pupils had been split up into two groups and called Rags or Tags. For the rest of his first year, Adam was a Rag. This was a galaxy away from his primary school, where it seemed that the individual was championed, even if that only resulted in a good brass rubbing or an encouraging performance as a wise man in the Nativity play. At this new school, it was all about discipline, and the best way to get that was to treat the individual with contempt and utilise a form of military code. Something Adam's dad would understand. Bullying too, within the ranks was another useful tool to divide and conquer, in fact all that was missing was a burly Sergeant Major. Unfortunately, it seemed that the pupils were more concerned with what their peers thought of them, than: 'Why is the food so undercooked that we become ill?' or 'Why is the shower water so cold that our private parts drop off?'

As a new boy, Adam was also provided with a guardian (a responsible boy in the year above) to show him the ropes, like the ins and outs of school etiquette and where to store his 'tuck' (a private provision box of treats like Toblerones, Crisps and Hobnobs. Useful to augment the prison food and comforting in a harsh winter).

Adam was forced to 'fag' - make toast for the prefects - and generally be servile, clean their common room, help write their 'parents open day' speeches, polish the head boys shoes, etc. Sometimes pupils had to beg on their knees to be allowed out of their common room, or they had to undergo some stupid 'forfeit' like warming a prefects chair by sitting in it, while one of them twisted his ears off. Often, understandably they found themselves wanting vengeance. As a result they would try to get them back. Thus was the germ, a cycle of humiliation put into motion. Bullying was institutionalised. It seemed as though it was part of the curriculum. The teachers even did their bit. I suppose it was all part of the character building ethos, like making them line up on the 'Quad' in the pouring rain for a role call to prevent a mass exodus. The result? A regular flu epidemic.

Early on in the term, Adam would sit in the dreary school library, idling away a few moments of free time, with occasional glances at a book. It was usually just before 'Gas', so-called because the prefects and designated teachers would gather together with those pupils who wanted to chat about things 'pertaining to the world'. This rather perplexed Adam. He knew that he could be quite shy, especially in a hostile environment, and speaking for any length of time in public seemed unpalatable: Perhaps a suspicious prefect might find out some piece of jargon, some little resident ammunition stored in Adam's person to be replayed at a later date.

'That new boy, he's a thicky! Did you hear him? The way he went on about Enid Blyton. Codswallop!'

Adam wasn't too disappointed though. The conversations were always full of bluster and little merit. In fact, nearly all the talk concerned picking up litter or doing a good deed for the benefit of the school. Funny thing was, Adam would have been more than willing to supply the matches had they wanted to burn it down. He had trouble keeping enemies out. He wasn't suddenly going to cut the rope to the drawbridge and allow them free reign inside his head.

Just before 'Gas' was rounded off, a newly found friend informed Adam that Stoke City had just beaten Chelsea in the League Cup Final. Adam was shocked, especially as he had no radio and there was no day time access to a television.

'Conroy for Stoke, then Osgood scored. Eastham got their winner'.

'Oh, no....' Adam replied.

'It's true, just heard'.

'How could we lose to Stoke?'

'Beats me', his friend replied shrugging his shoulders.

Then Adam suddenly thought to himself, 'If only I was at home. With Sam about there was no way that Chelsea would have lost to the Potters. He would have barked at the TV until the Blues had scored the winner. For certain. If nothing else he would have warned me of the outcome in advance'.

Yes, Adam had to admit it. He was homesick and missing his canine companion. It certainly didn't help to have to sit through the school's weekend film of 'Greyfriars Bobby' which was all about a loyal Scottish Terrier who keeps a vigil over his master's grave. And although the dog in the film didn't look exactly like Sam, Adam suddenly had unappealing visions of him spinning around in circles anxiously awaiting his return.

Adam was more than annoyed about the football result, because it didn't make any sense. Surely, the Cup winning team were on a roll. He was frustrated about it and he certainly needed a pick me up, but after some time he wasn't completely downhearted because he felt that Chelsea would soon be back at Wembley to win the FA Cup again and sooner rather than later. (Little did Adam know that it was going to take another twenty five years). Also, he hadn't been along to quite enough games at that point to forge that irreversible bond that being 'tamed' by your team will bring.

SCHOOL RITUALS

Alongside the unusual characters that inhabited the school, there were also some bizarre rituals obviously passed down through the schools illustrious history. The first one was heard just before seven o'clock every morning, consisting of a prefect shouting 'Flat Feet!' loudly out of the dormitory window. This particular ritual was supposedly derived from the sound of groggy boys stomping barefooted down the passages after getting out of bed.

'Flat Feet' was their very own human alarm clock and it woke everyone up depressingly early every morning with a jolt in preparation for their cold showers, which would be eyed with glee by their camp commandant and her two underlings. Now Adam knew why he was beginning to like baths more than showers.

The dining hall was another area of the school packed with ritual. It was a large wooden panelled hall with paintings of cranky former Headmasters on the walls. There were two central pillars, situated either side of the 'Heads' table. This was where the Headmaster sat with the prefects and the Head boy who sat to the right side of the Headmaster. The picture always reminded Adam of the Last Supper, and judging by the standard of the garbage doled out it was probably going to be.

In front of the main table, were five long tables where the minions sat and surveyed how much nicer things were on the top table. The elite cutlery, plates and silver service were nicely laid out on a crisp, white table cloth, whereas the ordinary utensils were left to be distributed haphazardly. You could be sure that plates were nearly always being dropped in the process or thrown around frizbee style and forks would always find themselves embedded in an unfortunate boy's head.

Then, after queuing up for what seemed like an eternity, the pupils were then allowed in to the dining hall. They had to stand militarily by their designated tables and wait for those at the head table to position themselves before being allowed to sit. A perfunctory 'Grace' was then said before the 'slop' was dolloped out. Then and only then were 150 ravenous bellies allowed to tuck in. Towards the end of the meal, the Headmaster would ring a little bell and inform the school about important events of the day and then the Head boy, servile and slime ridden at the best of times, would regale everyone with his side splitting jocularity.

The food at the school was more than plentiful but largely disgusting. At some point in every term a great number of pupils would go down with a frightening 'sick bug'. This was the schools answer to the bubonic plague, only worse. It was all part of the 'greater scheme of things', or so they were told. A process of flagellation that was high up on the agenda. It was easy to imagine the scenario: Headmaster and teachers of the school meet for the half-term coffee morning. One of the teachers pipes up and suggests an audacious scheme for the second half of term:

'Let's give the pupils some major adversity to overcome. This will develop their characters, help them improve their social and communicative skills and raise morale. Besides the boys will enjoy mucking in together to become one. Whole'.

More like a unified entity ready to be indoctrinated and depersonalised, with all individual impulses expunged. Just like in the British army. It was a clever mind game. Then the genial secretary would be dictated a Delphic utterance from the Headmaster to the chief cook:

'Item: No longer to burn the regulation sausages for the required two hours, but to flash fry them for a second. Item: All army surplus porridge to have its consistency reassessed and now to include large lumps and traces of the cooks unwashed beard'.

The result? A hundred very ill children. And if it wasn't your head in a bucket retching up your innards. It was buttock clenching, 'Oh my God, where's my other pair of pants?'

One of the strangest rituals which was kept closely under wraps but still consisted of its own rigid rules and regulations was known as

'Best Boy'. In the lower years of the school the boy who looked most effeminate would be chosen by an older pupil or 'Top Boy' as some sort of crude flunkie or 'other half' (Top Boys were designated in each year who acted as a kind of small time Mafia Don: Organising the healthy distribution of tuck, by stealing it, and also regulating 'Bob a jobs', a sort of crude tithe system, whereby members would exchange tuppenny bits for favours of a wide variety, consisting of lending out a blanket at night or donating a week's supply of Sherbert Fountains for example. Friendships were always easily bought and sold too).

If a best boy hadn't been designated by a top boy it could easily be decided by a prefect too. This was an unpopular and less secretive method, however, because it spread the word and might have made future liaisons untenable: Also, the teachers might find out. Not that some of them didn't have a very good idea.

The best boy, now singled out on pain of retribution, would then escort or accompany whoever desired some kind of comfort. Usually the cause was homesickness or loneliness, sometimes it was just a confused cry for help. Adam wasn't too sure if he was an oil painting at the time, but then again he realised he was no grotesque either, so the days were long when he knew he might just get elected Best Boy.

Sometimes the 'date line' service would go a bit far, and you would see two inseparable pupils walking around together in their free time for the rest of the term, as if they were joined at the hip. Adam didn't know if all these companionships led to discoveries of a more basic nature, but he was pretty convinced that some of them did. The absence of girls at the school was in his mind a fatal omission, even for boys of such tender years, and experimentation of another sort seemed widespread.

'Was this all part of life's rich tapestry?' Adam thought. 'Doesn't the world rotate in a most peculiar manner? This wouldn't happen down at Stamford Bridge'.

PUNISHMENT

Punishment was another important facet of the school. Discarding the well accepted fair play approach of a yellow card for a caution and a red one for further indiscretion, certain teachers would always see fit to launch straight in with their own personal brand of discipline.

One of the biggest excuses for this self styled crusade used to be the perfunctory pillow fights fought out between neighbouring dormitories. These always felt reminiscent to 'going over the top' on some reckless invasion. They were usually diligently planned, the rumours of which would fly around for weeks. Code names like, 'Blitzkrieg West Wing!', or 'Destruction: White House!' were invented, making it absolutely clear that plans were afoot.

Adam would always remember those last tense moments: The anticipation as the night draws on: Torches switched on and off in a primitive Morse code: Scouts posted at strategic points, while last minute tactics are whispered frantically: The final adrenalin fuelled seconds expire as undiscovered, they infiltrate the enemy's encampment: The sudden cry of 'Tally Ho!' by a polite, but nervy pupil armed to the teeth, as all hell breaks loose. As pillows smite the air, an atmosphere of St Trinian's is mustered, but without of course any hockey sticks or schoolgirls in tight leggings. Casualties on both sides are heavy. Valiant fighters suffering from various forms of hideous 'Cotton burn' and terminal 'Feather allergy'.

As the brave commando raid on 'Normandy - Dorm "J"' nears its bloody climax, a defender cries out in agony having been strafed by multiple sweaty pillows. An attacker reels in discomfort, partly from being winded but suddenly realising that the evening school meal has not been properly digested. Dust and feathers reign down on the luckless foot soldiers. The war rages backwards and forwards. Well mannered expletives are exchanged and deadly vengeance is in the air. The dormitory now begins to look as if it has been sacked, as beds and the odd wooden chair become upended as haphazard barricades.

Suddenly an adult rages: 'Stop this! Stop this! At once! Do you hear!'

A bright light is immediately switched on. Everyone freezes, even in mid flight, as statuesque as possible in a ridiculous and vain attempt not to be noticed. As the dirt and mayhem settles, exhausted faces everywhere begin to survey the destruction. Eventually, they all turn around sheepishly, wondering which teacher has caught them this time. Would it be the House Master who likes to punish them with a cricket bat or the deputy Head who uses his own leather soled shoes with the rusty metal nails protruding. Or are they in for a treat? Is it the deranged games teacher, who regularly takes a ten yard run up with a wet slipper?

Bad news. It is. Adam had vivid nightmares about this teacher's particular method. In some quarters it was rumoured that you couldn't sit down afterwards for a week. But, could he handle the punishment? Could he actually take it on the cheek? Adam bet that 'Chopper' Harris could.

In later years, Adam thought that old William Shakespeare might have invited the sore bum theory. Or occasionally sitting at Stamford Bridge might bring it on. But looking back on punishment at this school, Adam's arse was rarely the same colour as the rest of his body.

This particular night though, Adam would beat the system. After the PE teacher had erupted, Adam managed to cannily hide under his bed, while the others in the dormitory were frog marched out into the corridor in single file, a ragged sorry looking lot, to await the inevitable damp slipper (apparently, Adam had heard it was made wet to give it that extra whiplash effect, and it was deemed to be both a crude and exceedingly painful addition to the schools punishment catalogue).

Adam felt a sudden buzz when he realised that no one had noticed him. For the moment he had escaped. He listened to the distant instructions from the teacher and the nervous, muffled replies of his comrades. One by one they were lined up. The humiliation was completed as each pupil was watched by their fellows, as they took down their pyjamas, bent down and awaited the punishment. If a pupil didn't take it with a stiff upper lip and cried uncontrollably they were in for at least a month's ribbing. If they behaved with valour - not even wincing or raising an eyebrow on impact - they were lauded around the school and nicknamed 'tough arse'. Unfortunately, nearly everybody shed at least a tear if it was at the hands of the games teacher, because the ten yard run up alone was sufficient to strike terror into the hardest of posteriors.

Adam listened out for the manic run up and then the resounding thwack of the slipper. A yelp followed immediately after and then again and again and one more for luck. He soon relished the fact that he had managed to get one up on such a terrifying adult. He had tasted a bit of fun with a pillow fight and he wasn't going to have to be detained at His Majesty's pleasure for it.

As he lay under the bed, Adam thought of his pet dog who would frequently hide under his bed at home, and he imagined what it would be like to creep through the turnstiles at Chelsea without paying. When his cellmates eventually returned, with tear filled eyes, clutching their backsides, groaning and snuffling, Adam slipped slowly back into his bed and tried to act convincingly that he had been whacked as well. He acted immediately as a precaution in case they found out that he had escaped punishment.

His mistaken friends were so bamboozled, they thought he had taken the punishment really courageously and had hardly flinched. Adam certainly wasn't going to ruin it by revealing the truth. Anyway, it was enough. Adam needed his little victory for himself. He didn't need it for anybody else.

SCHOOL HOLIDAY

It seemed that before Adam had even become fully accustomed to the School, he arrived back at the train station full of anticipation of the holiday ahead. He would see Chelsea with one of his brothers and have decent food, and go to bed late and sit about and watch TV and if he wanted to he could probably spend an afternoon doing little or nothing at all. But there was a strange tension in the car journey back home. His Mum had come to pick him up which was unusual, and was talking about matters in a slightly off hand manner, the way that adults are so good at when trials and tribulations are plaguing their minds. Call it reserve or the good old 'bottle it all up' theory, but Adam knew that something was up.

'How was school?'

'Fun....'

'Shame about the weather'.

'Yes....'

'Your collar's not straight....'

When they stepped out of the car he realised why. The house was in a right old state. Adam wandered up the path through into the living room, and placed his satchel down. All the windows had been completely smashed in, and every pane of glass in the back door that led out to the garden had been lovingly removed. He looked at the shredded curtains and surveyed the upended, splintered furniture. The living room table was now matchwood and only fit for one of Dad's bonfires and the mantelpiece was badly cracked. What looked like broken plates and cups and saucers littered the floor. Adam thought that an extremely energetic pillow fight had just taken place or that some burglars had ransacked the house in an effort to find that elusive trinket. But he was wrong.

He strolled up to his room like an automaton and sat on his bed. As sounds of hasty clearing up echoed around the house, a Policeman rang the door bell. Adam wasn't one for explanations, so he just tried to carry on as if nothing had happened. Eventually, he looked over towards his Airfix model box, which sat by his bed. Inside the box lay the plastic entrails of a German Second World War fighter plane which he had left unfinished in his hasty despatch to School. It looked like it wanted to be put together, so put it together he did. In fact, Adam spent most of his first holiday making and painting a Messcherschmitt 109E.

Unfortunately, he never got to see Chelsea during that holiday, because there was no one to go with. His brothers were at an age when it seemed as if they were hardly ever about, and Adam certainly noticed their presence when they were.

It was an unusual position to be in. Adam had so wanted to come home from school, but now he just wanted to go straight back again. Still it was only three weeks and then he would be back again. Then look out. He'd put the world to rights.

HOLIDAY CAMPS

Whenever Adam was at home, it never seemed very long before he was off once again. On his travels. In fact, he always seemed to be in some sort of state of transit: whether he had just returned from school or was about to leave home or was on his way to the station or was busy climbing into the back of a coach. But whatever mode of transport, Adam soon became accustomed to the freight train of life.

Things became further complicated when he had to attend special camps to get him away from home even in the holiday periods from school. In the spring and summer breaks for the next few years, Adam was packed off for a week or two to outward bound holidays across different swathes of the British Isles.

In Wales, he trekked over the Breacon Beacons and admired the beauty of Anglesey. In Scotland, he roamed Teviotdale and pottered about Hadrian's wall, sauntered around the Isle of Arran and marched on a mobile camp from Inverness to Fort William, spying for the Loch Ness monster and climbing Ben Nevis. In England, he canoed down the length of the unpredictable river Severn without capsizing, marched about Cornwall and regularly frequented the south coast, where Sussex and Brighton rock became his temporary home. He also followed the trail of the Druids and Saxons from Stonehenge to Salisbury along the Offa's Dyke. Over a seven year period, Adam managed to explore many of the nooks and crannies of the great British countryside.

He learned how to pitch a tent in a force nine gale, skin a rabbit and cook it for tea, fish with a sharp stick, utilise the stars and the moon to find his way. Pack up his rucksack just right so that he could carry it all, understand the contours on the ordinance survey and even ration the provisions to last a whole journey.

His friends on these holidays were usually all in the same boat. Something had happened at home so they had to go away, or some had no parents and were looked after in care. Some could not look after themselves and had to be helped, but all were welcomed and were part of the family.

Some of the kids were very tough and had rebelled against their lot. Some of the other kids would have been tough had not their life experiences chipped away at their souls. Others, I suppose like Adam, were in a halfway house and weren't quite sure where exactly they fitted in. But one thing was for sure. They were there to have fun. And so as best they could, they did.

1973-74

Talk about a bad year for Chelsea. After all the cup triumph of the previous years and the team lording itself around the country and further-a-field in Europe, suddenly everything was quickly hitting the fan. The Manager and players were busy falling out. The fallout would eventually result in four first team players being left out of the side and

Alan Hudson being quickly dispatched to Stoke City for a new record transfer fee. The directors of the club backed Dave Sexton, even though his management style was fast becoming just starch in the shirts of the Paisley wearing, good time footballing, King's Road icons.

Eventually, Osgood would move reluctantly to Southampton for £275,000 in March and at the end of the season David Webb made the short trip to Queen's Park Rangers to complete the partial dismantling of Chelsea's, up to this point, most successful side. Not only that, but relegation was an ever present and fingernails were chewed constantly all around West London and beyond waiting for the final whistle every Saturday. In the Cup competitions, Chelsea couldn't even get past the first hurdle which they crashed against spectacularly and the skeletal East Stand development reduced capacity and drained the revenue away from the club's already exhausted resources.

But there was some good news, Adam had finally been in the Shed. John had decided to take him along to see a London derby against neighbours Queen's Park Rangers and for atmosphere alone it was a completely different kettle of fish to any previous match that he had been to.

Firstly, the noise. Where Adam had been sitting before in the West Stand he always felt a little detached however much he was in the thick of things. At the Shed End you felt like the match was being directly affected by the people in the Stand around you who were willing on their team with a swagger, however rubbish the match and with a rich use of London vernacular whatever the result.

Secondly, he was now standing up and this allowed for far more expression whenever there was a goalmouth moment. He could jump up or at least attempt it, something he had to do to see over tall people in front, and it made him feel more in touch with the game, although this wasn't hard with his enthusiastic brother giving a commentary worthy of Brian Moore as the game progressed.

The Shed End was packed to the brim, so much so that it seemed like the terraces would burst at any minute. Extensive building was still going on in the East Stand (a mass of cranes, concrete and corrugated iron) so everyone was huddled in the remainder of the ground and around the pitch to watch a classic feast of goals. Six to be precise, all largely out of terrible defending, but a 3-3 scoreline and honours even felt just about right. Rangers had a well earned point to take on their short trip back to Loftus Road, while the Blues at least had managed a point to stave off relegation worries. And that's what it was, a season of worries. Unfortunately, things were about to get a whole lot worse.

CLASSROOM

Unfortunately, Adam's academic performances were beginning to echo Chelsea's chaotic season: Upheaval leading to poor performances, sloppy concentration, leaking goals left, right and centre. In Maths and Sciences he regularly failed to turn up, even if he was present in the class. Arithmetic bored him witless, and the only fun he ever had scientifically was with his elementary children's Chemistry set at home, trying to make stink bombs or some dangerous yellow gunge that could cause a nasty rash or if swallowed by his enemies would result in a transformation of apocalyptic proportions. Adam wanted to gain a patent for his chemical inventions and become a mad inventor, but it wasn't long before his equipment was confiscated by his mum, which in hindsight was a wise move.

If there had been marks for daydreaming, Adam was sure that he would have been top of the class, no doubt about it, because he was either planning some ridiculous escapade in his head or doodling frantically on the page. Unfortunately, when reality set in he was commonly 'absent without leave' and his school reports were testimony to the fact. Adam always tried to ignore the lumpy Head of Form teacher as he rambled on and on:

'I'm pleased to say, the end of term results for 2B have been most encouraging. There is much hard work across the spectrum and you have equipped yourselves well as pupils for the educational challenges that lie ahead'.

'Challenges ahead?' Adam thought, 'The challenge ahead is for Chelsea to rebuild the team next season and climb back up that First Division table'.

Mr Tank continued after sucking in a large amount of air.

'All of 2B have passed their exams with flying colours, except I'm afraid, for two notable exceptions'.

At that moment a little lump developed in Adam's throat. He just knew that he was one of the exceptions. It was as obvious as a Zeppelin over London and the way the teacher went on, Adam was convinced the fat bubble was about to explode.

He sat at his tiny desk and as everyone's eyes began to look about in nervy anticipation, Adam toyed with the sleeve of his school shirt.

'Well, this needs a good wash', he reckoned (it would not be uncommon for their shirts to go at least a week without getting spruce. Mind you, that was nothing compared to their green school sweaters, they could go for half a term without so much as a dot of Daz. Even after a week or so, it wasn't difficult to detect a rich tapestry of dried porridge, Weetabix, school potato and traces of marmalade and butter across them).

'Taylor?'

'Sir...'

Adam breathed a sigh of relief. Some other unfortunate was biting the dust. While some boys smirked at him, others prepared their put downs for the school playground. 'Thicky' was a good one, 'Spazmo' even better.

'Next term, you will be in 3C'.

'Yes, sir'.

There was a cough and a splutter and then everyone held their breath once more.

'And likewise....'

(again the lump returned to Adam's throat and sure enough he found himself absolutely correct. Pity he hadn't been so correct with the academic side of things, he would have been top of the year).

'Nedman, you will also find yourself next term in 3C'.

'....Yes, sir....' Adam replied eventually, with a large dose added suggesting as if he was 'not really caring'.

'This will enable you both to work at a pace which is more in keeping with your needs. I feel that you two boys will excel in this more relaxed atmosphere and your grades will improve as a consequence'.

What he really meant was, 'I've had enough of you stupid little idiots - go down a form and rot in the abyss of your own making'.

'Thank you, sir….butt-head….' was Adam's quiet reply, which was still enough to be heard, so that not only was he now in a new form but also on a detention. The pace of the new form the following term was much more conducive though: Adam could doodle and daydream for hours.

DOG DAY AFTERNOON

Sam, the pet dog, had become an increasingly close companion whenever Adam was on holiday, and when he was away at school Adam always missed his company. Sam was a keen terrier with quirky tendencies and like Adam's sister was always 'there or there abouts'. He was intelligent too. He would growl loudly at the television during 'Top of the Pops', especially if there was a particularly Glam and glittery appearance by Mud or Wizzard. He always barked at 'Doctor Who', whenever a Cyberman popped threateningly into view, and that was always Adam's cue to hide behind the settee. During 'Match of the Day', when very occasionally Adam was allowed to stay up late, Sam tried his best to keep a respectful hours silence and was usually to be found following the Chelsea fortunes from his favourite living room seat.

Adam reckoned this canine understood a thing or two about 4-4-2, despite always being turned out in the Leeds strip - all white. But give him a ball and he'd do his best to mimic Charlie Cooke, only on exactly the same spot and round and round in an ever frenzied circle.

Sam always knew if there was a storm brewing outside or inside the house. He knew even before the kick off, because he would enter Adam's bedroom very stealthily and next minute he'd be hiding under the bed, trembling, breathing heavily and sweating in the way that only dogs can.

There they were. Adam and Sam. They were good friends during these uneasy moments. Sometimes Adam likened it to two expectant soldiers clocking each other before having to go into action, puffing on that proverbial last cigarette, praying for a truce and the guns to fall silent. Strange thing was that Sam not only knew when it would start up, but he also knew when the referee would blow the final whistle. He would do this little shuffle and then proceed to shake himself down. He would then look at Adam indignantly, 'Oh, so it's alright again', and with a wag of his tail he'd make for the door, as if Adam would charge him rent if he hung about.

One weekend in term-time, Adam took part in the School's Subbuteo, Table Football Championships, played in a dilapidated portakabin next to the boot room.

For some reason unknown to him, Adam's team was 'Blackpool' (in eye-catching tangerine) and he got knocked out - more like robbed - in the quarter final by Taylor, the other form dunce, now one of his best friends. His opponents team was supposed to be 'QPR' but you couldn't be too sure because half of the players had very serious ailments, like having no head, or one arm missing, one or two had a fixation with glue, another new transfer acquisition had forgotten to take his old clubs' shirt off and was masquerading as Stoke City. It was also confusing because both teams shared blue and white, though Rangers had the famous hoops. But a kind of camouflage resulted and that's how Adam reckoned that he had been beaten.

The pitch was also a disgrace. No way should it ever have been deemed playable by the referee (one of the less conscientious prefects). It needed a bloody good iron and a dash of paint on the lines. No doubt the Groundsman had been away on holiday. Adam reckoned his notice would most certainly be awaiting him on his return. QPR's goal was another bone of contention, being so furrowed it looked like Plough Lane. There was also a strange pit in the green cloth along the length of the left flank which halted Adam's fleet footed winger, and a crease mark in the centre circle that stalled his midfield. His goalkeeper seemed to spend a lot of the time just flying around in mid air above the pitch. The strikers were forever goal hanging, but up the wrong end, tangled inside their own net.

The two boys played the long ball game. They flicked it every which way. Sometimes, the ball went so far up and away that the game would have to be halted while they both went off and searched for it. There were some disturbing injuries too. One of the opposing players lost his base during a heated goalmouth melee, while Adam's favourite centre-half got crushed when he rushed off excitedly to the toilet during half-time.

It was to be a costly error. Up until that point the match had 0-0 painted all over it and Adam fancied himself in a replay. As they laid out their teams in their preferred formations for the second half, Adam crowded his goal, as he was now down to ten men (once the game had started no substitutes were allowed, but it wouldn't have made any difference anyway, as there weren't any more players in Adam's box. So, so much for 4-3-3. It was now more like 7-1-1). It was then that Adam sensed that something wasn't quite right. He didn't know what exactly, he just sensed something - you know how you do. Call it a funny feeling. Call it a premonition. Anyway, it was enough to throw him off his game and because he wasn't concentrating fully, right at the end, QPR scored with a dipping deflection which just left Blackpool's keeper standing, arms aloft.

As loud whoops of joy launched themselves out of the opponent's orifice, and the final whistle blew exactly at that second, Adam was informed by a prefect that his parents had arrived and that he was now excused from Hobbies.

When Adam met his parents, he was surprised because he had been fairly certain that they wouldn't be coming to visit him that particular weekend. But he wasn't complaining. He was whisked off to somewhere that produced copious amounts of decent food and chocolate sundaes. Yes, something was definitely up. His sister was down to see him as well and she was making far too much effort. 'That's strange', Adam thought, and he was correct. Perhaps during all those times when Sam was hiding under his bed, during a storm, the dog had lent Adam some of his own prophecy making kit. Because just as Adam sat in the back of the car, ready to be driven back to his place of learning he was told that Sam, 'wouldn't be around anymore'.

There was a long pause. The engine of the car ticked over as Adam's parents tried to put the news over as sensitively as possible. But he was prepared. He had a hunch that bad news was coming his way. He had already sensed it. When eating his ice cream he could tell that his sister was upset about something. His worst fears had been confirmed.

'He had to be put to sleep', his mum said.

'Sleep?....'

'Sam wasn't well....'

'Why?'

'He'd been ill for some time'.

'Ill?'

'He just wouldn't eat', added his Dad.

'I see....' as tears welled up, Adam stared at the floor.

'There was nothing we could do'.

The world crumbled around him. A big hole opened up and Adam fell in it. He wanted to tell them about his crushed centre-half in the Subbuteo competition but he didn't think they would appreciate the metaphor. He tried desperately to come to terms with the news, 'won't be around anymore'. How could that work? Surely, Sam would be back? Alan Hudson was, after injury. So was Peter Osgood.

This was a new concept. Grief. Adam hadn't really thought of Sam as just a pet, but as another member of the family. I mean he saw him about as regularly. In a funny kind of way hearing that Sam had been 'put down' made Adam feel like it would just be an extra long time before he saw him again. Just lots and lots of extra time, followed by more and more, but eventually, somehow or other he would.

'Sam is gone', Adam thought to himself. 'At least he won't be able to chew my Airfix kits anymore', he reasoned, 'and drive me mad hiding under my bed. But he won't be able to do his Charlie Cooke impression with my football either'.

It was beyond doubt. Adam's crushed centre-half had sustained a career threatening injury. He concluded that the player would now be labelled as 'crocked', but always mentioned in apologetic tones in future match day programmes.

Back at School, Adam slowly retrieved the pieces of his centre-half and laid them to rest in the Subbuteo box with a strip of cellotape wrapped around him. And eventually, once Adam had come to terms with Sam's sudden leaving, he thought;

'Perhaps I'll make a bid for my opponent's crafty Stoke City player as a replacement after all. He was handy he was, lording it around the centre circle'.

MUSIC LESSONS

Adam wanted to waste some time playing a musical instrument, so he had a trial with the violin. The problem was he learned how to tune it properly, so his school music lessons revolved around him screeching and grinding the bow down the length and breadth of the instrument for hours on end. The noise was so bad, dogs howled in the street. Children were evacuated from the neighbourhood. Grown-ups went mad and his bumbling, eccentric Germanic music teacher spent the whole time huffing and puffing, frantically trying to prevent Adam making the kind of din that would bring down aeroplanes and wake up the dead.

'No, no, no! Aarrgh! No! God no! Look - move your finger here!'

'Where?' Adam replied, looking dim.

'Here. Here!' the teacher would shout, as he tried to pull Adam's fingers apart and into the right shape. 'No, not there. Here! Here!! Place your fingers here!'

'Where?'

'Weren't you listening? Look, I showed you!'

'I couldn't hear…'

'But I showed you! I showed you!'

'Oh,….sorry'.

And then there would be a slight pause before Adam let loose once more, the sort of grating sound that made the torture of fingernails down a blackboard seem like a good hobby.

ZIGGY STARDUST

Adam's older brother Alan took him shopping one day during the holidays, which was a rare event. When they reached the high street, Alan turned to him announcing;

'I forgot to get you a birthday present'.

'I know....' Adam blurted, suddenly remembering. Mind you if Alan hadn't said anything you could be sure that Adam would have continued being none the wiser.

'So, is there anything you want?'

Adam glowed in anticipation.

'Er, umm....I dunno'.

'You don't know?'

'No. Well...er, yeah, well no.... oh, I know - that record you keep playing'.

'Which record?'

'The one with the loud noises on it?'

'Loud noises?'

'Yeah....guitar'.

'Loud guitar'.

'Yeah, it's got a man in a telephone box on it'.

'Telephone box?'

'On the cover, and it says, 'Play really loud'.

'Oh....what d'you mean, David Bowie?'

'Yeah, that's him!'

'Ziggy Stardust?'

'Yeah!'

'Okay....'

'Great', Adam thought. He didn't have any records at that point, apart from an old Camberwick Green album, the Best of Trumpton and Chigley, Thunderbirds'- 'No Strings Attached' played by the Barry Gray Orchestra, and an old, broken Thomas the Tank Engine extended play, which all his brothers had discarded in turn.

It was obvious. Adam really wanted to start collecting something a little bit more substantial. Something that might make him seem more grown up. Sophisticated even. The only proper records he'd seen up until this point (apart from his brothers closely guarded collection, were in his sister's possession and they were a load of old 45 rpm singles by the Beatles, like 'She Loves You' and 'Love Me Do' and other bands of that bygone period like Gerry and The Pacemakers, covered in scratches and fingerprints from hasty playing and negligent storage. Lots of love songs and slushy epithets of devotion that made Adam want to vomit whenever he heard them going round and round on his sister's turntable. Let's just say that he wasn't too keen on tunes about boy meets girl or girl meets boy at this stage because all that seemed to happen was a lot of silly snogging and Adam reckoned that you wouldn't want to do that forever. It was like Kiss Chase back at his primary school. You just didn't want to still be playing it while eating your school dinner of bangers and mash.

So when his brother Alan said that he was buying him a birthday present, he knew that it was going to be something a little bit different (Adam already owed John for taking him to his first Chelsea match).

They entered the HMV record shop and there were lots of racks of albums and brightly coloured posters on the walls, advertising new records whose band members didn't seem too dissimilar to Adam's brothers in appearance. In other words lots of hair and peculiar clothing, words like 'LED ZEPPELIN' and 'THE ROLLING STONES' jumped out at you and 'SPECIAL OFFER' and '45's' and 'LP'S'.

The counter seemed huge and high up and the shop was being run by some sort of Tony Blackburn look-a-like, whose groomed hair seemed all 'syrup of figs' and he practised his cheesy smile to all the customers in turn.

'D'you have Ziggy Stardust and the Spiders from Mars?' said Alan hopefully.

'Er, yes, just a moment', and off the shop assistant trotted around the side of the shop to where hundreds more albums were stacked. He stood next to the shelf marked with a large letter B and within seconds he had extracted a gleaming new copy of the very same album that Adam's brother had purchased only about six months before.

The Ziggy Stardust album cover was mysterious: the singer posing outside a side-street doorway at night, under an old streetlamp and a brightly lit sign saying 'K. WEST'. Bowie looked defiant with his modish blonde hair, posing cockily, guitar in hand. His green and black jumpsuit with the trouser bottoms provocatively rolled up to show off a large pair of black boots signified he might be some sort of musical bootboy straight off the football terraces or out of an infamous film like 'A Clockwork Orange' (The Ziggy Stardust album cover always reminded Adam of a striking poster he had seen which happened to have been taken from the Kubrick film that was pasted on the wall right outside Adam's favourite cinema in the Fulham Road).

To the right of Bowie, cardboard boxes and rubbish littered the pavement. To the left, a row of cars sat in the street. It could be just about any urban scene, anywhere you might think, except within it was something Adam thought extraordinary, and that of course was David Bowie himself. There wasn't anyone else like him. He was absolutely unique. On the back cover he slouched arrogantly in a telephone box. Was he waiting for a call? Or was he about to make one? Adam wasn't quite sure. Again the picture was dark and slightly murky as if it was all an enigma, even to the singer himself. And was he that masculine, in his laced up boots? There was a hint in the make-up on his face that perhaps he wasn't.

Over to the left of the back cover, towards the bottom, were the words: TO BE PLAYED AT MAXIMUM VOLUME. As John and Adam left the shop, there was the unmistakable smell of new vinyl, as if it had just arrived from the pressing plant. The effect was further increased by a large HMV record bag which Adam tried not to swing about too much as he returned home.

Once back, Alan put the record on. Adam had only ever heard it in the background before. This time the effect was instant. He was knocked out by the sounds and the words. The first track was called 'Five Years' and it made Adam laugh because Bowie's lyrics were straight out of some strange dreamlike fantasy world about a Policeman 'kneeling and kissing the feet of a priest' and someone 'queer' being sick at the sight of it. Then Bowie saw someone 'in an ice cream parlour, drinking milk shakes cold and long'.

Adam had never heard anything like it. There was something sad and ominous about the repetition of the Five Years at the end of the song. 'Did they really only have five years left?' Adam wondered. 'If we do, we better get a move on then'. He looked again at the back cover, with '1972 RCA Records' in small print down the bottom. It was then that Adam calculated, despite his minimum maths: 'Five years from 1972?' He paused for a moment. 'That'll mean the end of the world will be in 1977'.

The rest of the album continued the strange obsessions with more and more of a Sci-Fi element. Adam liked that too. Especially the title track itself. And he thought the guitarist, Mick Ronson, was superb. He had a heavy glam style, but he was also incredibly melodic and it was no coincidence that the songs on the album were as catchy as they were. 'One day I'd like to make some sounds like that', Adam considered, unrealistically.

The titles of the other tracks, were also full of mystery, just like the enigmatic album cover: Moonage Daydream, Starman, Suffragette City and the last track, Rock'n'roll Suicide, was a poetic barnstormer. The addition of an inner sleeve with all the bizarre lyrics and close up black and white pictures of all four members of the band was an added bonus and the album certainly sounded great whenever it was played over the years, as it stated, at 'maximum volume'. 'Not bad for the first proper record in my collection', Adam concluded.

WORLD CUP '74

The summer term of 1974 was full of hope. Adam was finally more settled in at school. He was beginning to know the ropes and had also managed to his surprise to make a few friends. He was also playing a lot of football in the school yard. The weather was brilliantly hot and the icing on the cake had to be the World Cup which was about to take place in Germany during the term.

England unfortunately, weren't represented after the disaster against Poland in the qualifiers and Scotland were knocked out early in the competition without making much of an impact. Allegiance to a team was crucial to fully enjoy the competition and as Adam had a Dutch relative and had visited Amsterdam on a couple of occasions with his parents, he decided to support Holland.

What a choice. Of all the teams he could have chosen to follow, Holland were going through something of a footballing renaissance: In other words they were beginning to play some amazingly silky stuff and focus more on the total, attacking game, as opposed to the dull, negative, defensive stuff that many other teams believed was the only approach to win great competitions. I suppose you could say that the Dutch were becoming more adventurous and flamboyant in their play rather like what the Brazilians had achieved on their way to winning the World Cup in 1970. Then, players like Pele, Jairhzino and Tostao had a massive influence and Adam could remember their names rolling off his tongue with ease by the end of the tournament, despite his relative youth.

So, Adam reckoned the Dutch were the new Brazilians and hot favourites and he concluded that he could do a lot worse than put all his support in their corner. They had Johann Cruyff for a start, and Johann Neeskens, and his favourite player of all - Johnny Rep.'What a fantastic name', Adam thought. He wished he had a name like that too. He would be popular with the girls having a name like that, even though his knowledge of girls at that point could be very easily accommodated on a small postage stamp. Johnny Rep. Wasn't that really the name of some revolutionary hero? The sort of figure that disciples would regularly die for and dedicate odes to?

Then of course there was the kit. Bright orange. Not light orange or dull orange but brighter than bright orange. Yes, a fabulous kit. In the same way that Brazil's 1970 yellow, green and blue kit was memorable.

Adam followed Holland's progress as much as he could. At weekends they were allowed to watch a few of the games, and when the Dutch players lined up before the matches to sing their national anthem, Adam kept trying to picture what he might look like dressed in clogs.

Cruyff was incredible throughout the tournament. Such a straight and proud stature on the ball, coupled with unbelievable vision. He was the definitive footballing silk purse, and all around him, sow's ears huffed and puffed about, trying to stop him. Like Pele before him, (and in Adam's more than biased opinion Chelsea's Charlie Cooke) Cruyff was turning football almost into an art form. Adam tried hard to recreate Cruyff's tricks on the school yard with little success, but at least he made sure that he always managed to be Johnny Rep.

Unfortunately, those industrious Germans weren't going to be bamboozled. The final was a frustrating, nail biting event. Every neutral wanted Holland, playing the beautiful game, the way it should be played, to lift the trophy. And surely they would. It was written. Or was it? Beckenbauer certainly had different ideas and due to a Gurd Muller winner, the organised, efficient Germans triumphed. Sadly, Holland's destiny was to be the plucky losers. The valiant finalists. The flamboyant failures. The skilful runners up.

Still, the Dutch had reached the finals and given many people like Adam a lot of enjoyment along the way and with the passing of their World Cup aspirations so it resulted in a passing phase for Adam: By the end of the next school term he too was on his way to another educational establishment. Not that he was bothered. He had few real friends at the school and never really fitted in. One of the only times Adam felt that he had fitted in was when he took a small part in the school play, but that was a make believe situation anyway, and a brief one at that, so you could say that it probably didn't count.

In fact when the news went round to his fellow pupils that Adam was departing at short notice because of family reasons they almost treated him as if he wasn't really one of them in the first place. On one occasion in the dinner queue Adam overheard them chatting about his parents having financial assistance from the Governors of the school and that was the reason why he was leaving. Whatever the explanation, Adam tried his best to move on. He was like a footballer who had come to the end of his contract and was now out of favour with his club. But like many things in life, ready for the next adventure just around the corner.

3

TURDS

So there he was. Another new place of learning. This one called itself a 'Friends' co-educational school and Adam had visions of everyone being amazingly cheerful to each other and helpful to a ridiculous degree. He thought everybody would always be at hand for those in need and when he finally left the establishment everyone would be there to wave him on his way to adulthood. What a mug.

This time however, girls were included at the school which was fortunate because Adam was aching to find out a little bit more about the opposite sex, even if it was going to be some time before he actually put his inquisitiveness fully into action. The school was also situated in the west country, near Bristol, so at least it was close to some sort of civilisation. So, on paper it was another opportunity for Adam to make his way in the world and he should at least look as if he was grasping the opportunity with both hands.

Again Adam had arrived late. By a whole term. But this time it wasn't too depressing, as he was becoming accustomed to being in the wrong place at the right time or the right place at the wrong moment. The downside was always having to make friendships with pupils who already reckoned they knew the ropes and each other and so once more he was typecast convincingly in the role of outsider.

Adam was soon to conclude however, that this time, although fortune had most definitely not shone down on him in terms of his new school, at least in the timing stakes perhaps things were a little more promising.

He had only been at the school a day when he was informed by some others, including his first friend Robbie, that the pupils from the years above them had nicknamed the first year third formers, including Adam, 'Turds'. New comers seemed about as worthy as pieces of excrement, so Adam guessed that they weren't considered worthy at all. At Adam's previous school, being called a 'rag' was bad enough, but now he was labelled as a turd. I suppose it was an absurd sort of compliment, a promotion. He wondered if there might be a medal to go with it?

So, it was clear. Arriving a term late at his new school made Adam not just an outsider, but a 'shitty' one to boot.

'Turds?' Probed Adam, ever the infant detective.

'Yeah. Last term they tried to hang us'.

'Hang us?' Adam gulped.

'The year above took us into their changing room one by one, and hung us up by our feet'

'What?!'

'Yeah, then they spat at us and whipped us with wet towels'.

'No?!' Adam's eyes widened rapidly.

'One of us even got hung by his neck cos 'Skull' didn't like him and he nearly died'.

'Skull?'

'Yeah, he's their leader. Each Form's got one. The leader of the upper fifth beat up the Maths teacher and got away with it'.

'How did he do that?'

'His dad's a Governor, so he only got suspended'.

Adam choked on the information for a minute.

'So, what happened with Skull?'

'The teachers never found out about the hanging'.

'Why didn't you tell them?'

'We were too scared'.

'Oh, blimey....' said Adam anxiously, suddenly realising that the next few years at the school were certainly going to be more than interesting.

There was a pause as Adam's new school books dropped to the floor and as he picked them up he realised that he was now incarcerated in a very hostile seat of learning. What's more, there was a completely new code of conduct and Adam didn't like the sound of the wet towels one bit. The thought of having a noose placed around his neck just for being late didn't help either. Being spat at just because they were considered inferior and turds certainly didn't warm the cockles.

The positioning of their changing area alone, was fraught with danger. To reach it they had to go through the lower and upper fourth's changing room and they would usually run the gamut of towels, belts, shoes and anything that came to hand, like soap, washing bags and shoe cleaning tins. Early mornings and late evenings were mostly spent trying to dodge the various missiles sailing through the air as they brushed their teeth, and 'coming round' from getting a direct hit on the crown from a scrubbing brush or broom handle was not an irregular occurrence.

The organised shoe fights in the changing rooms between Forms was more of an entertainment, and leveller, allowing the turds to get their own back a little bit if they were good shots and there was no greater sense of achievement to be had than seeing someone from a higher year connect with a flying size seven. They had to be quick to avoid the crossfire, yet patient enough to choose the right moment of attack, and a skilful tactician to deploy military manoeuvres in their group. Even Napoleon would have been proud especially when the day was won with a last desperate volley, with backs to the wall. Afterwards, pupils were lucky if they ever found their own shoes again and if they did they were always covered in scuffs and scrapes or at worst someone's front teeth.

Another ritual that the upper fifth enjoyed inflicting on the turds was known as 'bloodsports'. Firstly, the senior pupils would find out who a turd's best friend was, in Adam's case it was Robbie, and then they would press gang them both into their common room. The two friends would then be forced to fight each other until blood was drawn.

Luckily, before long, Robbie caught Adam's nose full on with his fist and as the red mist came down and Adam tried to make out the stars whizzing, cartoon-like, around his head, they were finally excused to jeers as they made their way out of the common room to sanctuary. They were reminded that they couldn't tell anyone about it and certainly not a teacher, if they did it could be on pain of death. They had to take everything on the chin, or in Adam's case, on the nose.

Luckily, in the year above was a popular pupil who was also a Chelsea supporter called Steve. Lucky, because getting to know him eventually prevented some of the bullying of Adam's year, as he was tall and had a lot of influence. And when Steve heard that Adam also went to matches and was a keen Blues supporter, they planned to go to a game the next time they could.

Regrettably, Chelsea's fortunes at this time had hit rock bottom and Adam had watched the school television teary eyed as the commentator Barry Davies sadly reported Chelsea's relegation from Division One after fifteen years in the top flight. Not only that, but Dave Sexton, their most successful manager had resigned and even though the magnificent albatross, the East Stand, had finally opened, it was now going to be playing host to the likes of Notts County and York City. More worryingly, was the TV footage of some serious fisticuffs at Tottenham Hotspur - the end of season fixture that sealed Chelsea's fate and salt was rubbed into the wound with a violent free for all on the pitch after the match, which the TV cameras captured dramatically. One supporter was used almost like a rag doll by a group of thugs who could almost have passed for Bay City Rollers fans with their wide bottomed jeans, stacked heeled shoes and scarves wrapped flamboyantly around their wrists.

With the new surroundings of Division Two at least Chelsea could rebuild for the future and that is exactly what they started to do with Eddie McCreadie as the new Manager and Adam, Steve and his dad went to their first match together against Sunderland and watched from high up in the gleaming East Stand. The result was a satisfying hard fought 1-0 Chelsea victory and everyone reckoned that from their vantage point you would be hard pushed to find a better view of a football pitch anywhere in the country.

THE HOLE IN THE FLOOR GANG

As a result of being called 'turds', Adam's year seemed to spend most of their time avoiding the other members of the school. This meant that during free time they tried to occupy themselves usually within their own ground floor common room or in the dormitories, that's if they weren't out on the school playground known as the 'Quad' kicking a football.

After classes one afternoon, Adam noticed a loose floorboard next to his locker in the corner of the large common room. In fact, the wood was so loose that he tripped over it and went flying. Louie, who had been another new addition to the school, but even more awkwardly, in the middle of the term, laughed as Adam hurtled through the air.

"Ere, watch it!' Shouted Louie as Adam collided into him.

'Oh, sorry!'

'I bet....' Louie replied in his unmistakable Somerset accent.

For some reason, Louie was already becoming unpopular with the rest of the year. It had nothing to do with his mixed race background or his chequered childhood. One of the Form's more outspoken girl's thought that his personal hygiene perhaps wasn't up to scratch and that he was a little bit fat, but even though he didn't wash very often and was known to wear rancid socks, Adam felt that he had to be given a chance. He was an avid football fan, following the frustrating fortunes of Newcastle United and his favourite player 'Supermac' Malcolm MacDonald and he was always handy to have around whenever they ventured into Bristol at the weekends, because Louie knew the city like the back of his hand.

'Look! The floorboard's come loose', Adam blurted.

'Yeah, you're right!'

Louie stepped forward, and slowly, as he lifted the worn wooden board, the darkness beneath revealed itself. The plank came up almost completely out of its berth and with the aid of a quick tug, a nail twisted and turned and finally released it.

'Blimey! You can see right under the floor!' Louie announced excitedly.

'Watch out!' shouted Robbie as he ducked, Adam nearly beaming him

Laurel and Hardy style as he stood up.

'Heh, look at that!' Adam froze, and they all watched in silent awe as a strange dust like mist escaped from the hole in the floor.

'Spooky 'en it!'

'Yeah....'

'Bet it goes all the way right under the school'.

'There could be buried treasure down there!'

'I bet there is....'

'Come on, let's go under the floor!', challenged Louie with a big grin, the dust settling.

'No, chance! Think how smelly it'll be', replied Robbie with a good point.

'All we 'ave to do is pull up another plank to fit through'.

'But there might be some rats?' Adam added for effect.

'Yeah, rats?!' echoed Robbie.

'There's no rats. You two's are just chickens!' claimed Louie adamantly.

'No we're not!' answered Robbie and Adam eventually, the two of them shaking their heads unconfidently.

'Are so! Well, I'm not. I'm not!'

Just at that moment two Form girls entered the common room and the three lads immediately stood up suspiciously and Robbie tried valiantly to change the subject, with anything to cover their tracks. He decided on 'conkers', which was hardly going to put the nosy lasses off the scent, especially as they were out of season. As expected, it didn't wash and as Adam was busy shuffling his body over to cover up the hole in the floor, 'Snowy', a pretty girl with long blonde hair, who everybody fancied, spied the suspect loose flooring.

'What are you up to?'

'Nothin....' muttered Louie, tight lipped, in the most unconvincing fashion you could imagine.

'Yes you are. What's that then?!'

Three craniums then turned slowly in synch and dumbly clocked the wooden board that Adam had just placed up against a classmates till. They even did a double take for good measure.

'Don't tell anyone! You promise?' Louie ordered.

Both girls nodded briskly.

'No tellin' no one! Or else!'

'We promise....'

'Swear?'

'We swear....'

There was a brief pause that only helped to add to the tension.

'We've....found....a hole in the floor', whispered Robbie.

'I found it'. Adam reminded everyone, glancing at Snowy as he said it.

'Really? Let's see!'

And the two girls hurried over excitedly to peer down into the abyss.

'Don't you tell anyone. It's a secret. Right!'

'We said we won't and we won't. We promised!' said Snowy's tall friend Annabel, adjusting her specks.

'Better not', said Louie crossing his arms and puffing out his chest.

There was another pause.

'What are you going to do?'

'We're gonna escape that's what'.

'Escape?'

'Yeah, down there. We've had enough of school. We're not comin' back'.

'Wow, can we come too?' pleaded Snowy hopefully.

'No way! We're not havin' no girls with us'.

'Oh, go on. Please....'

'No! We found the hole. This is our mission. Go play with your netball!'

Then, after looking at each other for a moment, the two girls strode off in a huff.

'Do you reckon they'll tell?' questioned Robbie after the common room door slammed shut.

'They'd be stupid to 'cos we'll know it's them', replied Louie authoritatively.

After the girls had gone back to their business the three amigos discussed the next stage in operations. Louie was all for exploring straight away without any sort of hesitation. Robbie was well up for the tunnelling but was slightly nervous at what they might discover and the fact that they could get trapped down below scared him. Adam was all for planning their next move. They needed to put the plank back and await their moment. Anything hasty and they might get caught. The next weekend, that would be their signal. They would have more time to explore the hole and they would also be dressed in 'civvies' so if they got dusty their school uniforms would not be spoilt. Also, they would have to put a 'watch' on the door of the common room to avoid detection. Torches would also be needed and some sort of utensil, perhaps taken from the kitchens, would be required for any digging purposes. Fortunately, Louie and Robbie were in agreement. The very next Saturday would see their first journey into the unknown.

The time passed quickly, as the three worked as usual in classes, which wasn't very much, in order not to raise any suspicions from any vigilant teachers. Had they suddenly improved their grades or excelled in their appreciation of English Lit and History, not to mention Geography, where a sudden flair for ordnance survey maps would definitely have rung the alarm bell, it would no doubt have led all the way back to the hole in the common room floor, like a bad smell. Or like Louie's socks.

They wanted it to seem as if nothing had happened. Which of course it hadn't. However, messages of great importance in secret code began to be passed backwards and forwards in lessons. One message that Adam sent to Robbie, who sat just across from him in class, went something like; 'L. a R. mt 1.27 nxt 2 bns Pss on'. Robbie's encoded reply was 'S. I. G (he was like Adam a fan of Captain Scarlet) and then 'C. U. R.' (American 'Mad' comics were his favourite).

They were convinced, to the enemy - the Gestapo teachers - their code was uncrackable. This was tested to the full, when during one lesson, a message of Robbie's dropped accidentally on the floor right next to their beady Maths teacher and even though the message was picked up and read out aloud while Adam and Robbie held their breath, its gobbledygook meant absolutely nothing at all. Except of course to the two code makers. Which was fortunate, because its contents confirmed that torches were at the ready and that Louie had recently pinched a large ladle from the Kitchens.

The other important area of operations in their 'phoney' campaign was to make sure the girls kept quiet. This was sorted out by nominating both Snowy and Annabel as chief spies and common room lookouts, so they had an active and important involvement and if they told on the boys they would surely face the consequences too. So at least there was some sort of guarantee that they wouldn't snitch.

In the clothing department, they decided that wearing their sports kit and tracksuit bottoms during any operations was paramount, so that any detection of dirt could easily be passed off by the school laundry as excessive exertions on the rugby pitch for the good of the school.

Meanwhile, the loose plank had been temporarily returned to its place and no one would ever have guessed that it was removable, even with close inspection, as dust and dirt had been placed carefully around its edges to make it seem as if it had never been tampered with, just like in one of Adam's favourite films 'The Great Escape'. They knew that eventually another floor board alongside it would have to be removed to allow them easier access to the dark world beneath, but that was going to be simple because the very next piece of wood, which was luckily concealed right next to Adam's locker, was already slightly loose.

Saturday came around at last. Luckily, none of them had any parents visiting that weekend to disrupt their planned escape. Most of the other boarders in the year were going on excursions or were being taken out by their parents for a weekends respite from the school, which meant that there would be complete reign of the common room territory. The few lucky day pupils were already enjoying their regular weekend freedom from the establishment's clutches.

Then came good news from the Front. Not only did they have the torches and a large soup ladle from the Kitchens, but Robbie had scrounged a school caving helmet complete with lamp attached which the older pupils used on field trips. Although it was at least two sizes too big for him, he looked the part, that's when he could see where he was going. Despite this, Robbie was certainly enthusiastic about the task ahead as he had been potholing once, and because he had the best equipment for the job, he was quickly named 'Tunnel King'. He was also short and stocky which made him ideal to lead the expedition, ladle in one hand, a ball of string to mark out the way, in the other.

Following in his wake would be Louie, the 'Cooler King', famed already at school for his amazing appetite for detention and his devil-may-care attitude, especially when it came to washing his feet. So he wasn't going to be at all bothered about getting dirty.

Last but not least, was Adam, who fell into the role of checking on communications between the lookouts and the chain of command during the early stages, deal with any logistical problems along the way and bring up the rear, but never too close to Louie's feet. He was prepared for any eventuality, so he had a large supply of chocolate biscuits, stolen from the Staff Room, to maintain morale.

Adam considered his role to be similar to that of Sir Richard Attenborough's in the classic 'The Great Escape' and at times he fancied himself in the part, recognising all the while that in real life, Attenborough, was on the board of director's at Chelsea.

As D-Day ticked, the three stared down the hole, and flinched with nervous energy at the dark uninviting domain beneath.

'Go on then, Robbie!' cried Louie, almost licking his lips.

'Alright. Keep your hair on!'

'It's all clear....' whispered their trusty girl guides hovering by the common room door as they twiddled with their hair.

'No one about....' Snowy added for good measure and as she spoke, Adam suddenly imagined the two of them both far away on some desert island collecting coconuts or trying to catch some exotic fish for their next meal.

'Here goes!' and Robbie was off, scrambling into the void through the space in the floor that had been widened cunningly, with a lot of Louie's brute force, during the days of preparation.

'Mind the dust....' Adam said uselessly.

'Dust!' mocked Louie.

He immediately burst out laughing and at the same time almost began beating his chest.

'I don't mind no dust! Come on, let's get down there!'

'I am!' replied Robbie, clunking about in all his equipment.

Good as his word, the Tunnel King was already half submerged and as he twisted his body down he started to disappear below ground zero. Just at that moment, Robbie's caving helmet cracked against the side of the hole and Adam and Louie burst out laughing.

'Ouch! That hurt!'

Once Robbie had recovered and was fully below ground he switched on his lamp and an eerie illumination highlighted the murky abyss and they could just make out for the first time the untidy contours below. There didn't seem to be as much dust as before but there was a lot of paper and old rubbish and some rusty pipes and wooden rafters crisscrossed about like railway junctions. There was no doubt about it, space was at a premium with only about two foot in height to move about in.

'I'm next!' said Louie and after leaving a hiatus in Robbie's wake, he switched on his torch and followed with gusto and it wasn't long before he too was swallowed up.

Suddenly the girls ears pricked up and Adam froze stiff.

'It's a teacher. A teacher!' Snowy hissed.

'Oh, shi.....' Adam murmured. 'Louie! Robbie....Louie!'

There was a shuffling commotion and panic from under the floor and then all went quiet. Louie gave out a final gasp as if to say 'How dare a teacher turn up now! I'll kill 'em!' and they all continued to freeze. Adam stared over at the girls who likewise stood bolt upright expecting at any moment to be caught red handed.

The moment seemed to last forever and then just as Adam sensed the door creaking open and an adult entering, the two spymasters gave out a big girlie giggle.

'Only joking!'

There was a tense pause.

'WHAT?!'

'Only joking!'

'Oh....you - '

From under the floor you could hear a great rumbling and clanking as Robbie and Louie moved in response. Then Louie let rip which was comical, as he sounded like he was in some long dark tunnel, which you could say he was.

'You bloomin' girls! I'll bloody sort you both out! You 'ear me! When we escape from 'ere we'll come back for you. We'll come back to get you - you see if we don't! Bloody girls!'

'It was only a joke....' said Annabel still grinning from ear to ear with her friend.

'Joke!' rattled Louie from another dimension. 'Joke! I'll give you a bloody joke! You'll see!' and as he ranted and raved he began to choke on some dust that had caught up on him.

'We'll be off then!' said Snowy indignantly.

'Fine!' Adam added.

'You won't have anyone to guard you -'

'WE DON'T CARE! NOW BUGGER OFF!!' cried Louie like a schoolboy possessed, his head now jutting manically out of the floor.

As the girl's left in a flurry, Annabel stuck out her tongue in Louie's direction and muttered something under her breath that sounded like 'bet you get caught'. Luckily for them Louie was too preoccupied to hear.

Once the girls had departed and the common room became quiet once again, they decided to wait for another of their year to turn up so that they could replace their look-out, before Adam too descended below. They didn't have to wait long because the 'Prof', a fellow pupil, so-called because of his bespectacled bookish demeanour, entered sheepishly to complete his Prep and once persuaded, watched at the door that the girl's had vacated.

The positive thing about the Prof was that he was largely trustworthy because he was always on his own, so it was difficult for him to get up to any shenanigans. He had few friends, if any, and his parents rarely visited him, so he was almost totally self sufficient. He was a rare commodity in the school, where virtually all the pupils cow towed to the teachers or showed off to their peers in one form or another. No, the Prof was different. He didn't care what other people thought of him. In fact, he was totally oblivious of them. His head was a jumble of mathematical conundrums of his own making, but it was a cranium that he seemed at home in.

What's more, Adam reckoned that if the Prof was captured and interrogated by the teachers that he would certainly go the distance. There was no way that he would risk Adam, Robbie and Louie's temporary companionship. Besides, as most people hardly even acknowledged his existence, he was being empowered with a position of trust, however tenuous. The 'Prof' - 'The Lookout'. If the teachers ever managed to force him to spill the beans about the secret hole, which was highly unlikely, his solitary reply would probably be 'E = MC squared' or 'I before E except after C'. To get anything more out of the Prof of any significance, would have taken a sustained cross examination. The teachers would certainly have to prepare for a very late night and obtain some spare light bulbs for that intensive psychological grilling.

With the greasy haired professor in place, with one eye on the lookout and the other busily scrutinising his Physics books, Louie returned once more below and it wasn't a moment too soon, because Robbie had already made great headway and they could hear him banging out a primitive Morse code with the soup ladle near the corner of the room. Only trouble was it was the wrong corner. Robbie in his confusion beneath, was heading towards the inner sanctum of the school and not as far away as possible from it.

Louie manically followed the path of the string that Robbie had left behind and as he struggled to stop the Tunnel King going too far, Adam went over and banged on the floor roughly above where Robbie was.

'The other way! The other way!' Adam cried, but he wasn't sure if Robbie was hearing him clearly as he just kept clanking back some more crazy Morse code in his own demented fashion.

There was now nothing left for it. Adam had to follow Louie down below and explain the situation. They wanted to leave the school, not end up buried at its heart. Now that would have been silly and such a waste of Robbie's youthful tunnelling talent. Once Adam had clicked his torch on, he slipped underneath as fast as he could and at that very instant he caught the Prof peering over his text book and giving him a belated thumbs up. Before Adam had even caught his breath he was under the floor.

As his torch propelled its beam, up ahead, beyond a twirl of rusty pipes was Louie, huffing and puffing at the exertion of trying to move in such a restricted space. It was fortunate that they weren't large adults because there would have been no way that they were ever going to see the light of day again and as the thought of premature burial crossed Adam's mind constantly, he tried to scramble along the string towards Robbie. The illumination from his potholing helmet made Robbie look like a weary miner and already his face was covered in dirt. He still seemed a long way away and a wooden support holding the floor up momentarily obscured him from view.

Adam paused for a moment to take it all in and took out one of his chocolate biscuits. The darkest recesses were spooky alright and there were unidentifiable shadows and shapes thrown in relief all over the place by their ghostly searchlights. If ever there was going to be buried treasure about, here was surely the place. The school Governess's jewels perhaps, or maybe something counterfeit like Monopoly money, in fact just any old coin would have done the trick. No doubt the discovery would stop them immediately in their tracks. No more thoughts of escape. No, with enough gold and silver they could buy the whole establishment. The teaching staff certainly wouldn't be difficult to purchase, judging by the teaching talent available. Adam reckoned they might fetch a couple of bob at most. Furthermore, they could buy themselves lots of qualifications and certificates and even pass a law permitting free time at all times and like Alice Cooper sing, 'School's out forever!' For ever.

But it was more likely that the treasure would make them quarrel for sole possession of its bounty. Who knows? Maybe they would take sides. Maybe they would gang up two onto one and then a final fight to the death would end with Louie suffocating the unfortunate victim with his cheesy socks while grinning manically. Adam gulped noticeably at the thought. What could be worse than that? Not a lot.

As he finished off his digestive, he kept all thoughts of betrayal to himself. To Adam's surprise he noticed that there was less dust than he had expected but there was still lots of old bits of paper, sweet wrappers and odds and ends scattered across the floor. Old discarded text books that dated as far back as 1965 littered the ground.

'Oi, Robbie?! Turn round! Turn round!' shouted Louie almost frothing at the mouth.

'Oh, no....' Adam thought. 'Maybe even Louie's getting scared?'

'It's this way! This way!' was Robbie's distant reply.

Just at that moment there was a loud crack on the floor above them and they all ducked down into the dirt to protect themselves. It was almost as if the wooden boards were going to cave in.

All was silent. As they lay stock still, they could suddenly make out an adult voice up above in the common room. 'That must be a teacher talking to the Prof and he's tried to warn us in his own way' thought Adam. They waited and waited. Adam and Louie tensely eyeballed each other, that's of course when their eyes weren't transfixed on the ceiling right above them. They were like two U-Boat occupants waiting powerlessly for the depth charges to hit and as the time ticked by, a bead of sweat dripped off the end of Adam's nose. They were goners for sure.

Fortunately, the chatter seemed somehow to die down and once again there were two loud cracks on the floor above them and they realised that it was an all clear from the Prof. What a genius. There was no doubt he had saved their skins and as soon as they were back above ground and successful in their escape they would make him an honorary member of their gang. A postcard would arrive for the Prof, some weeks later, which in itself would be a novelty because he never received any mail, sent by the three fugitives from a secret mountainous location.

Adam and Louie continued to make good progress towards Robbie, but in their haste the string had got tangled around Louie's legs and he had spent what felt like twenty minutes muttering 'Bugger!' and 'Shit!' while he disentangled himself.

Robbie was in such a small space now it didn't seem possible that anyone could fit themselves into it. The cavity was surrounded by foundations and rubbish and he looked in a bad way and it was also cold down there. The expression on his face told the whole story. He was close to panic. Unfortunately, just like the real Tunnel King from the film, Robbie suffered from an unusual form of claustrophobia.

'Robbie....you alright?' whispered Louie comfortingly.

There was no reply. Robbie just looked vacant and mumbled as if he was about to say something but then decided not to. They were all now hardly recognisable as their former selves, the filth having completely changed their features. Robbie looked especially transformed with his helmet covering his eyes.

'You'll be alright....we're gonna get you out of 'ere'. Louie repeated himself, but it was no use because Robbie was still not quite with them. And just as Adam was thinking about how to help him through the labyrinth to safety, there was a strange shuffling noise from along the far wall and when Louie's torch caught something scurrying about, that was it, Robbie was off like a flash, scrambling as fast as he could towards the direction of the hole in the floor, the soup ladle and the string long since ditched and his helmet almost falling off. As he passed by possessed, he shouted out, 'A RAT! A RAT!' and that was the signal for Adam and Louie to cry out as well and the three of them were almost trying to scamper over each other to reach the sanctuary of the entrance.

It was chaos. Adam couldn't be sure how they managed to emerge from the floor, but eventually they did. Adrenalin or madness must have taken over. One thing was certain, Robbie was completely out of it. The only other time Adam had seen him quite as upset was after the gang had tried to conjure up the ghost of an old school governor with Louie's Ouija board in their spooky old dormitory. They had asked whether a spirit was specifically present in the room and after a momentary pause they were scared absolutely witless as the glass moved virtually on its own towards 'YES' on the board. Robbie then screamed that he could see an apparition right by his bed, almost shrouding it, and they were off running for their lives.

As Robbie lay in a sweaty heap on the common room floor, the others struggled to remove the potholing helmet from his head. Louie gave it a final tug and off it came as Robbie let out another yelp as the strap had caught in his hair almost pulling a clump out with it. He was in a bad way alright with a great coughing and spluttering and as they tried their best to calm him down he rocked from side to side. The Prof, who was surprised to say the least by their manner and appearance, managed to find a glass of water from somewhere and that helped to avert Robbie's further distress. That was lucky because the biscuits in Adam's pockets were completely crumbled in the hasty exit from the hole.

Eventually, Robbie came round, to everyone's relief and as soon as they had recovered from their misadventure, they closed up the hole again, and automatically washed and changed out of their dirty clothes.

After a couple of days, rumours of an attempted escape from the school filtered around the corridors. The Prof was instrumental in this as he had seen it first hand and became an authority on the legend. The two ex-spies Snowy and Annabel knew more than enough and as a result gossiped with the best of them. In a peculiar way, even the piece of wood that covered the common room hole developed a life of its own. Many a time Adam, Louie and Robbie would sit in the changing rooms discussing the merits of another break out attempt. But for some reason lifting up the plank once more and returning to that netherworld was too much for them to countenance, especially for Robbie. Maybe it was the rats or the possibility that next time they might not be so fortunate, but whatever, they all came to the conclusion that the hole was history.

A week or so later, Adam and Robbie were kicking a football on the quad and generally minding their own business. Robbie had one of the worst shots in the world, this great technique of booting the ball up onto the roof of the school at every opportunity so they then had to do some climbing to get it back. Just as he was about to toe punt one more spectacular, another boy in their year came running over.

'Louie's gone down the hole again!'

'What?!'

'He's gone down the hole again!'

'No?!'

'Come on! Quick!'

And with that they raced back to their common room and sure enough, a crowd of pupils had gathered around the hole and you could hear Louie under the floor telling everyone to 'Get stuffed!'

Robbie and Adam tried to shout down to him.

'Louie! Come back!'

'No way! I'm off. I'm never comin' back!'

Then it suddenly dawned on them that they were about to have a Form meeting with their head of year teacher right in the very place that Louie was trying so desperately to escape from.

'Louie, you've got to stay down there! Stay down there!'

'I know! Damn right! I'm leavin'!'

'We've got a form meeting in here in two minutes!'

There was a long silence as the cogs in Louie's head eventually rotated.

'Oh.....Bugger!'

'Stay down there and keep quiet and we'll block up the hole!'

'Bugger it!!'

They did just that. Robbie expertly concealing the spot once again with a bit of dust and a strategically placed chair. It wasn't an easy thing to do though. Poor old Louie was now entombed in complete darkness having, in his haste, forgotten his torch and there was probably a good chance that some peckish rats might be right down there with him. How long could he stay there and remain quiet. Ten minutes? Fifteen? Twenty? Maybe twenty-five minutes at a push? Unfortunately, the forthcoming lesson was forty-five minutes long so Louie was going to have to be braver than brave and quieter than a mouse or it was all over.

Hastily, the Form tried to make ready for their class as if it was just like any another Tuesday afternoon, expertly feigning either excited chatter or bored indifference. The effect was so believable that they almost forgot that Louie was going to be taking part in the lesson, albeit from under the floor. The teacher entered on cue and without anymore ado went through the register as convincingly bored as the rest of them. Everyone was present and correct except for one obvious omission and when Louie's name was read out they tried to cover his absence by suggesting that one of them had seen him looking very green after lunch and that he had gone to the 'San', the school's plague ridden hospital wing, with a stomach bug.

It worked. The teacher was completely bamboozled, so all that remained was for Louie to go the distance. If anyone could, Louie could, and as the lesson progressed most of the pupils began to cross their fingers that no noises or scratching sounds emanated from the floor. Louie hadn't moved at all as yet, so that was something, but what if he had a sneezing fit, which was likely because Louie was known to suffer from bouts of asthma. Whichever way Adam looked at it, in the long run, it wasn't looking good.

The Head of Form continued with the perfunctory lesson which was basically finding out how all the school hobbies were going. As it transpired, Pottery, Photography, Embroidery, Stamp Collecting, Film Club, and Caving Club were all going well, minus a helmet. The 'Escape from School' hobby had certainly taken a new twist. Just then, a faint, dreaded noise was heard from under the floor and the whole class jolted as one. Regrettably, the camp commandant had heard it too.

'What was that?' said the teacher with some authority.

'What, sir?' replied Robbie, who then bravely tried to cover the noise by coughing loudly. However, this subterfuge was no use as once again, Louie stirred below.

'THAT?'

'Don't know, sir. A mouse?' countered Robbie once again in vain.

As he spoke, their head of year pupil, all nicely turned out uniform and parted hair, looked over to the teacher with a disapproving look and you could almost sense him making up his mind to shop Louie for the benefit of his future school career. But there wasn't any need, because there was suddenly a great cracking sound and as the chair over the hole went flying, Louie popped up like a demon, his face once again covered in dirt. After a moments stunned hiatus, the flummoxed teacher approached the defeated looking schoolboy while everyone else looked on dumbstruck. Louie obviously couldn't hold out any longer and like Robbie before him was coughing and spluttering and mumbling incoherently. The teacher didn't hit him immediately but it was a close run thing and once the seriousness of the situation was digested he let rip at the top of his voice.

'This is an outrage! What the hell do you think you are doing!!'

Louie tried to gather himself.

'Er....'

'Before you report to the Headmaster you will go and wash! You stupid boy! Now go!'

'Yes, sir....'

As Louie disappeared, his tail between his legs, the teacher then picked up the splintered planks and surveyed the hole.

'Who else was involved in this?' probed the Officer of the Gestapo.

Everyone shrugged their shoulders and just looked on. Despite the teacher's questioning, there was no way that anyone was going to own up and Adam and Robbie looked over to Annabel and Snowy looking nervous in the corner.

Sure enough, Louie was once more going to be taking the can. The 'Cooler' King was severely reprimanded with another gating, which meant that he had to stay in school all the time, and he was given a series of harsh detentions for a month which consisted of writing thousands of lines like, 'I must not dig holes in school property', 'I must not attempt to escape from Colditz', and 'I must not steal soup ladles from the kitchens and use them for making tunnels'.

As for their hole? That was quickly and ruthlessly boarded up by the staff with some sturdy looking nails and the whole of the year was warned about future break outs and that any insubordination would be punished with an iron will.

It was a shame, because the hole had afforded them their first genuine adventure, but 'never mind, there were bound to be more along the way', Adam reasoned. And anyway, it was obvious for everyone to see: You didn't need to escape from the school by going under the floor. It would be a lot easier to just walk out of the front door.

FIRST SNOG

As Adam sat doodling in a History lesson one afternoon, suddenly a folded up piece of paper landed on his desk. Luckily, it missed his head by inches because it probably would have knocked him out. It was the largest crumpled up message that he had ever seen and he didn't have a clue from where it had come. The message went as follows,

'I know who fancies you. Meet me in the suntrap after class and I'll tell you who it is'. L.

He turned around. The rest of the class were busy scribbling down historical facts and figures and while the teacher busily chalked on the blackboard something about the English Civil War, Adam studied the handwriting once more. He didn't recognise it. Even the L was deceptive because there wasn't a girl with that letter beginning their name in the class. He looked around the room again to catch any sign of who had thrown it but everyone seemed preoccupied. Maybe it was Robbie larking about? But Adam didn't think that it was, because even he had his head almost resting in a book.

As Adam looked at the message once more his heart started pounding. 'Who fancies me?' 'Who could it be?' 'Maybe it's Snowy?' which would have been good because Adam fancied her rotten. Many a time he had been transfixed in the breakfast queue by her long blonde hair and stunning looks. He was even beginning to have some pretty racy dreams about her aswell, with her scoring a winning goal at hockey for example, but then the reveries usually ended at the onset of Snowy taking off her school sweater or untying her shoe laces, because Adam could never quite remember what happened next.

But it was an L not an S, so it couldn't be her. Perhaps it was the female Scripture teacher who Adam thought was quite attractive, although she was married, and if God existed, which Adam felt was looking pretty unlikely, 'He' would probably not take too kindly to an adulterous liaison with a very illegal age gap. Still, some things never ceased to amaze him and discarding her Biblical studies for an afternoon, Adam was more than certain that she would have been able to show him a few things alright.

So after class, he nervously strolled down to the suntrap set idyllically amongst the school gardens. It was a hot, clammy day and he could see his destination looming up ahead. The suntrap was really just a lump of concrete and tiles with a crumbling red brick wall around it, but it was attractively covered in Triffid like plants and trellises giving the impression that you might actually be in Provence rather than the old, grey west of England. As a meeting point though it was streets ahead of the rotting scout hut or the rusty bike sheds, especially on a sunny day.

As Adam neared the rendezvous, he tried to remember the times that he'd played kiss chase at primary school. It seemed such a distant memory that he almost had to kick start his brain to recall it. He was up for the cup for sure, especially if it resulted in a bit of snogging action, but there was definitely a little uncertainty, his last school having put paid temporarily to any inquisitiveness with the fairer sex.

His heart was beginning to pump and mimicked the hasty motion of his legs as he turned the corner and stepped up onto the suntrap. 'Maybe Robbie will be there laughing his head off? Maybe no one will be there at all and I'll look a fool? Maybe I should just turn back now before it's too late?'

It was already too late. As he glanced across at the solitary wooden bench, there, sitting seductively at one end was Kate. Adam almost fell over, as she was the last person he expected to see perched there. She wasn't in his class so how was she able to get the message to him? He wasn't sure, but he had to admit, although he was disappointed that it wasn't Snowy who'd asked him along, the presence of Kate, a cheeky brunette with an attractive smile was going a long way to making up for it. And anyway, the note said that the person would inform Adam who it was that fancied him, so maybe, he hoped, it could end up being Snowy after all.

Adam quickly planted himself down at the other end of the bench from her and began twiddling his thumbs hesitantly, all the while trying to project a calm exterior. He was completely tongue tied. Unable to make even a sound. Fortunately, Kate was far from shy and broke the ice without further ado.

'So you got my note then?' she began, with a flash of her big blue eyes.

Adam could feel his blood pressure bubbling over, so much so, that all he could do was just nod desperately in response.

'You're here!'

'Umm.....'

'You came along'.

'Er......umm'.

'Do you want to kiss me?'

His head turned slowly towards her.

'You?' Adam wondered.

'Yes'.

'Er....'

'Cos I fancy you!' said Kate earnestly, as Adam felt the perspiration around his armpits.

'Oh....'

'Are you going to kiss me then?'

'Er....yeah.....umm'.

There was a long silence as Adam tried to look cool and unflustered. A totally unconvincing performance.

'Go on then. Kiss me!' and Kate stuck out her face immediately in order to give him some sort of target to aim at.

'Umm..... right ....'.

What to do. He was still sat at the other end of the bench from her, sitting awkwardly as if he had a serious bout of constipation, bolt upright with his arms now stiffly hanging to the side. He resembled a stringed puppet.

'I'm waiting....'

After another deadly pause Adam shuffled along, bit by bit, towards her. Eventually, when he had reached near enough, she placed one of her arms around his shoulder.

'Well?'

'I've got a sore throat....' he chirped up, unbelievably.

'Sore throat?!'

He nodded trying to give himself some more valuable seconds.

'I don't believe you'.

'I have....' and he let out a pathetic cough and rubbed his throat.

'So, you don't want to kiss me then?'

'Er....umm'.

He went back to the old routine again, but just as he was contemplating his next move Kate literally stuck her face onto his and held him in a vice like grip. There was no escape. After the initial shock, the memories of kiss chase came quickly back to mind and with a spot of lip fencing Adam began slowly but surely to improve his technique, so much so that when they stopped it felt as though he had been sucking on a Hoover for about ten minutes.

'Are you going to the school disco tomorrow?' Kate said eventually, staring into his eyeballs.

'Course....' Adam answered sheepishly.

He hated the school disco.

'You won't tell anyone will you?'

'No....' he replied sincerely.

First chance he got he was going to tell his friends and boast about how he had lost his tongue for at least a minute down Kate's throat.

'You'll keep it a secret?'

He nodded again, almost crossing his fingers.

'Good. Do you want to go out with me?'

'Er, yes....'

He didn't. He really wanted to go out with Snowy, but there was no way that he was going to look this particular gift horse in the mouth. He was going to snog it.

'See you later then', said Kate almost pouting.

'Okay....'

They kissed once more, almost for luck.

'Er....just one thing', Adam said tentatively.

'Yes?'

'Who did you get to send the note?'

'Oh, Robbie did', replied Kate without hesitating.

'Great', Adam thought. 'So when I get back, Robbie will be ribbing me constantly and no doubt Louie will already know and then it won't be long before the whole school knows too'. You see, Kate was lying as well. She didn't want to keep it a secret at all. She wanted everyone to find out.

As Adam left the suntrap with a hint of a skip in his step, he could almost sense Kate opening up her diary and making an official entry. He was intrigued to think what she might write;

Friday, 27th June: 'Lovely hot day. Don't want to do Prep. Met Adam after Games, in the suntrap, which was full of butterflies. He needs a lot of kissing practice - his mouth's like a sloppy sponge! I think I'll go out with him though, if he goes to the disco. The only ones who know about it are Robbie and Snowy'.

Adam returned to school and just as anticipated, Robbie knew everything and so did Louie, judging by the size of their inane expressions. He asked Robbie how he threw over the note without him seeing and Robbie just shrugged his shoulders and started laughing. He wasn't going to get much joy out of him. Louie followed suit with a big guffaw and then pronounced that he would never go out with a girl;

'Cos that's a right girlie thing to do!'

The next day was the dreaded School Disco. Adam knew that the whole thing with Kate would rely on him turning up and dazzling her with some brilliant footwork before she would even consider another bout of kissing. Unfortunately, there was a big problem. The reason that he hated the school disco so much was that he had two left feet, in fact even someone with no feet probably would have walked off with the disco dancing prize if they were up against Adam. Even though he could sometimes be sporty, especially if that included kicking a football through a school plate glass window, when it came to strutting his thing or shaking his stuff, forget it. He would have preferred solitary confinement for a year: having to walk over hot coals repeatedly: even to be shot by firing squad at dawn, anything if it meant that he could avoid the school disco.

But there it was. If Adam didn't turn up that was it with Kate. He was about to take a millisecond to decide that he wasn't going to attend, but then there was another problem. Since meeting up with Kate at the suntrap, his feelings towards Snowy had completely changed. In fact, they had transformed. The next morning when he clocked Snowy in the breakfast queue he hardly even noticed her, when before he would have had a glazed expression and a mouthful of Frosties following every sweep of her long blonde locks or shuffle of her languid frame. Now, for some strange reason he was looking out for Kate and her naughty grin as if he was trying on a new hat or a new shirt. It seemed so fickle that he couldn't quite work it all out and nor could Robbie and Louie who were surprised by his change in affection. But it was simple: Snowy who?

'Bloody 'ell! What did you and Kate get up to?' Probed Louie like a bumpkin detective.

'This and that!' Adam responded with a flourish.

'They swapped tongues! That's for sure!', concluded Robbie.

'Uuurrggghhhh!' cried Louie, almost spitting out his Shreddies.

So, Saturday night came around quicker than you could say Wall Street Shuffle or Boogie Nights. Whenever Adam had been to the disco before, which was probably only once, he had sat around the edges just listening to the music. And what awful, dire sounds. 'Sailing' by Rod Stewart, seemed to be permanently stuck to the stylus and the sugary Bay City Rollers were flogged beyond all reason. There was some vomit inducing Carpenters and Simon and Garfunkel, which made everyone shamble about like zombies and then without any explanation, everyone would start swaggering gleefully about with their hands in their pockets to Abba's, 'Waterloo'.

There was always some serious hippy stuff like Yes, Emerson Lake and Palmer and Led Zeppelin's 'Stairway To Heaven' taking half an hour at least to play themselves out and that was eventually the signal for everyone to start head banging, which became even more frenzied when Deep Purple's 'Smoke on the Water' was trundled out. The fairly recent, overblown 'Bohemian Rhapsody' by Queen, was usually the clincher, where everyone became completely demented air guitarists while others clutched their testicles as they failed to reach the high notes.

The only passable bits were when more decent music was aired, which wasn't very often. For Adam a bit of Slade, or Sweet were acceptable, alongside some Bolan or Hendrix and he loved 'Alright Now' by Free.

In fact, any old glam was good because that would be the signal for him, Robbie and Louie to go berserk on the dance floor and jump around on each other. You see that was okay because there was no dance certificate required. You weren't marked out of ten by the end. You just jumped.

Adam also enjoyed the odd comedy moments like 'Ernie: The Fastest Milkman in the West' and 'The Monster Mash' where everyone sang, 'It was a graveyard smash!' 'It went by in a flash!' in a silly Barry White-like voice, that could chill the dead.

Even those annoying litter fetishists from Wimbledon could raise a bit of a laugh as it meant that the three lads could dive about the place once again and be daft, which they were past masters at. 'Remember you're a Womble?' How could they ever forget.

So there they were. At the disco. Sat around the perimeter. Looking dejected in their ill fitting flared jeans and cheesecloth shirts. Picking their noses and surveying the toe tapping talent on the dance floor. Adam's digits curled up suddenly when the lights dimmed and 'Seasons in the Sun' came on. The original was so saccharine it made him think of instant suicide and the alternative 'terrace' version that he had heard being sung in the Shed; 'We had joy we had fun, we had Tottenham on the run, but the fun didn't last, 'cos the bastards ran too fast'. As the weepie came to its box-of-hankie's climax, Louie began shouting,

'I've 'ad enough of this crap! Let's smash up the record player!' as he gave out one of his trademark 'Hee! Hee!' sniggers.

It was a drastic step alright, but valid none the less. As a result, during the next song Adam and Robbie were preoccupied trying to pull Louie back from creating havoc on the sound system and what's more on the diligent sixth form DJ. They looked as though they were doing some strange tribal dance, with lots of pushing and pulling as they tried to stop Louie, not wanting him to get picked out by some of the older pupils because then there would probably have been a queue forming to give him a thump. Luckily, Louie calmed down a bit and as they returned to their corner, Adam caught a glimpse of Kate. She was dancing seductively with a spotty friend of hers across the way and both of them were dolled up for the occasion: Kate in a frilly top and her volcanic chum in comical dungarees. Not only was her friend from the year above, but she was also wearing a large, gleaming dental brace.

'Imagine snogging that!' said Robbie with a gulp.

'No bloomin' chance!' added Louie with interest.

Then Robbie started nudging Adam.

'Go on then!'

'What?'

'Go and dance with her'.

'Who?'

'Who d'you think? Kate of course!'

'No way!'

Then Louie started in on it.

'Go on, you chicken!'

'Get off!'

'Chicken!'

'Not!'

'Are!'

'Not!'

Then Louie started his fowl impression that made him look more like Mick Jagger sucking on an orange. Then there was the absurd sight once more of them pushing and pulling each other, only this time Robbie and Louie were trying to push Adam in the direction of Kate with all their might while he tried to return to his seat. Eventually, one big push took him right past the two gyrating girls and he ended up going flying. As he managed to pick himself off the crowded floor, a romantic boy and girl from the lower fifth who had been disturbed from their clinch looked down at Adam with daggers. Adam apologised repeatedly, blaming it all on Robbie and Louie for the intrusion.

As Adam returned to his place, he tried to look cool by doing what he thought was a soft shoe shuffle to Hot Chocolate, whose husky singer was crooning melodically away. He couldn't work out what had possessed him. Predictably, he tripped over just as he reached safety. Robbie and Louie burst into hysterics again and after Adam had brushed himself down once more, he looked over to find Kate laughing too and whispering not into Pizza face's ear, but into a tall boy's from the year above. 'Brilliant, now I've got competition' Adam realised, and unfortunately it was coming from one of the toughest boys in the lower fourth, who was known as 'Agro'.

It was clear that Adam's days as a Casanova were coming to an abrupt end even before they had really begun, unless of course he immediately started dancing around with the flare of Fred Astaire. Thing was, he had the flares alright, just none of the timing or anything resembling finesse. As luck would have it though, just as he was considering taking up dance classes in the holidays, the next song to hit the turntable was 'School's Out' by Alice Cooper and right away Adam, Robbie and Louie were flying about the place, singing loudly and careering into each other. This time Adam tried to make it look like he could actually dance a bit by varying the steps. But that was difficult when Louie was jumping on his head and Robbie was trying to trip him up.

Towards the end of the record, he looked over to where Kate had been dancing but she had completely disappeared. There was just the girl with the brace who was ambling aimlessly about. As he passed near, he plucked up the courage to ask where Kate had vanished to.

'I'm not telling you!' said Kate's friend.

'Oh, go on!'

'No…'

'Go on!'

'Oh, alright then. She's gone off with 'Agro!'

So Adam was right. Whilst he floundered about failing to impress with his clowning, Agro had strolled in like an arrogant bank robber and left with all the swag. Trouble was, Adam couldn't really lodge a complaint, unless of course he fancied having his youthful visage rearranged and the thought of having his school trousers filled with concrete certainly made him think twice. So, as best he could, he tried to put the Kate situation behind him and chalk it all up to experience.

Adam never did go out with her in the end, so his kissing technique would just have to wait for another opportunity, but he wasn't too downhearted, because as his mum always used to say.

'There are plenty more fish in the sea'.

SCRUMPY

Once they had started the second year at the school, Adam's Form were no longer dubbed as 'turds'. What a relief. A whole year's new intake would be smeared with that particular honour. However, despite their new found freedom, it was now their customary responsibility to begin trying out the local, traditional occupations that they had already heard so much about.

Some weekends they would journey up the Combe to mess around in the countryside, make a nuisance of themselves or just loaf about and get up to no good. One particular Saturday, the Hole in the Floor Gang strode over the hilly fields in search of some west country cider or 'Scrumpy' as it was known.

'I've 'ad scrumpy loads of times!', said Louie chewing on some hay and acting as if he was a registered alcoholic.

'Yeah? What's it like?' asked Robbie all ears.

'Well, it's like really sweet and you get it in this big plastic thing'.

'Plastic thing?' Adam probed trying to pin Louie down.

'Yeah, it's like a petrol can, only plastic'.

'I see....'

'You can get different flavours too', said Robbie with an obvious and gaping lack of knowledge of this particular subject.

'You mean you can get dry, medium or sweet! Sweet's the best cider, 'cos you can drink it easy', Louie corrected.

'It sounds a bit sickly?' Adam probed once more with interest.

'No, it's the best! Dry's too dry'.

'What about medium?'

'Well that's sort of in between. You can get a lump of Cheddar with it an 'all'.

'Cheese?' said Robbie turning up his nose.

With Louie's socks in the vicinity any more mouldy dairy would have been greedy.

'Yeah. A big lump of the smelly stuff. So's you can scoff it while you drink'.

Adam was about to award Louie a scrumpy certificate, as his degree of knowledge was more than impressive. 'I wonder if he's ever had any?' he thought. Louie replied almost telepathically.

'Drank a whole gallon one time, didn't make me sick or nothin'.

'I once got really ill on some rum', added Robbie holding his stomach to make us believe him. 'I threw up on my shoes'.

'Urrrgggghhhh!' Louie almost wretched.

Then it was Adam's turn.

'I drank a can of beer once. Then I fell over'.

And they were off larking about. Louie doing an impression of Adam collapsing, Robbie being sick. What was patently obvious was that none of them had ever had any serious experience of alcohol. It was just kids stuff. But soon they were going to be finding out about the real thing.

As they ventured further and further away from the school the attractive, rolling countryside took hold. They sauntered up a long, dirt track and passed an overgrown field which for some reason had a large crater in it. They climbed over the gate to investigate and just as they did a nasty smell was all about them. Louie looked at Robbie, then Robbie looked at Adam, but there was no way that it could be anything that even they might let off. Not unless they had been force fed the school slop for a term. Then they saw the crater. There was a wrecked and rusty old car lying on its side at the bottom, some sheets of corrugated iron and what looked suspiciously like one or two dead sheep.

'Poooorrrrrrggghhh!!!' said Louie holding his nose as he surveyed the scene.

'Get a whiff of that!' replied Robbie and within an instant they were scurrying away, back up the lane to their desired destination. The local cider farm.

Eventually, out of breath, they arrived and positioned themselves in a strategic vantage point overlooking the locale. After a moments observation they discussed the next stage. They couldn't go and buy the cider and cheese themselves, being so young, so they decided to wait until an older pupil from the school came along and then ask them to purchase the provisions on the their behalf.

Luckily, they didn't have to wait long and soon they had passed over their money, with a generous tip, to an upper fifth former who was not only large but well on the way to growing some stubble, so he could pass quite easily for an eighteen year old. Not that the owner of the cider farm was concerned, he probably would have sold his strongest vintage to the three of them, even if they had gone into the shop wearing silly moustaches and disguises. The thought of Louie and Robbie dressed up as adults with long sideburns and bushy beards brought a smile to Adam's face. Mind you, no doubt he would have looked just as peculiar, disguised in a stolen blazer and tie and puffing frantically on a pipe.

'What sort of cider do you want?' asked the Upper fifther.

'Strong!', said Robbie.

'No....what sort?! Sweet? Medium?!'

'Sweet!' Louie pronounced with another of his accomplished grins.

'Okay....'

As the upper former confidently entered the farm, they watched and waited. As the time ticked by and there was no sign of any liqueur they became increasingly nervous. What if the pupil shopped them to the owner and called the Police? They would probably have to clean out his scrumpy barrels or help him dry his cheddar. 'No, they hadn't received the cider yet', Adam thought, 'so until such time they were safe'. It would be their word against the owners anyway and surely no court in the land would ignore the facts. Just as he was having visions of the three of them dressed in prison clothing and part of a chain gang, breaking rocks with their bare hands, their lanky accomplice appeared with a see-through, plastic canister full of what looked like apple juice and in his other hand he swung a bag which Adam deduced must contain a lump of Cheddar's finest. He was correct, and when their purchaser jogged around to where they had positioned themselves they could instantly smell the sauce.

'I got you dry cider in the end, as he was out of sweet!'

'Great!' said Louie as if he had in fact ordered dry cider in the first place and once the crumbly cheese was passed around and they were busy stuffing it into their contented faces it wasn't long before the older pupil left them to their own devices. But not until he had had a swig of the fluid, which he downed with a hearty thumbs up. After he had warned them not to tell on him if they got caught, he was on his way. Soon they were on their way too. To find a safer place to drink.

There was no doubt about it. They had a gallon of cider. 'Dry' to boot. A whole gallon between them. More than enough. But who was going to have the first swig? Once they had found themselves a more remote spot, they tossed a coin to see who would have first turn and Robbie won. Without any hesitancy, he unscrewed the top and then put his head back and took a long gulp. As he was getting to his limit, Louie managed to wrench the scrumpy from his clutches and Robbie was coughing and wiping his mouth.

'It's dry alright!'

'Well, course it is! What did you think?!'

'It's not easy to drink'.

'Give it 'ere! I'll show you!'

And Louie took a big gulp down and afterwards let out a massive belch that echoed around the fields and reverberated off the cows.

Adam's turn. He held the container and looked into the clear, dark froth. There was a distinctive smell about the stuff which he thought wasn't too dissimilar to diesel fuel that nearly made him gag, but so that he didn't look a wimp in front of the other's he did his best to take just as large an amount as them. As he downed as much of the dry beverage as he possibly could the strong aftertaste drenched the senses like a shell case exploding in his brain. Instantly, his alarm system went into overdrive and as he passed the scrumpy back to Robbie, he let out a silent burp that almost managed to strip his vocal chords. Robbie began laughing and that was the signal for them to start a fit of the giggles which was as inane as it was drawn out. Adam was waiting for a punch line that was never coming and as they launched into their second, third and fourth helpings, the alcohol's grip became total.

By this point, they were having problems just standing up, but that didn't stop them running manically about from one end of the field to the other and back again. They even tried to climb a large apple tree which was ridiculous, because once they tried to swing about from one branch to another, all control over their limbs was impossible. The best climber, even in his sozzled state, was Robbie by a mile and once he had clambered virtually to the top he proceeded to chuck large cooking apples down on Adam and Louie from a great height. They found it hard to dodge the bombardment and once when Adam managed to duck just in time, Louie caught a large golden delicious in the face. Robbie chortled so loud he nearly fell out of the tree and when he eventually came down to earth, Louie managed to jump him and threatened to throw up in his ear. Then, almost completely forgetting the scrumpy container, which was now more than three quarters empty anyway, they became almost incapacitated and spent what must have been the next hour or so rolling around holding their stomachs and feeling sick. But you couldn't be sure, because time had probably stopped as it was now caught in a haze of alcoholic apples.

Adam's next sensation was feeling his head almost open up from inside as if someone was unzipping it and suddenly he hurled some chunks of undigested cheddar and a copious amount of distilled fluid right in Louie's direction. Whereas before, Louie would probably have gone mad, amazingly, this time he hardly noticed, but that was because he was just as drunk and still in a fit of laughter. There was no sign of Robbie, who had disappeared in a daze after his tussle with Louie and with around another hour of lolling about staring at the senseless sky, Adam and Louie then tried to search for him. Unfortunately, Robbie was nowhere to be found, so once they had managed to pull themselves a little together, which wasn't easy, they decided to scamper back to school and try and sleep off their stupors in the dormitory. They staggered about taking an eternity to walk even a few yards. By the time early evening was drawing in they finally made it back to the school grounds, but not before Louie had brought up most of the ingredients of his stomach, including some lethal looking diced carrots.

The next test was to reach their dormitory without anybody noticing. Incredibly, they managed to make it as far as their ground floor changing room where they found Robbie already collapsed and mumbling incoherently to himself, a plastic bucket by his head ready to catch any puke.

There was no doubt. The drinking escapade had done for them alright: Hook, line and sinker. And what's more, while they sat like gormless spectators in their changing room, occasionally coming alive to throw up all around them, their luck finally ran out when the History teacher discovered them. He wasn't best pleased and became even less so when all they could utter in response to his angry questioning was 'dry', 'scrumpy' or 'cheese!'

The punishment was swift and the trio were immediately gated and Louie was severely reprimanded once more as the ringleader, that's after all three of them had managed to fill up a bucket or two and then come round with an earthquake of a hangover.

One thing was certain. They were going to have a lot more respect for the local firewater in future.

FILM CLUB

Every other weekend the school put on a Film Club in the meeting hall where pupils could watch movies. What made the event just that little bit special was the laxity in the staffing. The teachers were so conspicuous by their absence you would have thought they had all gone home. They probably felt that little misbehaving could go on during the film and once the lights went down, it wasn't easy to see if something was going on even if there was. But Adam wasn't complaining. Far from it, and whatever the film; a suspect 'B' movie with some pitiful performances or some crackly '60's Hammer horror with Peter Cushing or Christopher Lee, a large expectant audience was assured. In fact, there was not many a pupil who didn't have 'Film Club' amongst their personal list of school hobbies. Adam did. And why not? The result was frequent softly lit rendezvous' with Sally, a popular girl in the same year, who was also like Adam, an avid film buff, her favourite genre being disaster movies like the Towering Inferno, in fact any film starring either Steve McQueen or Robert Redford. So, for a couple of hours on a Saturday evening the assembly hall regularly became a youthful cinematic haven from the rest of the school.

Even the Film Club's projectionist was one of the pupils and the job description required a fair amount of responsibility:

1) The diligent compilation of a list of films to be shown. For example, any 'James Bond' flick and 'The Pink Panther' films were always a winner, with of course the begrudging permission of the staff; so no 'Emmanuelle' or 'Deep Throat' unfortunately, although the day that 'Shaft' was finally screened, after much deliberation, there was great rejoicing.

2) Making sure that the film spools were changed over efficiently. Always a necessity for 'Lawrence of Arabia'. This epic came in at a whopping three and a half hours, so you certainly had to have a vigilant projectionist at the helm. There was nothing worse than watching a film segment out of order, or sitting down to your favourite Sergio Leone 'Spaghetti Western' only to discover the end credits playing out upside down.

3) Mixing the audio and visuals to optimum effect. The sudden loss of sound and vision was a continual hazard and more often than not you would find the screen becoming so blurred it felt as though you were watching whilst under the influence. For many girls at the school, the sudden assault of screaming volume during the film 'Love Story' was unforgivable.

4) Sensitivity to the world beyond the realm of the cinema. So for example, during one particularly rebellious period at the school, the classic film 'If', where Malcolm McDowell initiates revolution and shoots the teachers and Headmaster, was postponed to the following term.

A school projectionist's job was clearly no easy matter. However, the plaudits they received for a popular film well presented without any mishaps, like the projector overheating and going up in flames, more than made up for all the hard work. Mind you, to be honest, a lot of the time Adam couldn't have cared less what was being shown: 'Dance of the Vampires?' or 'The Thirty-Nine Steps?' 'Up Pompeii?' or 'Psycho?' It didn't make much difference.

To say that the pupils were a little bit preoccupied would be an understatement. They all had just one thing on their minds: a bit of slap and tickle at the back of the hall, or failing that a steamy snog during 'Where Eagles Dare'. They were all busy fumbling around with each other's erogenous zones, and what they would fantasise about during the week they would more than try and put into practice during Film Club: A hasty juggle with a girl's bra strap in the cheap seats: A more seductive encounter perhaps, to the accompaniment of the Barry Gray Film Orchestra.

I suppose they were all just trying to outdo each other's party tricks. Mind you, Adam certainly wouldn't ever forget the fun he had with Sally during 'How To Steal A Diamond' and 'Butch Cassidy And The Sundance Kid'.

AWAY DAY

During the summer holidays, Adam and Steve decided to travel to Chelsea's second division away fixture at Millwall. Although they weren't sure exactly why they did. The match was a London derby of the less appetising sort. A friendly it most definitely was not, and you could be sure that the local New Cross constabulary would have a little flutter in their tummies come Saturday - that's if they hadn't gone on holiday, or taken sick leave at short notice. Millwall versus Chelsea was known as a 'ding-dong' derby. Millwall fists would probably be the 'ding' and Chelsea heads would probably be the 'dong'.

The train journey was endless, changing from this line then changing to that. The boys were most definitely in a different part of town - there was no welcoming committee and New Cross Gate station seemed as if it had been refused council refurbishing grants since the Industrial Revolution. A steam train was expected at any moment. There was then a long walk to the ground partly because they got lost and it wasn't long before Adam and Steve found themselves behind schedule.

They were trying to keep a low profile, but being only just thirteen (Steve was only a year older) they didn't quite understand the meaning of the word subtlety. They both wore nylon Chelsea scarves tied around their wrists and Steve had brought his lucky Chelsea jacket covered in badges, of the large sew on variety, for good measure. Fortunately, both teams played in blue and white so at a hundred yards distance it would not be completely obvious they were 'Blues' supporters.

Not only did both clubs share blue and white colours, they also shared the same animal on the crest of their shirts. The Lion. Millwall called themselves, 'The Lions' and their ground, 'The Den' in Cold Blow Lane, continued the theme. I suppose you could say that Adam and Steve were just another two ignorant visitors coming to be fed to them.

Millwall's ground looked similar to the Shed End at Chelsea, only this time it was all the way round. If it was a food it would most likely resemble a bowl of concrete. Terraces on three sides. Rickety fences. A small side stand of seats for the more retiring supporters. They even had mounds of rubble outside for ammunition and old railway tracks, tunnels and breakers yards littered the barren dockland terrain, probably to hasten a quick getaway. Adam and Steve were a little bit concerned. Nothing of this was mentioned in the brochures. To their dismay, it seemed as if only one member of the local constabulary had bothered to turn up on his bicycle and he was an old extra from Z Cars.

They asked the amiable constable which end they should go in, and became a little quieter when mentioning that they were 'away' supporters. There were a lot of groups roaming around with more than team tactics on their minds. Some looked to be perfectly balanced - chips on both shoulders. Others were having trouble choosing weapons.

'You're up the wrong end boys, you'll have to walk round the ground', replied PC McGarry.

'Oh, right....' said Steve.

Just then, a hatch opened at the back of the Millwall Stand and a beefy skinhead who looked as though he had already digested most of the match day pies, leaned out and hollered, 'Lions! Lions!' His shouts were accompanied by a sharp thudding sound, as if someone's head was being repeatedly beaten against a brick wall. As the hatch slammed shut to cheers from 'home' supporters all around them still waiting to get in, Steve and Adam looked apprehensively at each other. The penny dropped with a thud. 'Oh, Christ! We're not walking round', they thought. 'Not unless we fancy viewing the seven wonders of Millwall from inside the nearest A and E department'. And they didn't.

'Can you help us officer, we're Chelsea fans. We can't walk round'.

Just at that moment a raucous shout of 'We hate Chelsea!' rang out and the hairs rose up on the back of Adam's neck. 'Walk round? No bloody way. Not without a Police escort and Montgomery's Eighth Army for protection'.

'Alright, I'll tell you what I'll do. You stick with me and I'll take you through the ground. You still have to pay mind'.

'Thank you, Officer'.

So off they went with the Pied Piper into the amphitheatre. Being juveniles, they managed to enter the dilapidated Forecourt turnstiles to the sum of about 70p and both purchased match day programmes to the tune of 10p each. On the top in bold letters were written the words, MILLWALL WELCOME then at the bottom in smaller letters, 'Chelsea'. In between, an extremely rampant lion roared. There was also an eye-catching proviso in the programme: A WORD OF WARNING followed by some stern advice; 'This afternoon's match with Chelsea can be very exciting and equally entertaining. However, it should not be used as an excuse for feuding between rival fans. Hooliganism is hideous and senseless and those who indulge in it at the expense of decent law-abiding supporters and to the detriment of the game and clubs alike seriously want their brains examined. We are well aware, of course, that a local 'derby' match means there is a possibility of friction between certain irresponsible factions: groups of youngsters who have little or no interest in the game. Football clubs can do without these types and the best thing they can do is STAY AWAY. If there are any here today, be assured, no matter who they pretend to support, the police will deal with them'.

Stay away? Adam wished he had, but for totally different reasons. It seemed to him that if the football clubs could do without 'these' types of supporters, they would be playing in empty stadiums. And the police could certainly not deal with the trouble. They would have had problems with a cat stuck up a tree. The wise words continued: 'We are warning the youngsters again about running on the pitch. This will not be tolerated at any time, before, during or after the game. If it happens today, then boys will be charged the same as adults at our next first team match. This is no idle threat. We will carry this out'.

Running on to the pitch was about the only way of appearing on 'Match of the Day' for free, only trouble was the cameras were not going to be turning up for this particular encounter, it being the bog end of the second division. Well, 'The Big Match' perhaps, but there was no way Jimmy Hill and co were going to be travelling down the Old Kent Road. The other reasons were to escape flying boots and fists and when a goal was scored the surge down the terraces sometimes made it unavoidable.

Despite all the threats and warnings, the match day programme actually celebrated Chelsea's enigmatic past and gave a good space to the away team's players statistics with a nice picture of the side, all grinning hopefully. It would turn out to be a brief respite.

As Steve and Adam walked into the ground behind 'plod', they could see that it was a big crowd for Millwall of 21,002, and the atmosphere was dangerous - all vitriol and burger stalls. They then passed through a blue door and suddenly found themselves in the players tunnel. Adam couldn't believe it and nor could Steve. Here they were right inside. Adam had always dreamed of walking up the tunnel at Wembley, and here they were at the next best thing. It's funny, but it made Adam's day, and he knew it had made Steve's. They sauntered on past the players changing rooms in a daze, not quite believing it all. Chelsea's changing room had 'Visitors' written on the door and there was a burst of nervous laughter and chatter. From the other side of the passage a door suddenly swung open and a burly physio exited. They had hoped to catch a glimpse of Peter Bonetti, Gary Locke or even Ray Wilkins, who Adam used to regularly confuse with 'Him' upstairs, limbering up and making themselves ready to exchange two points with Millwall for a lot of fond memories. Instead, they were looking right into the Lions' dressing room and a couple of their players were putting the finishing touches to their pre-match preparations - adjusting their studs and flexing their legs. One of the Millwall players smiled wryly at them as they walked on by. The home team certainly looked 'up for it' and Adam was beginning to reckon that Chelsea probably weren't, as was customary on days like these. The only Blues player who probably was up for it, was none other than the 'Chopper' himself, but today, Harris, would be watching the fireworks from the bench.

They came back out into the daylight, as if the ground had spewed them out, the Policeman about to break into a jig. This was worrying - they were now in full view of the whole stadium and a target for artillery and it was only about twenty minutes until the kick off, which would be early today, because everybody turns up five minutes beforehand. In those days people would turn up at midday to talk to the Groundsman or just watch the grass grow.

The tiny procession continued on its merry way from the tunnel right around the side of the pitch. Adam tried hard not to look at the crowd or catch someone's eye in the stands. The locals knew him and Steve weren't 'home' supporters. They were as obvious as florescent trousers. They could feel faces sneering, and 'Oi, wanker!' was mentioned at random as they strode past as if it were some special greeting. As they carried on reluctantly around the edge of the hallowed turf, something else caught their attention. Amid the very loud chants of 'Millwall', Adam could hear a slight echo reverberate a split second afterwards, behind them, as if in response. Not 'Millwall' or 'Chelsea', but 'Shit!' This must be the 'away' contingent that Adam and Steve had wanted so much to join and converse in all things footy. Then Adam understood. They were being marched up the wrong end. The only friend in their hour of need was taking them up to the furthest place from their compatriots. They were cut off, and Adam realised that today the Millwall fans would most definitely be obtaining their pound of flesh. Eventually they arrived near the goal and the cocky policeman opened the gate in the barrier to their selected pen.

'Get in there and stay by the goal. You'll be alright'.

'Oh, thanks....' Steve said with a gulp.

Adam and Steve didn't really want to stand around arguing, so they did just that, standing to the right side of the goal, near a crush barrier - a right couple of spare parts. There was suddenly a sense of wanting to look behind and to the side all the time. Adam's eyes knew that something was amiss - they should now be focussed out of the back of his head. Thank God Steve had taken off his lucky Chelsea jacket and Adam's Ray Wilkins shirt was in the wash, otherwise they were to be replacement footballs for the afternoon. Behind them eyes bore down, a very hungry set of Millwall 'Lions' licked their lips and waited to pounce on cud chewing prey.

'We've gotta get out of here', Adam said sensibly to Steve.

'Yeah, I know. But how? If we try to leave, they'll know we're Chelsea'.

They thought nervously for a moment.

'Maybe we'll just sit tight and pretend to be Millwall fans'.

'Good idea', said Steve, as they both hurriedly concealed their nylon Chelsea scarves.

It was strange. Adam had already given himself the last rites and absolved himself of a host of tiny transgressions; burning Mr Painter's plank; stealing stamps from one of his brother's albums; not sharing his sweets with those in need and such like. But now they seemed not to be the main object of the home supporters furtive attentions any more. Maybe it was their age, or lack of it, and the fact that they were marched down from the other end, suggested that they might in fact be a dangerous consignment of impetuous Millwall youth always ready to have a go. No, unsurprisingly, Adam didn't think so, and he was proud that they weren't. They were just happy to be genuine football fans at a game that wasn't particularly fashionable. Adam thought that they were incredibly lucky, and anyway they were about as much threat as Cliff Richard on a night out.

The focus of attention had switched. The players of both teams were now coming out of the tunnel, side by side, in a hastily arranged attempt to diffuse the terrace tensions. So, more than ever it was the time for a momentary glance at the pitch. Chelsea were wearing an unfashionable red away kit and Adam knew that they were in for a good old thumping, on and off the turf. He was right. The Chelsea fans up the other end seemed to be surrounded - an exclusion zone of about five yards encased them - and hundreds of Millwall reinforcements were proceeding from the left hand side over a paltry fence along the side forecourt and over the other conveniently nonexistent fence up the other. It looked like an endless army of cartoon ants insidiously creeping over, swelling the ranks up ahead. Adam and Steve came to the conclusion that there was probably no particular home and away end at The Den, because it was such a rare occurrence for any visiting supporters to even turn up, due probably to Millwall's unequalled hooligan reputation. Of course this afternoon it seemed clear that the Chelsea nutcases who had infiltrated the other end fancied a good kicking. The odds looked grim.

'Thank Christ, we're not up there', said Steve.

'Thank that friendly Bobby', Adam replied.

'Yeah, I know. There's gonna be trouble'.

You could just tell that they would both go on to achieve remarkable academic success.

The game began. The Chelsea players were soon doing their familiar impressions of 'not turning up'. Kenny Swain was in the team. A good player, but with a name like that he was always going to be second to the ball against the two 'Barry's' of Millwall - Kitchener and Salvage. This turned out to be a blessing in disguise though - a Chelsea victory and their heads would be placed on pikes. Millwall looked like they would score with every attack and this served to bring out the last ditch bravado from Colonel Custer and the King's Road troop with chants of, 'Millwall run from Chelsea! Millwall run from Chelsea! La la la lah, La la la lah!' The Millwall fans then taunted them back with the friendly, 'You're gonna get your fucking heads kicked in!' The Chelsea supporters then upped the ante, with provocative use of the raised right fist, implying that the home supporters were all masturbators and you didn't know if it was a harsh refereeing decision, perhaps an offside against Millwall, but that was it. The home supporters, massed by the excuse for a fence, launched themselves in a big swathe into the retreating Chelsea ranks. There was a huge cry from all around.

'Do the bastards! Do the Chelsea scum!'

Adam didn't think they needed any encouragement. It was pandemonium and when Millwall scored the first goal through Salvage the temperature went through the corrugated roof. Attila was certainly getting his money's worth for sure. And he probably sneaked into the ground for free. Adam thought that most of those involved had perhaps obtained a ticket with an inkling of the afternoon's entertainment, but it was of little matter. The fighting looked reminiscent of the Battle of Naseby, all flailing arms, legs, heads, in close proximity, with ordered advancing and retreating and classic pincer movements. Burlesque had come again to The Den, Cold

Blow Lane, this sunny afternoon and it wouldn't be the last time.

St John's one ambulance was soon crammed full to the brim, band-aids were at a premium and across the terraces Victoria Crosses were being awarded with aplomb. At last some more Coppers turned up, after oggling the dailies and supping that tenth mug of rosy. But they knew what to do. Adam and his mate were saved. Hurrah. Her Majesty's loyal Constabulary were here and they knew alright. Did they heck. Soon as look at you, they were wading in, hitting the wrong people: the helpful steward; the friendly neighbour at her first match; the reserve goalkeeper warming up at the side of the pitch - anyone but Mr Idiot. Still at least while the mayhem continued, Adam and Steve could enjoy once again the breath of anonymity, and they were both still in one piece.

It was nearing half time, and the hapless Blues were soon further behind, through a well taken Ray Evans free kick. Then it was three down through a Brisley header which took a deflection off the crossbar and the backside of Bonetti, who was already sporting a fitting black eye from a previous encounter. Chelsea were looking like sinking even further. 'Good', Adam thought, 'Keep it going'. He had of course his self preservation to keep in mind and Steve's, and any sort of comeback by the Blues would get messy.

During half-time, another very brief respite, both forces regrouped, debriefed, talked tactics, comforted the wounded, applauded the little heroes, chewed on burgers, spat out peanuts, slurped, belched, farted, jeered and cheered the half time results - West Ham were losing - and looked forward to, and prepared for the second half.

The second half began with a big worry. Next to Adam and Steve were three 'Chelsea girls' about the same age. Now this was a major problem. If the boys identified their allegiance they were dead, but if they ignored them they weren't going to feel very good about it. Also, they might be recognised as Chelsea fans and exposed. The young girls had become quite vocal in their support towards the end of the first half, chanting, 'Come on you Blues' and 'We love Butch' and even more so now that their team in the second half were attacking towards them. The Millwall fans all around, seemed to Adam's amazement to allow them quarter, a moment's grace, as if the trio were some quaint aberration.

The Chelsea girls had come to see Ray (Butch) Wilkins' thighs, and Gary (Starsky) Stanley's latest hairdo, and weren't really going to attempt to take the Millwall forecourt. They were more likely going to be forced to spread the full-time sandwiches or heat the hot-dogs. Then it all seemed to change. One brave chap lobbed over some saliva for good measure.

''Ave some of that, you slags!'

One of the girls, without turning, told the lad where to get off, very quietly, knowing full well the ominous precipice that they were now standing on. The Millwall fans chuckled.

'D'you hear that? The slag said, fuck off!'

From that moment, whenever Chelsea got the ball forward, which wasn't very often, spit would rain down on the luckless girls. But they continued to watch the game and sing for their heroes. They rode the situation out and managed to diffuse it, despite being in need of a change of clothes and a good hose down when they got home. Steve and Adam were astonished. They exchanged relieved glances, whilst acknowledging privately their own fragility.

Meanwhile, the fighting up the other end had become more vicious. Sporadic. Supporters were looking hesitantly around not knowing where the clonking was going to come from next. There was a nasty element in the air, as if at any minute a blade might be used alongside the customary boots and fists. Not surprisingly, Chelsea's hardcore had drifted and were split into smaller factions across the stand, an always fatal manoeuvre: Lack of cohesion; Fragmentation; Orders not reaching the front lines; Fear; Panic; Piss-poor morale.

Unfortunately, Millwall still had vast superiority and with it culled the terraces. A loud cheer went up whenever a group of 'melting' Chelsea were exposed and the image of a score of boots and knuckles licking into the cowering opposition, was like some demented animal on a roller coaster that you didn't think was ever going to stop. The whole episode just left a bitter taste, and Adam knew that come the final whistle, he and Steve still had to return home without the aid of a hearse.

While Millwall's followers were busy on the terraces winning the Battle of Britain, their brothers on the pitch swaggered about playing keep ball, doing pretty much everything but score a fourth - the coup de grace. But the players weren't too bothered with the match already won and so they proceeded to celebrate conga style, around the stadium. The Lions had used exactly the right tactics against this Chelsea side: Kick and rush and lump the ball into the six yard box. But even Adam had to admit they had played some pretty good football. To say that Bonetti, Chelsea's goalkeeper, had earned his wages that afternoon was an understatement. It could have been six.

The final whistle blew, Chelsea had been thoroughly conquered and the cheers rang out loudly all about. Then Adam thought, 'Shall we leave straight away or stay behind to let the home supporters return for their tea?' They both knew that whatever happened, the real nutters - and they could be the majority, would stay behind, possibly right outside the ground, and though there was no welcoming committee on Adam and Steve's arrival, there would certainly be a large one on their exit.

They began to walk sheepishly out to the exit with everyone else, through what can only be described as a wide tunnel with a ledge on either side. As they shuffled along, looking straight ahead, trying to grin as if they were in reality home supporters and 'well chuffed' with the result, to one side a couple of mean looking Millwall suedeheads stared menacingly down on the assembled throng. The two of them were up to a spot of divining.

'They're Millwall....'

'They're Millwall....'

'Look! They're Chelsea...'

Adam's heart sank. 'I'm going to be a statistic', he thought. But he was wrong. It wasn't them. It was just up ahead. Two Chelsea fans were being royally Dr Marten'd and steel toe capped, and there wasn't a friendly Bobby in sight. Perhaps PC McGarry had had his bike stolen. Anyway, miraculously, this bit of bovver in front seemed to save them, because in the melee they were both able to slip away unnoticed. Adam couldn't believe how they had done it, but they had managed to escape. They had managed to sneak out.

When they finally made it home, having luckily out manoeuvred the roaming Millwall gangs by ducking and diving on the tube network westwards, and hiding for twenty minutes in the toilets at Earl's Court, Adam's mum asked him how the match had gone.

'We lost 3-0'.

'Oh, dear....' she replied. 'That's a shame. Well, better luck next time'.

Better luck next time? Adam wasn't sure that there was going to be a next time. And little did his mum know that her son's salvation had been another's penance.

Adam felt sorry for the Chelsea fans who had felt the leather of the Millwall inside and outside the ground that Saturday afternoon and quickly thanked his lucky stars. He was worried his parents would find out about the trouble, but there was hardly even a mention of the match on the news. Towards the end of 1976, it would have taken a half time invasion from Mars and Armageddon to warrant even a footnote.

Some years later, whenever Adam heard the song, 'House of Fun' by Madness, with its 'Welcome to the lion's den, temptation's on its way', the fond memories couldn't fail but come flooding back.

MATCH DAY PROGRAMME

The 1976-77 season, saw a great resurgence under the astute guidance of the manager, Eddie McCreadie. He already had royal blue blood in his veins, having enjoyed a legendary Chelsea career and despite the odd setback at Millwall, Bristol Rovers, Luton Town and Charlton Athletic for example, Chelsea's football was both effervescent and strident in its desire to return to the First Division, the club's natural home.

However, the state of the club behind the scenes was disastrous. The protracted building of the new exclusive East Stand had virtually crippled the Club and every Home Match day programme asked for financial assistance from the fans for the cash strapped Club: 'YOUR CLUB NEEDS YOU' and 'CASH FOR CHELSEA' being regular features. The hunt for money was so intense that buckets became a fashion accessory.

Chelsea, the Kings Road swingers? Not anymore. They were three and a half million pounds in debt. But they would certainly swing if they couldn't pay the rent - the ground being situated in one of the most expensive areas in London, even if it was in the wrong borough. So, 'Cash for Chelsea', was, Adam felt, a worthy cause because if they didn't all help out they would find that not too far down the road, supporters were going to have a lot of free time on a Saturday afternoon. The thought of having to obtain a football injection at neighbours QPR or Fulham, even with the likes of Stan Bowles and George Best was out of the question, so Adam kept a 'Chelsea tin' under his bed which he would fill with tuppenny bits whenever he could. He would write down the amount of money collected in the tin at the end of each week and hoped one day to present his savings to the Chelsea Chairman, Brian Mears, himself. Collecting at that rate Adam would have been saving till Doomsday, but it was well worth it. At least he was doing something. And it certainly raised his morale.

Despite the financial ill omens, McCreadie worked wonders with his youthful team and managed to blend just right the old timers like Harris and Bonetti with the up and coming talents of Wilkins and Finnieston.

Unfortunately, Chelsea were now decidedly weak in Cup competitions and capitulated predictably away to Arsenal in the League Cup, fourth round. Adam listened to the mid-week match on his radio at school and chewed his nails down to the quick. Just before the kick off, he thought, 'If Chelsea win, then it means that Sally won't ask me out and doesn't fancy me. But if Chelsea lose, then it means that she does fancy me and will ask me out'. Adam came to the difficult conclusion that he wanted Chelsea to win. Unfortunately, Chelsea lost 1-2 despite a goal from their solid Scottish defender David Hay, and would you believe it? He ended up being asked out. Adam fumbled around with a red face for a couple of days and then through Robbie, he relayed an acceptance of the offer by note. It didn't quite make up for being knocked out of the League Cup by Arsenal but Adam managed to get in some much needed kissing practice once he'd overcome the initial embarrassment. He certainly needed the practice. Sally thought that he kissed like a cement mixer, but that didn't cramp his style. At least he was going for it. And one night, Adam and Robbie certainly went for it, venturing daringly over to the girls dormitories. To get there, they had to negotiate the treacherous 'subway', a forbidding, damp, concrete tunnel that linked the two sides of the school together. They even managed to dodge all the cockroaches that scuttled about its floor, there and back again, so they could spend a couple of hours in their girlfriend's spotless, cosy rooms. As a result, it wasn't long before Adam's lips and tongue soon felt strained and he began to wish that all future Chelsea matches should be won in order to stave off such risky rendezvous'.

Adam saw some great games in the holidays, half-term, whenever he could. The home League match with Southampton was particularly memorable. The Blues were 0-1 down and came back amazingly in the last fifteen minutes to win 3-1 with superbly wrought goals from Wilkins, Finnieston and Swain.

Chelsea fans sang extra hard that day with many of Adam's terrace favourites: 'Chelsea are back, Chelsea are back, Hallo, Hallo!' and 'Chelsea, Top of the League! Chelsea, Chelsea, Top of the League!' and especially 'Knees up Mother Brown'. Then the crowd would break out into massed chants of 'CHELSEA!' with rhythmic clapping above the head, in unison. 'Knees up Mother Brown' was usually sung when a team had just scored or were winning, or when the supporters were bored, wet or freezing cold, which was most of the time. It would get everyone going and there would be lots of swaying and movement on the packed terracing. There was also prodigious gesticulation and the odd expletive thrown in for good measure.

Before the game against the table topping rivals Wolverhampton Wanderers at Stamford Bridge, Adam stumbled on something out of the ordinary. Near the back pages of the Match day programme, which he usually scrutinised with the intensity of a train spotter at Waterloo station, was a music advert for a new record release by a band called 'The Damned'. It turned out to be the first Punk single ever released. Adam studied the black and white picture of the four young, messy haired musicians and took note of the caption that read; 'THE DAMNED' single 'NEW ROSE', on Stiff Records.

It was odd because that was all it said and this just increased the mystique. Adam thought the band looked original; short hair, wraparound sunglasses, leather jackets, badges, T-shirts and a bow tie and dinner jacket. One member of the band stared out in an aggressive pose, who Adam later found out was the drummer who called himself Rat Scabies, because he was once inflicted with the disease, and the others looked on vacantly unconcerned: the singer Dave Vanian who was an ex-gravedigger, the bassist Captain Sensible, fresh from his job as a toilet cleaner, and the caustic guitarist Brian James.

'They must have something to do with Chelsea?' Adam said to Steve.

'Yeah, maybe', he replied looking at the picture in his own programme.

Then Adam suddenly remembered the commotion that had surrounded the appearance of a band called the Sex Pistols recently on LWT's teatime, 'Today' programme. Although Adam was away at School, as it was during term time, so he didn't see it live, the news of the show spread like wild fire, especially the rumour that one of the cheeky lads in the band, Steve Jones, had said, 'You dirty fucker - you fucking rotter!', live on the telly. It was also reported in the papers, that a lorry driver was so incensed that his eight year old son had heard the bad language, that he kicked in the television set.

The newspaper headlines were everywhere, and the only way to miss the gossip was to be on a mission to Mars: 'WHO ARE THESE PUNKS?' - Obnoxious, arrogant, outrageous…the new pop Kings. 'THE PUNKS - ROTTEN AND PROUD OF IT!' - Worthless, decidedly inferior, displeasing... 'FILTHY TV CHAT' - A top level probe ordered by Thames TV. 'THE FOUL MOUTHED YOBS' - Inquiry over four-letter words. 'FOUR LETTER PUNK ROCK GROUP' - The bizarre face of Punk Rock. 'THE FILTH AND THE FURY!' - When the air turned blue. Uproar as viewers jam phones. 'ROCK GROUP START A 4-LETTER TV STORM' - Viewers in big protest over shock outburst.

Luckily, in the Christmas holidays Adam got a glimpse of the scandal when the BBC repeated the TV interview but with the naughty bits taken out. Adam thought that you couldn't tell exactly who was in the band and who wasn't. It was mysterious. The interviewer, Bill Grundy, seemed to be surrounded by a strange group of young guttersnipes that had just arrived from another planet. They were scruffy and unkempt, sporting cropped, coloured hair and apathy, but something about their look suggested that a lot of thought had gone into it. Their clothes were fashionably weird with rips and slashes tailor made. One was even wearing a swastika armband which certainly made Adam hold his breath.

Adam's friends at school hated them at first and called them 'stupid punks', being brought up as they were on the monolithic hairy Yes, Pink Floyd and Deep Purple. But he found these surly outsiders compelling, and one of them in particular, Johnny Rotten, who had already been labelled a 'ragged rebel' in the press, had a hypnotic quality, as if he was lost in his own world and how dare you enter into it without being invited. His eyes jumped out at you, his teeth all decay. He was certainly different.

As Adam sat on the terraces, listening to the pre match spin, he looked again at the picture in the programme. He decided that when he got the chance he would certainly find out a little bit more about this group The Damned, and the tabloid capturing phenomenon, Punk. The Wolves game was a see-saw cracker as well which Chelsea drew 3-3.

Fulham at home was always a hard fought local derby and a Christmas treat of the first order. It was an unbelievable crowd for a Second Division match of 55,003. Most of who were Chelsea supporters on their yuletide holidays. Adam, Steve and his dad impersonated exceedingly thin sardines in The Shed that afternoon. One of those times when you couldn't shuffle or blow your nose throughout the whole afternoon or even go to the toilet, so packed was it. Adam was fairly lucky as he held a 'strong bladder' record of about four hours, which allowed him to continue to watch in comfort and maintain his place on the terraces. Steve's dad spent most of the second half struggling to return from the delightful Shed toilets.

Also there was the added enjoyment of watching Bobby Moore and George Best turn out for Fulham which certainly helped. They played some great stuff, and promised much, yet in the end did the decent thing and handed Chelsea the two points on a platter. A rare goal from the man mountain Micky Droy at the Shed End and one from Kenny Swain wrapped up Adam's present rather nicely. They even managed to get Steve's dad singing along to some of the festive terrace favourites; 'Is that all, is that all, is that all you take away?!' and 'Jingle bells, jingle bells, jingle all the way, oh what fun it is to see, Fulham lose away!'

There were however, some bad upsets and unfortunate tantrums. Chelsea were thrashed 4-0 in a blizzard at Luton Town, which Adam put down to having to play with an orange football, and likewise at Charlton Athletic, Chelsea were on the receiving end of another 4-0 tonking.

Regrettably, both matches gave vent to a turbulent outbreak of Chelsea rioting. Charlton's Valley stadium was illuminated by bonfire's right across the terraces, while one unfortunate burger vender even had his whole stall pushed down a hill. One supporter who had ripped off a long plank of wood from the back of the stand, instead of using it for kindling, tried to stop Charlton from scoring by leaning over and swinging it near the Chelsea net. Unfortunately, even the crafty use of a plank couldn't stop the rampant Addicks.

At Luton, the town centre was completely smashed and looted. This was almost a repeat of the year before when on the Kenilworth pitch, Chelsea's irrepressible Micky Droy, became a vigilante hero by utilising his ample size thirteen football boot up the backside of an overzealous so-called travelling supporter who had ventured onto the turf. Not for nothing did Chelsea fans champion his strength of character with chants of 'Micky's gonna getcha!' Regrettably, wherever the Chelsea herd went, so it seemed did all the tabloids, and ugly fighting in ridiculous flares and tank tops never seemed far away.

In the ominous rematch with Millwall at Stamford Bridge, Adam and Steve witnessed various demonstrations of sparring, duelling, steaming, surging, team wrestling, group bundles, pitch invasions, mounted Police charges and terrace too-ing and fro-ing when the Millwall hard nuts tried in vain to infiltrate The Shed End. Most certainly, a late night was had by all the doctors and nurses at the local hospitals. It was a wonder the match was ever concluded. However, the 1-1 final score may have saved a few windows.

Apart from the violence, the banning orders and the 'anti-hooligan' all-ticket schemes, there was also great tragedy in the Spring with the news that Peter Houseman, one of Chelsea's most loyal and underrated players and his wife had been killed in a road crash. Adam heard about the car accident while reading the papers at school and was gutted for a long time after. Houseman was one of his favourite player's and it was extra sad because Adam felt he never received the acclaim that he so rightfully deserved. He collected a letter, 'Tribute from the Fans', from one of his programmes for his scrapbook which movingly commented that Houseman made up one fifth of the greatest forward line seen at Stamford Bridge. That it would never have been the same without his presence and that he would always be remembered for his magnificent performances against Manchester Utd, and how he finally recognised the support the fans had for him after his equalising goal at Wembley against Leeds. How he was the sort of person that you cherished more when he wasn't around, because it was then that you realised the amount that you missed him. The heartfelt words concluded in the hope that Chelsea would do something special for Houseman's family, because he had done so much for the Blues.

Yes, unfortunately, in many respects season 1976-77, had everything, including the kitchen sink. But most importantly, by the end, Chelsea were back where they belonged, in the First Division. Hull City's visit to Stamford Bridge concluded the season's fixture list and they were brushed triumphantly aside 4-0, in front of another large crowd that frequently invaded the pitch to celebrate. A memorable hat-trick from Steve Finnieston and a goal from the diminutive Ian Britton, had Adam licking his lips in anticipation of the following season: Division One. The final emphatic result certainly sent the Chelsea fanfare out in style.

SUMMER OF PUNK

One weekend during the close season, Adam met up with Steve in order to go to Stamford Bridge to get the latest on the build up to the forthcoming season back in Division One, and to purchase some programmes of matches from the last season which they had been unable to see. A visit to the stadium during this time was a must as there was no football being played and before long, serious withdrawal symptoms would set in. Adam would always wonder; 'Who have Chelsea bought?' 'Who have we sold?' 'Do we still have the same Manager?' 'Do we still exist?' 'Do we have a different away kit?' 'Are the burgers and the hot-dogs still as bad?'

Because of Chelsea's unpredictable financial position the supporters were never quite sure of the future. So, regular visits to the Ground gave them a feeling of continuity. A sense of belonging. A belief that everyone could do their bit. Perhaps it might only mean a few more coffers in the Chelsea piggy-bank or more likely a plastic bucket. Anyway, if it was a nice day, you could do a lot worse than visit their home, especially as a dramatic piece of Blues news seemed to occur when you least expected it. The ending of Eddie McCreadie's management of the club that very close season, being a fine case in point. The very gaffer who had galvanised the young squad into a convincing, winning formula and ultimately gained promotion with a flourish, had had a reasonable request of a new set of wheels, as a perk in his new contract, rejected. Adam couldn't help thinking that however lurid the furry dice or loud the leather upholstery, it was more than just another short sighted decision made by the crusty, ill advised, cash starved board.

Eventually, Adam and Steve reached the Ground and found the dilapidated Chelsea shop open. They had a good look at the Chelsea shirts, mugs and biros and eyed the various posters of the team on the wall. They found lots of programmes on view and some were from the games that they had missed out on. Others were from matches long since past and as they thumbed through the memories, Chelsea came that little bit more into their hearts. Adam finally went for a few recent away programmes and a couple of home matches, stretching his pocket money to the limits. But he felt content when he realised that his collection for the season was nearly complete. Steve did likewise.

After their craving had been somewhat satisfied, they wandered around outside the ground. To their surprise, Stamford Bridge seemed fairly quiet, although there were a few posters up advertising close season activities. One in particular caught Adam's eye. It was advertising a forthcoming rock concert;

'THE JAM / CHELSEA' - Live at Chelsea Football Ground.

The poster was in black and white in large letters, on the Shed forecourt wall and it immediately reminded him of the earlier Damned advert in the programme. He turned to Steve.

'Who are 'Chelsea?' Are they some sort of band? Maybe it's the players? Maybe some of the team are punks?'

'Dunno....they could be...' Steve said bemused.

The Jam, Adam had heard about already. The three piece led by Paul Weller had been on Marc Bolan's 'Marc' TV programme which he had seen (it was certainly miles better than 'Magpie') and he had heard their single, 'In the City' and quite liked it. Their look was all adolescent sneer - tidy, grey Mod with a large hint of the Union Jack. He didn't think that they looked particularly Punk, but the sound certainly was, being full of angst and intelligence. Whatever the case they were certainly stapled to the movement and they would be playing right there at Stamford Bridge.

Going to a football match at this stage was fine - even if at times the matches frequently turned into World War Three - and Adam and Steve were still sometimes known to be accompanied by adults, due to their lack of years. Unfortunately, he knew that attending a Punk concert at the age of thirteen was going to be absolutely impossible. Also, there seemed to be something forbidding about the whole thing and he knew that he had to find out a lot more about it and wait until he was slightly older before launching himself right into it. But he was definitely intrigued by the enigma of Punk - both in its look and sound - and he was determined to investigate it with all the intensity of a Sherlock Holmes or a Dixon of Dock Green.

After consuming a large hot-dog each and a can of Coke they decided to catch a bus from the Kings Road up to Steve's house in north London. Something they did if the weather was fine and they wanted to hang around the neighbourhood that little bit longer. As they wandered towards the Kings Road, they dodged the traffic and tried to glance at their programmes. An always impossible task. But soon, they found themselves venturing up the road towards the World's End and they knew that they would soon be able to find a place to sit and read. As they walked along there seemed to be a strange atmosphere. The odd police car roared past and there was an aggressive element in the air. Then just up ahead on the left, lots of people were gathered around a shop window. Some of them looked just like the group, the Sex Pistols, that Adam had seen on the TV who had been dubbed 'foul mouthed yobs'. Even if it wasn't them, it was certainly some Punks and Adam and Steve were about to see them right up close. Adam was a bit worried. Their appearance was weird and like nothing else he had ever seen in daylight. All he could think was how unique a style they had and how they stood out. He turned to Steve.

'Look, loads of punks....'

'Yeah....'

'Weird aren't they?!'

'I know....'

'What are we gonna do?'

'Catch the bus'.

'You reckon?'

'Why not?'

'Okay', Adam replied as they tightened their pace.

But that meant they had to walk right past the punks down the Kings Road. Adam steeled himself and Steve did likewise, although he seemed less concerned about it than Adam. The fact that he was taller probably gave him a little more security. As they came up close to the Punks, Adam suddenly noticed the shop to his left, with its sign above, that usually said 'SEX' in big pink letters. He had always considered it to be a strange place, a sort of outrageous and tacky clothes boutique and he had always hurried on past it whenever he walked down the street. This time he looked at it more intensely and there seemed to be a lot of activity. Strange people were going in and coming out of its forbidding interior and as they did so Adam noticed that it's name had changed, but it wasn't that clear what it was now called (he found out later that it was calling itself 'Seditionaries'). The windows were all boarded up and covered in wire grating.

'What's that mean?' he said to Steve.

'I haven't a clue....' Steve returned.

When the shop was called 'SEX', Adam always blushed at the sight; 'A shop calling itself 'SEX? Wow, I wonder what's inside? Who knows? Could be just about anything? It's gotta be a bit naughty. It must have something to do with snogging. Maybe it's to do with girl's breasts?'

As they hastily walked past the shop and turned the corner by the Man in the Moon pub, suddenly they saw a large group of freshly greased-up Teddy boys prowling around the street. Mind you to call them 'boys' would be inaccurate because most of them seemed like fully grown men. Burly greasers. And they were a lot bigger than Adam and Steve that was for sure. They were looking to have a head to head with the Punks - you just knew it, it was as obvious as the brothel creepers on their feet. They bobbed about moodily in their immaculate Tedwards, all wannabe James Dean's dressed in bright colours, while their Teddy girls strutted around, sucked on cigarettes, inflated egos and egged on troops that didn't need any encouragement.

They completely ignored Adam and Steve. Fortunately, these two were no threat. The Teds brushed past them and as they did some of them broke off and ran to the other side of the road where they bunched into a larger group by the traffic lights. They shouted 'We hate Punks!' and 'Fuck off Pistols!' Adam looked at Steve and sighed, 'Here we go again' he thought. It was clear. These lot weren't about to disagree about their choice of football teams. They were about to disagree about their choice of record collections.

The Punks milling around 'Seditionaries' (Adam found out later that it meant; 'agitators against authority, whose conduct or speech tends to rebellion or breach of public order') reacted quickly and grouped themselves almost as if to protect the shop and the whole area around it from the Teds threatening approaches. They looked determined - lurking about, even on the main road, as if they weren't going to give an inch. Just then, abuse and taunts hurled themselves back and forth, as the Teddy boys moved forward in an amateurish Roman formation. As bottles smashed in the street, a Police siren sounded. Incredibly, more and more innocent bystanders had gathered to watch the manoeuvres, including two little old ladies on their weekly shopping trip and surprised tourists cocked their Kodak's at the two sets of discontented youth. As Adam and Steve almost broke out into a run towards their bus stop destination by the Beaufort Market, Police moved in from all around.

The battle of the King's Road was now well underway, with about the same level of excitement Adam reckoned as the final duel in Star Wars between Luke Skywalker and Darth Vader but without the light sabres. One lanky Punk clashed with a Rocker right in the middle of the road oblivious to the traffic and as the two went about each other, exchanging punches viciously, they resembled crazy spinning tops.

'Let's get out of here!' shouted Steve.

'Look, there's our bus!'

'Come on then!'

Problem was, the bus was stuck in the melee as the traffic had slowed right down to a virtual halt with the ensuing violence. As Adam and Steve looked back nervously, there was a cry as the two tribes ran hell-like towards each other. Both groups had by now managed to mass in ever larger numbers, as if the whole thing had been pre-arranged. The scene soon descended into farce. Youths ran insanely about, down side-streets and around Chelsea Park Gardens, in between vehicles, mobbing and fighting and hollering at each other. Policeman tried desperately to catch the perpetrators, truncheons at the ready, but only seemed at best to be pulling off accomplished impersonations of the Keystone Cops.

'Chelsea! Chelsea!' the Punks cried, and 'White Riot!' and 'God Save the Queen!' echoed, which riled the Teds, accompanied as it was with lewd hand gestures and spitting, as Teds were well known for their patriotism and the picture of the Queen with a safety pin through her lip on the cover of the recently released single of the same name by the Sex Pistols, to coincide with the Queen's Silver Jubilee, was to them serious effrontery.

Relief. The bus had managed somehow to get through the warring bodies and made it's way slowly forward. Some of the Punks began legging it up the street as if in hot pursuit with what looked like Elvis Presley and Gene Vincent impressionists on their tails. The Punk's shirts were covered in slogans and the odd zip or tear. Some were paint splattered, as though Jackson Pollock had had a particularly bad hang over. The rest of the clothes resembled freshly pressed hand-me-downs. Adam thought that one of the Punks looked more like a Soul boy. His hair was straight out of 'Crufts' - a safety pin embedded in his cheek and you couldn't take your eyes off his attitude for a second.

It was obvious that the Punks were mixing up all the dress codes in a primitive fashion just to annoy people. Utilising anything at their disposal to look that little bit different: a boot lace tie and ripped up T-shirt: a black leather jacket and crazy coloured hair. Thing was, they couldn't quite match the Teds undoubted ferocity and decided to save themselves: Adam reckoned 'Runaway!' straight out of the 'Monty Python and the Holy Grail' film had probably been the cry as they scurried away comically in tight fitting tartan bondage trousers. The Old Bill were now moving in, in significant numbers and various stragglers from both factions began to find themselves lined up against the walls or 'banged to rights' inside a claustrophobic meat wagon.

While the local sheriff and his deputies tried to earn their badges, Adam and Steve hopped on the bus without hesitation and managed to take sanctuary on the top deck. As they slumped down and waited for the bus to transport them as far away from the war zone as possible, some sweaty, spike haired, xeroxed T-shirted Punks had the same idea and came and huddled up at the back of the vehicle. The bus conductor was concerned that the Teds might follow, so he asked the punks to leave immediately. They refused point blank with plenty of vile verbals, until a large intimidating Policeman appeared and made them vacate the top deck. Adam never found out what happened to them, but he was relieved that they had gone as they seemed intent on trouble and soon after the bus moved off with a 'ding ding' of the bell and a sigh of relief from the passengers.

Adam and Steve sat back and settled in their seat. Once again they had made it to safety without the assistance of Superman or any other super heroes for that matter and as the distant King's Road rioting subsided and the grubby Routemaster chugged its way up to North London towards Steve's house, they took out those recently purchased match day programmes and happily scrutinised their Chelsea Bibles.

MICK AND THE ROBINS

Mick, who was to become another good friend of Adam's, had already been expelled from two tough Comprehensive Schools in Bristol for rowdy behaviour and was considered officially as a bit of a handful. It was surprising then that he became eligible for assistance from the boarding school that Adam was at, but the school was keen to take on difficult teenagers, like Louie, who wouldn't be taken on anywhere else, or pupils who had disadvantaged backgrounds and couldn't afford an education, but showed potential.

It was all part of the School's Quaker ethos and Mick was supposed to be thankful that the State were coughing up all his fees, as there was no way his old man was going to. His father worked in the Bristol docks, when he could get work, and his mother had long since left the household. The school looked upon it as a benevolent outstretched hand. For Mick, although he knew it was probably his last chance, he cared little about qualifications and the like. He just wanted to rock the boat and have a laugh.

When Adam first met Mick, his reputation had proceeded him and his strong Bedminster accent singled him out and set him apart from the rest of the year. He also looked different. He was quite tall and had black hair which he liked to quiff back in an Elvis style, he was never without a comb, and he was always one for wearing a tank top and kipper tie with his school blazer. His out of school clobber usually consisted of wide legged, high waisted black trousers, or 'cowboy pants' with large side pockets and a white T-shirt with the short sleeves rolled up and he was never seen without his black leather jacket exactly like the Fonz's in the popular TV series Happy Days. He also had large front teeth which made him look tough and he had this way of flicking them with his index finger whenever he was bored. A lot of the snobs in the year looked down their noses at him and ignored him. Mick didn't care though. He could more than look after himself. And he knew that everyone was a bit scared of him. But with the girls he was an instant success, and he knew it.

This was further reinforced when only after a couple of weeks, Mick chanced one afternoon, to meet up with a group of the Bristol chapter of the Hell's Angels in a layby at the side of the school's busy main road. Both he and Adam had just been innocently on their way to the nearby sports field for Games, but Mick thought it would be a good idea to take some time out and chat with the biker crew who Adam could see looked definitely born to be wild. One of them was even cursing madly as he tried a hasty oil change on his large Norton. They had been visiting Cheddar Gorge, as if it was a family outing and were laden with supplies of scrumpy and cheese and although Adam felt somewhat ill at ease, Mick seemed to be in his element especially when he found out that the ring leader, who was perched on a spotless Harley, hailed from the very same area of Bristol. Meanwhile, Adam just couldn't get over how unexpectedly normal they all seemed. Certainly nothing like what the tabloids would have people believe. When he thought about it further, he just put their manner down in the end to the fact that both him and Mick were never going to be any threat.

Afterwards, word of the meeting spread quickly throughout the school, an eagle eyed games teacher having already reported it, and the result was a bizarre slap on the wrist for them both for 'talking to Hell's Angels'. For Mick though it was gold dust. Any problem from the upper year bullies in the future and he would let it be known that he had access to some more than persuasive intervention and Adam could certainly gain some benefit from it too, even though he realised that there had been notorious fights between the Bristol and Cheddar chapters, so it was always going to be fumbling around with a very loose cannon.

Adam found that although he didn't have an instant rapport with Mick, who didn't like Punk at all, because they were both mad about football and Mick discovered that Adam wasn't at the School under normal circumstances, they saw each other as somebody that they could be mates with.

Mick was a lifelong Bristol City fan, and like Chelsea, both clubs were now both in the First Division together. During the 1977-78 season, Adam went to quite a few City matches with Mick, as Bristol wasn't far from the school and Mick's dad lived quite near the stadium. Louie would probably have gone to the games as well, had he not been spending most of his free time in the school's solitary confinement wing.

Adam found himself becoming quite fond of their compact ground, Ashton Gate, with its picturesque view up to the Clifton suspension bridge. Years later Adam would even keep an eye out for their results which would never quite reach the heady heights that they had around the time Adam went to watch them. At that time they were worthy members of the First Division, due to Alan Dicks' astute management style (he had also once turned out for Chelsea) and they were busy springing a few surprises along the way with their passionate, determined play.

Their supporters home end was electric, with its claustrophobic, metal roofed stand amplifying the noise straight onto the pitch and the 'Robins' supporters could certainly follow their team. They knew how to sing alright. Most of their chants could strike fear into the faint hearted, especially with the likes of; 'You're goin' home in a fuckin' ambulance!' and, 'We 'ate Rovers! And we 'ate Rovers! We 'ate Rover's! And we 'ate Rovers!' but sometimes the chants were a little more comic; 'Oh, I've got a brand new combine harvester, and I'll give you the key!' and, 'I'm a cider drinker, I drink it all of the day!'

It was an amazing accent. The Bristonian burr. The sort of accent that could cut glass if it wanted too. Adam knew that he was in an alien environment, being a Londoner and Chelsea supporter, and that it probably wasn't advisable to hang about in it for too long, but Mick and his mates; 'Oggie', who was always on the look-out for a bit of trouble, and 'Spud', named because his surname was Murphy, 'there's more Murphy's than spuds in Ireland' or so Mick would joke, insisted that Adam go to some matches. Whatever the reason for Spud's moniker, the name was pretty suitable anyway because he looked the dead spit of a large King Edward potato. To Adam's relief, they all welcomed him even though he was from London and he felt honoured that they even tried to convert him from his allegiance to the Blues. If Adam hadn't already been a Chelsea fan, he probably would have been persuaded to follow the Robins, and Mick's passion for his hometown certainly rubbed off; Saturday's being literally the only day he looked forward to and he would love egging on his favourite players, like Tom Ritchie, Trevor Tainton and the legendary leg biter, Norman Hunter.

The crowd at Bristol City were definitely partisan, but you knew you were alive whenever their heroes went for goal. Sometimes City's attacking play was so frenetic it was like the attack on The Alamo, I suppose because the home end was so close to the pitch, unlike at Chelsea where the Shed sometimes felt like it was at least a mile away from the grass. And whenever they shouted;

'Go on Mabbutt!'

'Have 'em Sweeney!'

they never failed to raise their players determination on the pitch and a spectacular goal wouldn't be far away.

Adam felt that here was a club that hadn't really ever won much (even less than Chelsea had) perhaps mainly due to the lack of money in the coffers, but despite this the supporters loyally continued to follow their team through thick and thin. In fact a lot of it. And they knew their football, in what was for them a cracking season. They faced the likes of the mighty Liverpool and Brian Clough's legends Nottingham Forest and in most of the games they more than held their own.

There were some scrapes though, particularly when West Ham paid a visit. Some claret and blue individuals even managed to sneak into the City home end. Throughout the match, Adam could see these heads bobbing up and down and everyone would go,

'Oi, look there's a West 'Am!'

Then there would be a bundle and the brave, more like suicidal, away fan would be briskly ejected with a bloody nose for his pains. The Bristol City fans knew how to sing for their team. They also knew how to battle for it. At the home fixture with Leeds, where there was a lot of trouble, Adam wasn't surprised when he heard that there had been a fatal stabbing right outside the ground.

After the matches they would nip back to Mick's dad's place in Bedminster, where they would meet up with the rest of his mates, that's if they hadn't already seen them at the game. There the plan of action would be to kick a football about on Bedminster hill where there was a lop-sided pitch with crooked goals. As they played 'three and in' dressed in the wrong gear - wide cowboy-like trousers with large pockets and awful stripy V-neck sweaters, they could look down on the Ashton Gate stadium below them and dream about being professional footballers: Transported instantly from the deadbeat dead-end reality all about to a fantasy world of opportunity.

As Mick pretended to be Tom Ritchie and Adam failed to be Ray Wilkins, and great effort was used up trying to keep the ball up in the air for as long as possible in their ridiculous garb, they would then break out the cigarettes, which were so strong Adam called them 'coffin nails'. Afterwards they would feel really ill, but they all thought it made them look tough and older than their years. Spud reckoned that he could chain smoke them all day without even coughing. One thing was for sure. His lung capacity was bigger than any of the others.

The eventual visit of Chelsea to Ashton Gate was a mouth watering prospect and also for Adam a double-edged one: The club he began supporting, playing his temporarily adopted one. He knew that he would have to put up with the constant ribbing from Mick's mates and in the Bristol City home end there was no way that Adam was going to be able to cheer if Chelsea scored. He would maintain a healthy and life prolonging silence, even though Mick's mates probably would have stopped any trouble arising had it started. But one thing he knew for certain, he was definitely going to be in the wrong end.

On paper, the fixture certainly had it's interesting conflicts on and off the pitch: Norman Hunter versus Chopper Harris, two of the hardest men in football battling it out for bragging rights: Chris Garland trying to forget that he was once a Chelsea player and appear against his old club (unfortunately he didn't): Adam's mate Mick's love of Elvis Presley, Happy Days and 'The Fonz' against his own fondness for Punk, the Sex Pistols and 'Ready Steady Go'.

Bristol City set out their stall from the off. It was called 'home victory'. Chelsea did likewise. It was called 'away defeat'. When City scored their first, Adam stood stock still as all about went Avon bananas: 'We 'ate Cockneys! And we 'ate Cockneys, We are the Cockney 'ater's!

Mick and his mates ribbed him mercilessly, once they had come back down to earth. As they swaggered on the terraces, Adam did a fine impression of someone taking it royally on the chin, virtually hiding under a barrier. But it wasn't over by any means, well not before City had slotted another two past the despairing stretch of Bonetti. Mick was in his element once again and with his mates tore into Adam with interest, but he knew that they weren't going to hit him, they just shouted the names of the goal scorers repeatedly in his ear.

'Gerry Gow!'

'Cormack!'

'Rodgers!'

It wasn't long before the names were impressed, or more like tattooed on Adam's memory. The hammering dealt mercilessly out to Chelsea that day was for him like chewing on a large household brick without so much as a glass of water.

The whistle went and before Adam could file the defeat away in his personal out tray, Oggie and Spud reckoned that they fancied a bit of a fisty or two with the Chelsea faithful.

'Let's follow 'em up to Parkway station'.

'Aye. Let's do 'em!' Spud cracked.

'Cockney fucker's!'

Adam gulped. Mick smiled back. The win had definitely chuffed him and his shoulders were now placed even further back than before.

'You got a right stuffin'!'

Adam took it for a moment, then let loose.

'Makes us even then, cos we beat you at the Bridge!'

While Mick flinched, Spud laughed like a huge dinosaur, but it wasn't because he was going to have a go at Adam. They admired his front, especially as older supporters around them had worked out by the end of the game that he wasn't the usual 110% Robin.

'Come on. Let's have a go at 'em lot', said Mick wide eyed, looking up to the away end.

They all decided to leave the ground, following fast on the heels of the away supporters once they had been let out and cut them off at the pass. It wasn't much of a detour because all Mick's mates lived in Bedminster just up the road from the station, so you could say that they looked upon it as some local excitement. For Adam it was going to be a difficult evening - watching his youthful Bristol mates taunting the Chelsea and he was already well aware how easy it was to provoke the average Blues fan. He didn't think that Mick's mob were really going to get involved, being in their mid teens, but with Oggie you never quite knew. He wasn't scared of anybody. Not even the devil himself.

'Send 'em home on fuckin' stretchers!'

Then he looked at Adam as if to say, 'not including you', which was a great relief and off they all went up to the station to stalk their prey.

It was a long amble up a winding hill and round and round some roundabouts, traversing busy roads and crossing masses of erratic traffic lights and crazy Baleisha beacons. As they chain smoked Embassy and Spud hitched up his large trousers and flexed his solid arms, they tried to look as old as they possibly could. Oggie meanwhile tried to look as menacing as possible, which wasn't hard, especially when he attempted his party tricks, consisting of a vicious Chinese burn that would sting for a week or stubbing out a cigarette on your neck when you weren't looking.

Eventually, Mick suggested that we wait around for the Chelsea supporters and while they bantered at the side of the road, short of breath, Adam trying all the while to escape their awkward objective, many more Bristol City fans gathered and sang their allegiance to Alan Dicks' heroes (for a team that had been languishing ungainly in the bottom half of the table the whole season, the much needed two points scalped from Chelsea had raised them up to eleventh in the First Division table and relegation fears were quickly forgotten. In fact you would have thought that they had just won the Cup. Chelsea meanwhile, were looking sunk, their defence springing leaks all over, despite Chopper Harris' last ditch efforts).

'Our defence was like a teabag', Adam offered up as a pathetic excuse.

'Teabag?! Shite more like!' said Mick, and Spud was soon leading by a length once again in the laughing competition.

'Oh, leave it out....' Adam replied and amazingly to his relief they let it rest. He supposed the humiliating result was probably enough and anyway he was heavily outnumbered so it was far too easy a conquest to keep them entertained for long.

'Oi, look! "Ere they come!' said Oggie drooling at the prospect of a confrontation with the King's road travellers.

Just at that moment, the Chelsea fans appeared in a large formation further down the hill, a massed rank of menace, escorted closely by the Police, all blue and white around the edges. As they marched aggressively up the road, they were busy singing about how proud they were that they were Londoner's and how they would follow Chelsea, 'Over land and sea - and Leicester! We will follow Chelsea, on to victory!'

As soon as Mick and his mates heard the distant taunting they flung back their favourite cider drinking songs and their hate for all things Cockney, 'Come an' 'ave a go at the City A-G-R-O!!' Once within range, the gesticulation really started up, and with the Chelsea fans nearing all the while, Oggie tried to hit the away supporters with his speciality projectile - 'flying gob' - and Adam tried quickly to imagine that he was somewhere else.

When the Chelsea meatheads were in close enough attendance to almost smell them, Adam felt his blood start to run cold. They looked an intimidating bunch alright and a library's worth of violent tabloid headlines only increased the sense of forboding. As the knot in his stomach grew larger, some of the Skinheads within the Chelsea ranks tried desperately to break through the line of police, but they were unsuccessful. They were completely hemmed in. Adam was glad that both sets of troublemakers were kept apart, especially as it would have been unfortunate to have been beaten up by his own supporters, and the

Chelsea following looked intent on having a good ruck with the locals. It made no difference if the opposition were elderly, kids or just local shopkeepers closing up for the day.

'Fuckin'shitters!' shouted Oggie, as he and Spud eyeballed the cosmopolitan nutcases ambling past and Police helmets alongside pricked up trying to hone in on the close range verbal bombardment. The irate Chelsea fans quickly responded with obligatory 'wanker signs' and sneering remonstrations and it wasn't long before a bottle came flying over, which even Spud managed to duck. The result was a mini police snatch squad amongst the closely guarded group of marchers.

It wasn't long before the Blues supporters were nearing the station. For once, the Police had the situation pretty much under lock and key and Mick was well aware that there wouldn't be any trouble, although Adam was more than relieved that it was just a standoff because he didn't know how fast he could run away in heavy shoes and large trousers.

As the ranks of defeated looking away fans passed by full of oaths and threats, the locals almost waving them on their way to the train station, the four lads decided to retire to Mick's dad's loudly wallpapered house. After a great sigh of relief from Adam and a short stroll away from the danger zone, they made it back, but not after reminiscing on the day's activities and more than once hearing Oggie boasting on about what he would have done to any unfortunate Chelsea supporter that got in his way.

'Them bastards would have got a right fuckin' kickin'!'

Again he looked at Adam as if to say, 'not you mate' and Adam tried once more to put his nerves back in their box.

As it turned out, they had completely missed the football results service, and even Starsky and Hutch and their tea had grown cold, but at least they'd had some genuine excitement, so they didn't really mind. And Mick's dad was more than pleased, as it turned out, because he was an armchair Robin.

PUNK DETECTIVE

By now Adam had found out a lot more about Punk and was already fast becoming a devotee of the Sex Pistols. Louie had purchased a copy of 'Never Mind the Bollocks' in Bristol in the holidays and they played it at every opportunity in their common room in their free time. The album's lurid, yellow and pink cover with large black cut-up writing looked striking - absolutely perfect. Louie's favourite track was 'Bodies' and he used to sing along with gusto about a bizarre girl named Polly from Birmingham who had an abortion and lived in a tree. Robbie's favourite song was Problems and again he would try and outdo Louie in the singing department, 'Have you got a problem? The problem is you!' Adam's favourite was Holidays in the Sun, because it was dead catchy and the lyrics and vocals were totally inspired. Then the three of them would try and 'take off' the guitarist Steve Jones with some larking about with a broom handle. His sound was awesome - like a third world war and coupled with Paul Cook's pile driving drums, Rotten's vocal cacophony and the newly installed Sid Vicious' posing, they were unbeatable. There was no doubt that the boys were becoming older and considerably wiser, even though there was absolutely no hint of it in their school reports, which enabled them to appreciate the music even more and feel that they could join in with it.

One of the first things that Punk seemed to have achieved was to alter and play around with an individual's identity by changing their name. Not only was it a piece of rebellion - rejecting the system; name, number, rank etc; for some punks it was also to avoid the attentions of the Department of Health and Social Security. With all the illicit gigs paying cash in hand to the bands, it was essential to create a smokescreen to the attentions of the Inland Revenue so punks could continue to play and 'sign on'.

The movement was challenging authority, because here was a rebellion that was not merely fractious, it also seemed as though it might be intelligent. Here was a cause that had more than a chapter heading of knowledge and a lack of dress sense to boot.

There were some brilliant made up stage names. Here's just a few of Adam's all time favourites: Poly-styrene (her anti-consumerism summed up perfectly), Captain Sensible (who took his name from a clothes shop assistant who cried out 'Oh, it's fucking Captain Sensible!' when the future Damned guitarist had been messing about impersonating a pilot), Ed Banger, Laura Logic, Jak Airport, Rat Scabies (the madcap 'gobbing' drummer also of the Damned), TV Smith, Tory Crimes (the original drummer of The Clash), Lance D'Boil (a terrific cure for acne), Johnny Moped, Stiv Bators, Beki Bondage, N.A. Palmer, Jet Black, Vi Subversa, Jah Wobble, Palmolive, Dee Generate (the 14 year old drummer of Eater who replaced the first drummer called Social Demise, who had trouble taking time off school), Joy De Vivre, Splodge, Richard Hell, Ari Up, Jello Biafra, Nancy Luger, Ivor Bigun, Rob Gotobed, Honey Bane, Nick Cash (probably not his real name), Slimy Toad, Rob Goodfornothing, Spizz Energi, Klaus Flouride (the slight, bespectacled bassist from the Dead Kennedy's who looked like he might in fact be an accountant), Sue Catwoman, Ricky Slaughter, Gaye Advert (the bassist of the Adverts who was without doubt the pin-up of Punk, with her gothic eye make-up and black biker jacket. Adam had a major crush on her), East Bay Ray and last but certainly not least, Steve Ignorant of punk anarchists Crass.

People were trying to reinvent themselves in their own particular cartoon image: Not someone else's, not the family's, not societies. It was a statement. A rejection of conformity and all the so-called 'received wisdom' that had gone before.

This was important. People were deconstructing. Punk was taking an almost lateral, alternative view of the world - a world that seemed out of joint. Everything was taken apart just as if it was a component in a motor engine. Once it had all been checked out, it was put back together again but in a different form. So that in future you couldn't be so simply pinned down, labelled, boxed and filed away. This always reminded Adam of how he used to play with his Action Man, dressing it up in completely contrasting clothing when he got bored.

Was the sum of the parts what you really were? Perhaps you were in fact the parts of the sum. The disparate parts. That's why 'Identity' or the lack of it was mentioned again and again on so many records of the period. What sort of identity? A sham one? Or was it the real thing?

The music too was broken down to its bare essentials: heavy on the drums; blistering guitar, throbbing bass; and hasty, purposeful vocals. The sparse, simple compositions of no longer duration than a couple of minutes, as if all the musicians were trying to play as fast as possible because they had a bus to catch, echoed some of the more brutal Glam songs of the early to mid 70's, and the shorter rock'n'roll songs of the 50's and early 60's. On the whole, brevity was the art of wit and the shorter the song, the more likely people were going to remember it. Furthermore, a lot of the musicians were novices and youthful, so short songs were the result of an uncomplicated directness.

Once Punk had exploded across the UK, hastily set up bands had to have material to play, and quick. Otherwise they would miss the boat. Even better if people already knew the song. As a result, many Punk bands played cover versions of songs that had been memorably catchy or were just downright brilliant. Glam again was a good starting point because of its outrageousness: Vice Squad did a memorable reworking of Sweet's, 'Teenage Rampage': Siouxsie and the Banshees did a great cover of Marc Bolan's, 'Twentieth Century Boy'.

Bolan's putrified career was given a whole new lease of life with the advent of Punk. He was one of the only few 'old farts' that Punks accepted into the fold as a Godfather of the movement. This was probably because he was a one-off, a unique songwriter with an outrageously glamorous stage persona that towards the end knew no bounds. Also, he tried to shun the self satisfied rock establishment and searched desperately for his rock'n'roll roots. Just before his tragic death, which Adam's brother Alan told him about as his girlfriend lived near the site of the accident in Barnes, Bolan toured the UK with The Damned, and his regular TV programme 'Marc' featured lots of Punk groups, and he had a regular column in 'Record Mirror' magazine.

Because the songs were short and catchy, excellent terrace-like anthems were created. In the case of the Sham 69, their song 'If the Kids are United', was accompanied by terrace chants of 'United!' and rhythmic hand clapping, as if hundreds of football supporters had been asked to contribute to the recording. This was also very Glam influenced with its nod to bands like Slade, who at one early point in their career modelled themselves on Skinhead boot boys. Around the time that Sham 69's single, 'Hersham Boys' was released, Chelsea fans in the Shed End were singing the chorus of the song with 'Chelsea' replacing 'Hersham'.

Life was imitating art. The terraces were reverberating. The music was chanting. Tunes that could be easily hummed or whistled, so there were no convoluted fifteen minute marathons here, with endless guitar solos and lyrics that concerned themselves with the petals of a flower as seen through the eyes of someone on a particularly depressing acid trip, were the order of the day. The lyrics usually concerned themselves about what it was like to be young, ordinary and living in the unpredictable, crazy world of the 70's: In a city. In a consumer society. In a disposable ethos. On a planet that was saying more and more, 'Buy now, forget later'. As a consequence, this new 'do-it-yourself' approach to rock music had much more drive and purpose. More integrity than anything that went before it, and it was a right royal kick up the back passage to all the self-satisfied, stagnated, super bands that were parading themselves around mammoth stadiums, and were sitting back and watching their cash registers overheat.

Punk was an assault on the nation's dulled senses, a major wake up call, and the way that everyone had previously perceived their environment and culture was now entirely under review. 'Something Better Change', as The Stranglers powerfully chanted was a common rallying cry and for a while it seemed as if things might indeed change for the better. Alongside the seriousness of the message, people just wanted to have a bit of fun and be entertained and at the end of the day, it was always still just good old rock'n'roll - only now dressed up in a more accessible and diverse package and possessing a very long tongue in the cheek.

The results were immediate. A lot of people found that they just couldn't resist. Punks were galvanising themselves and were having lots of fun while they went about it. The example being set was simple. What you are is important. Who cares about where you are from: Scum, wastrels, downtrodden, the dispossessed, the minority, the smelly. It doesn't matter. You can all be elected and you all have something to say. Boy or girl. Black or white. Green or Orange.

X-Ray Spex, one of Louie's favourite bands, had lead singer Poly Styrene, who was a loud, unconventionally striking, mixed-race girl with buck teeth who wore outrageous outfits and screamed and yelled, 'Oh Bondage Up Yours!' in a high pitched wail. Not only that, but she was also intelligent and had an articulated lorry load of charisma. Just by her attitude she was lobbing a hand grenade right into the heart of the male dominated rock domain and it wasn't a moment too soon.

'Yes'. Punk was saying. 'You too can do it'. 'You too can get up on stage'. There is no exclusion. 'Can't play?' 'So what!' 'You still might have something to say?' 'Why not do it yourself' The underage Punk band Eater did just that getting up on stage with £30 guitars purchased straight from Woolworths as did the Buzzcocks who brought their equipment and instruments to their early gigs in plastic bags.

The act of doing was an event in itself. An act that was to be cherished, however destructive, and a great sense of achievement was had from trying to beat the system. The system that so desperately wanted to classify you and destroy you, the individual.

This was something that the hippies had tried to achieve but couldn't, because they were probably too concerned with peace and love and magic mushroom navel gazing. Yes, 'Sex and Drugs and Rock'n'Roll' - Punk certainly was, as Ian Dury so aptly coined it, but it was also rock'n'roll that could be equally memorable and life changing.

Another very effective shock tactic used by Punk was to invert and subvert all the old musical cliches. For example, the hippy movement always made a great play on the words 'peace and love', even if all around was the Vietnam war and disillusionment. The Clash wrote a song called, 'Hate and War' and this was a direct shot at '60's flower power and was emphatic in its honesty. So many songs prior to Punk had 'I love you' in them that there was almost nothing left to say in that department, unless of course you were equipped with a large paper bag to throw up in afterwards. The Sex Pistols mocked this brilliantly by inverting 'I love you' with the words, 'I'm in love with myself'.

Further clever twists on tired cliché were the Pistols' admission that they had 'No Feelings' when feelings, especially for other people, in a song were always meant to be so terribly important. The Beach Boys surfing candy floss 'Fun, Fun, Fun' was wittily harangued by the American Punk, Iggy Pop with his song 'No Fun' which the Pistols covered superbly. In the 'good old days', a future was something to look forward to, but now there was 'No Future', absolutely none. There were now lots and lots of 'Problems' everywhere when previously, problems had been for the greater part swept under the carpet. Instead of wanting to be like everyone else it was now becoming more interesting and fashionable to say 'I Wanna Be Me'.

Even being negative was a positive: You could now admit to being partial to a little bit of 'Submission', to being the occasional 'Liar', 'Pretty Vacant', a 'Cheat', 'Artificial', repeatedly asking yourself 'What's My Name?', discovering that you were 'Out of Order', even 'Ugly', being a 'Suspect Device', or 'Damaged Goods', a 'Back Biter', having 'No Pity', even being a tiny bit 'Crazy'. Such was the unburdening of the National psyche. Yes, if you were going to be a little degenerate, why not admit it and tell everybody about it in the first place.

CUP GLORY

In the third round of the FA Cup, Chelsea scored a memorable victory over the reigning League and European Champions, Liverpool.

Adam and Steve arrived at Stamford Bridge especially early to soak up the unique Cup atmosphere and it was a large crowd of 45,449. They felt they stood little chance against such mighty opposition, but the FA Cup was always an unpredictable competition, and just about anything could happen in the next ninety minutes.

Even Peter Bonetti had caught Cup fever, and in the match day programme he showed that he was in comic mood: His best moment in life? Being born. The team he cheered as a boy? Bonetti United (star player Bonetti). Modern player most admired? The Bionic man - he has such a good pair of hands. Hobbies? Sun bathing, lying in bed, holidays, cruises, breathing. Other sports played? Scotch (without hop), Squash (without orange), gammon (without back), tiddly (without winks). Matchday Superstition? Always putting one foot in front of the other when going on the pitch. Strangest happening in career? Playing against a team which had a giraffe at centre-forward - he was too good in the air. Favourite away ground? The Palace (Buckingham) - you meet some nice people there. The change he would like to see in football? Changing from goalkeeper to Chairman. A bright idea for football? Luminous footballs - bright enough?! Career ambition? To retire as a millionaire. Today's ambition? To be as serious as he'd ever been in his life about winning the match and helping Chelsea start a 1978 Cup run that goes all the way to Wembley.

Chelsea took to the field to a resounding chorus of 'Blue is the Colour' over the tannoy system and as the fans sang along in The Shed their spirits were instantly lifted. Having home advantage was also crucial. They would sing the ball into the net if they had too.

Unfortunate for Liverpool was the presence of Clive Walker in the Chelsea side who had recently burst into the first team with his amazing speed and dazzling wing play. Today he was going to take the Reds to the cleaners. Adam just knew it. Walker's inclusion made up ably for the absence of Chelsea's midfield maestro and deity, Ray Wilkins and even though the side still overflowed with youthful inconsistency, on their day - watch out.

The veteran bamboozler Charlie Cooke still graced the Chelsea line up and that meant that with Clive Walker, there were two too many ball jugglers on the pitch for Liverpool comfort. After sixteen minutes of high octane knock-out football, Walker collected the ball innocuously enough on the left and it seemed to bobble forward in his stride. The Liverpool players Phil Thompson and Joey Jones were concerned - a terrier had the ball - they backed off as he sped forward and the next thing Adam saw was Walker's left peg launching an unstoppable swerving missile into the top of the Liverpool net.

It was one of the greatest goals Adam had ever seen at Stamford Bridge. Ray Clemence, the Liverpool keeper didn't even see it. Even if he had there would have been little he could have done about it. As he stood in his net like a spare part and cursed his lame defenders, everyone went berserk. The packed Shed swayed this way and that. Scarves, flags and arms raised themselves skyward: When Butch goes up, to lift the FA Cup. We'll be there. We'll be there!

'You'll Never Walk Alone', was taunted back at the European Champions, and 'Chelsea are back, Chelsea are back!' echoed around the ground and it was soon time to break out the throat lozenges:

'Perhaps we can win?' Adam said to Steve.

'Give Walker half a sniff and it'll be a rout'.

During the first half, Charlie Cooke was unfortunately injured and Steve Finnieston, came on (this would turn out to be Cooke's last ever appearance for the Blues), which in this instance actually helped Chelsea put the ball in Liverpool's net. Cooke had been marked tightly by the opposition who were in awe of his legendary box of tricks. Finnieston was an out and out striker and less well known by Liverpool, so he was allowed acres of space.

Six minutes into the second half Finnieston beat Clemence swiftly to his left and it was 2-0.Adam and Steve couldn't believe it. They were in heaven and as they jumped around screaming, 'Yes!' 'Yes!' 'Yes!' they suddenly began to believe. It was now all Chelsea, and Liverpool with the likes of Dalglish, McDermott, Hughes and Kennedy were beginning to resemble headless chickens, running all over the pitch chasing Walker to absolutely no avail.

In the fifty fifth minute Tommy Langley swooped on a dodgy back pass and crisply made it 3-0. The terraces were opening the bubbly, toasting individual performances, cheering each time Chelsea just retained the ball or passed back to the confident Bonetti. The atmosphere was becoming hysterical:

'Why can't we play like this every week?' Steve pondered.

'I s'pose it's because we're Chelsea', Adam replied unsatisfactorily.

Just as they were both beginning to gloat, Liverpool scored and went about trying to make a game of it. But it was no use. Walker still had other ideas and from Bill Garner's unselfish pass, he helped himself to his second goal which the attentions of Liverpool's hard man, Jimmy Case, couldn't prevent.

After another consolation goal for Liverpool, the game ended in 4-2 delirium. Liverpool had been knocked out of the third round of the FA Cup for the first time in twelve years. Suddenly, Adam had visions of Wembley's twin towers and the parade of the gleaming trophy around the pitch. Unfortunately, it was only the third round. Soon enough, reality would strike. The next game in the League, Chelsea were thrashed 1-5 by Coventry City and they eventually went out of the FA Cup in the fifth round to, would you believe it, Leyton Orient. Such was their inconsistency. But at least they had the odd player who on his day could make you dream. Such a player was Clive Walker. The press went absolutely bonkers and Walker was compared to an oxy-acetylene burner, a blitz, a revolutionary, a being from another planet, and a completely daft, infectious, wonder winger from another age.

More importantly, Chelsea rubbed it in just a little bit more by beating Liverpool 3-1 soon after in the League match at Stamford Bridge. Walker was let off the leash once more and had another fine run around to the dismay of the forever back pedalling Liverpool defence.

FIRE EXTINGUISHER

Adam would do anything for a dare. He didn't know exactly why. It was probably because he was worried that he might be as thick as two very short planks, so the only way he could express himself was through doing something silly. He knew deep down that he was sometimes a bit inhibited on the social front and that he occasionally had trouble communicating effectively. He concluded, like Louie, that the best way to impress his peers and especially the girls in his year was to appear to be slightly dangerous and capable of doing things that others wouldn't have the guts to do.

His mate Mick fully understood this, but he didn't usually need to resort to Adam's irresponsible tactics because he was already dangerous enough. This was to be the beginning of a downward spiral and it wasn't long before Adam had cut himself off from the mainstream part of the school and began to question all the received bullshit, which everyone was expected to digest.

One hot day, the form were queuing outside the 'language laboratory', a large studio of booths where pupils would sit individually with headphones clamped to their heads as the cranky French teacher tried to drill their noodles with oral 'Francais'. They were feeling stifled alright, both by the sticky weather outside and the prospect of slumping for an hour in the claustrophobic booths, reciting 'la baguette, le croissant, l'hotel, le cafe, bonjour, merci, qu'est que ce?', and endless mind boggling grammar and following Jean-Paul's repetitive trips to the Boulangerie to purchase le pain. Pain it most definitely was and after about five minutes you could be sure that the last thing they wanted to do was visit France. Instead they would have much preferred to have bombed it with their text books.

It didn't help that their French teacher, as well as being cranky, was as camp as a tent. His more than apt nickname was 'Feelers' and he was a regular spectator in the boys changing rooms when they showered after Games. He would make out that he had some important information to impart to the pupils about visiting the Eiffel Tower or the Bastille for example, but really all he wanted to do was to have a peek at their youthful tackle. As you can imagine, he came low down on the table of teachers that were respected, but there was little that could be done about his changing room habits, because noone was prepared to open a very scandalous can of worms and face the wrath of the Board of Governors.

Other teachers managed to gain some respect, either by being alcoholic

(Adam would marvel sometimes at the History teacher's nocturnal habits and his level of consumption gave him the smell of a distillery in lessons) or by their complete battiness (the bumbling Physics teacher regularly electrocuted himself whenever he demonstrated how a dynamo functioned or would scorch his clothes and hair with his careless messing with a Bunsen burner). It seemed to Adam that even Inspector Clouseau could be a more responsible adult than some of the teachers. In fact the only teacher that Adam respected at all wasn't even a teacher, but the school caretaker, who was well known for having been a football scout for Chelsea in his former years, but was now retired. Many a time he would watch as Adam and his friends played football in the yard and even though he considered Adam to have a 'good engine' and 'two good feet' the school only thought of football as a 'kick about' and that was never going to be enough for Adam to take it any further.

So there they were. A long line of depressed, spotty youth, waiting for their pervy instructor to turn up (if they had been naked in the shower you can be sure that Feelers would have turned up early). The queue was hot and bothered and they were bored. Mick turned to Adam.

'Let off that fire extinguisher for a laugh. I dare you', his Bristol accent twanging.

'You dare me?!' Adam replied with a glint in his eye as he surveyed the gleaming red safety implement, pinned to the wall above a bucket of sand.

'Yeah, I dare you!'

Adam looked again at the extinguisher. 'It must be full of water', he thought naively, 'It's hot today, so what better than to spray a bit of water around. It will raise our spirits and cool us all down', he concluded logically.

Before he had taken a breath and considered another course of action, he had pulled out the silver pin, tossed it away (rather like Clint Eastwood had thrown grenades in the war film Where Eagles Dare) and depressed the lever. There was an instant of inactivity, as the pupils in the form stared in huddled disbelief as Adam held the extinguisher's plastic tube towards them. Suddenly, it burst into life and to his horror, the extinguisher wasn't full of a little harmless H2O, but a whole tank full of CO2 fire fighting foam. As it belched out spurts of suds madly in all directions, Adam tried to put his finger over the end of the tube but it made no difference. 'Sod it!' he thought, 'It's too late! There's nothing I can do!'

So he began spraying everything in sight. Everyone tried to scramble away down the stairwell, and the girls were all screaming and yelping, trying in vain to protect their hair, but it was no use. The extinguisher's spray was merciless. Three pupils cowering next to the door of the 'lab' with their French folders held high above their heads were completely submerged in an indescribable foam, so much so that they soon looked like lumbering creatures in a massive bubble bath. Then Adam switched his attentions and had a direct hit on a form colleague trying to escape out of a small window. Once he'd succeeded in covering as many people as possible (he'd even caught Mick, who was laughing so loudly that he managed to swallow some) Adam then moved on to the walls, ceiling and fixtures and fittings.

It was as if he was in possession of an angry snake that just wouldn't stop spewing, but there was no way that he could let go. Some foolhardy pupils even tried to advance slowly towards him shouting 'Stop it! Stop it!' in a concerted attempt to take the extinguisher off him, but Adam was a school kid possessed and not easily defeated so that just made him squirt them all the more until they couldn't even speak. As they finally gave up and retreated, weighed down by the sludge, Adam grinned, rather like Christopher Lee used to do in an especially Hammer-like horror.

Pupils' beady eyes stared through mountains of foam. Hair styles were all tall and whipped. White dripping beards hung off slushy faces. It wasn't long before the whole scene looked rather like an Alpine region, and you couldn't work out who exactly was who, a Yeti perhaps or maybe even a polar bear. If some bright spark had turned up for the day's French class with Ski's, sledge and a map of the Alps they would not have looked at all out of place. Some people were now so covered that they had decided to stop moving and looked like statues from a museum.

Unfortunately, the extinguisher just didn't know when to stop and soon the whole stairwell and corridor were completely clouded. 'Blimey', Adam thought, 'I didn't expect this!' even Mick was beginning to panic and looked like he wanted to high tail it at any minute. Then, as fortune would have it, to Adam's relief, the extinguisher gradually emptied itself and the tube began to splutter and jerk before spitting out one final large droplet and then all was quiet chaos.

'Oh, blimey!' Adam said cleverly to Mick.

'Let's get out of 'ere!' he shouted back.

They ran as fast as they could, through the fast settling mayhem and eventually managed to scramble outside into the bright sunlight, pursued by an army of ghostlike figures understandably hell bent on revenge.

Problem was, they weren't the only ones. The deputy Head, a particularly fanatical disciplinarian who was nicknamed 'Himmler', was so incensed that he and the Chemistry teacher, another mad eccentric who once allowed Louie to construct a bomb in class, had to enter the language labs, looking ridiculous in second world war gas masks (the foamy residue was supposedly dangerous if inhaled) that Adam knew that the fallout from the 'dare' was clearly going to last for weeks.

Once the area had been checked out, cleaned and made safe (you would have thought the school had been polluted by a ton of Anthrax), the deputy Head took Adam and Louie aside, which was strange because Louie had had nothing to do with it but he was always a main suspect, like Dick Dastardly, because of his background and general rebellious demeanour.

The boys were stood up rigidly against one of the rusting Portakabins as Himmler screamed at them.

'Which one of you did it?! Which one!'

There was a pause as they cowered.

'Well?! Tell me!' the teacher shouted, pacing menacingly backwards and forwards.

Then suddenly, without any warning, Louie began laughing into his school tie, tears nearly coming out of his eyes. Adam couldn't believe it but then he realised why: The gas mask had left a dark round outline on the deputy's face and it made him look like he'd been shovelling coal.

'Stop sniggering!' said the 'Fuhrer' and Louie got a clout round the face for his pains and immediately straightened up. It was only really a hard slap but Adam knew that the deputy Head wanted to have a proper go at them. You could see it in his eyes. Adam was pretty good at recognising aggressive tendencies by this point and as he stared, Adam looked back thinking that he couldn't do anything to them, apart from 'gate' us within the school for two weeks, because they were in an establishment that didn't believe in corporal punishment. Weighty principals were holding teachers back from giving the boys a good thrashing. It was then that Adam realised that in the physical stakes they were untouchable and were far too young to end up in prison.

When Himmler caught Adam grinning at the situation and turned and got hold of him, roughly by the collar, he wasn't best pleased.

'Do you realise what a foolish, childish little prank that was!'

'Sir -'

'Do you?'

'Sir, it wouldn't stop -'

'Shut up! You stupid little cretin!'

'But sir, I thought it was full of water'.

'Water! Why you....'

And with that he cuffed Adam hard around the face. Luckily it wasn't a fist, but it was near enough to be a knock-out blow and his jaw ached after the shock of it.

As Adam rubbed his face, and winced fairly convincingly, he thought an Oscar nomination might be in the offing, as the deputy Head stared into his retinas.

'Do you know how much damage you may have caused?'

'No, sir?'

'£30,000 pounds worth!'

'But - '

'Lucky for you the doors to the language laboratory were locked, otherwise we would be looking at a criminal matter!'

'I'm sorry sir. I didn't think that would happen'.

'Sorry! You'll be sorry alright'.

Once more instead of a short, sharp, shock method employed by his former school, which didn't really deter anybody either, Adam and Louie were forced to stay in uniform in the school grounds for the allotted time, and Adam was repeatedly reminded by the teachers on duty of the huge amount of damage that would have been caused had the lab's door not been locked. He was lucky alright. To pay off £30,000's worth of damages would probably have kept him in 'Bob a Jobs' for the rest of his life.

Amazingly, Mick got away with it completely, but I suppose he had only dared Adam to let the extinguisher off, and Adam certainly didn't have to take him up on it.

As a result of the extinguisher episode, Adam and Mick began to increase their rebellious activities even more and it wasn't long before they were embroiled in another escapade.

Once, when a local school's rugby team and arch rivals played against their school the two of them sneaked into the changing room, where they had left all their belongings and while they were out playing their match Adam and Mick placed toothpaste into the crotches of their underpants and managed to conceal the damp stringy insides of felt tips inside the shower heads. What a result. On their return from their match, two unsuspecting boys were soon covered in ink as they dived in for a post match wash and some others had even got as far as putting on their pants only to find that good old Colgate was in completely the wrong place.

Unfortunately, it wasn't long before the two culprits were caught. They were top suspects, probably because the visiting team were using their very own changing facilities and the smell of foul play led right to their lockers. Short of taking finger prints off the toothpaste tube and insides of the felt tips and deducing who in the year had grubby teeth and no colouring implements, the teachers were very thorough. All it left for Adam and Mick was to make themselves ready to bite the machine gun bullets. And the punishment was endured valiantly, the two being made to visit the school and apologise in person to the disgruntled pupils.

UPTON PARK

It was a sunny Easter bank holiday, so Adam and Steve once more decided to a take an away trip to Upton Park for Chelsea's First Division fixture with West Ham. Rather like the Millwall game the season before, they had another long journey to the East End, however, this time they left themselves ample time to stand about on the terraces inside the ground prior to the kick off. They had also looked at a map prior to leaving home to make quite sure that this time they didn't get lost in unfamiliar territory.

They had also learnt well from previous experiences not to take any identifying scarves or lucky Chelsea jackets. They managed to turn up on the spur, incognito, so to speak. Just like that. When they arrived it was still only 1.45pm, an hour and a quarter before the kick off and there was hardly anyone in the Ground. The empty stadium still felt claustrophobic, with its covered terraces standing very close to the pitch and the metal roofs resembling large baked bean tins. Adam also noticed that there weren't too many escape routes: 'Never mind', he thought. 'There probably won't be any trouble', even though deep down he knew pretty well there was a good chance of a bout or two or three.

Adam and Steve were going to support their team and not even Lucifer himself was going to prevent their admission. They had an added incentive for going to the game as Steve had bumped into both Peter Bonetti and Ray Wilkins, in a sports shop in Oxford Street just a few days before and had obtained their stylish autographs for his scrapbook. With the possession of their signatures how could they not show their appreciation by turning up for the next match? How could they not follow their heroes?

The atmosphere was distinctly unwelcoming. It felt as if they were hemmed in, in a cattle pen, whilst the emerging home populace began to amass and scrutinize them like animals in a zoo. Apart from Adam and Steve, only a few other Chelsea fans were clustered in the away terrace (they were relieved that this time at least they were in the official away end). Even so, they looked about trying to work out the exact identity of the supporters around them, but they were now wearing less and less scarves and badges. Eventually, a forlorn cry of 'Chelsea!' went up and they both breathed a sigh of relief when they realised there were quite a few more comrades entering into their end to join them. The mood became a little more optimistic when the songs, 'Super Blues' and 'There's only one team in London', rang out.

Adam looked at his watch. It was 2.15 pm. Unfortunately, the underlying cold welcome hadn't subsided. More and more West Ham fans were entering the Ground and to the Chelsea fans left, beyond a fence, chants of 'I'm Forever Blowing Bubbles', the West Ham theme tune, rang out. Then a pant wettingly loud, 'United!' 'United!' followed and Adam suddenly gulped with apprehension. He looked at Steve. He was busy gulping too. The Chelsea fans around them were trying to muster themselves into some sort of responsive choir but were heavily outnumbered: 'If you all love Chelsea, clap your hands. If you all love Chelsea, clap your hands. If you all love Chelsea, all love Chelsea, all love Chelsea, clap your hands!' And, 'Lah, lah, lah, la, la, la, lah, la, la, la, lah, Chelsea! (sung to the end tune of 'Hey Jude' by the Beatles).

Despite the West Ham fans ominous vocal presence everyone tried to remain calm: Steve sucked extra hard on a mint. Adam continued to flick through the match day programme which had a distinctive claret and blue cover and 'HAMMER' written prominently on the top. Over a faint photograph of the Upton Park stadium was a sketch of a player celebrating a goal, his fists clenched high above his head. Inside the programme there was nearly as much talk of violence as there was of football. Falling attendances due to widespread trouble was definitely the topic of the day and Chelsea's manager Ken Shellito reckoned that the 32,000 attendance for their recent match against Manchester United at Stamford Bridge was about 20,000 below expected. The manager thought it was down to the effect of an irresponsible minority and yet there now seemed to be a continued indifference by many people. At the Chelsea v Manchester Utd match, there wasn't too much trouble inside the ground, but there was plenty outside, especially after the match. Ficticuffs and train stoppages now were both expected and routine when the hooligans were let loose after matches.

This was certainly food for thought and Adam chewed on the possibility that he himself might be returning home in a wooden box. 'This could be my last match?' he reasoned. To keep his mind off such depressing thoughts, he noted down the important team changes, checked Chelsea's position in the League (mid table) and noticed that West Ham needed the points, because they were in a relegation position. He turned to Steve.

'I reckon it'll be two points to West Ham'.

He didn't know what had come over him. Steve called him a 'prophet of doom' and looked down at his own programme and made a prediction of the score.

'Two-nil to us', Steve said.

'No. Two-one to them', Adam replied.

They then made predictions on the size of the crowd. Always trickier away from home as they weren't as accustomed to what an unfamiliar stadium looked like packed with spectators inside it.

'25,000', said Steve.

'21,000', Adam said confidently, trying to narrow it down.

Eventually, they bought themselves a cup of tea and a Mars bar each and just as Adam was about half way through devouring his chocolate bar, a huge chant of, 'West Ham Agro! West Ham Agro! Hallo! Hallo!' went up, from their left and suddenly Adam found himself right in the middle of a chaotic terrace surge: Coins and plastic cups of tea began to rain down. Phlegm, angst and other missiles followed. Everyone just ran, as boots, fists and heads started to go to work.

It was mayhem. Adam couldn't tell who was who or where anything was because nobody seemed to be wearing any scarves. During the following season, two large groups of Chelsea fans fought each other in the Shed end because they couldn't tell if either faction were Tottenham fans or not. Of course after the initial exchange of swipes and blows, they soon realised. It was due mainly to paranoia and hasty triggers because the Shed enders didn't want their terrace 'taken' by another group of supporters. They wouldn't ever be able to live with the shame. In fact, the Shed was taken on only one major occasion when a large group of West Ham fans infiltrated their way inside so ridiculously early that there was no one there to stop them, apart from some bemused kids and a hot-dog seller. Chelsea fans didn't want a repeat performance of that fiasco so they became as vigilant at Stamford Bridge as the Home Guard in Dad's Army. Of course, it goes without saying that after the mistaken identity with the 'Tottenham' fans, profuse apologies and a lifetimes supply of lager was meted out to all and sundry at the nearest pub after the game.

It was clear that Adam had completely lost touch of Steve and at the instant he tried to survey the terraces for a sight of him, a half-full bottle of liquid hit his left arm soaking it. He stumbled under a terrace barrier and as he did he was helped on his way with a hefty kick in the leg and the swing of a punch that luckily didn't quite connect from a huge West Ham skinhead. As Adam fell further forward down the terrace, and put out his arms to stop his fall, he suddenly detected the unmistakable odour of urine that must have been in the container. He knew that he couldn't hang about and make a formal complaint about his soiled jacket, because the large numbers of West Ham hoodlums who had infiltrated the pen looked very annoyed. So Adam carried on running, clutching both his half-consumed Mars bar and his injured leg across the terraces. Eventually, he shook off his assailants, probably because they were busy doing impressions of Giant Haystacks and Big Daddy, and from being almost completely surrounded he managed to somehow find himself an escape route.

Eventually, he hid up the side of the terraces like a powder monkey, behind a group of burly supporters and contemplated whether they were West Ham or Chelsea fans. Fortunately they were Chelsea supporters, as one of them had a tiny CFC badge on his jacket, not that it made much difference because everyone and anyone was a juicy target, but at least Adam was able to take stock of his predicament for a moment, scoff the rest of his Mars bar, fortunately clutched in his right hand, and look back across the terraces to search for his mate. It was clear that many supporters had dispersed onto the pitch to escape the ensuing violence. Adam later found out that Steve was one of them, thinking that he might be able to get on the BBC's Match of the Day. However, they were soon accompanied back onto the friendly terraces by a diligent Policeman so the match could start.

It wasn't unusual for Steve to get into a spot of bother with the Constabulary without really meaning to. He had once been ejected from Stamford Bridge for saying, 'Fuckin' hell! You're fuckin' useless!' during one particularly disappointing Chelsea performance. At Fulham's, Craven Cottage, the season before, they had arrived a bit late again and as soon as the players came out onto the pitch Steve shouted out, 'Piss off Maybank!' For this small crime, Steve was immediately collared by a Constable and ejected out of the ground. There was even a chant of 'loyal supporter' for him as he was escorted away. But there was some reason to Steve's vocal outburst (Teddy Maybank had played three matches for Chelsea unsuccessfully and then joined their nearest neighbours Fulham without so much as a bye nor leave. This didn't condone Steve's caustic tongue, but when Maybank overdid the celebrations on Fulham's third goal in front of the travelling Chelsea supporters, you could certainly begin to sympathise).

During the second half of the game against West Ham, Adam managed to finally meet up again with Steve, who had been wandering around aimlessly trying to find Adam amongst the walking wounded on the war torn terraces. Steve reckoned that because he had ended up running on the pitch he was definitely going to be watching Match of the Day that evening to see whether he would be featured alongside Jimmy Hill's chin and John Motson's sheepskin coat. Regrettably, he had no such luck. Steve then turned around and looked at Adam.

'What's that funny smell?'

'Dunno....' Adam replied, quickly concealing his damp arm.

The match with the Hammers followed a similar pattern as the previous experience at Millwall. Chelsea were never at the races and willingly handed over the two points to West Ham with a 1-3 loss, both Billy Bonds and Trevor Brooking played blinders for the claret and blues and as Brooking ran rings around the Chelsea defence, everyone in a Royal blue shirt just looked on in admiration.

Still, yet again Adam and Steve had survived a fair sized kicking by the skin of their teeth and made it all the way home, and that was despite there being nasty punch ups all the way back to the Tube and along the District Line. At many stations there were pitched battles and a group of Chelsea fans got jumped as far west as Earls Court thinking they were back in 'their manor' and safe, and Steve, boarding another Tube train home, watched in horror as Blues fans were surrounded on the platform and badly battered. The fighting even took place on a moving train among the frightened shoppers and tourists and kids out for the day.

'Come and 'ave a go at the West Ham a-g-r-o!'

'Come and have a knuckle sandwich?!' No chance, Adam thought.

In such chaos the chances of a fan falling or being pushed on to a railway line was always a distinct possibility and there was a good chance that you would read about it in the obituaries the next day. As Adam stood nervously waiting for his train, right next to the edge of the platform, it certainly brought a lump to his throat. Without doubt, following his team was never a completely hassle free experience.

Although Steve was disappointed that he wasn't featured on Match of the Day, he wasn't too worried, probably because he knew that he had both Peter Bonetti and Ray Wilkins' autographs and that was certainly something to cherish. Luckily, so did Adam, as Steve had cleverly and unselfishly asked 'The Cat' and 'Butch' to sign two pieces of paper in the shop.

That Sunday, instead of checking the tabloids for the West Ham match review, which he knew would make for depressing reading, Adam carefully stuck the piece of paper bearing Peter Bonetti and Ray Wilkins' flashy, indecipherable signatures inside his Chelsea scrapbook.

FAN CLUB

Some days Adam just despaired at the violence. Watching football had become like walking blindfold through a minefield, stumbling around, knowing that at any moment he might be making a connection. There was hope though. It wasn't all doom and gloom. Even followers in The Shed were trying to set a good example:

THANKS SHED

'I'd like to thank the kind person who found my glasses and handed them in after the recent match against Notts Forest. While I was in The Shed celebrating Chelsea's winning goal, someone's scarf accidentally knocked them off, and I thought that would be the last I would ever see of them. Instead, I am able to carry on watching in full vision - just another case proving that we do have true supporters in The Shed'.

This warmed the cockles alright. You could bet there were also litter collections at full time and a whip round for the latest Chelsea fan made redundant. The Shed enders were not unknown to wait behind for the away supporters too after the match, just to pat them on the back:

JOLLY WELL DONE

'My compatriots and I say, 'Jolly well done!' The best team won. And may I add that your victory of 4-0 was absolutely comprehensive and well deserved. A most agreeable and satisfying conclusion to the afternoon's entertainment. Please feel free to join myself and honoured companions, Doug, Gums, and 'Arry for some friendly discourse at your leisure in our local hostelry. Then perhaps you may allow us to escort you to your designated perambulator and wave you on your way to your picturesque abode set in idyllic greenery that is forever Carlisle'.

Like heck. The returned glasses were an impressive revelation, but what if it had been the guy's wallet? Certainly nothing that would have been printable in the Match day programme, that's for sure.

Of course there were many supporters who weren't writing to thank anyone in particular, but just to make a request. The letters page 'In Off The Post', was always good at revealing the desires of the average Chelsea fan:

CHELSEA GIRL WANTED

'I've supported Chelsea since I discarded my nappies and see them as often as my wage packet allows. Would it be possible for a young female Chelsea supporter, age 15-19, to write to me so that we can arrange to meet at matches. I'm nearly 18 and my likes are attending rock concerts, collecting records and Steve Kember'.

You could imagine Chelsea becoming an International Dateline Service: 'My likes are; Astronomy, Astrophysics and Tommy Langley' or 'Mountaineering, Hijacking and Johnny Bumstead'. Adam's likes around this time were probably 'Travel, Masochism and Trevor Aylott'. I wonder what yours might have been? You certainly don't need to be a Chelsea supporter to play the game. But it helps.

Some neutrals even wrote in just to congratulate everybody:

THANKS FANS

'May I say how very grateful we were for the kind reception and guided tour we had recently at Stamford Bridge. I'm certain that with that attitude and the sort of football Chelsea have so often played this season, the club is bound to do well. I must also express what I feel reflects most highly on your supporters. I took my young son to the away game at Cambridge and, as he supports your club, we stood with the Chelsea fans. They were a very happy crowd and their behaviour was very good-natured. One incident stood out for me. When your winning goal was scored, understandably the Chelsea supporters were overjoyed, but my attention was taken by a young man next to me who was not jumping and shouting. He had his arm out, making a protective shield for my son in case as he said, 'He got squashed'. This, I feel, says a great deal for him and the kind of supporters you have. Since then I have had occasion to visit the Chelsea ground, and have had nothing but kindness from everyone. This sort of thing, I think could well be adopted by quite a few other clubs to the advantage of the game'.

Lucky he didn't take his son to Chelsea versus Millwall.

Even fans from other clubs wanted to get in on the act, hinting that they might prefer to follow the Blues:

PRAISE FROM WATFORD

'As a Watford fan, I must say how I wish we had support like yours - it was the best I have seen in eight years of going to Vicarage Road. The large contingent of your supporters never stopped singing from when they arrived at 1.30 until they were on the trains home at 5.30. In the ground their noise was deafening, and you couldn't hear the Watford fans. With support like yours, you belong in the First Division, and I hope you go up for the sake of your tremendous fans. Good luck'.

They are absolutely correct, because Adam was there as well. It was a really good match and Chelsea won 3-2.

Then there were some Chelsea fans who were so ecstatic they just couldn't contain themselves:

LUCKY JACQUELINE

'I've been a Chelsea supporter for many years, and now my six-year-old daughter Jacqueline is a fan, too. I thought I would tell you about what happened on our bus-ride home from that great win at Orient. We were followed upstairs by some jubilant Chelsea fans, one of whom started talking to my daughter. She had plenty to tell him about Chelsea, and it ended with him giving her a £1 note to spend at Christmas. With it she bought her mum a lovely potted plant. If possible, would you print this to thank that happy Chelsea fan? I think Jacqueline must be a lucky mascot, because she has never yet seen Chelsea lose'.

I'll wager that didn't last. For Adam, seeing Chelsea lose was all part and parcel of the joy of supporting them. He just tried to keep it to a minimum. Amazing game though. Quite incredible. Chelsea predictable? You want your brains examined. They won the match 7-3 with a hat trick from none other than the unforgettable Lee Frost. Adam reckoned even 'Ossie' was looking over his shoulder, and quaking in his boots.

Then again supporting Chelsea from your hospital bed wasn't totally out of the question:

TONIC VICTORY

'A month ago I had an operation in hospital, and felt down in the dumps on that Saturday, especially when I heard that we had gone a goal down at Cardiff. What a marvellous tonic it was when we came back to win in the second half. Well done, lads!'

Some didn't even need to be in hospital. They would just follow Chelsea right there in their front room:

HARRY DOES IT AGAIN

'The other Saturday my Mum and Dad were out and my Mum's friend was looking after us. In the middle of 'Match of the Day' she let out a roar. I wondered what was wrong. She told us it was cramp, and she was really in pain and almost crying. Just then I remembered seeing Harry Medhurst treating some of the players for cramp, so I tried his treatment and it worked. She was very relieved indeed. Thanks a million, Harry'.

So if it wasn't potted plants, spectacles, Steve Kember, Cambridge or Vicarage Road, it could be a Hernia operation or just a little nip and tuck here and there and you would soon be writing in to the Chelsea family.

SOMETHING FOR THE WEEKEND

Mick's days at the school were numbered. After the toothpaste debacle he never really recovered. In fact, he found it hard getting over Elvis' demise and one night he just disappeared with a friend from the year above. Instead of going under the floor, like Adam, Louie and Robbie, he had been successful and made it out of the main entrance, never to return.

Mick's place was quickly filled by another state school pupil from Basingstoke who also had a large file. He had been caught with his mate stealing fixtures and fittings from a new housing estate in the town and was punished with the option of Borstal or the 'Friends' school. Later on everyone would joke with him that he had made the wrong choice, because Borstal would probably have been more preferable. His friend, Dave, who managed to escape by leaving the country, even outwitted the best detectives that Interpol could muster. So, the 'new boy' had a little bit of previous as a youthful kleptomaniac, so to speak.

One afternoon, as they idled away the lunch hour in their cramped changing rooms, someone mentioned that they thought the recently arrived socket burglar looked similar to 'Plug' of the Bash Street Kid's in the Beano, and as they were all in agreement, Plug's apt name just stuck.

It was soon apparent that Plug would carry on where Mick left off as he was just as interested in making a nuisance of himself. He had the air of a rebellious spirit and possessed a wicked sense of humour, but he was also well respected in the cranium department, being able to hold his own in more than one subject, despite needing to do the least possible amount of work to keep up. His French was more than accomplished too and he was brilliant at fixing anything electrical. What's more he loved punk. His favourite band was Sham 69. Adam was more than impressed to find out that Plug had already seen them live and his favourite article of clothing were his 'industrial slippers', an awesome looking pair of steel toe capped boots. Although he wasn't at all keen on sport, Plug admitted to a liking for Millwall Football Club which made Adam shudder a little at his fairly recent memories of Cold Blow Lane.

Plug also had a funny way of jumping out on people dressed in his bulky shoes, rather like Kato, Clouseau's irrepressible servant. One afternoon,

Adam was in a hurry to make a lesson, but desperately needed to go to the toilet and as he jumped down the concrete stairs on his way to the mediaeval looking latrines, Plug leapt out from nowhere and caught Adam full square in the groin with his steel toed building site boots. Up until this point, Adam had not really had a chance to get to know Plug that well, but this acted as an initiation of sorts.

'Why did you jump onto my boot?' Plug said with a sly grin.

'Jump?!......' Adam choked, gasping for air.

'Yeah, you jumped!'

'Well, what about my bollocks?!' was Adam's high pitched reply, as he clasped his crushed nuts in the corner.

Once Adam had recovered, incredibly they soon became close friends, although Adam was always a bit careful when Plug wore his slippers. It wasn't long before they were exchanging Punk records or singing along to Sham in their common room, especially their current single 'If the Kids are United' and the classic 'Angels with Dirty faces' which Adam had also seen on Top of the Pops. Jimmy Pursey, the lead singer, had introduced the appearance to his mum saying, 'Who's on Top of the Pops then?!' with a mischievous sneer, instead of the normal intro on the single which had him crying 'Who's got a dirty face then?' over an unforgiving guitar intro.

Sham 69 had, by now, a large Skinhead following throughout the UK and though they had trouble with the Fascist element who regularly tried to destroy their gigs, Adam and Plug were more keen on the fashion than the extreme politics. Despite this, they all wore yellow, Rock against Racism, 'Pogo on a Nazi' badges, because they thought that it would annoy their Headmaster and set them apart and with Plug's influence they decided that they would become a Skinhead gang as it was the most rebellious thing that they could do with their hair and they thought that it would impress the girls. Spiking hair up hadn't really outraged anybody enough so they thought a really close cropped number 'one', or 'two' would do the business. Surely there was no way that they would be told off just for getting a short haircut, or so they thought.

The difference was that they wouldn't be going to the local hairdressers to get their hair done because they knew that they wouldn't have a clue how to cut it. Most people still had extremely long hair and in the west country they were just a little behind the times. Dedicated followers of fashion? Maybe, but about a hundred years later. They would probably all leave the barber's looking more like Franciscan monks than lethal skins, so they all agreed that they would cut each other's hair themselves with a large pair of scissors the next weekend in the common room.

At the weekend they did just that. Plug who had already had a crop before, went first, and Donna, a lively Welsh girl with a wicked laugh, was roped in eventually to do the shearing. She was already well versed in helping out the fashion conscious pupils and Adam had already let her pierce his left ear with a long needle and some ice a few months before, so she could be trusted to deliver the required follicle to the nearest millimetre.

When Donna had completed Plug's skinhead, which took some time getting it just right, everyone gawped at his new image, trying really hard to recognise him from his previous state. He looked like trouble alright. His dark hair and underfed appearance transformed him and when he hobbled around in his industrial footwear he almost became a cartoon character.

Adam was next, and again Donna did the cutting and as she busied herself with the scissors he almost panicked watching locks of hair hit the floor. When it was completed, Donna stood back and surveyed her work.

'That's a good one that is'.

Everyone started sniggering, as Adam now looked like Desperate Dan and it was a strange feeling having his face completely exposed to the world. He spent the next half an hour running his fingers through his crop and tried to come to terms with the new person he saw in his reflection.

Next up was Robbie and he came out terrifically, looking almost like a Marine or GI. In fact the drastic haircut probably suited him best of all. After the three were sheared, Donna left them to show their new look around the school. The effect was immediate. Everyone was scared of them. Some didn't even recognise them as fellow school pupils. Their new harsh demeanours caused such a commotion that even the surly youths from the local village became fascinated and were always threatening to come up to the school to 'sort out those punks and skinheads'. Whenever, they attempted it, usually near to the weekend and well under the influence, even once trying to ambush Adam and Plug, with the aid of a childish flick knife, fire was usually met with fire from the rest of the school.

During the cutting ritual, Louie had been away and when he returned to find them in their new guise he was more than impressed and instantly asked Robbie to cut his hair for him as Donna wasn't about. He obliged and as they all held their breath, Robbie took the scissors to Louie's bonce. He cut away with such verve, that they feared for Louie's safety, but he just kept laughing.

'How's it lookin'?' he'd say over and over as they ribbed him.

'Oh, it's looking great Louie. Just great!'

'Good!'

As Robbie clipped away amateurishly with a silly smirk, clumps of Louie's hair just disappeared. The end result was in sight and it wasn't pretty. He looked like a badly plucked chicken with different chopped lengths of hair and bald patches all over his crown and although it said 'Skinhead' in large letters, it was definitely of the scary variety. Louie didn't think so though. He loved his unique haircut so much he now wanted different clothing to match it. To his particular specifications. And his friends were quite capable of obliging. It gave them a great opportunity to add the finishing touches to his new look. Adam made him a homemade punk T-shirt: taking one of Louie's white shirts and writing in lurid felt tip, things like 'Anarchy' and 'X-Ray Spex' and 'Pretty Vacant' across it. With a little bit of mud and dirt rubbed into it, some scissor cuts like razor slashes and some safety pins fixed around the neck, and not forgetting 'gobbing' over it, for that straight off the hanger authenticity.

The next thing was for Louie to be shown off to the world. He did just that at the next school assembly and after the initial shock of Adam, Plug and Robbie strolling in with their finely trimmed barnets, the main event, Louie, breezed in fashionably late and as he sauntered across to his place, in his razored hair and favourite Do It Yourself T-shirt, you could hear a pin drop. After a gasp from the teachers and pupils and some nervous laughter, the irate Headmaster had the young punk ushered physically to one side and as the rest of the school hung their mouths in disbelief, and gabbled over the morning Hymn, which they would always change the lyrics to anyway, Louie almost took a bow and immediately went on his way for yet another reprimand and punishment for his pains from the Head. Eventually, the other three followed with a warning that they had to grow their hair, but the damage was done. They had certainly made an impression and Louie's tardy entrance became legendary. Not only that, but their hair would probably need at least two months growth to look anything like normal. Louie's probably three. And as far as Louie's offending T-shirt was concerned, it was never seen again. One of the teacher's took it home to incinerate it after school.

While Louie did another dose of stir, everyone found it hard to keep in touch with him, solitary confinement now becoming the order of the day thanks to the more oppressive regime. On one rare occasion, Adam managed to chat with him in their grim toilets, over a poorly rolled cigarette, at the end of another taxing day at the establishment. Louie turned to him, his head trimmed so ragged you could still see bits of his scalp sticking through. He wasn't a pretty sight. Skinhead? Thanks to Robbie's hairdressing skills he looked like he had done a month in Chemo. He had this way of wiping around his nostrils with the back of his thumb when he was thinking and when he spoke, although he looked expressionless, there was emotion in his voice.

'I can't take no more of this. It's a joke. They've 'ad it in for me from the very first day. All them teachers. They've wanted me out....'

He paused for a moment.

'Anyway, if I stay 'ere, I'll only become a bully an' that....and I don't want that. No, I'm gonna leave. I don't wanna be like all the others. Sad fuckers!'

He paused as he looked up and thought for a moment.

'Only thing is, I can't go home. My mum - she just bosses me about....'

'What about your dad?' Adam replied carefully.

'What about my dad?!' Louie remained stone faced which was unusual for him as he used to have a mischievous grin.

'Well, can't you talk to him?'

Louie shook his head.

'I haven't seen 'im for years and even if I did he'd just batter me about and start shoutin' at me. He's useless.....anyway, what do I care about 'im? I'm better off on my own. I don't need nothin'. Don't need exams. Nothin'....I'll get by. You'll see. At least I can live with myself'.

'And your Punk T-shirts...' Adam said flippantly, and Louie managed a smile in response.

And that was it. There was another long pause and Adam sat there, uncomfortably, trying desperately to think of something to say to make him feel better but he just couldn't. It was impossible. Eventually, he attempted to mention how unfair he thought everything was but then he felt that he might not express it the right way and rather than make a complete idiot of himself, remained tight lipped. But it was crystal clear. The Cooler King had cracked. And sure enough, Louie's prophecy came true and he ended up being asked to leave the very next day, but not before he had set fire to the school's newspaper room after reading an incendiary article about Margaret Thatcher, who he detested.

When he left the school, with the aid of a Panda car, after saying his goodbyes to Adam, Robbie and Plug, Adam knew that he would never forget Louie's spectacular appearance in the morning assembly and in particular his daring exploits under the common room floor.

BAKED BEANS

The school dinner queue was another minefield of trouble. Pushing in was the order of the day and a moment never passed without some smart Alec trying to get to their dinner first. Not that getting to the food before anyone else was a good idea. The secondary school grub was somewhat better than at Adam's previous school, but that meant that it was only just about edible. Baked beans were heavily on the menu as if they were some sort of wonder drug and even though there were various different meat dishes served up, they had a remarkable way of all tasting the same. This was due to everything being overcooked in order to stave off food poisoning, so Adam usually found himself chewing on a charred lump of chicken or a blackened fish finger.

Lack of vitamin C was another problem, as there never seemed to be any fresh fruit around and even if there was, they weren't very accustomed to eating it. They were given prunes and plums regularly in puddings but Adam couldn't eat them because they made him spend far too much time on the toilet and the other various pies like rhubarb and gooseberry were usually vile. So urgent was the need for the Galloping Gourmet, even in his dressing gown, to visit the school that Adam regularly concerned himself with the prospect of catching rickets or scurvy or some other unfortunate disease.

The scarcity of tasty vegetables was another depressing footnote on the school menu. Carrots were soggy, peas were mushy, tomatoes were tinned, potatoes were smashed, runner beans were stringy, and the swedes were grim. Adam longed for something simple that not even the chef could destroy, like a basic salad or a raw carrot for example, especially when he heard that they could help you see in the dark which meant that getting to the girls dormitories late at night could be made a great deal easier.

Variety of flavour was another area which the school chef needed to buck up on and get with the times. 'Hot' meant the inside of your mouth would be burnt horribly for about a month, as if you had drunk a large glass of sulphuric acid. So keeping away from chillies and curries was essential, which was a shame because there were only two foods that Adam didn't really like eating, and they were Christmas cake and Christmas pudding, because he had gorged on them more than once as a child and been very ill. Adam had also over eaten strawberries, so he was in two minds about them as well. But everything else he ate with the ravenous intensity of a slow moving dustbin so having to avoid certain foods because the chef was a little over zealous with his pots of spices caused great anxiety and nutritional deficiency.

No wonder the school sports teams rarely triumphed, when they had to endure a long harsh winter surviving on scotch eggs and cheese on toast. Mind you the opposition teams looked as though they had pretty meagre supplies as well.

So it was with this sense of culinary despair that Adam queued up one afternoon for school dinner. There was a lot of pushing and shoving and jockeying for position. Usually the older pupils would be allowed in at the front of the queue, due to the school hierarchy and as he stood near the door to the dining hall another pupil in his form pushed right in front of him when he wasn't looking:

'Oi! I was here first!'

'No, you weren't'.

'Yes, I was!'

'No, you weren't!'

'Look. Get out of it!'

'No, I won't!'

'You pushed in!'

'No, I didn't!'

'Yes, you bloody well did!'

'Did not!'

'Did!'

'I did not!'

'Yes, you did you wanker!'

'Wanker yourself!'

With that shot across each other's bow the argument cooled for a brief moment as the dinner bell was rung and the queue shuffled forward inexorably towards food. As they obtained their first and second courses from the formidable looking canteen ladies, so formidable in fact that some of them were known to have beards and moustaches, and murmured their disbelief at the chef's incompetence, they wandered aimlessly around the dining hall with their plastic dinner trays looking for a suitable feeding post.

Adam had decided that he wanted revenge on the lowlife who had quite clearly pushed in the queue. His honour was at stake. The gauntlet had been thrown down. Was he going to pick it up? Yes, he was.

He waited patiently for the queue jumper to park himself down on a table by a window and then he plonked his tray down right next to him, which came as a shock, because Adam usually tried to eat with Robbie and Plug and failing that he would try and sit with some of the girls in his year, whose titbits of conversation were always enlightening.

There he sat, trying to ingest soggy cauliflower cheese while making absolutely no conversation with his nemesis in the next seat who tried in vain to ignore his presence. As Adam eventually laid into his baked beans and slurped his glass of water, his worst enemy trumped up:

'Showed you!'

Adam paused for a second:

'Showed me?!'

He thought to himself: 'Showed me what?' He pondered again for a moment, just as his enemy announced.

'Showed you how much someone can be a dickhead!'

Before anyone could shout, 'Fight!', 'Fight!', 'Fight!' Adam launched himself at him with all guns blazing. He managed to collar him just as he was swallowing a tired morsel of food and as Adam's hands tightened around his neck his expression went green. He tried to fight back wildly, by flapping his arms and legs about which only resulted in him knocking his food tray up in the air and spreading his stodgy rice pudding and jam all over the floor. By this point, so intense were they that they had completely failed to notice that the dining hall had become full and they found themselves scrapping for dear life in front of the whole school. Initially, the teachers on duty could do little about their falling out, such was the fury of their intension.

As they struggled, and Adam's enemy tried to fend him off with a dessert spoon, they then tried to exchange blows, which was reminiscent of a very poor saloon fight from the TV series the High Chaparral. Neither fighter seemed to connect properly and the sounds of grunts and groans were so laughably out of time that they soon went back to grappling which they were much more convincing at and it wasn't long before they were trying to grab each other in a life threatening headlock. They continued their manic Sumo wrestling and crashed about, knocking over chairs and bumping into the tables. Just at that moment when the teachers were about to intervene, they parted from each other for a second and at that very instant Adam moved swiftly, picking up his food tray and hurling it at the cowering pond-life with all his might. Unfortunately, he ducked just at the right moment and the tray overflowing with baked beans, carried on and hit a large, framed portrait painting of a former Headmaster behind him on the wall.

Before Adam could move in again on his enemy, a teacher had managed to halt his progress and other pupils were moving in quickly to stop the commotion.

'Right! Outside the Headmaster's office! Immediately! Both of you!'

After waiting for the food to settle, they walked on their way along the gang plank in the direction of the Heads HQ. They were still cursing each other under their breath, and as they plodded, they turned back to see that up on the wall, the proud upstanding Headmaster who had peered down at them so valiantly for many a year was now covered in baked beans, so much so that you could hardly make out his pompous, grinning face. The Headmaster turned to Adam in his office.

'Fighting in the dining hall! This will not be tolerated. Two week's gating and you will both have to clean up the mess in your free time. That includes the portrait of the honourable H. W. Graves'.

'That's the old Headmaster', Adam reasoned, who he hit with a bulls-eye right between the ears with his sloppy dinner. He didn't know if H. W. was the sort who had always eaten his five a day? But one thing was for sure, he certainly received a portion of school baked beans that day.

CIDER WITH ROSIES

It was a balmy summer's evening. The covert plan was set. At dead of night, Adam was to meet up with Plug and Robbie at the prefixed location, by the 'greenhouse wall' and then they would venture stealthily up to the girls dormitories to meet up with whoever they could persuade to share their adventures with. Girls that were a 'good laugh' were more than welcomed, as most definitely were the girls with attractive appearances. Most importantly, they needed to be interested in the three lads fun and games: to help drink the large, secret supply of cider: to smoke 'Embassy Number Ten' cigarettes until dawn or the onset of 'greenness' - whatever came first: to tell jokes and shaggy-dog stories incessantly and generally lark about (in these particular areas Plug usually reigned supreme): and if the boys luck was in, to dabble about in some even more enjoyable pursuits.

Fortunately, none of them was in a serious relationship at this point so they had much more chance of girls coming out to play, knowing that they wouldn't face the inevitable wrath of their 'other half's' in the queue at breakfast the next morning, and there is nothing as intoxicating as an evening without recriminations. That is, so long as they didn't get caught.

On one previous mission, where they were all meant to meet up as planned at dead of night, Adam foolishly placed his foot down on the handle on the toilet cistern as he did another impression of The Great Escape, clambering indelicately out of the ground floor changing room window. The flushing noise was so loud that a patrolling teacher soon came to investigate. As the 'screw' came sniffing about armed with a torch, Adam panicked and hid hurriedly under a car parked nearby. Unfortunately, the model of vehicle was of the small Italian variety and not only could he not really hide under it - his head was exposed and his Doctor Marten boots stuck out underneath the other side like a very sore thumb, so it wasn't long before he was in front of the Headmaster again and a 'gating' and a dose of solitary confinement, 'cooler' style, was on the cards.

As a result, Adam was going to be extra catlike this particular night. His eyes were certainly wide awake. If he had possessed a Ninja outfit he probably would have worn it. Despite the lack of appropriate kit, Adam was keenness personified - Robbie had come up with the brilliant idea of taking 'Go' energy tablets to keep them awake. Certainly, there was no shame as bad as sleeping right through till the morning - waking up to find out that you had missed an unforgettable night's entertainment with the girls, the rumours of which would circulate for weeks.

So, there they were, in the changing rooms. Alone. The three of them swallowed their heart racing energy tablets simultaneously and synchronised watches. Tonight was going to be the night. Plug reckoned it would be easy to make more of an encampment in their favourite spot up the Combe with bundles of hay from one of the local farmer's fields. Perhaps they might also consider having a small fire under the stars while they consumed their Scrumpy and frolicked with the girls? Adam and Robbie reckoned it sounded like a night to remember.

Soon Adam was in his bed, cloaked in darkness and looking forward eagerly to the night's revels ahead. The boys dormitory was uncharacteristically quiet but for the odd snore, cough or blowing off from one of its inhabitants. Under his blanket, he listened keenly with an ear plug to his radio. That night on John Peel's Radio One show, he played some of his personal favourite tracks - the Sex Pistols 'Pretty Vacant', The Fall's 'Bingo Master's Breakout' and when he span 'Teenage Kicks' by the Undertones, Adam's face lit up, especially when Fergal Sharkey sang about getting teenage kicks right through the night. Adam was definitely intending to.

The other song that certainly kept him awake was Tom Robinson's '2, 4, 6, 8, Motorway', with its irresistible riffing and Adam drummed out the beat against his mattress. If anybody nearby was to wake up at that moment he knew that he'd certainly be under suspicion for playing with himself, but he wasn't bothered and carried on.

It seemed like forever before the time to escape came about and the batteries in Adam's radio had long since passed out. Everyone else was in the land of nod. 'Let's hope Plug and Robbie don't have any hitches getting out of their dormitory', he thought. Every stage had been diligently calculated. Nothing could go wrong. They had solved the problem of getting into more suitable clothes for the adventure in cunning fashion: you certainly didn't want to meet up at the rendezvous dressed in your Rupert the bear pyjamas or cotton gown and nightcap, so casual clothes or 'civvies' were sneaked up to the dormitory before 'lights-out' and hidden under the bed. On the liquid front, the cider had been pre-stored in its gallon container inside an old oak tree up the Combe, so everything was ready.

Adam looked at the clock in the corridor. It was proudly declaring, one o'clock. Time for action. He hopped out of bed and dressed swiftly. The 'Go' tablets had kept good old shut-eye at bay and was still distributing a healthy slice of energy throughout his body. He felt in tip top condition and as he slowly pulled up the sash window, trying to avoid creaks, one or two of the sleepers he would unashamedly leave behind him groaned in their slumbers.

Because the evening had been hot, the window was already ajar and Adam slipped out into the night. The moon was present brightly in the sky and knowing that he was now exposed, he slid down the tiled roof above the changing rooms - halting for a split second as he thought he saw something move away to his right; 'Maybe that's Plug and Robbie?', he thought. Adam stayed frozen, his legs outstretched. It wasn't Plug or Robbie. It was a lean fox, scampering about. Adam half expected it to come up and ask him if it could join them up the Combe, but at the moment of its approach Adam dropped down to the ground, bending his knees to cushion the fall, narrowly avoiding a spiked metal railing which could have ruined his evening.

So far, so good. No teachers in sight and nothing had been disturbed. Adam then began to run towards the rendezvous point, which was just around the corner and slightly up a hill. As he approached, he could just make out two figures by their designated wall and as he closed he began to laugh with the realisation that part one of the evening had been accomplished successfully:

'How'd it go?' Adam tried to whisper.

'Okay....' said Plug. 'Except Robbie slipped and nearly put his boot through a window! What about you?'

'Yeah, fine. No one knows a thing'.

'Good', said Plug. 'Come on. Let's go!'

With that the three of them began running up the lane towards the girls dormitories and up ahead the building glowed faintly like some Pandora's box.

They halted suddenly, as they ventured near the Headmaster's cottage. One by one they crept past the creepy house trying not to laugh and began speeding up again once they had successfully negotiated themselves past the hated Goblin's hut. Once they were far enough away, and under the sanctuary of a tree, Plug turned to them again, short of breath.

'After I leave, I'm gonna send that bastard some jam sandwiches in the post, all wrapped up in a box, and he won't know who they're from'.

'Serious?' Adam said.

'No, tell you what....how about sending him a turd in a box! I'll bet he'd never forget that!'

Adam and Robbie cracked up laughing at the thought, especially as Plug would no doubt time the package around the Headmaster's birthday, and the rotting sarnies or old schoolboy's dump would be an unfortunate and unexplainable addition to his birthday celebrations.

But more pressing concerns were up ahead. Girls. The more the merrier they thought, but they knew they couldn't be too greedy - even they had to be careful. They sat down for a few minutes under the cover of the tree and planned their next move. Plug lit up one of his favoured French cigarettes, which the others reckoned he only smoked because it meant that no one would scrounge off him as they had a funny taste, and they took turns in puffing as frequently as possible: Robbie knocked his knees together and blew large smoke rings into the atmosphere: Adam tried to keep from coughing uncontrollably: Plug practiced looking suave. But really they were just three nervous, comical commandos.

'Who d'you reckon will come out?' Plug started.

'Donna, Mandy - Rachel for sure', said Robbie.

'You reckon?' Adam posed.

'Yeah, and maybe Abby'.

'Abby! Christ, I hope so. She's gorgeous!' Plug gleamed.

'Maybe Sally as well....'

'Sally?' Adam looked at Robbie. He glanced back. That was a chink in his armour alright - his on - off, now ex-girlfriend from the Film Society who had fairly recently dumped him. He suddenly had a feeling that Robbie had his eyes on her. 'Maybe she fancies him now?' he thought.

'Yeah, she's a good laugh'.

'No, she won't come out', Adam parried.

'Wanna bet!' Robbie stretched out his hand toward him.

'We'll see....' Adam stuttered, refusing the offer.

There was an awkward pause.

'Who's going up to the girls dormitory then?' Plug cut in sensing something.

'I'll go', Robbie said, before he could stop himself. It was strange because they usually tossed a coin to make such decisions, even though Plug joked sarcastically that their motto was, 'all for one and every man for himself'.

'Fine', said Plug, 'but you've gotta make sure no one grasses'.

'Don't worry. I'll tell Donna. She'll keep them quiet', Robbie reassured.

'Some of those girls have got right big gobs'.

'Like who?'

'Like 'Randy' Mandy and Donna 'Kebab!''

'Look. I'm telling you, I'll sort it....'

Plug looked over to Adam. Eventually, he nodded back.

'Right, let's get goin'!'

Plug then flicked the cigarette butt away and they were off again, moving quickly towards the girls dormitory, like chimpanzees in boots. When they drew near, a bright light above the large front door illuminated them in a flash:

'Quick! Round the side!'

They sped around the side of the building and dived into a wooded area nearby. As they raised themselves up, they paused for a moment to release a piece of foliage from Robbie's shirt:

'How come there's that bloody light!' Robbie croaked.

'Look, they keep it on all night....'

'So what are we gonna do?' Adam challenged.

'Robbie's gonna go up and rap on the toilet window. Donna will be there'.

'She better!'

'Just keep in the shadows'.

'Yeah, okay'.

And with that Robbie was off to the window. Adam and Plug crouched down again and spied on Robbie's foolhardy advance through what seemed like a large shrubbery.

'What the Hell's Robbie doing now?!'

Robbie had suddenly lost his marbles for a second and had sprinted across and was now waving his arms manically and jumping up and down right in front of the light.

'Fuckin' hell, what an idiot!' Plug frowned.

Then just as soon as he'd started, Robbie was round by the toilet window and tapping on the pane with a combined look of fear and hysterics. Suddenly another light came on in the front of the house and Robbie ducked down. Adam and Plug followed suit, almost head-butting each other in the process and there they remained, their faces down in the earth praying that Robbie's recklessness hadn't given the game away.

Still they paused, so much so that Adam and Plug were hardly breathing. However, the adrenalin of the moment kept their hearts pounding and as they lay still, that was all they could hear, apart from the 'tawit-tawoo' of an owl watching their progress from a branch above. But they were alright. The light turned itself off again and Robbie turned round and did the thumbs up. They breathed a great sigh of relief as if they had just puffed on the world's biggest cigar, and they were up again following Robbie's every impulsive move.

Then a faint light from inside the toilet window came on and the window slowly but surely opened. They held their breath again. Who could it be? The Headmistress? (They certainly didn't fancy her - being a right old dragon). Incredibly, it was Donna, and Adam and Plug looked at each other with a sense of relief and apprehension.

'If Donna gets over excited we're finished!' Plug concluded.

'Yeah, I know'.

Robbie was nattering away almost like a Commander in the Field. Donna was a keen trooper alright and as she took in the information the grin on her face grew to the size of a pumpkin. Then Donna was off and Robbie hurtled back to tell the others his news, which was encouraging.

'Donna reckons Mandy's up for it!'

'Surprise, surprise....' Plug intoned.

'And she's gonna get Kate, Sally and Rachel!'

'What about Abby?'

'No, she don't feel very well'.

'Oh, well....Did you tell Donna to keep her mouth shut?'

'Yeah, she's got it all sorted'.

'Brilliant!'

They looked excitedly at each other and as they clenched their fists in triumph, the first girl was climbing daintily out of the toilet window.

This time the three of them went to help, as Mandy clambered out in a loose fitting top, laughing all the while. Plug gestured to her to be quiet and she immediately did a loud Shush, as if she had already started on the Scrumpy herself (Mandy was certainly a loose cannon that was primed to go off at any minute. But one thing was for sure - no one was ever bored when she was around). Next out was Kate, who Adam had had his first few embarrassing snogs with in the second year and she grinned as she descended to earth aided by Robbie, who then quickly helped a nervous Rachel to her feet who was a pretty blonde girl, and like Mandy, in the year below. The last two were Donna, who's strong Welsh accent you could still make out even in a whisper and finally, Sally, who suddenly found herself helped by both Adam and Robbie as she climbed out.

All present and correct. The girls then took a few seconds to adjust their casual clothes and giggle amongst themselves when they looked at the boys. Adam, Plug and Robbie surveyed each other scornfully and concluded that their appearance was both haphazard and dirty from all the running and jumping about:

'You look right states!' Donna cackled.

'No we don't - '

'You do!'

'Look, shut up! We'll get sussed!' Plug grumbled back.

'Keep your hair on', said Mandy.

'Look, put a cork in it! Both of you!'

There was a pause for a couple of seconds, then Mandy burst out in hysterics once more. Adam looked at Plug who just crossed his arms and looked annoyed, while Robbie had his eyes fixed busily on Sally who reciprocated in kind.

'What's the plan then?' said Kate.

'We're going to the same place. We've got the cider'. Adam instructed.

'Great!' said Rachel, chirpily.

'Well? What are we waiting for?' Plug announced.

'Yeah, let's go!' declared Mandy and off she sped like the 'Roadrunner' with the rest of them trying to catch her tail.

As they ran, Plug broke out the all important regulation tobacco to all concerned, whilst carefully covering up his lighter so they couldn't be seen from a distance as they paused briefly to light up, and once they resumed their running, it wasn't long before they neared their destination. The moon reflected just enough light for them to see by, and as they smoked like manic steam trains and strided over a decrepit stile, dodging the odd crusty cowpat or two, their old oak tree came reassuringly into view. They had finally reached the large open field and the smell of hay, pasture and dried out mud battled with their nostrils.

'See those bails?' Plug began.

They all nodded except for Donna.

'Donna?'

'What bails!?' She teased.

'DONNA!!'

'What?...'

'You know what!'

'What?!'

'Let's get that hay and build a camp by the tree!'

'Oh, alright....' Donna sighed as she winked at Mandy.

They ran off, in all directions gathering armfuls of hay and as they did so Robbie ran straight to the tree and after a struggle, pulled out the gallon container with the cider in. He yelled and swung the scrumpy triumphantly around his head as the others continued their hunter gathering and Adam could tell that Sally was well impressed with Robbie. 'Oh, it doesn't matter, it's probably nothing', he thought, and immediately caught Mandy's eye who was watching him trying not to swallow a large clump of hay.

'You know what?'

'What?'

'Donna fancies you.'

'You what?!' Adam choked.

'You 'eard....'

'No, I didn't'.

'Yes you did', she smiled.

'No, I didn't - '

'Oh, leave it out'.

'Leave what out?'

'Look, shut it you!'

'What?'

'You know what!'

'Why?'

'You know why!'

'What?'

'Stop it!'

'Wha -'

'You know what!'

'Why? -'

'Aaaaaargh!!'

With that Mandy swung herself round and tried to land one on him. Luckily, Adam managed to duck just in the nick of time, otherwise it was a certain journey to casualty.

'Heh, let's 'ave some cider!' she barked.

'Good idea', Adam said relieved.

Mandy rushed over to Robbie and managed to grab the cider from him while he was still in the process of drinking it and some of it inevitably splashed all over his face:

'Fuckin' hell, Mandy!'

She ran off giggling and gurgling erratically, and after a few laps of the field, stopped right next to Adam and took another huge gulp of the medium-sweet contents (dry cider, as they had already found out, was vile and tasted like petrol, while sweet cider was a disgusting syrup, so medium-sweet it had to be).

Adam laughed with her and tried to help her towards the area where the others were busy completing the camp. Plug and some of the others were now busy trying to make a little fire in the middle of the circle of hay and try as they might their energetic attempts at lighting it were coming to nothing. It was clear they needed more advanced fire making skills (Adam was an ace with the kindling, learnt from his dad's many bonfire's and on numerous camping holidays away from home) and before you could say, 'Fawkes', a fine heartening glow was building from the centre of their camp.

They all lay down inside the haphazard perimeter of hay. There was a lot of chatter and laughter and then some more laughter and then some more chatter. The local rocket fuel was passed around excitedly to the accompanying sounds of loud swigs and the wiping of mouths on the back of hands, and while Adam waited for the cider to stutter it's way around again, he suddenly became aware of the seating arrangement: Donna was lying right next to his left with a silly grin on her face: Mandy was for some reason lying very provocatively next to his right and he began to feel as if he had been accosted by two amorous bodyguards. To his dismay, Robbie, who was chewing a long stalk of hay, was further round to the right, with Sally lying very close to him, in fact Adam reckoned at that moment way too close, because he now had his arm around her. On the other side of their artificial camp site, Plug was trying to come to terms with the considerable advances of Kate while Rachel sat and tried to make conversation with everybody.

They started on the jokes, which Plug could draw quicker than the Sundance Kid however inappropriate and soon they were all in hysterics.

'What part of Popeye never rusts?' He said.

'Dunno....' said Robbie, about to laugh anyway.

'The part he puts in Olive Oyl!'

And Robbie was howling louder than anybody.

'D'you know what happened when the last Pope died?'

'No....' said Robbie, snot coming out of his nose.

'Another one just poped up!'

Then Plug would try another.

'An old man went to the doctor; "Doctor, you've gotta help me. Every morning at six o'clock I have to pass water and move my bowels'. "So what's wrong with that?" says the doctor. "You don't understand! I don't get up until nine o'clock!"

And another,

'Did you hear about the man who had five pricks?'

All the girls' eyebrows rose in synch.

'No....' said Donna, hastily.

'His pants fit him like a glove!'

And there was pandemonium.

And another,

'Did you hear what happened to the man who had sex with his canary?'

'Canary? No....' said Rachel, trying desperately to suppress her giggles.

'He got twerpies, and the worst thing is that it's untweetable!'

And for the next half an hour, Robbie would be shaking his head and slapping his thigh shouting, 'Twerpies! Untweetable!'

When the comedy slackened, mainly because their jaws were aching from the laughter, a shaggy-dog story soon pepped them up again and they were off once more. The cigarettes and cider were beginning to do their work and everyone, even Plug was beginning to slur like one of the Wurzels. Mandy, who always enjoyed wearing a ton of eye-liner and lipstick on such occasions looked as if she had been smudged. Donna continued to rib everybody constantly and once they had begun on the ghost stories and the fire had subsided into embers, they all seemed to be huddling even closer together.

Adam looked up to the stars, and could just make out Orion's Belt through the gnarled branches of their favourite old tree and began to count his blessings. They had managed to escape away from the school for however short a time, without getting caught and were having a night that they would probably never ever forget. 'If only life could be like this more often', Adam pondered unrealistically.

Just as he was coming to a conclusion on the meaning of existence and everyone else was likewise fighting the inevitable effects of the cider, Adam suddenly caught Donna peering over at Mandy as if in some sort of recognition. At the very moment that he looked back at Mandy, she clamped her limpet-like lips over his and as he tried in his drunken stupor to work out what was going on, she'd flashed her supple tongue between his teeth and was busy slooshing his tonsils about. Adam thought about stopping for a split second, because he didn't really fancy Mandy but something about her manner; all teeth, lips and tongue was irresistible and as they wound themselves inexpertly around each other, it wasn't long before Donna began to get involved too.

In fact, before you could shout, 'Eureka!' both girls were taking it in turns to rearrange Adam's dentures. Not only that, but his neck was soon becoming wrenched, literally, right out of his head, and all the kissing from side to side made him feel as though he was on the stern of a ship during a great storm. He had never experienced this kind of attention before, not even in his wildest dreams, and he soon concluded that the snogging that used to regularly take place, once the lights had gone down at the school's weekend Film Club, came in a very limp second.

To Adam's initial surprise, he found out that Donna was in fact an expert kisser, and despite her size - she wasn't hugely fat, but he quickly discovered that there was certainly plenty to grab hold of and whenever he managed to put his arms around her she purred seductively in Welsh.

Mandy likewise, was hardly skinny - being proudly voluptuous - and it was obvious that her body once uncovered was well capable of raising eyebrows at a hundred paces, even at the age of fifteen.

Before Adam had relocated his neck and head back to their proper places, Donna was busy yanking at his trouser belt. He suddenly panicked, 'Oh no, I'm going to end up in the nude in front of everybody!' 'Maybe they're both doing this on purpose, to make a fool of me?' 'They're probably in some sort of pact and I'm the fall guy - a stool pigeon!' 'In a moment the others will jump out, flash-bulbs at the ready!'

Adam looked round, which was virtually impossible with Mandy's mass of hair in the way and her energetic technique of writhing it all about, but as he tried to spit out a bunch of her curly blonde tresses, he noticed that the others were either asleep or in a similar drunken position. He caught Plug in exactly the same predicament and Adam realised that they must have looked like two particularly hairy hippies - four eyes and masses of hair - as they surveyed the scene. He tried to work out where Robbie and Sally had got too, as he couldn't make them out anywhere, but at that very moment, Mandy pulled him back forcefully to the business in hand.

Now things were getting really worked up and as Donna resumed her tug of war with his belt, even using her teeth, Adam continued snogging Mandy, and tried to undo her bra which protruded from her already unbuttoned, flapping shirt. This task probably took about half an hour at least, as he fumbled hopelessly about with the strap, fretting all the while over the various combination numbers.

'Success!' Mandy's impressive breasts finally launched themselves into view and this had an immediate effect on Donna and she began to groan with her own intent. He gulped loudly to himself and thought, 'God, help me!' partly because he secretly looked up to Donna's tough exterior, expertly piercing his ear the year before, and he knew that she was probably going to eat him alive anyway, especially after he had been informed that she fancied him. But whatever, the facts were simple: Adam was putty in their hands and after the initial shock, he was beginning to really rather enjoy it and get into the swing of things. They knew it too. 'Why stop now?' he thought excitedly. 'No, exactly?! How stupid of me!'

As he tried to focus from one of Mandy's hypnotic breasts to the other in a befuddled haze, the options were suddenly doubled: 'Christ! Donna's undone her own bra!' 'Flippin' heck!!' 'What am I gonna do now?!' As he stared beady-eyed at Donna, and she began to chortle, complete confusion set in.

Before you could mumble the words, 'The Joy of Sex', the three of them were rolling around like an overflowing postman's sack trying to get out of the rest of each other's clothes. Adam felt as if he had been suddenly thrust on the set of a particularly bawdy Carry On movie. But he couldn't quite work out who he was meant to be: Sid James or

Kenneth Williams. His problems were clear, he needed to brush up on his technique and quick, but more crucially, he now needed to relieve himself badly and just as he tried to pull himself clear to go and find a nearby tree, the belt on his trousers gave way and Donna's hand was inside his trousers manically surveying the contents. As he felt her sharp fingers against his skin, he began to worry about his underpants. 'I've got the wrong one's on!' He thought, 'those stupid looking white Y-Front's from Marks and Spencers'. 'You idiot!' 'Why didn't I wear my rugby jockstrap?' 'That would've impressed them alright!' (Plug reckoned Adam's comedy grundies were handy only in the event of a nuclear war - in preventing fallout).

As he persecuted himself and took his dress sense to the cleaners, Adam was now completely prostrate between the two feminine handfuls. Incredibly, he began to relax a little more when he noticed that neither of the girls seemed too concerned or put off by his smalls. They were definitely more interested in the real Adam and they both proceeded to find it out with the brazen skill of pottery wheel apprentices. As he gulped for air, he tried to locate his remaining clothes - by this point his shirt was huddled around his waist, the arms still attached somehow to his wrists, while his trousers were now down by his knees. He felt as if he had been tangled in a strait jacket and before he could locate his belt, which had probably been thrown to the four winds and do some sort of hasty damage limitation, Donna was tugging at his M&S briefs, while Mandy erotically took off what very little she had left on.

'HELP!' Adam thought once more. But there was no one around who was conscious enough to care or doing anything about it. Both Mandy and Donna continued to kiss him like pneumatic drills and as he lay punch drunk on the deck with the two referees in close attendance, he suddenly thought, 'Sod it! It's not like this sort of thing happens every day, you know, so why don't I just lie back and enjoy it?' 'Why don't I just lie back and think of England?'

So he did. He put his problems with technique to the back of his mind and tried extra hard to tie a knot in his need for the toilet. Soon he found himself switching hopelessly between the irrepressible attentions of Mandy and Donna and as the frenziedness continued, he tried a poor impersonation of Roger Moore by trying to undo the zip of Donna's trousers whilst duelling tongues with Mandy. 'If this goes on much longer', Adam thought once more, 'I'm going to need resuscitation equipment!' and then he concluded, 'My fingers and tongue haven't had such a good work out since my second year piano and clarinet lessons!'

Incredibly, Donna's trousers slipped down with relative ease and she helped that little extra by shunting them down her legs. 'Voila!' Adam thought, in his elementary CSE level French. They were now all naked, except for Donna's underwear, which was a lot more presentable than his and amazingly, he managed to pull off an even more passable impression of James Bond and moved them, he didn't know how, slinkily down her legs.

The next hurdle was stark: Adam had only two moves when confronting a girl's downstairs department: Softly, to the left a little bit, with his fingers and then back to the right, round and round in ever decreasing circles. But here were two girls together? What should he do? He eventually decided to alternate the procedure between them in a sort of inept mirror image (though by this point they were all so hot and bothered and tipsy that any old technique would have satisfied) with a few improvised tricks thrown in for good luck, like imagining that he was playing a grand piano, or dancing the 'Twist' horizontally, with his arms held rigidly out to the side.

Miraculously, their breathing became noticeably deeper, which was probably a complete fluke, and he suddenly 'guffawed' as the girls got all hands to the pump in return. 'There's no turning back now!' he deliberated, as the girls arms bounced frenziedly off the ground and he stayed diligently at his post, the blood rushing quickly to his head. Once more an intimate rugby scrum resumed, as the girls moved in even closer and they found themselves working up into such a tempo of tossing and turning, that before Adam knew exactly what planet he had landed on, he let out a loud groaning sound and pitched forward like a crazy jack in the box.

The dust settled. It was clear. He was all played out. So was the 'Go' tablet. He concluded that Robbie's wonder pill should now be renamed the 'No' tablet, and he mumbled inanely to himself like a drunken pirate.

When he eventually rubbed the sickly grin off his face and looked about, he noticed that the two viragos had survived and were still lying in an alcohol daze next to him. Before they could stop him, he hitched up his trousers haphazardly and scampered off to relieve himself. He was also able to notice that their hastily prepared camp site now looked as if a large bomb had hit it. Bundles of hay were everywhere and the fire had burned a blackened crater in the ground. The cider container lay surrounded by piles of cigarette butts. Tiny bottles of whisky and gin were lying about, 'So the girls bought their own supplies', Adam concluded, as he emptied himself by a prickly hedge, with a second earth shattering sigh of relief. He certainly didn't remember drinking any of the whisky, but there was a good chance that he probably did. When he'd finished spelling his name haphazardly in the long grass and thrown up what seemed like a whole Off Licence's worth of drink, he returned as if nothing had happened and lay down again with Donna and Mandy who had made perfunctory attempts at covering themselves up while Adam was gone. They huddled up together once more and as the first signs of the dawn crept up, they snuggled down and went to sleep.

When Adam awoke, a large brass bell was clanging inside his head and the sun scorched his retinas with no sense or regard. Plug was wandering about holding his head and panicking:

'Shit! We've gotta get back. It's nearly eight o'clock!'

'Bollocks!' said Robbie, who Adam suspected had been with Sally all night.

'Don't worry', said Donna, smiling as she buttoned up her shirt. 'We'll sneak back into school....no problem'.

'What, with all the teachers about?'

'Yeah'.

'No way!'

'Look, stop arguing, we haven't got much time', Sally cut in.

'What about the mess?' Adam countered.

'Forget about it!' Mandy butted-in as she pulled him away towards the direction of school.

They moved off at pace, leaving everything behind that they didn't need. Adam's trouser belt was a goner for sure, and as they left the site pretty much as it was, only a hurried cleaning operation had managed to just about clear the worst.

It wasn't long before they had all made it back to the girl's dormitories. They looked a right picture. All of the ladies were having particularly bad hair days and their clothes were dishevelled. Apart from that, they all stank of cider and smoke from the fire. Adam, Robbie and Plug's hair was far too short to be ruffled but they made up for it by the tiredness on their faces. Adam reckoned the 'Go' tablets had definitely worn off on Plug and Robbie as well, because they looked wrecked.

They reached the dormitory building at a fair pace and luckily the downstairs toilet window was still slightly ajar. In the girl's clambered. However, when Donna tried to climb back in, Adam nearly launched her right into the toilet bowl with an overzealous push, but at the last moment she regained her composure and footing and was safe inside. 'If the girls are quick they might be able to blend-in without being noticed', Adam thought. 'For me, Robbie and Plug it's going to be much more difficult'.

'Jesus Christ! The Headmistress!' Plug warned.

The three of them high tailed it instantly around the back of the girl's lodgings like three frightened squirrels, something Plug found particularly difficult in his industrial slippers.

'We better wait here a second! Adam advised.

As they squatted down by the side of a wall, they watched as the Headmistress wandered down to the main school, oblivious of their presence.

'What are we gonna do?' Robbie probed.

'We'll have to cut through the fields'.

The Headmistress disappeared from view and they were off again, careering once more through fields to the side of the school. They kept on until they were right up by the meeting hall and from a narrow vantage point they could see towards the turds changing room:

'Look!' Adam shouted. 'The changing room window's open!'

It was a piece of good fortune as it meant they could sneak in and out, while the pupils were getting ready for breakfast and make their way to their own changing rooms the other side.

Robbie checked that the coast was clear and when he gave the signal they sprinted as fast as they could towards the window. As soon as they reached the window after hurdling an iron railing they jumped through and entered the lower form changing rooms. Luckily there was hardly anyone about as pupils were off having their morning showers and anyone startled by the sudden invasion knew to keep quiet about it or else.

Finally, they made it to their own changing rooms and sanctuary. For the time being they were safe. They immediately tried to hide all traces of the night's adventures and as they showered with large grins on their faces their fellow form pupils tried to find out what exactly they had been up to. They certainly knew that the three had been up to no good:

'Were you up the Combe?'

'Maybe....'

'Did you have some cider?'

'Might have....'

'Did you get off with some girls?'

'Maybe....'

And so on.

Even though they were all knackered from the lack of sleep and their throbbing hangovers, they managed to make some sort of appearance at breakfast, so as not to raise any suspicions. As they munched tiredly on their Shredded Wheat, what seemed like half the school was staring over at them, as though they were three brave soldiers returning from the battle front. While eyes fixed themselves upon them, they continued eating and tried to look calm and collected. Adam couldn't believe how fast the rumours had spread and Plug concerned himself with the likelihood of being found out. Temperatures rose further when Donna and Mandy and the three other girls finally made it to the end of the queue for breakfast:

'Who did you get off with?' Robbie gleamed at Plug, while the girls were being informed by a canteen lady that breakfast was over and that there was no food left.

'Kate....' Plug gloated.

'No?!'

'Yeah, straight up'.

'I didn't think she'd be up for it'.

'Well, she was.'

'Blimey!'

'What about you?' Plug turned to Robbie.

'What?'

'Who did you get off with?'

There was a pause as Robbie thought for a moment.

'I thought you knew?'

'No, I was well out of it', Plug admitted.

'Sally....'

'Sally?! I thought you were with Rachel?'

'No....Sally....'

Adam across looked at Robbie, as he grinned back. So, Adam had been right after all. His heart sank. But he knew that he was in no real position to get possessive over his ex when he had dallied around himself.

Then Plug and Robbie looked at Adam inquisitively. As Adam sipped his tea he smirked, partly out of embarrassment and partly out of surprise.

'So what about you?' said Plug eventually.

There was a pause as Plug and Robbie edged nearer.

'What about me?' Adam parried.

'Who did you get off with?' Robbie angled.

'Dunno....'

'Yeah, you do?!' said Plug almost nudging him.

'I can't remember....' Adam replied with a shrug.

'Yeah, you can'.

'I can't'.

'I don't believe you', Plug persisted.

'It's true?'

'Oh, yeah?!' Robbie laughed.

There was another pause as Adam looked at them for a moment.

'Okay....Mandy and Donna'.

'Mandy and....what both of them?!' Plug probed, as some of the girls began to look over.

'Yeah....'

'Together?!'

'Yeah'.

'What, all three of you?'

'Yeah....'

There was a long pause as Rob and Plug both gawped at each other and then the pin finally dropped.

'BLOODY HELL!!'

They both exhaled and then the three of them descended wildly into hysterics.

After breakfast, it was off to assembly, which wasn't easy, feeling as dog-tired as they were. Although they were all concerned that they were going to get caught, it went off without any hitches, apart from Donna winking at Adam from across the hall, during the hymn and afterwards they came out feeling ten foot tall:

'D'you reckon Donna will spread it around.' Adam said to Plug.

'No....she won't. If she does, it'll make her and Mandy look like right tarts'.

'Yeah, I s'pose'.

They all walked off to class confident that they had gotten away with it. However, during the lesson, Adam couldn't stop nodding off and Robbie would dig him in the ribs whenever his head started to droop. When Adam wasn't falling asleep he was thinking that they had left far too much evidence back at the scene of the crime pointing to their involvement and Adam knew that his trouser belt was out there somewhere by the camp site, with his name in big letters on the back of it.

Just before the end of the class his worst fears were confirmed when the vice Head entered the classroom and asked for Adam and Robbie to go immediately to the Headmasters office. On the way, they met up with Plug and as soon as they saw him they knew that the game was up. Just as Adam was about to speak to him, the Headmaster appeared and bellowed at them.

'In my Office! NOW!'

They dropped their smarmy guises instantly and shuffled quietly into the Heads office. A second later the Head entered with steam literally coming out of his ears.

'A local farmer, has informed me that some pupils have trespassed on his property and have vandalised his hay stacks and started a fire which has burnt some of his grazing land. I know that at least one of you is involved because an object was found by the farmer with one of your names on it'.

At that moment the Headmaster turned towards Adam and glared at him with a look that almost turned him to stone, 'my bloody belt I bet', Adam thought to himself.

'A member of staff has also been well informed that you three were the ringleaders in this misadventure. I'm sure you cannot deny it. The farmer has also notified the Police, who are ready to take action if necessary. Make no mistake about the seriousness of the situation. This is criminal damage. All three of you will be punished by the farmer in the way that he sees fit. The Police have said that they're happy for the farmer and the school to deal with this recklessness. Let me tell you, we will not tolerate any behaviour that brings this school into disrepute and you will all apologise personally to the farmer concerned. Alongside the farmer's punishment, to teach you a valuable lesson, I'm gating you all for four weeks and you are not allowed to mingle out of school timetable for the same period. Furthermore, you will be confined to the school grounds where you'll remain in uniform. Do you have anything to say?'

There was a gaping chasm of a pause as they thought long and hard for a moment, something they certainly weren't accustomed to. Another dose of solitary confinement. Great. One other thing was clear. There was a snitch in their mist. 'Even one of the girls who was with us possibly', Adam reasoned. Maybe Donna and Mandy hadn't had a very nice time after all. Perhaps it was his piano playing.

'Well, what do you have to say for yourselves?'

'Sorry, Sir....' they mumbled unconvincingly, as they tried not to think too hard about Plug's future express delivery to the Headmaster, courtesy of the Royal Mail.

'Sorry?!'

'Yes, Sir....'

There was another pause and you could hear the distinctive tick of a large Grandfather clock.

'Er....Sir?' Plug sparked up bravely.

'What is it?!'

'Er....who was it that said it was us?'

'That's something that I'm not prepared to disclose. Let's just say, that I have it on good authority. It's hardly a coincidence is it?'

They stood there like three prats scratching their heads. There was nothing they could do. Sneak or not, they were heading for the farmers retribution and make no mistake. Adam reckoned they were certainly about to get their hands very dirty and there wasn't going to be much chance of them rolling around with the farmers daughters. They were much more likely going to be found in a pen washing the pigs, or about the fields collecting cowpats or checking the consistency of the local silage.

Before long they found themselves lined up right in front of the farmer. After they apologised pathetically to him one by one, with lots of 'Sorries' again, he told them what their punishment would involve. He was short and squat and had more than a passing resemblance to Captain Pugwash (he would have been his absolute doppelganger in a Tricorn hat) and as he tweaked his beard and spoke in a rasping voice again, they tried not to laugh.

'You will spend the next three days workin' on my farm, to make you think 'ard about what you've done. It'll teach you to 'ave some respect for the countryside and for private property. It might even make you understand what 'ard work really means. But be warned, I'll not put up with any messin' about. While you are 'ere and workin', you'll do exactly what I tell you. If you don't, then the Police'll be involved'.

He then paused on purpose for full dramatic effect.

'Right, I think you can start on the pen now!'

'Oh, great....' Adam muttered to Plug under his breath.

'The pig pen'.

The three of them looked at each other and then at the size of the enclosure. It was huge and absolutely filthy. At least the pigs had been taken out, as Adam didn't particularly fancy wrestling with them while they tried to clean up the place. However, the pong was unbearable and dung and rotting food were everywhere. Whoever it was that said that pig's are clean animals should have seen the state of the lodgings they were supposed to clean out: A hundred incontinent elephants would have struggled to match it.

It wasn't long before Adam's treasured Doctor Martens were covered in muck. The concrete floor of the pen had to be hosed down so they spent ages sweeping sludge across it and back again. Some of the crap heaped up as they cleaned, but it was a long process and eventually they had to get in there and take it out with their bare hands.

As they worked, they pondered on how the girls had managed to get away with it. The only girl punished was Donna, who only had to suffer a one week gating. A puny punishment. The Headmistress obviously didn't have the same information sources that the Headmaster had been privy to in his inordinate wisdom that had done for the boys.

It was obvious. Getting caught was not good. And they were beginning to make a habit of it. What was worse was the fact that they were missing all their ordinary lessons and would have to make up the classes later, building up even more resentment for the future. And attending Film Club was now out of the question. Despite this, Adam still managed a contented grin whenever flashes of the previous night's revels crossed his tired countenance.

Eventually, after a lot of sweat, and the very real problem of trying to stop each other from falling asleep right there and then, they finished the pen which took the best part of the afternoon. All they needed now was a photographer to capture the historic moment. Then they started putting the hay bales back together that they had manically pulled apart and cleared up all the farmers fields around the school. This took the rest of the day and would be their punishment for the following day too.

On the third day they returned to the farm yard where they had to do more filthy cleaning jobs and by the end they were almost on first name terms with all the farmer's chickens, geese and cows. It was beginning to look like they were doing Doctor Doolittle out of a job.

But did it make them contrite, that was the question? Did it make them respect private property? Did it make them more conscientious of the countryside and their environment? Adam wasn't too sure. But had they learned their lesson? That was another important question. Adam certainly wasn't convinced and he was pretty certain that nor were Robbie and Plug. In fact, Adam decided that given the chance, he would have gone through the whole experience all over again, just to have five more minutes with Mandy and Donna up the Combe, and he suddenly found the expression on his face widening rapidly again at the thought.

BASINGSTOKE

A crappy little town in Hampshire? A lump of concrete surrounded by hundreds and hundreds of roundabouts amid rolling hills and greenery? A new overspill town created after the Second World War that had one of everything? One cinema. One train station. One shopping arcade. One bank. One Pub. One Post Office. One multi-storey. One school. One off-licence. One public convenience? Well, it seemed like it, and yet you could be sure that there were probably five hundred roundabouts (more per square mile than any other town in the whole of Europe). But this was Plug's home and during the summer holidays Adam got the chance to visit him.

His family lived on Brighton Hill, which was to the south of the town. Near his house were some customary local shops, a pub called the Pig and Whistle, a large factory called 'Cannons' and just around the corner, Basingstoke Football Club, that's of course near the large Brighton Hill roundabout.

When Plug showed Adam around the town from the vantage point of a bus, he seemed quite proud of the place. From repetitive history lessons at school, Adam had learned a little about the massive Parliamentarian siege during the English Civil War of Basing House, which was on the outskirts, to the east of the town, so at least he knew something of the place's heritage. Oliver Cromwell's army had taken months and months to wheedle out the doughty Royalist defender's and the final bloody siege in 1645 was one of the major events of the war and was also remembered for the barbarism of the Roundhead victors. All that remained to tell the epic story, however, was a few impressive looking earthworks and parts of old overgrown outhouses, the original house being largely raised to the ground.

One of Plug's favourite locations was a large Victorian, council owned house, called Cemetery Lodge in Chapel Hill, near the railway station.

'It's a wicked place', he said earnestly.

The Lodge reminded Adam of the kid's TV cartoon, Whacky Races, with its crazy Gothic looking tower and its wooden pillars and it's mock turrets and castle-like decorations and an unusual porch area raised well above street level with an iron railing. It had loads of character and some open grounds with large trees and on a hot summer's day it was certainly a good place to lark about. Eventually, it would be sold off for next to nothing to a corrupt local official, who later on would have a major influence on one of Plug's all time least favourite locations: the Anvil.

'It's a carbuncle on the arse of the town!' Plug reckoned.

He was right. The entertainment complex was hideous. A complete eyesore. Built as a venue to house the growing local demand for music and comedians, it seemed to have no further aesthetic function at all. It was like a lump of twisted concrete literally dumped in the Town. Constructed by the same corrupt local official who originally bought up the picturesque Cemetery Lodge.

They walked around the town centre and the shopping arcade and had a look at what was on at the ABC Cinema, which wasn't much, a re-run of 'Saturday Night Fever' with John Travolta. Not their cup of tea at all. 'Scum' with Ray Winstone had just been doing the rounds and that was much more up their street. They rated it a top film and a sobering reminder of their oppressive boarding school.

As it was a sunny day they then walked round to the Bass House pub where they were due to meet up with Plug's former school mate, Dave. Outside the public house was a good place to hook up as it was so central being located within the shopping centre. Adam had already heard a lot about Dave and he was almost becoming legendary, being mentioned as Plug's friend who had been caught with him burglaring, but had escaped the country and Interpol's clutches. Now he was back in Basingstoke, although keeping a low profile and yet he was brave enough to meet up in town.

They waited a while outside the pub, leafing through a copy of music magazine 'Sounds' to pass the time, but eventually Dave turned up, sporting spiked dark hair and a worn, black leather jacket covered in badges. He grinned as he saw Plug.

'How's it goin' mate?'

'Yeah, alright'.

And after introducing Adam, Plug chatted to Dave about how he had been doing. Dave mentioned that he was only back temporarily although he hadn't made up his mind whether he would be staying permanently abroad. He was keen to find out what their school was like, because had he stayed in the country he would have also ended up there with Plug. They reckoned Dave was luckier, having fled to Germany and he was already busy picking up the language.

'So who d'you support?' Dave asked Adam eventually.

'Chelsea', he admitted.

'Ah, they ain't havin' too good a season are they!'

'Not really. Who d'you follow?'

'The Saints'.

'I've seen loads of good matches with them. They even had Peter Osgood for a while'.

'Yeah, I know. And before my old man took me to the Dell, I nearly supported Chelsea myself'.

'Really?!' Adam replied surprised.

'There was this Basingstoke schools, five-a-side competition, when I was about seven and Peter Houseman of Chelsea was there'.

'Houseman?'

'Yeah, and when I got a chance I asked him if he reckoned our school would win and he said maybe, but that it'd be hard 'cos there was loads and loads of good teams. He was really nice to me and he gave me his autograph'.

There was a pause for a moment.

'You got Peter Houseman's autograph?'

'Yeah, I really liked the way he signed his name. The long, curly way he did the S of his surname looked great, so I started signing the S in my surname the same way. Still do now'.

'Blimey', Adam responded. 'Houseman was one of my favourite players. I was gutted when he died'.

'It was sad alright. 'Cos I really liked him I nearly became a Chelsea fan, but then my dad took us to Southampton and that was it'.

Adam was quite surprised by Dave's story and afterwards the three of them spent the rest of the day strolling around the town centre chatting about punk and the gigs that they wanted to go to. When they returned to Plug's house they listened to Ian Dury's album 'New Boots and Panties' in his bedroom. The record was brilliant and Plug already knew all of the lyrics. There was one song, Plastow Patricia, that really stood out because of its completely uncompromising beginning with a load of strong swear words that Dury belted out. It was the sort of record that Adam was always told to turn down for obvious reasons.

Plug and Dave talked for a long time about Basingstoke and how their mates were all doing and different parts of the town, so much so, that Adam almost needed a map to keep up with them. There was no doubt about it, Basingstoke was a sprawling area full of different suburbs and neighbourhoods, but an interesting place none the less.

Kingsclere

Popley

Winklebury

(Winkle Pub)

Oakridge

TOWN CENTRE Basing House

(ABC Cinema, Station)

(Bass House)

West Ham Roundabout

Buckskin

(Fire Station)

East Ham

Kempshott

South Ham

Brighton Hill
(Shops, Pig and Whistle, Cannons)

Oakley

INCREDIBLE RECOVERY

Steve had the good fortune to witness one of the most amazing games ever played at Stamford Bridge. As he was in the year above Adam at school he had already left that summer and was now at a school in north London doing his 'A' levels. Adam was well jealous of him because it meant that he could attend more matches than Adam and that season Chelsea were in a relegation dogfight and needed every bit of support they could get. Whenever he spoke to him on the phone Steve would say:

'I've been to more games than you so far this season. I've been to eight matches. You've only been to four'.

'Five', Adam would reply, trying to catch him out.

'Four'.

'Okay, four. But I went to Everton at home, first game of the season, which you couldn't go to'.

'So? We lost....'

'Yeah, but it was the first game of the season'.

'So?'

And on and on it would go.

There wasn't a lot Adam could do about it being away at school and Steve used to rub salt in the wound by chanting:

'8-4!' '8-4!' '8-4!'

Adam felt even more envious when he spoke to Steve after the Chelsea v Bolton Wanderers match at home. Steve was having great difficulty in stringing a sentence together. In fact it seemed as if this extraordinary first home victory of the season had rendered him completely speechless. Steve had stood in the Shed End as usual and watched as Bolton completely coasted it - netting three times with such ease that he was about to leave for home, expecting Bolton to score another three or four in the second half. It was the smallest home crowd of the season, 19,879 and Chelsea were nestled second from bottom in the First Division having won only one match so far.

There was only twenty minutes to go. It looked like no way back. Or so Steve and everyone else thought. Suddenly there's a substitution, Clive Walker, their mercurial winger, strides on to the pitch with only one thing on his mind - goal scoring. Yes, he had once more decided to flagrantly disregard the script. He almost immediately centres for Tommy Langley to stab home the ball and suddenly it's 1-3. Steve thinks, 'Oh, at least we've scored a consolation goal. Perhaps I'll stick around'.

On 82 minutes, Kenny Swain manages to slot the ball in the net, through a mass of white Bolton shirts and it's 2-3. Steve thinks, 'Oh even better, another consolation. Blimey, perhaps we can even save the game? Perhaps we can even get a draw?'

On 87 minutes, after another dazzling terrier-like run, Clive Walker angles his shot past McDonagh, the Bolton goalkeeper and its 3-3. Steve shouts 'Flippin' Hell! It's 3-3! Maybe we can win? Maybe we can?'

On 89 minutes, Walker whacks a hard cross-drive which is sliced into the Bolton net by their own centre-back Allardyce and as the final whistle blows, Steve is in dreamland. 'I don't believe it! It's 4-3! 4-3 to Chelsea!'

Apparently the whole ground, excluding Bolton's disbelieving contingent, went completely crazy. After the whistle, delirious Chelsea fans raced on to the pitch and thousands of supporters jumped up and down and hugged each other on the terraces for a long time after. Steve said it was one of the best atmosphere's he had ever experienced.

The players were ecstatic. Clive Walker had managed in under twenty minutes to become 'Man of the Match', and Chelsea had won for a second time that season. Yes, Steve was right. That was some game that was. That was some victory.

FIRST GIG

Adam had tried to see the The Clash when they headlined the 'Rock against Racism' Carnival with X-Ray Spex in Victoria Park in the spring of 1978. But due to being away at school it wasn't possible for him to go. Adam was determined to see them however, and his opportunity came later in the year.

Meanwhile, the Clash had released the single 'White Man in Hammersmith Palais', which became one of Adam's favourite records with the, by now, emblematic fusion of guitar thrash and reggae of Mick Jones and Joe Strummer. They were to appear at the Roxy Theatre in Harlesden, in north west London, to promote their forthcoming single 'Tommy Gun' and Adam was hoping that the punk-reggae outfit Special Aka, from Coventry, would still be the support band. Whatever the line-up, Plug got lucky and obtained two tickets.

There were some frustrating postponements to the gig, the result of some major feud between the Clash and their manager Bernie Rhodes who around this time was becoming more and more confrontational towards the band. But eventually the concert went ahead, much to Adam and Plug's relief.

The journey to Harlesden took hours; an endless tube, a monotonous overground train, then a bus, and finally a long winding road for good measure. Adam didn't really know what to expect as he had only been to one small punk gig before, and the two bands Prag Vec and Angletrax were not only weird, but played in a Theatre, The Young Vic, in Waterloo, which Adam had been to with his mum to see a panto when he was younger. (This wasn't the only time that a Punk band had performed in a well known theatre venue, probably due to the frequently overt political and theatrical nature of the songs, and even if some bands weren't particularly agitprop, they were certainly dramatic). Adam went to the Young Vic gig with his sister who at the time was more keen on Genesis and The Eagles, and hated Punk, so understandably Adam considered the Clash gig his first proper concert.

Plug had a bit of experience too. He had been to the Reading Festival and had seen Sham 69 try to play their rabble rousing set, whilst all about descended into a full scale riot between Punks and Skinheads, so he was 'blooded' as they say, but between them they were still most definitely wet behind the ears. They had only just turned fifteen and had heard about the riot at the Clash's concert at the Rainbow the year before, so they thought that there might be a chance of a repeat performance. If nothing else, it was certainly going to be an entertaining evening.

The Harlesden environment was harsh - a concrete dustbin came to mind and urban mania screamed out at them as they walked along. When they finally reached the venue, both of them now short of breath, Adam turned to Plug.

'Blimey! This is it. The Roxy!'

'Yeah. Bit dodgy looking in' it', said Plug full of enthusiasm.

The front of the Roxy resembled a dilapidated, sleazy sex cinema and the atmosphere seemed muted. In the high street, punks were strolling around aimlessly trying to avoid being run over by the general public. There seemed to be an undercurrent of despair. Punk as an active movement was rocking on its last legs. In fact it was well into its death throes, but Adam and Plug thought that being so young they would have a damn good thrash around in it and see where it led them. The Sex Pistols were defunct and the intelligence and elitism of the early period had turned into mass market ignorance - all packaged and labelled. However, Adam felt that even a dead horse flogged beyond belief was far preferable to most of the garbage around. Not for nothing did they detest the octogenarian Pink Floyd and those other skeletons The Rolling Stones.

The two of them sat outside the Roxy on the pavement, up against a wall, waiting to be let in. This was a novelty. They had managed to turn up early and they even had enough time for a bit of 'leaning against a lamp post' and 'slouching next to the rubbish bin'.

'Want some of this?' said Plug as he passed over a half empty can of lager.

'Cheers', and Adam took a swig.

'This is gonna be a right laugh',

'Yeah, I can't wait to see Strummer', Adam mused, grinning away.

There seemed to be a right mix of styles all about. There were a variety of Punks in all colours, shapes and sizes, a smattering of skinheads and even a few Teddy-boys, although to call them 'boys' would be inaccurate as they all seemed like fully grown men. Burly greasers. They were certainly taller than Adam and Plug. Mind you that wasn't difficult.

For some reason on the poster outside the venue, the rockabilly band Whirlwind were advertised as the last minute support and as Adam put two and two together, he suddenly concerned himself with the likelihood of there being a major pitched battle inside the venue, reminiscent of the one he had witnessed with Steve down the King's Road the year before. Some Teds frequently carried weapons and they were always an unpredictable bunch at the best of times. They would never usually give quarter, especially to their enemies. Thing was, Adam felt their statement wasn't that dissimilar - Teds were outsiders too - it's just that they were tidier dressers.

'What are we gonna do if there's a riot?' Adam pondered nervously.

'Leg it....' Plug laughed. 'No, it'll be alright! There's too many punks'.

The doors to the Roxy finally opened and Adam and Plug slowly shuffled themselves inside. Adam's heartbeat accelerated in anticipation as they entered. He already had a score of football heroes and now he was becoming busy amassing musical ones. In the theatre's foyer they were handed out free Clash 'Tommy Gun' T-shirts, which depicted the band posing against a background map of Africa.

'Superb', Adam said to Plug with a huge grin.

He loved collecting things. Adam placed the free T-shirt over his own and carried his tatty black Harrington bomber jacket. The white T-shirt looked brilliant, because when they entered down into the interior of the club, it glowed, due to the ultra-violet lighting. It was as though Adam had suddenly become invested with an electrical current. Others wearing the shirt radiated neon too.

The next thing he noticed, apart from the venue's tacky red upholstery was the low lit stage with it's cluster of amplifiers, drums and microphones.

The Roxy looked subterranean, a damp alienating place. 'This is going to be fun', Adam mused. There were two specific occupations that he wanted to witness and perhaps take part in. The first was to have a really good pogo and the second was to deliver some saliva, first class at the Clash. I suppose you could call it a primitive form of appreciation society (the Punk group The Damned had inspired 'gobbing', with the drummer, Rat Scabies', throaty spitting, and the drug amyl-nitrate consumed by the bucket load caused a lot of punks to salivate. Sid Vicious had been lumbered with originating the 'pogo' - jumping up and down to get a better view while watching the Sex Pistols perform at the 100 Club Punk Festival in 1976 and the two practices put together, quickly became a primitive ritual). Adam had seen the effect of spitting on the Chelsea girls at the Millwall game two years before and he had also read about Joe Strummer contracting Hepatitis from it the previous spring. The singer even spent some days in hospital. But appreciation was appreciation and Adam was definitely going to show some, especially if the band played 'London's Burning', 'White Riot' or 'Garageland', three of his favourite tracks.

Adam and Plug sat in the stalls and lurked. Half of the cinema seats had been removed to allow a large space for mayhem, and the place was filling up quickly. It was easy getting beer even though they were well under age, and if they met any problems they already had a sure fire plan - before they left home they had stocked up on a few cans of lager to send them on their way.

As they soaked up the dank sweaty atmosphere, they told each other how brilliant it was to be part of something vital, however late they were. Anyway, Adam had always been late for everything and so had Plug. He would certainly never again feel the incredible pulse that both anticipation and dread were having. This was new territory.

'Playing records is one thing', Adam calculated, 'seeing it all right in front of you another'.

'Yeah, it's a buzz alright', replied Plug gazing around wide-eyed.

Before long, the DJ started spinning some sounds to wet the pallets of the assembled constituents. Lots of Buzzcocks, the Damned and Siouxsie and the Banshees (their first single, Hong Kong Garden had just reached number seven in the charts and was being played repeatedly. It's subject matter inspired by the continual harassment by racist skinheads of Siouxsie Sioux's favourite Chinese takeaway in Chislehurst. The lyrics were a kind of tribute to the owners). Adam told Plug what a great record he thought it was and as they hummed and tapped their feet they knew they were going to be in for a right old treat.

Suddenly, before the bliss of the Banshees had played itself out, the support band Whirlwind burst out onto the stage like bad acne and the reverie was cut short. They seemed like a strange, quiffed beast, surlily looking out at the party of messy urchins who begrudgingly stared back.

'Look at the state of 'em!' said Plug on the verge of hysterics.

'Yeah, and the music's pretty bad too', Adam added towards the end of their first song - some grease laden ode to the long gone fifties and the recently departed Pelvis.

Throughout the remainder of their heavy rocker set, the odd plastic beer glass sailed over from disgruntled punks, whilst a solitary group of Teds in loud brothel creepers plied their wares in front of the stage. Around them, the massing ranks of ragamuffin haired youth screamed, 'We want Clash!' and 'White Riot!' You would have thought Adam and Plug were certainly out to get their money's worth, because it wasn't long before they both joined in as well, crying out at the tops of their voices.

Before this gig, they had both just been devoted apprentices, but now they were paid up affiliated members and they wore their T-shirts with pride. Adam had found himself some kind of new religion. It was all to do with nothing achieving. How could they lose, when they already had? Chelsea were always under achieving, when you least expected it. 'I'll do a bit of my very own', Adam thought.

Luckily, Whirlwind were off the stage as fast as their name suggested and in their place was a cranking surge of adrenalin. The Clash were coming and Adam knew that nothing could stop them, unless of course their tour bus had broken down. A ridiculous picture of the band calling the AA came to mind, which was unrealistic because the Clash all hailed from North Kensington and the cityscape surrounding, so at worst they could train it to the venue like Adam and Plug. Furthermore, Harlesden was well within spitting distance of the high rise home they raucously sang about in their song 'London's Burning'.

Adam and Plug moved forward, near the front to get a better perspective, their young chins in line with the stage. Classic records came thick and fast now, louder and louder and the space around them was dense with black leather, zips and discontent. It was a veritable jagged razor and it felt as though everybody was sliding along it together. Suddenly, the roadies who had been busy making ready, disappeared and everybody stood on tiptoe 'in the starting gate', waiting for their idols to appear: Waiting for their heroes to flick the switch.

Adam turned once more to Plug.

'There's Strummer!'

'Where?'

'Over there, behind the amplifier…'

'No, it ain't'.

'Yeah, it is!'

'No, it ain't'.

'Yeah, it is. I'm sure it is'.

'No, it ain't. It's a roadie'.

'No, it ain't!'

'Yeah, it is'.

'No it ain't!'

'Yes it is! That's a roadie that is. He's tuning Mick Jones' guitar'.

One thing was certain. Plug was just as fired up as Adam was and it was obvious that he wanted to have a good jump around too.

Then from out of the abyss came a sudden screech of feedback, and a blast of high octane drumming. A searing light challenged the eyes and a large montage backdrop of world flags blazed into view. They teetered on the brink. The mob was at home with itself, just like at the football

- ready to surge, ready to lose itself in it's own will. It was irrepressible - they had ticket stubs in their back pockets to prove it. Next second, Joe Strummer appeared through a mist, like an apparition, followed by Mick Jones and Paul Simonon and everybody cheered.

They were decked in familiar garb - black shirts, tight fitting epauletted jackets, stencils, the odd strap and zip, their T-shirts and guitars splattered with statements, not so many as before, but still boasting things like 'Noise' or 'Heavy Duty Discipline'. Strummer's shirt had 'H Block' stamped across it in bold letters, so his political leanings were clear. He had once said in an interview; 'Like trousers, like brain'. Now Adam knew what he meant. A startled, angered expression jumped out - all amphetamine and sibilant sneer. Strummer clutched his rhythm guitar in rigid machine gun expression while the band crashed straight into 'Janie Jones', a song that concerned itself with all the trials and tribulations of modern living.

Eventually, Adam and Plug leapt forward and lost themselves in the pogoing. They couldn't really help themselves and to be honest they really didn't have any choice, because everyone else was up to it. It was like diving right into the deep end. When they became more accustomed, and rid themselves of any remaining self consciousness, they even used each other's shoulders as a launch pad to get that little bit higher. What a strange ritual it was. A seething mass. Everyone knew all the words and mouthed them out as Strummer spouted his electric storytelling. His energy was phenomenal. He could have powered the National Grid (this was the same sort of buzz Adam had found in a big crowd at Chelsea, when the 'Blues' had managed to win a match in the dying seconds). 'Nothing can be better than this', he thought, 'except maybe losing my virginity'.

In the break between the next song Strummer asked if they all liked the free T-shirts and the devotees shouted out their approval. He had such a rapport with the crowd, that it seemed as if he had them right in his pocket. Then someone, maybe one of the disgruntled Teds, shouted out their disapproval (at a previous gig Strummer had shouted out 'We're the Clash! If you don't fuckin' like us you know where the door is!' to someone who had criticised the band) and he certainly wasn't in the mood to take any prisoners this time. He hissed out something incomprehensible that sounded like, 'Oh, well, fuck off then!!' through his twisted teeth and then there was another loud cheer from the audience. Whatever, the heckler got the message. As far as Adam was concerned though, he wasn't going anywhere. He was staying put.

The Clash's catalogue continued, with some of their new material from their second album, 'Give 'Em Enough Rope' which was about to be released. They still played some oldies much to Adam and Plug's relief, because they found it difficult going nuts about stuff that they had never heard before (it transpired that this would be one of the Clash's last UK gigs before the lure of conquering America put paid to their previously held Punk credentials, especially ironic as they had professed such strong dissatisfaction with corporate Yankiedom with the song 'I'm So Bored With The USA'. Yes, a sniff of a sellout was perhaps in the air, but luckily Adam and Plug caught them when both musical proficiency vied with on stage bravado resulting in a heady cocktail). Mind you it was good to have a rest in between belters like, 'Cheat'; 'What's my Name' (about the crisis of youth identity); 'Hate and War' (Mick Jones taking over the lead vocals); 'Police and Thieves' (the superb cover of Junior Marvin's reggae classic), and the brilliant 'Career Opportunities' (about Jones' employment at the Post Office opening mail during an IRA bomb scare). How could it get any better? But it did because they then played 'Garageland', one of Adam's favourites, which was a proud acknowledgement and retort to media criticism about playing in a so-called 'garageband'. The pogoing became even more frenzied. Saliva started to rain down. It dripped off microphones, clung onto the drum kit, flew past Mick Jones, who alongside Paul Simonon was busy exuding the coolest cool ever witnessed, and lodged itself in the front of his amplifier.

'No fuckin' spittin'!' shouted Strummer, as he thrashed his instrument to death. His polite request fell on deaf ears, as Adam landed a lump right on Paul Simonon's spiked hair and Plug had a near miss of an especially green hue on Topper Headon's hi-hat. So much 'gob' and stringy phlegm was now hitting the stage that their heroes soon looked as if they were covered in elastic.

Despite the audience's throaty attentions, The Clash played their thunderous new single 'Tommy Gun', which was received with another great roar and everyone's fists in the air. Adam could see the band lapping it up, enjoying the excitement of addressing the converted and all the while the gig neared its irrepressible climax. The Clash finally played the show stopper 'White Riot', about Strummer and Simonon at the 1976 Notting Hill Carnival riot, and the whole place exploded.

It felt good natured though - a Punk fell down right next to Adam and was quickly propelled back onto his feet by total strangers. It was a cartoon, no one was really going to get hurt. Besides, the Teds seemed to have all cashed in their chips and vanished.

The exhausted mob in front was now streaming sweat, and alongside the pent-up aggression was a rousing urgency: Adam chanced to pogo next to a particularly striking Punkette, who managed to launch herself even higher than he could, even with a heavy biker jacket and large boots; 'That's impressive and very useful on the curriculum vitae', he reckoned. And just at the very moment that he considered introducing himself, she was lost forever among a tumbling mass of bodies. 'Oh, well', Adam thought, 'that's life', and carried on pogoing.

After one last scream of sonic, the Clash stuttered to a crescendo, disconnected their guitar leads and left, after thanking everyone for loyally making the pilgrimage. Adam stared at the empty stage, his eyes all a blur. His ears were ringing like Notre Dame - Quasimodo was inside his head giving the ropes a damn good pull. If his ears could have bled, I'm sure they would have done. The crowd chanted, 'More, more, more!' and 'London's Burning'. After a few minutes, the band dutifully complied, diving back onto the stage for masterfully raucous renditions of 'London's Burning' and 'White Man (in Hammersmith Palais)', the guitars, bass and drums buzzing about as if they were a nasty itch you just couldn't scratch. Then the band disappeared once more into the dark and the auditorium lights came up. The dance floor began to clear. Rubbish and cracked plastic glasses littered the vacant auditorium. Steam from the massed ranks of pogoers began to lift.

Adam briefly lost sight of Plug, but soon identified him again, lingering among the quickly dispersing punters.

'That was fuckin' excellent!'

'Fuckin' amazing!' Plug replied eventually, gleaming with sweat from all the jumping about.

'Strummer's incredible!'

'Yeah. Gotta get the new single'.

'Definitely!' Adam concluded.

They stood about in the venue for as long as possible, trying desperately to hang on to the experience, because no one had informed them before that life could be quite that good. They always thought that everything was either past it's sell by date or that there was something dodgy with the label - so nothing quite seemed to fit. Unfortunately, they were soon moved on by burly security. And before Adam had even fully returned to earth, gravity pulling him back down all the while, he found himself sliding reluctantly out of the Roxy. His Tommy Gun T-shirt soaked right through, and his legs about to give way, but he was happy and he could tell that so was Plug.

After embracing the cutting night, which took about fifteen minutes scoffing a soggy bag of chips, they tubed it homeward to sweet suburbia, two exhausted but inspired disciples ready to spread the word.

SEWAGE

It was the infamous 'winter of discontent'. Rubbish and debris were stacked high in the Nation's bins and refuse pits. The rotten Labour Government had 'batoned down the hatches' and were 'keeping their powder dry' while everyone else was prevented from 'smelling the roses'. Strikes were rife. Yet a strange apathy was abundant. At school it was a similar tale.

One morning Adam's year awoke to find a major problem with the plumbing in their changing room. In the shower area, which was at a lower level to the rest of the facilities, sewage and left over food had risen hell-like from the kitchens. The height of the stinking fluid was about a foot and rising. The smell was so foul that they could hardly stay for long in the area and once they had surveyed the scene they made jokes about what everyone fancied for their breakfast:

'Oh, I reckon that half eaten sausage, bobbing about next to that soggy piece of bread!'

They complained immediately to their superiors, but falling on deaf ears as it usually did, nothing at all was done.

Afternoon arrived, and they were becoming further agitated. The sludge had now levelled off, but was still close enough to the main area of the changing room and the stench was unbearable. How could pupils carry on if one of their 'safe havens' - the changing rooms - were now tainted with rank detritus caused by one of their many grievances - the kitchens?

They couldn't, so they went into immediate action. A Form meeting was called with as many as possible involved, but it was really the same old group of agitators and a few followers. Their demands were simple. They wanted the mess cleared up immediately, and fast. Then after further thumb twiddling, a radical solution was hatched:

'Why not press gang 'turds' to act as cleaners?'

The plan was approved unanimously and the only doubt remained what would be the reaction of the Six formers. It was concluded, however, that they were largely 'squares' so they would definitely keep out of trouble and if they tried to oppose them they would live to regret it. The other doubt, the teachers reaction, was laughed completely out of court, because they were either oblivious, or doing nothing to fix the problem.

So, during 'break' off they went on their press ganging search. Rounding up 'turds' and lower formers. The easily bullied ones, the weaker ones, the 'little ones'. Anyone they didn't like was especially acceptable and passed the medical immediately. They chased and caught up with frightened boys all around the school, which Adam found although to some distaste, largely enjoyable. Onlookers thought that it was just a more serious game of tag, but Adam and company new different. They knew it was for real.

Adam found it a buzz to be in control. The worm had turned and now they were dishing it back out with interest. Now they were the bullies. Untouchable. Or so they felt. And Adam was one of them. He suddenly had a purpose. Even if it was stupid and nasty. There was a purpose none the less.

It was some metamorphosis. From a dreamy, retiring nature at the start of his school career, Adam had become a respected bully himself and he fully realised that there was a long list of adherents and patrons that had lined up before him.

The fishing haul was a resounding success. About ten turds of various demeanours had been herded into the changing room ready to do the dirty business. More importantly, not one teacher had found out. Then the turds were set to work. As they toiled reluctantly, they were taunted mercilessly as they mopped out the stew of shit in the shower area.

By special code the news soon got round to the rest of the form about the work detail and it seemed that suddenly everyone wanted a piece of the action. Adam marvelled at how 'safety in numbers' had brought out the worst in themselves and their fellow form members. One boy in the year, who had been considered Head Boy material all the way through school, equipped himself with a long broom handle and proceeded to flog the back of one of the turds. It was a free for all. Then the turd started to cry, so he was thrashed even more. The pupil tried desperately to clean up the mess, even using his bare hands to pick out the bits of fetid food, but there was nowhere to put it, apart from in an overflowing bucket. Everyone chuckled at the pathetic sight.

Even 'prof' who had been teased ceaselessly about being a mad professor (Adam had had a dramatic fight with him after putting half cooked bacon in his Rice Crispies one breakfast just to see if he would react) watched the proceedings with great glee, revelling in the spectacle. Probably because he wasn't on the receiving end for once. Yes, tables were turned.

Adam found it ironic that some of the worst culprits were the 'do gooders' and the 'holier than thou's'. They were all enjoying giving out physical and verbal abuse because it was there for free. The problem was, Adam also knew that the same 'group of lads', as the Headmaster liked to call them, would eventually take the blame.

He sat down with Plug and Robbie at half time to survey the scene. Not much had been cleared up. The cleaners were all covered in rotting liquid filth and were scared silly. One in particular had taken a vicious beating and was in the corner bleeding. It didn't look good. Adam was beginning to think that they had gone too far, especially when work resumed and another boy was pushed headlong into the sewage slop. But stopping such a roller coaster was going to be difficult. You could understand exactly why 'Lord of the Flies' had been on the English Literature syllabus, except this time the teachers, by doing not a great deal for years, had acquiesced the whole way along the chain of command.

As the teasing and beatings continued relentlessly by the future head boy and others, Adam began to feel ill. He just couldn't stand it anymore.

It was all leaving a distinctly foul taste in his mouth:

'We're gonna be finished Plug. We'll get scapegoated and we're not even the worst....'

'I know. Fuck'em! I don't care anymore. I wanna go back to Basingstoke. This place is a shit hole'.

And with that they carried on watching. Doing nothing. Adam now felt worse than when he had been one of the main culprits. Sure, he had started the trouble, but hitting turds and humiliating them repeatedly was not part of the plan and it was something he just couldn't stomach, even though he was virtually anaesthetised to violence. Also, it was now obvious that even though they weren't going to hang anybody, they were fast becoming as bad as the leaders or 'Skulls' that had gone before them. Even worse was the fact that Adam had come to some sort of realisation, and had remembered some sort of primitive moral code but at the vital moment had forgotten where he'd put it. He looked over at Plug who was also busy looking into himself. But it was too late.

The result of the cleaning party was critical. Retribution was in the air and the usual five names were read out in the next day's morning assembly. As the names were called out by the Headmaster they all had to stand up in front of the whole school. Far from being humiliating this made them feel like heroes and they smirked round at each other. The fact that they were all Skinheads made it a lot easier for the teachers to identify them, but as Adam had said to Plug he knew they weren't the worst - but Head boy material and his friends got off scot-free. Adam was so incensed that their names had remained off the miscreants list that he wanted to 'grass' on them himself and expose them for what they really were, but he knew it wasn't right to go and tell on someone. It was not amongst their code of honour: 'Shut your mouth and do the punishment', was their motto.

Adam, Plug and Robbie were top of the list. The teachers wanted them out. They just needed a good enough reason because mass expulsions were not popular with the Governors as it hardly reflected a positive light on the School. And in terms of a School League table they were definitely staring another relegation right in the face.

After assembly they were ordered to wait outside the Headmaster's office. One by one they entered his HQ and lined up in front of his huge desk trying not to laugh. None of them really cared any more about the consequences. They just wanted out. The Headmaster informed them of the severity of their behaviour and that this was the final straw in a long catalogue of misbehaviour. Punishment would be swift. After speaking to them as a group, he then spoke to them individually while their comrades waited nervously outside in a line.

As Adam stood in front of him again, the Head browsed through his extensive file which was just as Plug had said. Adam just wished that he could get his mitts on it himself and find out all the juicy gossip. He smirked as he thought of the time that Plug and Louie had broken into the Heads office armed with torches and made themselves at home in the middle of the night: Quaffing from the Head's Brandy decanter: Leafing through the Governors reports: Cutting off the end of a Churchill cigar and spinning in the leather upholstery. The two cat burglars had certainly had a night to remember, that was for sure, and what's more they never got caught.

The Headmaster peered over Adam's reports and told him to take the smile off his face.

'I hope that you realise the gravity of the situation. We at this School will not tolerate bullying in any shape or form. When I spoke to you after your last misdemeanour, you promised to change your ways and become a responsible member of the School. But far from it. You have failed me. I gave you a chance and you have let me down'.

'But….my parents wanted to take me away, sir - '

'Don't interrupt me! You will not interrupt me! Do you hear?'

'Yes, sir….'

Adam had got his goat alright. He knew that Adam's parents had already offered to take him away from the School and put him in a day School in London which Adam would have found much more preferable, despite the problems at home, but the Headmaster wanted to keep him, for the money it would cost for him to stay, even though some of it was being topped up by the State:

'You are insubordinate, rude and lazy. Too easily led by friends whom you choose with little discretion. There is no sense of worth in your behaviour. Let me tell you, this is a very serious matter. Even the Police have been involved in more than one of your past indiscretions. In fact, you are lucky not to have been placed in a reform school before now'.

The headmaster was referring to Adam's annoyance at being dumped by his ex who then went straight out with Robbie. Adam reacted in a very immature fashion which he soon deeply regretted. Once, when Sally was walking on her own, Adam confronted her about dumping him for one of his best friends. Adam obviously felt that she hadn't offered him a sufficient reason and he suddenly lost control and kicked and punched her full in the face. He followed up this crass stupidity by pouring some rancid yoghurt, taken from the kitchens, on all her form books in her locker, which he'd broken open and vandalized. The next thing Adam knew he was in front of the Headmaster again but this time with a Police officer standing right next to him who was going to place him in a reform school.

Sally had been so upset by Adam's behaviour that she had tried to do herself in. Luckily, they managed to save her just in time and get her to Hospital. However, the seriousness of the situation led the Headmaster to try and deal with Adam himself in future, in some sort of personal crusade, and he persuaded the Police to suspend any investigation and luckily, Sally had dropped the charges. Adam was relieved to say the least. He was also deeply upset about the pathetic lashing out. The years of witnessing violence in many areas of his life was beginning to have a profound effect on him. Tension was to be found in a lot of places: at home, at school, at the football, at gigs, down the street, up the street, in his face, in fact, pretty much everywhere. When Adam considered it all, he realised that this sort of behaviour was more and more common currency.

The Headmaster continued with all the sincerity of a Government health warning;

'It is clear that whilst you continue to flout authority you will add up to nothing. Personally, I think that you will never make anything of your life'.

That really hit home. "Never make anything of my life", Adam thought. 'I'll show you….Here I am at the age of fifteen and I've already been chucked on the scrap heap'. What a joke. He now despised even more the proverbial carrot and stick. He now wanted, as Louie had done, to make his own way in whatever he did. He didn't need School. He didn't need poxy qualifications. 'I'll do it all myself', he reasoned naively.

When Adam left the Heads office he was prevented from communicating with anyone. It was obviously to stop any plans of further insurrection. He was told to stand in a corner by the kitchens and await further instructions. There he stood for the next two hours staring cross-eyed at the wall. He knew that they had created a right old stink. Plug, Robbie, and the others had faced the same treatment in front of the Head and were now placed ludicrously all around the School as far away as possible from each other. Plug was the nearest to Adam and he could just about make him out down the long corridor checking out the wall tiles near the School library. When no one was around Plug waved and started laughing. Adam waved back. A teacher patrolling about saw him and shouted:

'Turn and face the wall!'

After the teacher had gone, Adam waved once more to Plug, but unfortunately he was looking the other way. As Adam stood statuesque, he began to think about his ex girlfriend, Sally. The relationship had been on shaky territory for some time, partly because he also fancied another girl from the year below, but wouldn't admit it, that is until it was beyond denial. Adam was at an age where he didn't want to be tied down in a heavy scene and trying to appeal to as many girls as possible was definitely ego boosting. Because of the announcement in the Assembly, Adam knew that the five of them were now everyone's main topic of conversation around the School and if some of the girls in their year didn't like their behaviour they would certainly be impressed with their defiance. 'Great...', Adam thought, 'If I get out of this sticky situation I won't need to chat anyone up so much because they'll be queuing up'. Which was good news, because chatting up girls probably wasn't his strong point.

As time drifted by and he began to replay the events of the last two days once more and speculated on what would happen next, he was this time called by the deputy Head into the School library, looking so furious that his head resembled an oversized beetroot. Adam put on what he thought was a disdainful swagger and nodded to Plug as he entered the library.

What met his eyes nearly knocked him back. The Library had been completely rearranged. All the tables had been placed together in a long line down the middle of the room and virtually every teacher in the School was sat along either side of its length. The Headmaster and Headmistress sat full of pomp at the head of the table. As Adam entered and took in the sight, all attention fixed itself on him. No one spoke. There was a pause as Adam scanned the teachers for a moment. They stared back. The visual fencing was highly intimidating yet something about it was strangely intoxicating. Eventually, he was motioned to sit down on his own at the other end of the table, where an empty chair was placed ready.

'You know why you are here?'

The Headmaster began. Adam nodded lazily.

'Well do you?

'Yes, sir....'

He sat there, awkwardly as if he was in Rumpole of the Bailey, trying to fend off over twenty pairs of eyes probing him in the dock.

'I can't hear you'.

'Yes, Sir'.

'This whole sorry tale of yours has developed over a number of terms. In fact, at least a year ago your games teacher took you aside and privately consulted you about your behaviour....'

Adam looked once more down the long table at the games teacher who was busy looking wearily at his arms folded in front of him. 'I'm not going to get much support from him', Adam reckoned and he was correct. The Headmaster continued.

'Yet you completely ignored his good advice and continued on your own destructive path. I must stress that your current attitude and that of your so-called friends will not be tolerated in this School. Your problems at home cannot and will not be used as an excuse for your flagrant disregard of order. If you are to return to this School after your three week suspension you must change your attitude, become a responsible and trustworthy pupil and you must grow your hair and remove your earring....'

There was silence again for a moment as the teachers scrutinised Adam.

'Despite your recent misbehaviour we are prepared to give you one last chance. We hope that you will see sense. We do not wish to you use the ultimate sanction against you but we will if necessary. Myself, the Headmistress and all of the Governors and staff hope that you will return to the School after your suspension a reformed and compliant individual'.

The dust settled. Adam suddenly thought of the rotting slice of ham which Plug had rebelliously imbedded between the antique pages of one of the Library's large Thesaurus's. 'Grow my hair? Take out my earring? You must be joking!' he thought. 'I'm quite attached to it, thank you. As for the rest you can stick it up your arses'. The whole saga was humiliating and Adam realised that they would repeat this process with Plug and Robbie and the others just for the fun of it. They were revelling in their power trip, reminding him of football thugs surrounding a victim just before kicking them in. But this was just a more sanitised and condoned method, without the laced up boots and the hospital appointment.

Eventually, the Headmaster summed up, and then asked some of the teachers to say a few words about the more positive aspects of Adam's stay at the school. That amounted to his enjoyment of football and a talent for making chocolate cake in Home Economics. Also the woodwork teacher contributed, describing how Adam's initial brilliant creation of a chess board gained him well earned top marks only for the individual pieces to then be concluded over a two year period ending up in a D- on his end of term report and the comment;

'Adam has made slow progress with his chess set. It is time he finished it and moved on to something new'.

After this pointless exercise the Head turned once more to Adam.

'Is there anything that you would like to say?'

There was a pause. Everyone turned towards Adam again in anticipation. He stared back at them defiantly. He wasn't going to let them walk all over him. He was going to show them a brave front in the dock. He considered for a moment and then blurted out.

'If I come back, I want more of a say in things....'

There was a hushed silence. Even Adam couldn't quite believe what he had just said. Then the Headmaster spoke again:

'You will return to this School on one condition and one condition only. That you strive to be a positive and constructive member of the School'.

The Heads' eyes once more bore down.

'You will now go to your dormitory to pack your belongings and wait for the taxi to take you to the train station'.

'Bollocks!' Adam thought. 'I don't want to come back to this lousy, stinking shit heap!' Besides it meant for the first time that he could watch Chelsea on a more regular basis and they had some important matches coming up against relegation.

He strode out of the Library in defiant mood, even though he was escorted by a teacher all the way back to his dormitory. He was still not allowed any contact with his friends, or any contact with the rest of the School. He wasn't even allowed to see the girl that he had recently started fancying or call home.

Adam sat down on his bed. The teacher, who was doing a favourable impression of the head Prison Officer from the popular TV series 'Porridge', eventually left him on his own to pack his things. After a few minutes of mulling over the ridiculous proceedings in the Kangaroo Court, Adam turned on his tape player. He lay on his bed listening to the Pistols, Sham and The Clash. As the first few bars of 'White Riot' jumped out, he thought, 'What's the point of being suspended? The joy of gorging on the big apple of London for a few weeks, only to return to School in perhaps an even more degenerate state than before. No, this is it', he decided. Just as the climactic chords of the Clash song came to a screeching end and the lyrics, 'A riot of my own!' played themselves out again and again in his head, he began to smash the dormitory up. 'No return!' Adam concluded. He was going to require only a one way ticket later in the day. That was certain.

Adam felt that he was making his own private statement even if it sacrificed his whole future. And besides, the School had taught him nothing. So he felt that he had nothing to lose. He began to trash some chairs, smash mirrors, break cupboards, rip up linen, wrench beds apart, bend off the shower heads and block up the toilets.

It was a pretty sad little rebellion, he knew that, but he felt better for it. When he eventually stopped himself, he lay back down on his bed, luckily left intact, and thought, 'I've smashed it up. Why don't I try and put everything back together again', as if to say, 'Here is your order, here is your world, but really it's just fake, because it's useless, it's all flawed'. Adam thought it was a unique idea, and wasn't even bothered if the teachers didn't understand it, as he knew that he would be expelled now anyway.

Eventually, the taxi arrived and luckily, before anyone had discovered the destruction he had caused, Adam was well on his way home. The driver was friendly and they chatted about Bristol City and Chelsea fortunes and the recent postponement of matches due to the bad weather.

Once on the train, homeward bound, Adam began to worry about his parent's reaction: 'Will they ever speak to me again? Will they throw me out of home?' He was still annoyed that he was allowed no contact with any of his friends back at School, 'What had happened to Plug and Robbie? How was his new girlfriend from the year below?'

In the long run, Adam just felt that it was probably for the best and as the train sped it's way to London, he munched on a stale British Rail sandwich and a packet of crisps, preparing himself for the next chapter of his life.

4

SID

After three weeks of soul searching and trying to avoid the understandable wrath of his parents, Adam was finally taken on at an inner London Comprehensive School. Most of the time during his suspension he had attempted to attend a Chelsea match but the terrible winter weather was putting paid to nearly every fixture for what seemed like more than a month. Not that it mattered too much, because Chelsea were having a particularly rotten season.

At least Adam had spoken to his girlfriend who was upset when he told her that he had been notified of his expulsion, for smashing up the dormitory. There was no way he was going back to the School, unless he had a cunning disguise, and he knew a large tin lid had been placed on his relationship and he would probably never see her again. He was now busy doing odd jobs for his parents, as the Headmaster had demanded that Adam pay back the total amount of the damage he had caused. As a result, he was unable to see anyone, although he spoke to Plug briefly on the phone who was returning reluctantly to the School after his suspension. Plug had some serious news hot off the press.

'Vicious's dead!'

'What?!'

'Sid Vicious is dead.'

'No!'

'Yeah'.

'How?'

'Heroin overdose'.

'When?'

'Last night'.

'Christ!'

When Adam looked at it in depth, the news of Sid's death was pretty inevitable. Although he was considered to have little musical talent - he was certainly unable to fill the shoes of Glen Matlock in the song-writing stakes and his bass playing left a lot to be desired - he made up for his lack of musicality with a totally self-destructive rock'n'roll lifestyle. Sid was without doubt the definitive article. The figurehead of Punk. The inventor of the pogo. He looked the part and he played it right to the end. Even though his death was clouded in a murder allegation that he had knifed his girlfriend Nancy Spungeon in the 'Chelsea' Hotel in New York, and his sleazy, drug filled last days were a sad and pathetic epitaph, Adam still felt shock and sorrow that this 'worthless' icon had bitten the dust: Because Sid enjoyed inflicting so much harm on himself, it seemed as if he might in fact be indestructible. Surely, there was little else that could threaten a damaged child let loose in the playground of Punk. Yet, unfortunately, the scourge of Heroin could.

Adam felt that Sid Vicious was a sort of prism of the whole movement: Both the apex and the base all rolled up into an unpleasant but necessary whole. He was Punk and Punk was him. What you saw is what you got and he carved out a career for himself in serious headline-grabbing trouble making. He certainly ruffled the feathers of the establishment in his own inimitable style and I suppose that was what he wanted more than anything: To be somebody. Or something. Though in a peculiarly innocent way even he wasn't quite sure who or what.

Anyway, with Sid dominating the Newspapers in such nihilistic fashion it seemed that Punk, tired though it was, would never go away. Regrettably, his end was another major nail in the coffin and with it the Sex Pistols looked as though they would finally implode. Their days were certainly numbered. Although not before Sid's version of 'Somethin' Else', by Eddie Cochran, was released and sold like extremely hot cakes all the way up the singles chart. People obviously liked it, but Adam felt there was something distinctly corrupt about the whole business: Trading off one already long dead rock icon against another fresher one.

Adam's girlfriend sent him a nice leaving present though. His copy of 'Never Mind The Bollocks', was by this time scratched and unplayable and ready for renewal and as luck would have it she sent him a brand new copy of the album with a thoughtful message written on it:

'This record was bought on the same day that Sid Vicious died!'

There were lots of love and kisses and a promise of undying devotion written on the back of the cover which was always a draw back on a classic Punk record, yet within a month Adam was to hear from Plug by phone that his girlfriend was now another ex as she had started dating someone else at the School:

'Wish her all the best!' Adam said to Plug with just the slightest hint of sarcasm.

So that, as they say, was most definitely that.

SANDWICHES

Adam's new School, a large, imposing inner London Comprehensive was about as far removed from his previous one as you could go. Firstly, you didn't have to wear a uniform and you could go home around 4.00pm which was a novelty since Adam had been used to staying on School premises for what seemed like an eternity until the too infrequent holidays came along.

The School was so big that its buildings resembled a large office block more than a school, with lots of windows and a long wire fence surrounding it. There were more pupils in just one year (around 400) than in the whole of Adam's last School so the fact that he was a very late inclusion into the School made it even more difficult to integrate himself. Unfortunately, exams in the shape of 'O' levels were only just around the corner and he found out to his shock that nearly every subject had a different syllabus, so he knew that he wasn't going to do too well when he came to sit them.

Another major problem was the slight Bristol accent that Adam had acquired hanging out with Mick and his mates in Bedminster and his old School being situated in the West Country certainly didn't help. The pupils at his new School had all heard that he had been turfed out of a boarding environment in 'Yokel land', so they treated him with a large helping of distrust and questions like, 'Where's your Pitchfork?' were commonplace.

These first few weeks in Adam's new centre of learning were one of the loneliest in his life, as he was openly ignored in the class room and in break times he was becoming worried about his own safety. He had thought that at boarding School that he was quite a tough kid but at his new School he was fast becoming aware that he was nowhere near top of the League in that department. He was more likely to be found down the bottom of the Third Division with Mary Poppins. This was made patently clear by a rumour that a dangerous pupil had recently been expelled for bringing an axe and ammonia spray into School just to 'have a go' at one of the teachers. Adam's mini rebellion at his old school seemed like child's play in comparison. Also, fighting in large groups by both boys and girls was a regular occurrence, either between local Schools or between Forms on the nearest park or down at the local shopping centre where a lot of teenagers spent their lunch breaks. There was also a gang of racist Skinheads who always seemed to be at loggerheads with the large Black and Asian contingent at the School. He soon realised that keeping a low profile was definitely preferable to getting kneecapped by the different warring factions. On his own he was an easy target ready to be picked off at will, so camouflaging himself was the name of the game.

As it was impossible to get anyone to talk to him (due to the four or five years that most of the pupils had been together, and maybe it was just because he was a complete stranger) Adam spent much of his time on his own. Eventually, he found himself some sanctuary, ironically right outside the Headmaster's office. It was ridiculous but it was pretty much the only safe haven in the school. During every lunch break Adam would stand right outside the Head's office in order to eat his sandwiches in peace and take a break from the rest of the school. It became such a regular occurrence that the Headmaster was eventually able to set his watch by him.

'What are you doing?' The Head would say with a hint of sympathy in his tone (Maybe he knew that Adam wasn't really that bad a sort after all).

'I'm eating my sandwiches, sir', Adam would counter.

'I see....'

Or,

'You again?'

'Yes, sir'.

'Where are your friends?'

'I haven't got any, sir'.

'Why not?'

'I don't know, sir', shrugging pathetically.

'I see....' he would reply once more and then walk off briskly as if there was a bad smell in the air.

I think after a while the Head was worried about Adam becoming part of the furniture. Anyway, there Adam would stand, next to the office by a large rubber plant, enjoying his sandwiches while all around the school, pupils were busy getting up to no good.

His mum made him a variety of different sandwiches over this period, one of his favourites were those with Sandwich Spread in them. Adam spent a lot of time in lessons thinking, 'I wonder what's in my sandwiches today? Tomato? Or pickle?' He never looked at his sandwiches until the very last moment so as to give himself a surprise. This was because the canteen food wasn't the best and every menu consisted of chips and beans followed by beans and chips or if you were really fortunate, chips and chips. Also, food fights would usually be the order of the day and as Adam was a suitable target and known as the 'Bumpkin' he wanted to keep well out of the way of rancid cabbage and flying Spotted Dick.

Eventually, with the repetitive break times taking their toll, Adam came to the conclusion that the best way to make friends was to play football on the school yard. Although this was fraught with danger, there being various gangs who would usually fight against each other and dispute

226

everything, including the result, it was the only solution to avoid him being placed permanently in a large frame outside the Headmasters office.

RECORDS

As Adam was enthusiastic and supported a London team, much to everyone's surprise, he soon became a fixture on the yard at lunch breaks. There were also plenty of Chelsea supporters who would stick up for each other and soon he began to make friends.

One of them was also in the same year and was a brilliant goalkeeper. His name was Alex, and although he dressed more like a Mod, he was an avid Punk rock record collector. He lived near the school and it wasn't long before Adam went round his house for a cup of tea and to look at his vinyl collection. His older brother was a keen Punk rocker too, who had seen the Sex Pistols live at the 100 Club in 1976 and that impressed Adam enormously. He had never seen so many singles and albums packed away in boxes and Schweppes crates. They had a massive record collection. Alex had all the early Pistols, even the deleted A&M 'God Save The Queen' single, in mint condition which was worth a fortune and he had a wide variety of other rarities and bootlegs, coloured vinyls, and records by little known bands such as The Desperate Bicycles and Those Naughty Lumps. He had a van load of brilliant American Punk and an original copy of 'Blank Generation', by Richard Hell and the Voidoids, a terrific track, with inspired lyrics about youth alienation which his brother had given to him on his birthday. So inspired was it that Hell had come up with the idea of a blank space both in the chorus of the song and on the lyric sheet, which was all about belonging to a ..... generation.

Alex had another great US release, 'I hate the Rich' by The Dils and he had all of the releases by The Ramones, The Dickies (Adam loved their cover of 'Banana Splits') , the Dead Boys, the Tubes, Patti Smith, Television, early Blondie and the transexual Wayne County and the Electric Chairs.

Adam's mate even had lots of continental Punk. He had some French Punk in the shape of the Stinky Toys and a copy of 'Paris Marquis' by Metal Urbain (Rough Trade's first single release) which Plug had already kindly translated for Adam at school. He also had some illusive

German and Dutch rarities too.

Of British Punk, if Alex didn't have it, then it wasn't worth talking about and his collection was more than impressive. He had 'I am a Dalek' by the Art Attacks which Adam loved because it had particularly silly lyrics impersonating a Dalek and reminded him of Doctor Who. There was 'Terminal Stupid' by the Snivelling Shits, another 45 in the collection, which was another top tune, championing complete youth knuckle-headedness.

He even had the first two singles by the Punk band, Chelsea. Adam would end up collecting most of their records and see them many times down at the Marquee. Alex had all the Clash singles, the Damned, The Jam, Sham 69, the Cortinas, the Lurkers, The Slits, UK Subs, Subway Sect, Crisis, Menace, ATV, Slaughter and the Dogs, The Members, X-Ray Spex, Public Image, The Stranglers, Eater, The Adverts, UK Decay, Killing Joke, Generation X, 999, Spizz-Oil, Penetration, Ian Dury and the Blockheads, Magazine, Wire, The Vibrators, The Saints, Elvis Costello, The Wall, The Skids, The Ruts, The Buzzcocks, Tubeway Army, Siouxsie and the Banshees, Stiff Little Fingers, Crass, and Adam and the Ants, all in different coloured vinyls and zany, eye-catching picture sleeves.

Alongside the records, Alex also showed Adam his fanzine collection, an independently produced newspaper, that were usually a couple of pages of xeroxed information about different Punk bands, though some of the fanzines could be quite elaborate magazines about everything concerned with Punk. Their cost ranged from about 10 to 25p. Adam was amazed. Fanzines were almost like comics, which Adam had devoured in his early years. They seemed to cater for all interests and the first one Adam bought had a brilliant article on Adam Ant, the interview taking place on a park bench. Usually the main focus of the fanzine was on going to gigs, collecting records and Punk paraphernalia in general, but the all important fan in the street was never taken for granted. One fanzine claimed to give 'Great street level insight to the top fan enthusiast'. Some of the names of the fanzines were memorable too: Ripped and Torn, Short Circuit, It Ticked and Exploded, Sniffin' Glue, Life in a Void, In the City, Alternative Ulster, The Quality of Life, Dayglow, Negative Reaction.

BONE IDOL

Alex was to make Adam the best Punk compilation cassette tape he had ever heard, with a lot of his rare stuff included and put it all on one C120 cassette tape, so Adam had a good hour and half of optimum recreational listening when he got back home. In the following months the cassette would drive his parents completely mad. Just when they thought the tape had come to an end, there was a moment of fumbling around in Adam's bedroom as he turned the tape over and placed it back in the cassette player, then seconds later the opening track would blare out again, which happened to be 'New Rose' by The Damned (the very record that Adam had seen originally advertised in the Chelsea matchday programme). It had a mind blowingly good introduction. First you heard the singer Dave Vanian announce; 'Is she really going out with him?' Then a thumping tribal drum beat launched in, quickly followed by a glorious galloping sledgehammer guitar riff and then a loud, throat wrenching 'AAHH!' by the singer, taking the song into the first verse. It was a delicious cacophony. In Adam's opinion one of the best Punk songs ever. Whenever he listened to it he just couldn't contain himself. He would sing along to the lyrics in a loud wailing voice even if he didn't know exactly what the words were and the more out of tune the better. He would mimic the guitar parts with screeching and howling and tap out the drum beats manically on a tea mug or the bedside table. Adam didn't find it easy sitting still. In fact sometimes he even started climbing the walls of his bedroom, when some especially demented singing and drums like crashing dustbins broke out again later in the song. One thing was for sure. It can't have been easy-listening for his parents and it was lucky that the pet dog Sam wasn't around anymore, because he would have gone nuts.

Adam was often ordered to turn it down, on pain of being thrown out on the street and he always found it difficult to wait till there was no one about so that he could put the volume back up to the max. For Adam it was just a matter of taste. The next track after 'New Rose' was the Damned's 'Problem Child' and unfortunately for his parents and the neighbours it had a similar effect on Adam as the previous number had. The guitar work was searing. The drumming lunatic.

Alex had recorded for Adam another great song by the Manchester Punk band the Drones, called 'Bone Idol', which he thought would make a brilliant image for the back of his black leather jacket (Adam eventually saw the band live just before they split up at a club down Oxford Street with Dan, another good Punk friend of his). The picture sleeve for the record showed a skeleton sitting on a toilet seat smoking a large spliff. It was stark - white on black. The words, 'Bone Idol', were written above the picture also in white. The back of the sleeve had a picture of the band and 'I just wanna be myself' the title of the B-side printed in big letters over it.

Next time Adam saw Alex he proposed a bit of artwork;

'Everyone's either got Adam and the Ants'- 'Whip in my Valise' on the back of their jackets, or a picture of a rabid dog with Slaughter and the Dogs written above it'.

'Yeah, you're right', Alex agreed.

'I'm gonna put the 'Bone Idol' picture on the back of my jacket?'

'How?'

'I'm gonna paint it'.

'Paint it?'

'Yeah. It'll be a laugh. And it'll look really good'.

'Bit difficult to paint it, I reckon', Alex countered.

'No trouble', Adam replied.

A few days later Adam bought the single from the 'Wretched Records' stall in Soho market and returned home to paint his leather jacket. This is where his years of painting Airfix kits as a kid would come in really useful. He copied the picture sleeve exactly down to the last detail in white paint. He had to be very careful because he was using gloss paint to make it both waterproof and really stand out, so he couldn't afford to make any mistakes. Luckily, Adam managed to create the same skeletal outline and the toilet seat looked identical. He made the 'spliff' a tiny bit longer and this made the picture even more comic. Then he left the jacket to dry, well contented with his work.

When Adam returned later, he studied his jacket, the words 'Bone Idol' standing out dramatically above the skeleton. It looked great, and what's more he reckoned it would probably be unique. The next thing was to wear it out and about: on the tube or while shopping or waiting for a bus or just about anywhere, even perhaps at Stamford Bridge. He wore the jacket to a few gigs and sometimes punks would come up to him, after clocking the picture;

'I really like the jacket, mate. Who did it?'

'I did'.

'You did? It looks more like a stencil'.

'No, it's painted. I painted it'.

'Well, it looks great. Everyone's either got Slaughter and the Dogs or Adam and the Ants on back of theirs'.

'Yeah, I know', Adam would reply sheepishly and walk off happy with his days toil.

He also painted 'Chelsea' on the back of the jacket at the top, which was always a little double edged;

'Chelsea are shit they are!'

'It's not the football team, it's the band', Adam replied.

'Oh….they're good they are. 'Right to Work' - good single that. Yeah, good band!'

Or,

'Chelsea are a crap load of tossers!'

'It's not the band, it's the football team', Adam informed.

'Oh, good man, good man! You know, I get down to the 'Bridge' myself, occasionally'.

You see you always needed to be one step ahead.

Badges were the finishing touch on the front of the jacket and Adam had a wide variety on the folded lapels. One particular favourite stated:

'Support your local Police. Break the Law'.

Another said:

'Fight War Not Wars', above a haunting image of a helmeted soldier.

There was a limitless choice of badges and any statement, caption or thought for the day could be economically captured on them. Adam's taste in music and his favourite bands were obvious for all to see as he 'caught that bus' or 'visited the launderette'.

Mixing styles was popular with Punk. For example, at any one time Adam would probably possess a pair of thick soled 'brothel creeper' shoes (Ted), leather jacket (Rocker - Soul boy), DM's (Skinhead), 'drainpipes' (Rocker), Bondage trousers (Punk), Mohair sweater (Soul boy), Dinner Jacket (Mod), luridly coloured socks (Ted), Slogan T-shirts (Punk), Harrington (Skinhead), Bum-flap (Punk), Ripped up Pegs (Soul boy), Bootlace tie (Ted), PVC's (new wave) and jumble them all together. It was fun mixing up the uniforms of different subcultures. Adam thought it used to really annoy people.

The first Punk garment that Adam ever purchased was through a mail order catalogue. He ordered a cheap pair of black PVC drainpipe trousers from some shady outfitters in the City. The arrival of his acquisition took about a week and was awaited with great anticipation. When the parcel arrived Adam retired to his bedroom for a fitting. Unfortunately, the drainpipe trousers were so tight that he had to hold his breath just to get them on and sitting down was not an option unless he undid the waist button and the zip, which he soon realised would be very revealing in the High street. Everything would have been hanging out. It was silly. Adam really needed to have tried the trousers on in a shop. He concluded that ordering clothes by mail order would result in him looking completely ridiculous: Either the clothes were so tight that they were absolute torture to wear and it wouldn't be long until he required first aid, or they were so loose that pedestrians were bound to trip over him.

However, Adam persevered with the PVC's, thinking that as long as he stayed standing they looked pretty cool and with the addition of one of his home made punk T-shirts, he certainly felt the part. One day he was preparing to go out in his new trousers when he made the unfortunate mistake while getting ready of smoking on the job. The cigarette somehow got too close to the PVC for comfort and before you could say 'Anarchy' his highly inflammable purchase was beginning to melt whilst he was still inside them. This was most certainly the quickest change of clothes Adam had ever undertaken. He felt it was a shame he never got to wear the trousers outdoors. Anyway, that was now impossible, because one leg had completely melted away.

Accessories, like padlocks on chains and studded wrist bands and belts were a useful commodity. For quite some time Adam wanted to copy Sid Vicious, who frequently wore a small padlock and chain around his neck. A nice thick chain with a Chubb on the end, or any other chunky lock was ideal. Adam found one that was just like Sid Vicious' only even bigger, but made two silly mistakes: fitting the chain too tight and also mislaying the key to the padlock.

As a result, he spent the next few days trying to get the chain off again. He finally had to file it away, which was a most awkward and embarrassing operation and his parents despaired as they could hear pained filing noises coming from his bedroom. Eventually, he got the chain off, at that triumphant moment it felt as if he had escaped from Alcatraz, only to discover that his neck was now completely covered in metal filings, that were a nightmare to wash off.

Hair dye was another important feature of the fashion conscious punkster, originally stolen from the Soul boy obsession with hair colouring and highlighting. Adam on the other hand could never quite sort out exactly what he was trying to do with it. Experimentation was all and unfortunately, subtlety was nowhere to be found. Well, especially not on the hair follicles.

Adam's first dyed look was a bright blue rinse over a number one crop. He wanted to resemble the Chelsea kit. The brighter the better. The only problem was the blinding crazy colour, which was so bright that once dry, Adam's head resembled a royal blue light bulb. He should have carried a government health warning at all times advising people to look at him only with the aid of sunglasses and to keep well away, because he might be radioactive. Adam usually tried to go out only after dark for the benefit of the populace and this would also help to avoid the inevitable hassle from frightened onlookers.

Adam also experimented with bright green hair dye which was a short lived look, because it made him seem like one of the undead. Orange was more favourable, because although it was bright and ostentatious, it had a cheerful feel about it and was preferred by family and friends. Neighbours expressed their preference for it as well.

Adam's personal favourite was bleach. This could make you look as though Sting was your older brother, or that was the attempt anyway, girls always seeming to like the image of the pouting Police vocalist. One afternoon in the school toilets, Adam decided to put in as much peroxide as possible to make what he thought was a real stinging statement. Unfortunately, he forgot to use any conditioning liquid, which came with the peroxide to lessen the bleaching effect and his hair turned out whiter than white with great horrible yellow clumps in it, as if someone had eaten a particularly bad meal and decided to throw up on his head. Not only that, but his hair started to fall out in lumps on his pillow due to the acidic peroxide and he had a few nervous weeks worrying that he might lose all his hair and might have to resort to a thinly swept Bobby Charlton parting.

SHAM'S LAST STAND

It was the summer holidays of 1979, and Adam had just left school after failing his exams. He was feeling empty and directionless just like Chelsea, who had already been relegated to the Second Division once again after winning only five matches.

During his first spell as an unemployed statistic, Adam applied for apprenticeships with Gas companies, and he had even tried to become an electrician, Christ knows why, because he was totally useless at Physics and anything wired together by him would probably blow up in the not too distant future. It was a forlorn attempt at trying to find himself a niche in the world, a sense of purpose, but Adam knew deep down that there had to be more to life than checking people's meters or queuing up in a long line every two weeks for what was virtually pocket money.

So Adam started to consider the possibility of being in a band. This however was unrealistic, because he had no musical ability that he knew of, in fact the one time he had a try on a fellow pupil's guitar in the music room at school he could hardly play a note and the classically overplayed riff from 'Smoke on the Water' by Deep Purple was all that anyone could or would play and even that was way beyond Adam's musical horizons. Despite this hurdle, he knew that he had a good ear for a tune, especially having been well educated by his brother's in the musical department. All he needed to do was to scrutinize the bands that he went to see and learn from them. The other problem was that in front of large audiences Adam was sometimes affected by crippling shyness, so much so, that occasionally he would have to go and throw up or hide in the toilet for three hours to escape reading out aloud in class. But from now on, he would at least try to put wheels in motion, because he didn't want to end up a member of the rat race, to him that seemed like a living death.

Around the last week of July, Adam and his mates Plug and Dave decided to go to see Sham 69 at the Rainbow in Islington. The gig was billed as 'Sham's Last Stand', although the band's fortunes had been on and off for a few months because of the outbreaks of violence at their gigs. But this concert seemed like it really would be their last. Sham had had many successful singles, the awesome 'Angels with Dirty Faces', the irrepressible 'Borstal Breakout', the football terrace anthem 'If the Kids are United', the stomping 'Hurry up Harry', the emphatic 'Questions and Answers' and the barn storming recently released 'Hersham Boys' which was clambering up the charts and had been on Top of the Pops. But Sham's success could still not control the unpredictability of their audience, who considered a good night out meant that lots of people had been hospitalised. Everyone knew that the gig would be alarming in the violence department but it was probably the last chance of seeing them. Also Adam had really liked them for some time, so this was the opportunity not to be missed.

The music press considered Sham 69 as a socially conscious working-class band from 'the Sticks', the outer London suburb of Hersham, and for that reason were still considered very much Punk. They also had one of the most charismatic lead singers in Jimmy Pursey, who sang without question from the heart. Their sound was critical too, like a wall of amplification, it assaulted the senses. The guitarist, Dave Parsons also had a knack of coining a simple but brilliant guitar riff that would be both catchy and memorable. Detractors accused them of being a stadium rock band or a sub standard Slade, but by the middle of 1979, in Adam's and many other's opinions, they pissed proverbially all over The Clash who were now far too busy coiffeuring their hair down Sunset Boulevard and hanging out of Cadillac's in the good old U.S of A.

Despite this however, Sham had always attracted a hardcore Skinhead following, probably because they owed more to the football terraces than a prevalent art school approach to Punk. 'What you see is what you get', and this was both a blessing and a burden to Jimmy Pursey, or Jimmy 'Sham', the man of the people. More importantly, this street 'cred' or grassroot feel to the band was used by the right wing, especially the National Front, as a vehicle to spout it's bigotry.

During the late 70's, Fascist groups had begun to move into music as a populist alternative to what was seen as boring, stuffy old politics, and left wing organisations like 'Rock against Racism' and the 'Anti-Nazi League' quickly sprang up to counter them. The irony was that the original Skinhead movement had been an appreciation of 60's roots reggae and Ska, but unfortunately, it's 'uniform' was both urban and aggressive so it was ideal for foot soldiers of the far right who could win on the street what they found difficult to win at the ballot box.

Sham's large skinhead following was also from all over the United Kingdom and this made for a lethal concoction, when for example the Kent Crew would decide to have a pop at the East End Skins to see who was the hardest. This was a blind alley that there was absolutely no way out of, and Sham 69 were more often than not the revved up vehicle careering out of control.

The background picture certainly made Adam uneasy, and he knew that he had been probably wearing the wrong outfit for some time, combining in his appearance what he knew was a Punk look with a Skinhead feel: close-cropped dyed hair, painted leather jacket, bondage trousers and Dr Martens. Sometimes he would wear army fatigues or a donkey jacket. For some stupid reason for the Sham 69 gig he opted for a bright blue mohair sweater and ripped up trousers. This was going to be a big mistake.

Earlier in the day, Jimmy Pursey had appeared on the TV as a guest on 'Juke Box Jury' and he seemed in high spirits despite Sham's imminent demise. There were plans afoot to link up with ex-Pistols Steve Jones and Paul Cook and continue as the Sex Pistols. Furthermore, new material was being worked on (including a storming version of 'Day Tripper' by the Beatles and a ten minute 'Borstal Breakout'). Other material was also being developed for inclusion in the soundtrack to the film 'Quadrophenia' (it was a partnership that was hampered by contractual wrangles and disagreements and never really took off, although they did appear live with this line up).

When Adam and Plug arrived outside the Rainbow concert hall

to meet Dave, there was already a large presence of Skinheads; all Sta-Prest, Fred Perry's, tattoos, DM boots, cut-off bleached jeans, Harringtons, belts and braces, crew cuts, Crombies, Sovereign rings, Loafers, chewing gum, steel toe caps and cigarettes behind the ear. It was like an appreciation society for Alex from 'A Clockwork Orange', but judging by the look of some of the meatheads present even the Droogs would have settled for a quiet night in with pipe and slippers. Adam suddenly felt a combination of fear and adrenalin, that heady cocktail he always recognised at dangerous Chelsea away matches. The funny thing was that he had to admit this fear had become somehow intriguing. Adam found it exciting. It was a stupid, crazy risk, like playing Russian roulette with five bullets in the revolver.

They finally met up with Dave, and handed out the tickets that they'd bought the previous week and entered the venue. They tried to get a drink at the bar as soon as possible, thinking that some booze might help to numb the senses if there was any trouble. The interior of the Rainbow was enormous. It normally seated around 2,000 people downstairs and around another 500 upstairs. Now it looked even bigger than normal, because all the seats had been taken out. Adam suddenly calculated, 'That's been done to fit more people inside so they can make more money out of us and bugger the consequences'. Dave agreed with Adam that the atmosphere was definitely not all sweetness and light;

'Fuckin' hell, it's all Skinheads!'

'Yeah, I know', Adam replied. 'I feel right out of place'.

Luckily, Plug fitted in fairly well. He happened to have close cropped hair and he looked the absolute deadringer for the lad on the cover of one of Richard Allen's 'Skinhead' series of books. He was also wearing an army jacket and boots. The three amigos stuck together, supped their beer and hugged the pillars and shadows at the side of the auditorium. And waited. The place was filling up fast and the sound system was being put through its paces with the likes of Stiff Little Fingers, who Adam would see later in the year at Brockwell Park. They were a Northern Irish punk band, from Belfast, who had a mind altering - in your face - song called 'Suspect Device', about the tension and strife in their native heartland. Menace's thumping urban myth 'G.L.C', was followed by the pathological Ska-Punk of 'Babylon's Burning' by The Ruts, which had recently charted. Talk about getting the evening underway.

However, the Skinheads didn't seem to enjoy the choices of the resident DJ and accompanied the selections with jeers. They wanted a lot more original Ska from the 60's. They were not averse even to a request or two, shouting for a bit of present Two Tone from Madness, Selector or Special Aka. What they were all unified about was their allegiance to the main band; 'We want Sham!' they cried. Adam had been reading in some of the music papers that week, that a lot of Sham's Skinhead following would do their best to prevent them from playing. What a paradox. The band they loved, yet wanted to stop. Interestingly, there seemed little evidence of an ulterior motive in this action, as people believed there was with some of the Sex Pistols almost manufactured trouble. This was just pure naked aggression for the hell of it.

The first support band of the night, were the Little Roosters and they appeared on the stage and quickly got underway. But there was a feeling of discontent. No one had come to see the support band, and if they were rubbish they would more than likely be forced off the stage and returned quickly to where they had come from. A sigh of relief soon gripped Adam - they weren't bad, and they played simple rabble rousing two minute anthems, and although they lacked that little bit of extra cohesion to really make them memorable, they were good enough not to annoy the swelling audience.

As plastic glasses were refuelled, the first band left and again the Rainbow Disc Jockey struck up some more tunes for the discerning punters. Only this time it was 'I Fought the Law', from the Cost of Living EP, by The Clash, which had also recently charted. It was definitely The Clash because this really riled the large skinhead contingent, especially now Mr Alcohol was beginning to have his effect. Different groups started roaming around the auditorium, shouting 'We hate Clash!', 'We hate Punk!'. And if it wasn't that, it was, 'We hate Chelsea!' or 'We hate West Ham!' 'Wonderful', Adam pondered, 'a right old selection of football thuggery has arrived'. He felt as if he was in an episode of Star Trek, surrounded on all sides by Klingons, desperately seeking Scottie to transport him to safety. Adam wanted to be anywhere else but there, except perhaps Millwall's 'Den', but it was a close run thing.

Luckily, the next support band arrived on stage - lucky because Dave had decided to wear his favourite Clash T-Shirt to the gig and most of the attention switched back again to the stage. It was Tenpole Tudor, a devotee and substitute in the Sex Pistols, who would be best known for his silly hit 'Who Killed Bambi'. His stage demeanour was all histrionic fumbling, and his vocal delivery spluttered like Iggy Pop on Helium. Despite this, Tenpole got a surprisingly large round of applause, probably because the last thing he was going to do was to threaten the Skinheads hard earned machismo. He had an absurd comic element that wouldn't upset the apple cart, and his recent single, 'Swords of a Thousand Men' had done well in the charts and was a catchy number. His band had a quirky, almost camp feel about them - all Sid Vicious's dressed as Musketeers.

More importantly, Tenpole could laugh at himself, and he needed too because as his set progressed and the funny, cheeky silliness subsided, so-called humorous chants of 'Poof', 'Cunt' and 'Tosser' resounded around the auditorium and bounced back off the walls. This was without doubt the show that Adam didn't take his Grandma or his new girlfriend to.

Adam, Plug and Dave watched intently as Tenpole Tudor launched into his high pitched whining. He sang just like John Lydon would have done had Lydon suddenly decided that he was a little bit more happy and content with the world. The PA system was also noticeably louder now and the impressive lighting rig came into its own, shedding red, blue and orange hypnotically around the stage.

The mass of Skinheads had begun to loosen up and enjoy themselves, at everyone else's expense. They massed in the middle of the huge dance floor to jump, strut, flex, pose, threaten, cajole, taunt and strike up stroboscopic attitude. You certainly knew if you belonged, and Adam didn't. He had the wrong mind set and the wrong clothes. In fact it was worse than that, he was a mixture of styles, a hybrid, a 'ponce' hijacking as he was, 'looks', from different subcultures, and Skinheads were most particular about loyalty - it was usually stamped on their knuckles. Nuremberg came to mind and the 1936 Olympics, so did a hot cup of milk and an early night. In retrospect, that would have been so much more preferable. (This gig wasn't the same sort of malevolence as the violent 'Crass' gig's that Adam queued up for but never managed to get into. This one was far worse and he would have swapped it willingly for any of the others - even a notorious Dead Kennedys gig at the Music Machine where a vicious glass fight between Skinheads and Punks broke out near the bar).

'What the hell's gonna happen when Sham come on stage?' Adam queried.

'We'll go down the front and do a bit of pogoing', said Plug.

'Yeah, it'll be alright. There'll be so many punters, no one'll be able to move about', Dave added.

They were probably right. Even if there was trouble, when Sham came on they'd be down the front packed in near the stage, so they'd be safe. Besides, Jimmy Pursey, the voice of the kids, would see them alright. He'd make sure they came to no harm and anyway Plug and Dave hailed from Basingstoke, which was even on the same train line to London as Hersham, where Sham 69 originated. As a result, they almost considered themselves 'Hersham Boys', anyway something close to an allegiance, which felt like it might protect them in their hour of need.

Tenpole Tudor finally left the stage, to muted applause and wolf whistling. This almost seemed to be the signal for the Skinhead crews to purge the venue of their enemies. Punks were being pulled out into the middle of the dance floor where various lump heads would be waiting to try out their industrial slippers. It was a free for all, anyone who fancied agro just helped themselves. As noses splintered and heads cracked open, the Rainbow management were busy divesting themselves of all responsibility. The bouncers that were in evidence had decided to let the Skins rule supreme, because they were heavily outnumbered by about a hundred to one, and so they royally shat themselves. They weren't the only ones. Adam was beginning to succumb to extreme fear too. If it went on for much longer he'd probably need a change of underwear.

As fellow Punks and assorted youths littered the outskirts of the dance floor with kicked in faces, Adam surveyed the scene and it didn't look encouraging. The violence was psychopathic but clinical. Targets were being literally picked out of the crowd for slaughter:

'What the fuck are you gonna do about your Clash T-shirt?' Plug shot across Dave's bow.

'I'll be alright', Dave replied with a nervous gulp.

'Oh yeah! The Skins are gonna do us, mate'. Plug countered.

Then, before the three could argue any further, there was a sudden blast of sonic as if from within the depths of the venue. Sham were about to appear, and the ominous overture to 'A Clockwork Orange' rang loud and clear. As the menacing introduction grew in intensity, a cutting announcement came over the PA system and almost before Adam realised the band emerged defiant, ready to crank themselves up with an ear splitting roar. They didn't hang about, smashing straight into their first single, 'I Don't Wanna', and the whole auditorium exploded. The sound level was thunderous and whacked right up to eleven. The drumming was titanic, all crashing dustbins. Dave Parsons strutted and pulverised his guitar, a classic cherry red SG Gibson, seen on many a classic photo or picture sleeve. Treganna's lively, solid bass playing was like good mechanics: making sure the awesome engine ran at optimum pitch. As for Jimmy Pursey, he wasn't so much singing as retching out his anger for all the world to see. After only one song you could usually find his tonsils lodged against the back wall. The short and to the point opening number ended to a huge cheer and Adam could tell that this evening, Sham 69 were definitely not going to be taking any prisoners. Unfortunately nor were a large majority of the audience.

Sham's next song, 'What Have We Got' reinforced their intent, its usual chanted reply of 'I got you' changed to 'Fuck All!' This was a brilliant rallying cry and as the three lads chanted and tried to force their way further to the front, many of the Skins had the same idea. How Adam was still alive at this moment he'd never know, but the blood was certainly pumping, with his heroes belting out their anthems right in front of him. Unfortunately, a stage invasion was definitely in the air. It was only a matter of time. Sham's next song 'Red London', a socially aware tune that riled the Skrewdriver loving element and didn't fit at all snuggly with the identikit Fascism that was being flaunted to the misery of all rock'n'roll loving youth, lit the fuse.

It wasn't so much pogoing, as a swaying mass of bodies and contorted flesh. The Skins now possessed the large space in front of the stage and were 'Sieg Heiling' en masse. Adam would never forget the hate on their faces. They didn't give a fuck about the music. They didn't give a fuck about anything. Pursey certainly knew this and tried desperately to prevent more trouble in between the songs. He exploited every avenue. Joking with them. Pleading with them. Even trying to talk with them on a one to one basis. But it was to no avail. His pleas fell on deaf ears. Fisticuffs were erupting all over the place as Adam, Plug, and Dave tried to dodge various missiles that were now stage bound. It was such a shame because Sham were literally on fire. The songs they played and the integrity they played them with was awesome. One of the most incredible performances Adam had ever seen and this was under serious provocation. The band continued valiantly with 'That's Life', a great tune about a day in the life of an ordinary bloke. After the song, an aggression filled gap then signaled the next number, an absolute classic. Everyone held their breath, as did the band and then the whole place went up. There was an ear splitting scream of feedback from Parsons' strangled guitar and Pursey slowly spat out the words:

'Who's got a dirty face then?!'

Then the bass and drums kicked in as well with a staccato, pile driving phrase and everywhere fists, heads, elbows and boots came into crunching contact. It was a Rottweiller with a bone that just wouldn't let go. Before the first chorus was even over, the Skinheads were getting a foothold on the stage. They were doing their best to stop the gig. They wanted their fifteen minutes of infamy. Their fifteen minutes of power. By the second chorus, boot boys had infiltrated the stage to such a degree that Pursey's microphone was sure of being stolen at any moment. Skins screamed 'Angels with Dirty Faces!' and 'Sham!' as worried roadies and inadequate security tried to push back the tide. But the 'one' that they managed to eject off the stage was soon replaced by two more nutcases eager to stand up and be counted.

Dave Parsons was beginning to look forlorn, now hardly able to play, so surrounded as he was by short haired herberts. The band moved back further as the mob closed in. It was becoming farcical, and before Adam could fully appreciate what was happening right before his eyes, the safety curtain came down and Sham had disappeared. And with it their hopes. Pursey was seething. His celebratory final gig now in absolute tatters. But there was nothing that he could do.

It was bedlam. In front of the curtain Skinheads reprised the various football chants and loud Sieg Heil's were spitted out again with relish. After the few minutes of stunned hiatus, an announcement came over the PA system that Sham would only return if everyone left the stage immediately. The Skinheads were the culprits, there wasn't any doubt about that and eventually some members of the audience in front of the stage tried to pluck up the courage to demand that the thugs get off the stage so the band could return.

Dave who was by this time more than fed up of seeing his beloved band's farewell destroyed by imbeciles, pleaded, Adam couldn't believe why, with one of the burliest, hardest looking Skins prowling the front of the stage.

'Oi, mate! Get off the stage. We want Sham....'

Adam and Plug exchanged worried glances. Up to this point they had both been diligently concerned with self preservation and now Dave was going down the road of no return. As the Skinhead wheeled round and leered down at them, the veins in his head pulsated:

'Fuck off, you wankers!'

Dave tried again.

'Look, I don't want no trouble. I wanna see Sham'.

'You fucking cunt!'

'Please mate. Look - '.

'Fuck off! And yer fucking Clash!'

'But - '

Just as Adam was thinking, 'Dave, why did you wear your favourite Clash T-shirt?!' the nutter dived off the stage straight onto him. It all happened like lightning. Before Plug and Adam could even consider coming to Dave's aid, a head-butt had rained in on him, followed by a hail of knuckles and flashes of sole. This Skinhead could certainly handle himself alright. It was his speciality. The blitzkrieg bop.

Dave hit the ground with a thump and the Clash hating Skin continued to abuse his footwear. Dave was soon curled up into the foetal position and was taking the beating valiantly. Adam and Plug could do nothing but watch their mate get punished repeatedly to chants of 'You cunt!' Then without any explanation, the Cyclops backed off, proud of his work and Seig Heiled fervently over our flailing friend before walloping Dave one last time. He then rejoined his troops triumphantly out on the dark dance floor, almost to a round of applause. Amazingly, while this skirmish played itself out, the edge of the stage had now become completely vacant.

As Adam and Plug picked Dave off the floor, dusted him down and moved him to safety at the side of the auditorium, the curtain went up and Sham returned, again to a huge cheer. Incredibly, Dave had nothing broken. The head-butt had caused a bruise on his forehead and his nose was running red from a fist which ruined his shirt, and he had a couple of sore ribs, but apart from that he was okay, if a little dazed. He was just more than pleased that he was still breathing and that Sham had reappeared.

Pursey took a few minutes to thank the audience for allowing the band back on and he pleaded with those whose thoughts were still on sabotage:

'We wanna play. We wanna play for you. Fighting won't help!'

Unfortunately, Sham continued where they left off with 'Angels with Dirty Faces', and the feeding frenzy continued. Perhaps a slow ballad might have taken the sting out of the Skinheads tails, but Sham didn't have much in the way of soft ballads or love songs in their repertoire. The atmosphere around was disquieting. The band were now travelling on a one way elevator ride to hell. Eventually, 'Angels' finished in a flurry of feedback, guitar and drums, but there was going to be no respite because immediately afterwards the first few devastating bars of 'Borstal Breakout' rang out. The band were in awesome form, Pursey literally assaulting the song. On record, the song was introduced by a psychotic cry and the slam of a prison door, while the middle section of the number was accompanied with smashing glass and the sounds of a full scale riot. You could argue that it wasn't perhaps the right song for the occasion, but Sham continued the gut wrenching terrace anthem regardless. As Pursey continued his vocal tirade, the mayhem offstage turned even uglier. A full scale ruck was now underway between loyal Sham fans and the Hitler youth. Regrettably there was only ever going to be one winner. The Skins reinvaded the stage and as the sledgehammer chords of 'Breakout' dwindled, you could see that for Pursey the final nail in the coffin had struck home. He looked pallid. Above the battle, he shouted out what seemed like a muffled, 'What's the fuckin' point!' and threw his microphone to the ground with disgust. He then wandered upstage in a rage, and as he passed the drum kit he pushed the bass drum over and shouted:

'I've had enough!'

Then he stormed offstage. The rest of the band in hot pursuit. That was it. Sham 69 were history after only having played for about twenty minutes.

After Sham had gone forever, the Skinheads continued to punch anyone in their path. Luckily, the trio were off to the side of the stage and near a side exit so they didn't hang about waiting for Pursey to re-emerge again. Their thoughts were now even more set on self preservation.

They clumped up some concrete steps towards a large exit door and gave out a huge sigh of relief as they burst out of the Rainbow into the humid night air. It was time to take stock.

Considering the situation, casualties were slight. Dave, although foolhardy, had survived the lion's fury and Adam and Plug were silently impressed by his single mindedness, even though they were lucky not to be involved too. Plug was always immune to any physical confrontation, unless left with no alternative and could certainly talk his way out of a sticky situation. Adam, on the other hand, probably deserved a good pasting, especially when he thought about what he was wearing, but he just walked around pinching himself and deliriously put it all down to lady luck. But he didn't count all his chickens at once, because they still had to make that more than dangerous journey home.

As they debriefed, Dave, who was never able to miss an opportunity turned round.

'Oi, look, we're right by the stage door. We can meet the band'.

'Maybe get their autographs!' Adam countered.

A motley crowd were already hanging around waiting for their deflated heroes to appear. The three lads then stood about chain smoking and tried to look cool, Dave doing his very youthful impression of a ruffled Malcolm McLaren. Suddenly, Tenpole Tudor appeared from the stage door and Dave was off like a rocket, chatting away. You had to hand it to him, he had no shame.

Tenpole turned out to be quite friendly but you could tell that he had found the gig tough going. He looked exhausted. Dave told him how much he had enjoyed his set, and questioned him about the future with the Pistols. Tenpole, noticing Dave's recent battle scars, talked about being beaten up at the gig. As they chatted many other people were gathering.

However, there was still no sign of Sham. There were rumours that Steve Jones and Paul Cook might put in an appearance, as they were working on the Sham-Pistols project with Jimmy Pursey. 'Blimey', Adam thought. 'The Pistols!'

As Dave bantered with Tudor, Plug began chatting too.

'You're past it....'

'Sorry...?' Tenpole turned surprised.

'You're past it, mate'. Plug repeated.

'You what?'

'You're too old'.

'Too old? Bollocks I am!'

'You're too old to be a Punk'.

'Oh, yeah! I'm younger than Johnny Rotten!'

'No way. Anyway, he's better than you'.

'Maybe, but I'm younger'.

'You reckon? I'm sixteen. How old are you? Twenty nine?'

'Fuck off!'

'Please yourself....'

'I'm a fucking Pistol!' Tenpole pouted.

'So what?!'

'What d'you mean, so what?'

'That 'Who Killed Bambi?' What a crap record! 'W H O K I L L E D
B-A-M-B-I!', Plug aped.

'Piss off!'

'You're an old tosser you are!'

'You what....fuckin' calling me a tosser?!'

'Yeah!'

Tenpole moved forward menacingly.

'Look, he don't mean it, mate....' Dave intervened.

'Yeah, I did. You're an old twat!' Plug challenged.

'Right, you fuckin' little shit!'

'He don't mean it -

'You can fuck off an 'all!' Tenpole fired back at Dave.

'Old twat!' Plug persisted.

'Oi! Fuck off! You little arseholes!'

With that, Tenpole trooped off with steam coming out of his ears, while
Plug held his ground. Adam certainly admired his front even though
he couldn't believe it. At times, Plug had even more than Sainsbury's.
If he had a bee in his bonnet he would always say what he felt, straight
up, even if his head was on the block.

Meanwhile, Adam had been busy surveying the Islington terrain for a
sighting of any of the Pistols but unfortunately, like all rumours, there
seemed little substance to them. He turned back to Dave who had
heard that Sham were staying inside the venue for some time because
of the trouble, so it would be ages before they would see them. Finally,
a vote was taken and it was decided, two to one, that they might as well
hit the road. So, they went on their merry way, back to the Tube station
and the sticks.

Easier said than done. For the next hour and a half they played a
frighteningly drawn out game of cat and mouse with roaming gangs of

skinheads. Most of the time they played the mouse. It was impossible. Just as they had managed to avoid one particularly fierce group another mob would appear. Adam felt that he was still in for a good kicking for sure and by the way that Plug and Dave were acting, both were suspiciously quiet throughout the journey, he knew they were thinking exactly the same thing, although Dave was obviously considering a return bout. This time though he would probably end up being given the Last Rites as a bonus, whereas before it just seemed like a bucket of cold water and a sponge.

Adam didn't know how, but the three of them managed to change Tube trains at Kings Cross, not an easy thing when the eyes are everywhere, scouring the subways and escalators for imminent danger and at any minute expecting to be jumped. It reminded Adam of that gang-war film, The Warriors, another of Plug's favourite films, about the unpopular 'Warriors' crew who have to get back to their home turf with what seemed like the whole of New York's bad apples out to kill them.

Fortunately, they had made it to the Piccadilly Line and their train, but once on it, it didn't seem to be going anywhere. The driver must have been having a cup of tea or something. Or perhaps he was friendly with the skinheads. Adam thought just about anything was possible being so shit scared.

Because it was getting late there were people returning home after a drunken Saturday night out and as Adam watched from the open carriage, the tube train just sat around idly in the station filling itself up with lurching bodies.

'When's the train gonna leave?!' said Plug, trying to suppress the lump in his throat.

'Christ knows!' replied Dave massaging his sore lip.

'If the train don't leave soon, we're dead!' stated Plug with authority.

'Come on.....come on....' Adam added nervously for dramatic effect.

There was a pause, then a little bit more panic.

'Oh, fuckin' 'ell!'

Just at that moment they heard a distant football chant and then within another second a large group of skins broke out onto the platform, as if almost from the depths of hell.

'Shit!' Adam blurted out, and Plug and Dave immediately peered out of the carriage down the platform at the impending doom.

'Oh, no....' muttered Dave.

'We're fucked!' said Plug, simply.

This particular group of 'number ones' were in good voice, being particularly well oiled and they looked around for any enemy they could batter. Whatever the shape or size. Adam was hoping naively that they might be considering having a night off for once after all the aggravation. You know, that they might decide to be friendly for a change. Like it was all becoming a bit of a chore. Adam wondered if they ever became bored with all that macho violence? All that insane kicking? All that antisocial behaviour? Maybe they were going to turn over a new leaf, shake hands and wish everyone a good night. But no, that wasn't likely.

Just as soon as the three had clocked them, the Skinheads all clocked back and to the accompaniment of loud jeering and stomping DM's, the three passengers noticeably retreated further back into the carriage. Before Adam had time to pray for the Tube to move off, driven by his fairy Godmother, one of the more mouthy skins hurtled towards them with only one thing on his mind. Destruction. Amazingly, just as he reached the compartment the train's automatic doors creaked shut and he found that he couldn't quite wheedle his large frame between the doors. Much to the skins annoyance, he was left to bark and snap through the window from the platform as his frothing mates caught up. As he ranted violently and kicked the train door, Adam and Plug had the great pleasure of watching Dave proudly giving the 'wanker' sign back through the window as the train got underway. Thank Christ the train didn't stall. They might have ended up as drawstring lamps. If Adam hadn't been so nervous he would have died laughing but at least Dave had had his little bit of revenge.

But now they had a new problem. Paranoia. Dave had humiliated the Skins and they would more than likely chase after them.

'What d'you do that for?!' cried Plug.

'For a laugh', admitted Dave.

'Those skins'll wanna kill us now you berk!'

'No they won't....'

There was a pause as Plug shook his head.

'How will they get us?' Adam butted in.

'Yeah. How?'

'They'll come after us'.

'They won't'.

'You reckon?'

'We're too far ahead of 'em now', replied Dave with an edgy grin.

As the underground train sped south westwards and they counted down the stops nervously between each station, it wasn't until Earl's Court and the District line that they could let out a huge sigh of relief. Because that meant that there was only one more train change and sanctuary. So if that gang of skinheads was going to pursue them after all, they had a lot of catching up to do. It was reckoned that the only way they were going to catch up was with the aid of a helicopter, so they could jump ahead further down the line. But that was unlikely. Besides they wouldn't have all fitted in. At least one of the skins looked very large and would no doubt have taken up at least two seats all on his own. In fact, the chopper probably wouldn't have been able to take off.

Thankfully, at Earl's Court there wasn't a skinhead in sight, just a motley bunch of Heavy Metal fans sauntering back from a gig, and as luck would have it Adam, Plug and Dave gratefully boarded their final train. After they had concluded that there was no way that they were going to be ambushed or 'headed off at the pass', the journey now being well underway, the three cheered out aloud and swung triumphantly around from the hand grips above their heads.

SUPERMARKET SWEEP

Adam's first job after leaving school was as a shelf stacker in a local high street supermarket. Not the best career in the world, but it meant that he could now afford to go to more Chelsea matches, punk gigs and buy records and obtain clothes, despite the jobs meager hourly pay. Also, a couple of old mates from school like Dan, worked there as well and they were a definite help in Adam obtaining the post, having put in a good word. Also, the mind numbing hours certainly went quicker as Adam could lark about with people he already knew.

Whenever Adam worked at the store, he had to be relatively presentable, so he grew his hair back, as a spiky barnet and punk clothing weren't allowed. He had to comb his hair down flat which just made him look startled or as if he had just got out of bed and had rushed to the store in a rush. The supermarket outfit was horrible too, in it's grey and brown and was far too large and Adam always felt awkward in it - flapping about almost like a constipated penguin - and even worse was the fact that he had to keep it done up all day, even in hot weather. He also had to wear black trousers with a white shirt and tie, so it was by far and away the tidiest outfit since his uniform at secondary school. For him tidiness was always a problem.

The only concession for Adam, was the fact that he was allowed to wear his cherished Dr Martens, which was lucky, because by now they were virtually soldered to his feet. His gait and appearance in the complete supermarket uniform was quite comical: a sort of messy Charlie Chaplin, without the moustache.

Adam was assigned to his own tiny metal locker in the locker room and he always used to have a real problem trying to fit his 'Bone Idol' jacket and bondage trousers inside. Whenever he turned up for work at the front of the supermarket, the managers, and there seemed like loads of them, would nod disparagingly to one another and then mock his appearance.

'Look at the state of him!'

Or,

'Heh! Bone Idol! Where's your toilet seat?' they'd shout.

Adam and his fellow shelf stackers, despised these jumped up fools who thought they had more than an ounce of power and who bossed them all about. It was as if position and authority had been handed down to them directly from the Almighty and Her Majesty. But the reality was, that they had just stuck out the shelf stacking for a longer period than anybody else and worked their whole lives at the job rather than Adam, whose very loyalty was questionable. There was no doubt about it, for Adam this employment opportunity was going to remain short term. There was no way he was going to try and work his way up the supermarket ladder to become a 'Mr Tesco' or a Sir Sainsbury in his fifty fifth year only to kick the bucket from all the stress the next. Also, failing that, he didn't want to just end up in a warehouse somewhere bollocking people for delivering rotten avocados or castigating some poor employee for directing a shopper in the wrong direction on the shop floor: Adam sometimes did this on purpose, sending the shopper to the opposite end of the store from where they actually wanted to go for a bit of fun. He would usually meet up with them later on in the day and they weren't best pleased.

'Excuse me?!'

'Yeah?....'

'D'you know you sent me the wrong way!'

'Pardon?'

'You did, you sent me the wrong way!'

'When?....'

'I had to ask a manager and I was in a hurry!'

'Oh, dear....'

'I asked you where the flour was?'

'Flour?'

'Yes, flour!'

'Oh....sorry. I thought you meant flowers....you know plants'.

'How silly of you, how could you not know what I meant?'

'Well, I - '

'It's just typical of young people today!'

'What is?'

'Being directed to the wrong place!'

'Well, I'm sorry, but if you'll excuse me I'm a little bit busy'.

'Well, make sure you don't do it in future!'

'Yeah, sure. I'll try not to....'

The customer would then stomp off in a huff as Adam sniggered to himself and continued stacking the shelves with great enthusiasm.

Adam's other tactic was to try and keep out of the way of the managers as much as possible and he would spend a lot of time careering about the aisles with his metal cart, fully laden with washing powders, cereals, tinned fruits and cooking oils. They were given pricing guns which were a complete nightmare, they would always be breaking down and having to price a long line of toilet rolls at 49 and a half pence was fraught with frustration: the gun would misfire and spit out a line of stickers with nothing on them or the ink was so faded that you couldn't tell what the price was anyway.

Sometimes when they become bored and the shop was empty in the early morning, they would play dodgems with their carts or use them as wheelbarrow's and give each other lifts round the shop floor. If they were caught the managers would then go into their prepared speeches like little Churchill's.

'We at this supermarket are proud of our heritage. Working for the customer is our priority. Good service is number one. At present there is far too much idleness and misbehaviour in this area. Slacking must not be encouraged. We all have to pull in the same direction, otherwise chaos will be the result. So we need to see an immediate improvement from now on. Make no mistake. Any further instances like this will have to be punished with dismissals'.

The warehouse was the only place where Adam could find sanctuary, there being less managers about and the many aisles of stacked up supplies gave him good cover from detection whenever he wanted to skive off a bit of work. Sometimes he would break into the supplies and scoff chocolates and other goodies. Easter was an especially good time when lots of chocolate eggs would go missing in mysterious circumstances. Sometimes he would sneak out of the store with chocolate bars concealed on his person, always a risky business as they were regularly frisked by the security guards when knocking off work. He manoeuvred around the body search by placing the chocolate bars down his underpants as that was the only area the security staff wouldn't venture. So there he was, lined up ready for a search and as if he was wearing a cricket box or particularly large codpiece, but he would always get away with it:

'What have you got?' He'd ask Dan, once they were a safe distance away from the Supermarket and out of the range of binoculars.

'I've got a big Toblerone and a load of Smarties!' he'd reply, pulling out his swag. 'What have you got?'

'Er....some Cream Eggs and a large Fruit and Nut!' and Adam would proceed to count out the eggs with a big grin on his face.

'Excellent! We've got a right feast!'

And they had. Adam was relieved to finally get rid of the chocolate from out of his trousers, because it definitely cramped what little style he had.

The money from the job came in very useful and during this time, on his weekday nights and Saturday afternoons off, he would go to gigs or important Chelsea matches. The Marquee became a regular haunt and Adam would see plenty of cracking bands there: The Adverts, the Pretenders, the Rezillos, the Buzzcocks, the Lurkers, 999, Adam and the Ants, the UK Subs, Chelsea, Splodgenessabounds, who had a terrific single with a chorus of, 'Two pints of lager and a packet of crisps, please!' and Spizz-Energi, who also had a brilliantly daft single called 'Where's Captain Kirk?' which ended with the lead singer Spizz, shouting, 'Where's Spock? Where's Spock? Where's Spock?!'

Adam's inevitable dismissal from the supermarket was just a matter of time. He managed to spend a whole day stacking the shelves full of washing powder. The problem was that he had managed to get all the prices wrong, so come five o'clock, it was clear that the Supermarket had lost out on a lot of business right from under their noses. After having completed his designated task, he did think it strange why the Soap Suds were leaping of the shelves like hot cakes, but he just assumed there must be some great savings and special offers. Unfortunately all the discounts had been unwittingly handed out by himself. Some of the Powders, were mistakenly half priced in some cases and by the end of the day and the customary money counting, the Supermarket discovered that it had lost over two hundred pounds in business from Adam's incompetence.

As he scoffed contentedly on a smuggled chocolate bar in the locker room and prepared to leave for the day, he was informed that the shop floor Manager wanted to see him in his office by the loading bay. Eventually, Adam trudged over to his Headquarters, knocked unsuspectingly and entered.

'What have you done on the washing powder shelves?'

'Sorry?'

'What have you done with the powders?'

'Umm, stacked 'em....' Adam replied dozily, swallowing the last of his Milky Bar.

'Yeah, but you priced them all wrong!'

'No, I'm sure I - '

'You've made a right bloody mess up!'

'But - '

'Get your belongings. You're sacked!'

'But, I didn't know how much - '

'Well, you should've asked one of us about the pricings!'

'But how could I have done, if I didn't know the pricings were wrong?'

'That's not our problem. You have to carry the can'.

Carry the can? Adam was trying hard not to carry anything.

Adam then had to go to the main office where they asked him to hand back his special overall, but just before leaving, he told them that he would rather take it home and burn it. This didn't go down at all well with the Managers who had all worked really hard to get where they were and Adam could more than sense their delight as they waved him on his way out of the Supermarket trolley door.

HAPPY NEW YEAR

New Year's Eve. Soon to be a new decade. The 70's were about to cop it. Thank Christ. The question was, how to celebrate? Adam's school mate, Dan, an avid Madness fan, had heard about a Two-Tone party taking place in Clapham and he reckoned it would be good for a laugh.

Since Adam's mate Steve had gone abroad to work, Dan and Adam were going to a lot of Chelsea matches home and away. Dan was a Chelsea Skin and dressed uniformly in Abercrombie, Two tone, Loafers, Perry's and braces, etc. He also liked Punk a lot and he was similar to Adam in his liking for the Skinhead style.

Dan reckoned they would be able to crash at the party, or if they got lucky with the fairer sex they could meet up the next morning because the first Chelsea fixture of the 80's was a morning kick off at Luton Town and they could catch a train with the Chelsea away supporters at St Pancras. Chelsea had things to celebrate too: Recently being top of both the Second Division and the Football Combination, where they were above Arsenal.

At the home matches Adam had already met some of Dan's mates, but it wasn't till they went away that they really came into their own. A couple of them were friendly with one or two of the notorious Chelsea following. When Adam asked Dan about his mate Pete, who Adam had met a couple of times briefly, Dan said:

'Pete's a laugh and he knows Icky....'

'Who's Icky?'

'Hickmott....He's a nutcase. Leads a Chelsea crew. Sometimes carries a walking stick and makes out he's crippled'.

'And he's not?'

'Nah, as soon as he sees trouble he uses the stick to hit people!'

'Don't the Coppers take it from him?'

'They don't realise until it's too late'.

'Fuckin' hell….How does Pete know him?'

'His brother's a mate of Icky's from work'.

'Is he coming to Luton?'

'We're meeting him tomorrow at the station'.

'What about Icky?'

'Dunno. But they're gonna take the Town'.

'Great', Adam thought. 'I'm walking right into a war zone'. What a way to see in the New Year. Trouble was he needed his Chelsea fix and Dan was a mate, even if they didn't always see eye to eye. Thing was, in the middle of the increasingly dangerous terraces, home and away, Adam usually felt safe, especially if some of Dan's mates were about. That is as long as you were a Chelsea fan. If not then it wasn't such a good thing. They had the reputation of being some of the country's worst hooligans and were not at all bothered about rumbling with Millwall, West Ham, Leeds, Cardiff, just about anybody, anywhere, even if they were heavily outnumbered. One of Dan's favourite football stories was about when he went to Aston Villa away:

'A handful of Chelsea sneaked in the Holte (Villa's massive home end) and stood about'.

'Stood about?'

'Waiting for kick off…'

'What happened?'

'Soon as the match started, you could see them, from where I was in the away end, steaming in'.

'Did they get battered?'

'No fuckin' way! The Villa legged it. On the pitch. Everywhere. Someone said it was the Icky crew. Took the whole fuckin' end! Fifteen of them. The Villa just shat 'emselves!'

'Blimey....'

'Complete nutters!'

At the end of the tale he gave out a little laugh. Adam could see that it gave Dan an uneasy buzz alright, but he just dismissed it in the end as probably nothing that unusual. Dan spoke about his older Chelsea mates as though they were heroes, but Adam looked upon them as being foolhardy. There was always going to be someone around the corner who was bigger and harder than them, although when Adam heard about the exploits of some of Dan's friends he began to wonder. Besides, Adam just wanted to watch the matches. He didn't want trouble. He knew that Dan wasn't really a thug but he also knew that even at sixteen, if Dan was confronted, he could definitely look after himself.

They eventually made it to the party in Clapham after buying some cans from a local off licence and were welcomed into the house by the host's girlfriend. Although it was still fairly early, the party was already in full swing, this being a serious celebration to see in the new decade. Most of the party goers were Skinheads, apart from one or two Mods, which Adam didn't find too awkward as he'd toned down his punk appearance for the night, in the hope that he might be able to 'pull' later on. Sometimes Adam could look so rancid that it was rare for girls to even come near. Unless of course they were as dishevelled as him. This particular night Adam looked more like a messy Skinhead. Dan meanwhile, had bought himself a brand new Crombie jacket in the Christmas sales which he was more than proud of and as the stereo blared out 'The Prince' by Madness, everyone got down to some serious moon-stomping.

The party was packed. When it wasn't Madness on the turntable it was The Specials, and when it wasn't The Specials it was Selecter. I don't think Adam had ever done so much moon-stomping. Dan was in his element and took part in a moon-stomping competition in which he eventually came second: he had a great knack of looking completely demented, like some sort of pneumatic drill when he danced, and while he was busy taking part in the heats Adam was in the kitchen trying to find a girl to chat up.

As luck would have it, a blonde Skinhead girl turned to him just as he was rummaging around in his plastic bag trying to reach for another can of lager.

'D'you know Dan?'

'Yeah. We went to the same school'.

'You like Ska?'

'Yeah....it's alright'.

'You a Skinhead?'

'No, Punk....'.

'That's funny…'

'Why?'

'You look more like a Skinhead'.

'It's just tonight. I'm a Punk really'.

'Who's your favourite band then?'

'Dunno....can't say…the Pistols...Sham'.

'Sham 69?'

'Yeah....'

'I think they're shit!'

'Well, I saw their last gig at the Rainbow. They were brilliant'.

'Pursey's a prat!'

'No, he ain't'.

'Yeah, he is. He can't even sing.

'You don't need to. Look at John Lydon with PIL - he can't sing, but it never stopped him'.

'I like Buster Bloodvessel'.

'Who's that?'

'The singer of Bad Manners'.

'Don't know them…' Adam said, his back to the wall.

'You know, that huge fat bloke with the long tongue'.

'Oh, oh yeah....'

'He's brilliant'.

'And you reckon he can sing?'

'He's well good'.

'A bit fat though!'

'Course he is. 'Lip up fatty man. Lip up fatty, fatty reggae!'

'What?' Adam countered.

'NE NE NA NA NA NA NU NU!!'

'Yeah, right....'

It was pretty clear. They weren't suited. The last thing Adam wanted at that point was a heated discussion about his record collection which he was growing increasingly proud of.

With the exchange concluded, Adam was out of the kitchen and back to the main party. He certainly didn't need someone slagging off Jimmy Pursey on New Year's Eve. Even if he had bitten the dust. Adam also didn't need a cross-examination into his appearance. Besides, he was only a Skinhead for the duration of the New Year's Eve celebrations and the football match the next day, and after that it was most definitely back to normal. Or more like, abnormal.

While Adam was out in the kitchen, 'Gangsters' by The Specials, had been spun, but as he returned to the living room, there was a slight pause and then a voice shouted out, 'One Step Beyond!' and Dan was off stomping again. The Madness track signalled the final throes of the competition which Adam's mate was holding against a big, mean looking Skinhead who you certainly didn't want on your case. As Dan swaggered manically from side to side, a pork pie hat temporarily placed on his head, he clenched his fists, while all eyes surveyed the duelling duo.

It was pretty obvious who was going to win. Although Dan put in a valiant performance right to the last, he was never going to throw in the towel, his opponent stomped even more hysterically, with his tongue lolling about and his eyes almost popping out of his head, so it wasn't long before the whole room broke out into loud applause and the big Skin held his sweaty arms aloft in triumph.

'I need a lager!' Dan announced as he came over to Adam.

'You did well'.

'I was fuckin' miles better than him!'

'Oh well, it don't matter'.

'Yeah, it does. I should have won'.

Eventually, he calmed down and they all sat around drinking and chatting about gigs and records and every so often, almost on cue, they would all get up to dance again, especially if the tune was a classic. Even some frenetic pogoing started, when The Jam were played for the benefit of the resident Mods. The next song, 'Eton Rifles' went down particularly well. When the Angelic Upstarts or the Cockney Rejects were played, things went completely ape. These two bands were the more acceptable face of Punk to the Skinheads, as both outfits were trying to be a cross-over in their look if not their sonic, and as the Upstarts song 'Police Oppression' blasted out from the stereo, the sounds of a heated argument and a great crash of smashing glass came from the front living room.

'What the fuck was that?!' Dan blurted out as he swigged his lager.

'I dunno....'

'Sounds like trouble'.

He was right. While the pogoing had continued unaware, a brick had been launched from the front garden through the living room window and was now sitting comfortably in the middle of the settee, with broken glass all about. Luckily, no one had been sitting in that particular spot at the time or they certainly would have had a new year night to forget.

As people scrambled away in shock, the ear splitting music came to a grinding halt. A cocky Skinhead then held up the offending article.

'What fuckin' wanker chucked this?!'

As everybody looked out towards the front of the house, another Skin shouted.

'Someone's been hurt!'

A girl standing near the window had been covered in shards of glass and she had what looked like a nasty cut on her arm. As she crouched down and looked at herself bleeding busily, her worried boyfriend tried to help as best he could. Suddenly the big Skinhead appeared again.

'Everybody, outside quick!'

'There's gonna be a ruck...' added Dan.

Without a moment's hesitation, everybody from the party, except the walking wounded, moved outside to see what was going on. No one seemed to have any fear. Maybe it was because fighting seemed to be such a common occurrence. Almost as if it was what you did between having a cup of tea and a cigarette.

Outside, two groups of Skinheads were facing each other by the front gate to the house, and their snarling faces and angst ridden demeanours suggested that they weren't very happy.

'Which one of you threw the brick?!' The large Skin taunted.

'What fuckin' brick?'

'You fuckin' know!'

'Oi, fuck off you wanker!' taunted one of the imposters.

'No, you can fuck off!'

'Come on then!...' another raised the tempo wisely.

'Fuckin' gate crashers!'

'We ain't gate crashers!'

'Oh, yeah. Throwin' a fuckin' brick!...'

'Piss off!'

'Just cos you couldn't get in!'

'Fuck off!'

'No, I won't fuck off! A girl's been hurt. Who threw it?!'

There was a pause as the enemy took stock.

'It weren't none of us...' Their leader chirped up again.

'Fuckin' liar!' the determined skin growled through gritted teeth.

'Brilliant', Adam thought, 'what a right festive occasion this is turning out to be'. Some Skinheads had tried to enter the party under false pretences, thinking that they would get in just because they were Skins who had no place else to go and it was that charitable time of year. But it was an unwritten law: even on New Year's Eve, gate crashing was an unpopular and unsavoury pastime.

Just at that moment, almost in a blur, the boyfriend of the girl who was bleeding on the carpet, pushed through the crowd and literally jumped out in front of the gate crashers.

'You cut my bird! You cunts!'

The gate crashers, beginning to realise that they might have gone too far, backed down slightly in the face of naked fury. The boyfriend then locked horns immediately with the first in the group in front of him and like someone possessed took the first of the gate crashers out with a flying kick. Then before you could say, 'Should auld acquaintance be forgot', all hell broke loose. It was like a huge bundle. Skinhead fighting Skinhead. However, when the big Skin who'd won the moon-stomping competition threw his heavyweight prowess into the ring alongside the nutter seeking vengeance, it wasn't long before the gate crashers were high tailing it away down the street as fast as their white laced Dr Marten's could carry them.

'Thank fuck for that'. Adam sighed to Dan who was revving himself up to chase after them.

'Let's get 'em!'

'You joking?!'

'No!'

'Leave it. It ain't worth it!'

Adam felt that there had been enough displays of violence already for Dan to be stupid as well. Besides, the Police were bound to be along at any moment even if they had their hands full with the rest of the Nation's drunken revellers, and anyway it was still only 10.45pm. An hour and a quarter to go till midnight.

In fact, the Police had already been phoned by the host of the party and were on their way. Meanwhile, the last of the intruders had been seen off with a punch and a kick in the bollocks and as he tried to run away clutching his crown jewels, he promised retribution which was laughed out of sight. After a moment's pause, Dan turned back to Adam.

'The party'll be finished when the pigs turn up'.

'What are we gonna do?'

'Get out of here....we won't be missed and we had nothin' to do with the ruck anyway'.

'Where are we gonna go?'

'What about Trafalgar Square?'

'Yeah....but what about the time though'.

'We've still got well over an hour'.

'D'you reckon we'll make it?'

'Easy. Come on, let's go'.

They soon made themselves scarce, which wasn't too difficult. Most people had gone back inside to clear up, or were like the two lads, disappearing into the night knowing that the Old Bill were soon going to be making an appearance.

Adam and Dan began walking in the direction of Battersea and it crossed their mind that the gate crashers might still be around the neighbourhood. Fortunately, there was no sign of them and they began to pick up their walking pace when they discovered that there weren't many buses, it being New Year's Eve and there was no Tube station nearby.

They were looking forward to getting to Trafalgar Square. They knew that there was going to be thousands and thousands of people swaying about enjoying themselves and even though it was far too nippy to jump in the fountains, they were both gearing themselves up to snog as many girls as possible come 12.00am AD 1980. From Battersea, they kept south of the river and passed through to Vauxhall where up ahead they could just about see Big Ben poking its head provocatively through the cold misty night. As people passed by they held up their cans of lager, the supplies retrieved before leaving the party, and wished them a Happy New Year:

'We could do with some of this good cheer more often', Adam joked.

'Fat chance!' Dan concluded.

The crowds were now getting busier and busier with just one thing on their mind: Reaching Trafalgar Square on time to see in the next decade. Adam and Dan had kept up an almost military pace and were nearing their destination. They crossed the river at Lambeth Bridge and made their merry way past the Houses of Parliament and on past Parliament Square up Whitehall. They had less than half an hour to go. As they upped the pace again and swigged on the last of their supplies, they passed Downing Street on their left and Dan considered lobbing his beer can at Number Ten:

'No Maggie Thatcher and no Government!' He shouted in a loud voice. Suddenly the festive mood changed and it seemed that a whole squad of Police had just despatched themselves from out of the shadows. Due to their more than heavy presence, Adam advised Dan that they had to move on, and that it wasn't worth it. Dan wanted to hang around Number Ten giving the Prime Minister some New Year grief. You could tell that the lager was starting to kick in. Adam was concerned that Dan was going to get himself arrested and that meant them probably missing the celebrations and the all important Luton match. When Adam told him that the Police cell was going to be really unwelcoming, and freezing cold, luckily Dan saw sense and they carried on their way once more, although it was more difficult now with tired legs and the fact that a large crowd had gathered at the end of Whitehall in a huge bottle neck right in front of Nelson's Column. What's more, there was now only fifteen minutes to go.

As they slowly shuffled into Trafalgar Square like a couple of weary sheep in a huge flock and mingled with the thousands of ecstatic reveller's hell bent on having a good time, Adam began looking around quickly for a way of stocking up on their dwindling alcohol supplies. But there was no way that they were going to be getting anymore. Everywhere was closed and there was no way out. The Police had cordoned off certain areas and some crowd barriers prevented a rapid despatch. Adam turned around as Dan meanwhile scrunched up his empty can and threw it on the ground.

'What are we going to do now?'

'Hang on....' said Dan.

He then proceeded to sneak out a small bottle of whisky from the pocket of his new Crombie jacket:

'Finished the beer....now for the reserves!'

'Brilliant!'

As they laughed, Dan took a big swig on the whisky as if it was water and after gritting his teeth and taking in a sharp breath, he offered over the bottle. Adam took a long tug, nearly choking on the fluid, but it did the trick alright and his stomach felt instantly warmed.

They looked about again. The neon clock on top of a tall building near the Square announced that there were just eight minutes to go. Eight minutes left in the shitty Seventies. There were thousands of people milling around. Some had already jumped in the fountains and were trembling ridiculously from the cold and the wet. Some had clambered on top of the Lion statues and were proudly professing their good cheer to the Nation. Others were rehearsing their 'Auld Lang Syne's' in huddled groups and a couple of large Union Jacks fluttered about. Everywhere, couples were busy getting closer to each other, though some no doubt were probably getting further away, what with all the temptation on offer. As expectations soared, Champagne bottles were getting ready to pop.

After another couple of minutes of loitering about, Adam and Dan suddenly found themselves amongst a large group of Gothic Punks, who had also been standing about moodily in a circle. Although they looked a little out of place, they joined up with them, as the Goths turned out to be quite friendly and soon they were all sharing out their beverages, which included some lethal cocktail in plastic bottles. As they chatted and made ready to count down the decade, Adam looked into himself and thought of what resolutions he would try and take with him into the future: 'To make a crack of playing in a band': 'To never give in no matter what people might think': 'To follow Chelsea back to Division One': 'To find himself a Punk girlfriend, and if she happens to have large breasts, then so much the better!' For Adam, at that moment in his life, it didn't seem too much to ask.

The last of these resolutions was already looking pretty promising as there were some striking Goth girls in the group, the only trouble was that they all seemed to be paired up with their boyfriend's who looked like vampires returning from a rock convention in a local mortuary:

'Don't reckon we're gonna have any luck with this lot', Dan said.

'Yeah, you're right. They're all Bela Lugosi's!'

Suddenly, almost without warning, the New Year countdown began and as soon as the fateful hour struck, everyone let themselves go in one collective explosive celebration. Everybody was hugging each other, jumping up and down and waving their arms about wildly. Suddenly, it seemed like the world was your friend. 'Strange', Adam thought again. 'At any other time of the year there was a good chance that it would be the opposite'. Due to the overwhelming sense of compassion, Adam and Dan didn't have to work very hard at finding any girls to snog. There seemed like an endless supply roaming around seeking a

New Year kiss or two, or three, even if they happened to be with their boyfriends.

Inevitably, it wasn't long before they had lost touch with the Goth's, which was a bit of a relief. They would be better off on their own. Dan was soon getting on famously with a pretty 'Modette' looking girl, right next to one of the statuesque Lions and it almost seemed as if they were going to solder their tongues together. Either that or their faces. This caused no end of jealousy to the Modette girls' boyfriend who was standing close by kicking his heels. His oversized Parka, with a large target on the back, hung about him sadly, and as he surveyed Adam's mate snogging his girlfriend almost to death, he began to get annoyed.

'Oh, fuckin' hell Julie!'

But she wasn't listening. She was much too busy swapping saliva with Dan. After what seemed like about five minutes they finally stopped to draw breath.

'Happy New Year!' Julie said, her subtle lipstick now all askew.

'Yeah, Happy New Year!' Dan replied, with a big grin.

'Julie, come on!' said Parka boy, miserably.

'See you then....' Dan said to the girl eventually, his eyes on stalks.

'Yeah....'

She kissed him again:

'See you - '

'I said come on!' and with that the Mod was off quicker than a Vespa, with his amorous girlfriend in tow.

As they scampered again into the crowd, Dan looked triumphant.

'She was a right stunner'.

'Yeah, not bad', Adam replied.

'Not bad?! You need your eyes tested!'

'She was too Mod looking…'

'What?'

'She was a Mod'.

'So?'

'Well, I'm a Punk….'

There was a slight pause as Dan recoiled.

'It don't matter'.

'Yeah, it does…'

'Not if they're tasty birds it don't', he concluded.

Then they were off again ambling round the fountains and wishing everyone the best. They must have kept it up for a fair while, because Adam's face was beginning to ache from all the smiling. Suddenly, it was 12.30 am and they knew there weren't going to be too many late Tube trains home. The problem was trying to tear themselves away from the euphoria, because despite the cold weather it looked like the whole world was out partying.

Eventually, when the crowds started to disperse, Adam and Dan began to walk back reluctantly down Whitehall and on towards the Thames. Walking past Number Ten again, brought out a reprise of 'No Maggie Thatcher and no Government!' but this time from both of them and with even more ferocity. The Police once again moved about as if they had been hiding behind trees all night and as they almost jumped out at the two revellers, Adam and Dan realised that they had better be on their way.

As they sauntered over Lambeth Bridge once more and turned tiredly towards Vauxhall, up ahead they could see the looming railway bridges and the overground station:

'With a bit of luck we can get a train home', said Dan

'What with British Rail? You reckon?'

'They'll be later than the Tubes'.

'Wanna bet?' Adam replied, ready to shake hands on it.

They finally reached the station, just as a blister started to pierce through the skin on Adam's left foot and his worst fears were realised. The station was closed:

'I don't fuckin' believe it!'

'Told you…'

'Useless fuckin' trains! Living in London and you can't even get a train home on New Year!'

'I know....'

'What are we gonna do now?'

'Freeze our arses off!' Adam joked.

They looked around agitatedly for a while, as sleet began to settle on their jackets. The Tube station was completely empty and even the shutters were down and locked. The adjacent mainline station looked as though it hadn't been given a lick of paint since the First World War and everywhere was depressing brick and graffitied grey concrete:

'Hang on, look! The overground station's still open!'

Up above, they could see some activity, although it was probably just a station guard packing up for the night with his lantern. They ventured past the empty ticket office and hurried up the stairs to the platform. There was no one about. No trains. Nothing. What to do?

'Let's try the waiting room. It's freezin' out here!'

'Good idea', Adam said, rubbing his hands together frenziedly.

Entering, the room's warmth smothered them immediately like a blanket. A little gas fire at one end was on full and to one side a down and out was lying on the bench deep in slumber. Adam and Dan sat down on a creaky bench to the right of the fire and weighed up the situation:

'Well, there's no more trains. We might as well crash here and get the first Tube up to St Pancras at six'.

'What about him?' Adam countered, just as the tramp began snoring as if his life depended on it. It seemed as though he was trying to keep an imaginary feather up in the air.

'Christ, he's loud!'

'Where else can we go?'

'There's nowhere....'

'At least he don't smell too bad'.

'That's what you think', Dan said. 'I won't be giving him a New Year snog that's for sure!'

They both laughed out loud at the thought, and as they cackled, the body began to stir. After a few moments the old codger's eyes opened slightly as he raised himself up:

'Eh? What's that? Eh? What....so it's funny is it? Funny....me lying here!

Funny, eh? Is it?'

'Well now you come to mention it....' Dan replied, trying to conceal his sniggers.

'And a bollocking New Year to you!'

It was clear the old man was not in a festive mood.

'Cheers....' Adam said.

'Wisecrackers.....eh? Comedians?'

'If you like', said Dan, sensing a routine.

The pensioner scrutinized them both up and down as if he had mislaid his glasses.

'You're all the bloody same. You lot. People like you.....bloody kids, that's what. I tell you - it's all bollocks it is. Bollocks!'

'We know mate....'

'Bollocks!'

'We know!'

'Oh, you do, eh?'

'Yeah....'

There was a big pause as the tramp's mind slowly ticked over:

'How's that then?'

'We're Chelsea supporters....' Adam reasoned tiredly.

After a split second, the old man burst out into hysterics and nearly fell off the bench:

'Chelsea!?' Then after a pause for what little oxygen was left in the room he broke out laughing once more.

'Yeah....alright, alright!' Dan moaned.

'What a load of old fuckin' bollocks!'

'Who d'you support then?' Adam said, cutting in.

'No one....not even myself!' and he was off in drunken hysterics again.

'We're off to Luton tomorrow. Morning kick-off'.

'Good for you', he turned to Dan and stared him out for what seemed like a minute. Then under his breath he exhaled:

'Bloody hooligans....that's football'.

'Well, we ain't'.

'What?! Hooligans?'

'Yeah....'

'You look like it to me'.

'Fuck off!' said Dan, almost spitting.

He was becoming increasingly annoyed. Adam just wanted to try and make the best of things, but any way he looked at it, things were pretty bleak. Seeing in the first few hours of the new decade with an argument, while they sat in the waiting room at Vauxhall train station wasn't what Adam had envisaged. But there was some comfort. At least the room was nice and warm.

After the initial broadside from Fagin, he then settled back to his kip. He was a funny old codger, alright. In his sleep he began to berate everything and everybody and after an hour or so of that, between Adam and Dan's banter, they began to feel a bit sorry for him. They felt even more when he turned in his sleep and fell off the bench, but not until the lads had spent about half an hour in a fit of laughter. After their mockery had subsided Adam began to think about their unexpected companion. Despite his outspoken nature, he was a pretty harmless sort of fellow. His bark was certainly worse than his bite. Adam concluded that it wasn't completely unreasonable for the old man to even have been a little like himself and Dan in his youth. It was just a case of perhaps taking the wrong turning at the crossroads. Or finding yourself one day falling through the poverty net with no chance of escape. With that little reverie playing in Adam's head, he soon found himself nodding off.

When Adam woke up in a crooked mess at the edge of the bench, Dan was already up and pacing about the waiting room, full of anticipation of the new day ahead. The crisp dawn was well under way and as Adam yawned and stretched, he noticed that the old lodger was beginning to stir too. The fire was for some reason turned down low and the cold was now tangible through the gaps in Adam's donkey jacket.

'I didn't sleep a wink thanks to that old bastard!' said Dan.

'Yeah, I know. I only got an hour or so myself'.

'You snored nearly as badly as him'.

'No way'.

'You did. I thought you two were having a competition'.

'It must be my blocked nose. I've had a bit of a cold'.

Adam was also sporting a thumping hangover from the nights revelries,

273

Dan too, but as soon as they found their feet they were on their way again. It was 6.30am, and as they departed the diminishing comfort of the waiting room behind them, the old man muttered something to himself that Adam couldn't quite make out.

Wiping the final evidence of sleep from their eyes, they quickly reached the welcoming Tube station and soon the first happy travellers of the new decade were on their way to St Pancras. When they arrived at the familiar forecourt, after leaping up the Tube escalator, they found the station virtually empty. Only the odd cleaner or station guard strolled about. 'Hardly surprising', Adam thought, 'The whole of the Nation is probably in bed with a communal headache'.

'There's about two hours till the special to Luton', said Dan.

There were a couple of pre-organised Chelsea Supporters Club trains taking fans 'officially' to the match, but which was more likely in order to keep an eye on the unpredictable away support. The organisation was so lax though that virtually anyone could and did get on them.

'Let's get some breakfast. I'm starving', Adam said, rubbing his stomach.

'Yeah, me too. Good idea'.

They then spent the next hour or so sitting in the only open greasy spoon near the station, scoffing on bangers and beans, floppy slices of bread and butter, and downing endless milky cups of tea. As the time passed, more Chelsea fans were starting to turn up in groups for something to eat before catching the train. In amongst the hustle of the cafe Dan recognised a lanky friend of his:

'Oi, Keith!'

'Heh! Alright'.

'Yeah, I'm alright'.

'Happy New Year!'

'Yeah, Happy New Year! Oh, you know my mate....'

Keith who reminded Adam a little of 'Lurch' from the original TV series The Addam's Family, slowly turned to him.

'Yeah....How you doing?'

'Alright, thanks', Adam replied.

'So what d'you do for New Year?' Dan began.

'I was with Gary and Steve. We went to this great party in Camberwell. You should've come. Wall to wall birds. Fuckin' right laugh! Got completely arseholed. Pulled this tasty crumpet. Should've seen the jugs on her!'

'She's not coming to the Footie then....?'

'Nah. Had to leave her behind. It was too early. Anyway, she's into Rugby'.

'Oh, fuck that!'

'Don't worry. I did!'

Keith started laughing like a drain, then Adam and Dan followed suit, but it was slightly strained as they were both thinking that Keith had had a much better time than them. Adam and Dan had been snogging girls. Keith, if he wasn't telling porkies, had had his hands full.

'What about you. What d'you do?'

'We went to this party down Clapham'.

'Any good?'

'Nah, it was shite. There was a load of trouble. Fuckin' skinhead ruck! We had to leave cos the Old Bill were gonna turn up. Then we ended up Trafalgar Square'.

'I heard it was a riot up there'.

'Yeah, it was alright....'

Luckily, as Dan chatted, he didn't mention the rest of the night spent in the Vauxhall station waiting room. Adam was too tired to blush anyway even if he had.

'Have you seen Pete?' Dan said to Keith, changing tack.

'No. Not since Leicester - Boxing day'.

'Well he's definitely up for it. He says Icky's mob'll be there'.

'Yeah, there's gonna be a fair sized kicking. Mate of mine said loads of Chelsea up there already....whole of the town centre's been closed down and boarded up - fuckin' 'Filth' everywhere'.

Once they were done, they all paid up for their food and hurried back to the station. As the discussion continued, they stood about on the concourse waiting for the special. Eventually, the notice came up and they were off to the platform with a whole load of other Chelsea supporters, although again Adam couldn't easily tell because hardly anyone was wearing scarves. Chants of 'We are the famous....the famous Chelsea!' echoed around and it seemed as if everyone was already in good Bank Holiday heart.

They boarded the train and immediately the three of them took up one whole area of four seats with a table in between. The spare seat was for Pete when he turned up. Now the topic was all about the match.

Chelsea's manager, Geoff Hurst and assistant Bobby Gould, were doing a fine job and the Blues were sitting third in the Second Division. Unfortunately, they no longer had Ray Wilkins gracing the midfield, he had already been gobbled up by Man Utd, and Peter Bonetti had been replaced at the end of a brilliant career by the more than eccentric Yugoslavian goalkeeper Petar Borota. But the Yugoslav was fast becoming a fan favourite because of his unpredictable and sometimes hysterical goalmouth antics: instead of catching the ball, he always liked to juggle it first. Also, he wasn't averse to a little bit of swinging on the crossbar to amuse the supporters. But behind the clowning and the ridiculous permed hair, was a great shot stopper.

Despite Wilkins' transfer, the Chelsea midfield was still fairly talented with the likes of Ian Britton and Micky Fillery chasing and probing. The strikers, Tommy Langley and Clive Walker were more often than not, excitingly Cavalier. Even Ron Harris was still there in a utility position and despite his years, he was still biting legs with interest. With all their quality, everyone was confident that they would defeat Luton on the pitch. Off it? It was pretty clear. The town was going to be raised.

The train filled up quickly and everywhere supporters were breaking open their personal supplies of lager as if they were smuggled contraband and soon the carriage was a swaying mass of Chelsea loyalty: 'We will follow the Chelsea, over land and sea - and Leicester! We will follow the Chelsea, on to victory!' Then straight away someone with a gruff voice would shout out, 'Altogether now!' and arms would be raised up to the ceiling en masse once more, everyone stopping their lively conversations to join in again. When the supporters got bored of that song, they would soon start on another: 'Maybe it's because I'm a Londoner, that I think of her, wherever I go. I get a funny feeling inside of me, just walking up and down, maybe it's because I'm a Londoner, that I love London town!' Then someone would shout out, 'Get off me sister!' and amid the smirks this would lead into another request: 'You are my Chelsea, my only Chelsea, you make me happy, when skies are grey. You'll never notice, how much I love you, until you've taken, my Chelsea away! Lah, lah, la, lah, lah. Lah, lah, la, lah, lah!' Then everyone would stand up in unison, vociferously chanting out 'Chelsea!' until they all needed a break to put their larynx's back in place. It was well known that sometimes the simple repetitive chant of 'CHELSEA', to the tune of Amazing Grace, could last nearly the entire length of a match.

Suddenly, Pete turned up out of the blue, after scrambling all the way down the train to find them.

'Alright, lads!'

'Heh, Pete....'

'Happy New Year!'

Just at that moment the train lurched forward on its way and there was another huge cheer. Another Chelsea song started up immediately and Pete quickly took up his seat reservation amid the chaos. Once comfortable, he then tried valiantly to speak over the singing.

'I'll only be here for a bit....I'm supposed to be meeting up with the rest of the lads....'

'Yeah?'

'We're gonna take the Luton'.

'What about Icky?' said Dan.

'They've all gone by coach'.

Because he was a little older, Pete instantly gained respect. Though he wasn't that tall, he was built like a brick outhouse, so that probably had something to do with it. If you were going to have a fight with someone, Pete would definitely not be top of the list. And Dan had a theory, it was always the shorter ones who were the real nutters, because they had had to defend themselves from the word go. Anyway, Pete had a look in his eye that suggested that there was a certain bravado about him and in the short time that Dan chatted with him, Adam was becoming pretty convinced that fear was probably not in his vocabulary.

The Special soon reached optimum speed - what seemed like about thirty miles an hour, but eventually the massive murkiness of London drifted away and they found themselves venturing deeper into the rolling frostiness of Hertfordshire. The sight of a couple of cows and a lone sheep brought out the resident comedian in Pete; 'Sheep shaggers! Sheep shaggers! Sheep shaggers!'

After a few final gulps of lager, Pete wished them well and told them that he would try and meet them after the match back at the train station. This they all knew would probably be impossible, but they said they would look out for him anyway. As the Flying Scotsman began to near its destination, slowing down once more to a crawl, the unfamiliar Luton skyline, all vacant blocks and back-to-backs appeared in view.

Run down? Dan reckoned it was a shithole. Once more the less than subtle Chelsea songs came thick and fast:

The famous Tottenham Hotspur went to Rome to see the Pope,

The famous Tottenham Hotspur went to Rome to see the Pope,

The famous Tottenham Hotspur went to Rome to see the Pope,

And this is what he said, 'Fuck off!'

Who's that team we call the Chelsea,

Who's that team we all adore,

We're the boys in blue and white,

And we fight with all our might,

And we're out to show the world,

That we can score!

Bring on Tottenham or the Arsenal,

Bring on spastics by the score,

Barcelona, Real Madrid, Tottenham are a load of Yids,

And we're out to show the world,

That we can score!....

We hate Luton and we hate Luton!

We hate Luton and we hate Luton!

We hate Luton and we hate Luton!

We are the Luton, haters!

My old man said,

Be a Chelsea fan,

And don't dilly-dally on the way.

We'll take the Arsenal in half a minute,

We'll take the West Ham and all that's in it.

With hatchets and hammers,

Carving knives and spanners,

We'll show those Tottenham bastards how to fight....

and sung to the theme tune of the once popular television series The Liver Birds, which was usually reserved for Liverpool supporters: 'If we see you on the corner, with a red scarf round your neck, Chelsea boys will come and getcha, and we'll break your fuckin' neck! Lah la la la! Lah la la la! Lah la la la la la lah!' As supporters started swinging on the baggage shelves and pulled the fixtures and fittings apart, things became even more sinister: 'We Are E-vil!' was sung, which then turned even more worryingly into, 'We Are Na-zi's!' There was no way Adam was going to chant that and when some fervent Seig Heiling began, Adam shot a look to Dan who was about to stretch out his right arm skywards.

'That's sick that is!'

'It's only a laugh', Dan replied.

'A laugh....?'

'Yeah, it's a joke'.

A couple of people looked round at Adam not singing, and a few others who hadn't proclaimed themselves as Hitler Youth were stared out, as if they were killjoys or traitors. Adam didn't think it looked like much of a joke. The strong connections with the National Front and British Movement had been well documented in the Chelsea support for years, but that seemed to suggest that it was just a minority opinion of some marginalized, crazy faction. However, the fervour of the present singing and saluting on the Orient Express suggested otherwise and most of the carriage had taken part in it.

It was the first time Adam had heard such a manifesto in such large numbers. Before, it had usually been the odd individual or nutcase. Now it was widespread and undeniable. Luton's multi-ethnic environment was certainly going to come under fire. So was their football team, because they had at least three black players in their squad (Luton was one of the only clubs at the time with regular first team black players, another was West Bromwich Albion, with the brilliant Cyrille Regis and Laurie Cunningham).

Chelsea, on the other hand, had none and the type of reception at

Stamford Bridge that the first, black Chelsea player would receive, didn't bare thinking about. It certainly didn't help when there had been Conservative Politicians like Enoch Powell ranting on about the flood of immigrants supposedly taking white men's jobs and the consequences leading to 'rivers of blood'. As far as Adam was concerned, that was just lies, fuelling both blind racism and encouraging the bigoted scum to rise to the top. It was all so frustrating because it was now becoming impossible just to go and enjoy a day out at the football. You could have a good day out at the races. So why not at the football? Which is all Adam wanted to do. Have a good day out. Unfortunately, Adam couldn't help but get caught up in all the trouble.

Finally, the train halted in the Luton station and the rusty doors flapped open. Supporters descended from the rapidly deteriorated carriages like a large eager army, trying to keep close knit so as not to get left behind. As soon as they arrived towards the station exit, they realised that despite the freezing weather, the Police were out in numbers. They had Police on horses, Police with dogs, that barked incessantly and large numbers of foot patrol PC's ready to keep the Chelsea fans from wreaking havoc on the trek up to Luton's Kenilworth Road home.

Suddenly everyone found themselves herded together right outside the station forecourt, which after about fifteen minutes became unbearable, when Adam suddenly found himself forced to cop somebody else's body odour or have to peer up the runny left nostril of a fellow supporter. It was as if the Police were doing it on purpose. Hemming hundreds of fans in. Tarring everybody with the same brush. 'You're all hooligans', they were saying, 'You're just animals. Let's treat you all the same'. When in fact, there were many genuine supporters and there were both old and young and even a few women along too, although you would have been hard pushed to count them needing more than the fingers on one hand.

Some Chelsea fans soon got the hump and started to taunt authority: 'Harry Roberts' is our friend, is our friend, is our friend. Harry Roberts' is our friend, he kills Coppers! Let him out to kill some more, kill some more, kill some more. Let him out to kill some more, Harry Roberts!' The subject of that song was pretty clear. So was the next: 'Kill, Kill! Kill the Bill! Kill, Kill! Kill the Bill!' That was the final straw and the Police waded in purposefully, extracting the perpetrators and the first few arrests were begrudgingly made. This managed to rile up the

Chelsea supporters even more and everyone started pushing forward and swearing at the boys in blue. One of the Policeman, trying to make an arrest of a half-cut, burly troublemaker had his helmet knocked off in the process and this was accompanied by loud jeers and the theme tune from Laurel and Hardy: 'Da er da er, Da er da er, Der der der der, Der der der der. Da er da er, Da er da er, Der der der der, Der er! Der er!'

Everyone chuckled to themselves, as the odd wise cracker shouted out some profundity and the Police once more looked about with egg on their faces, trying in vain to identify known troublemakers or just weed out the worst offenders.

Suddenly they were on the move at last and everyone shuffled forward about two foot, like a Frankenstein monster trying to find its feet. Moving in unison. One, great big chain gang. 'Welcome to Luton', Adam thought. He looked across towards Dan, who was busy raising his eyebrows to the heavens as they stumbled along. Keith, who's height made him resemble a crow's nest, reported back everything that was going on up ahead:

'The Old Bill are nicking someone up the front again'........'Hang on there's another ruck!'......'Group of Luton up the left - well bricking it!'

As they carried on their slow progress through the streets, Keith would continue describing everything around him. It was like having their very own tour guide, but the problem was he only had a chapter heading of knowledge of his surroundings and there was little of historical note to report.

'It's a right old tip', he kept saying.

After what must have been about half an hour of stopping and starting, they reached the main town centre. Keith's mate had been right. The whole town had been boarded up and all the locals with any sense were staying behind bolted doors. Especially, the large Asian community. Occasionally, from one or two of the houses there was a ruffle of a lace curtain and it was clear that someone had been nervously spying on the passing horde.

They then made their way through the graffiti strewn shopping arcade, which was again all boarded up and as they plodded, you could hear the sound of crunching glass underfoot. Someone had obviously not pulled their shutters down or nailed up their plywood in time. Adam tried to think of another match that he had been to when the local inhabitants had literally disappeared, but he couldn't. It came as no surprise though. Since 1976, Chelsea fans had rioted in the town on an almost annual basis.

The floodlights to the Stadium soon came into view up ahead. The ground was tiny and decrepit with a couple of apologetic tinned roofs and it was nestled between lots of crumbly, terraced houses.

'This is a right fuckin' comedy club!' said Dan dismissively.

'Call it a football ground? Fuckin' khazi!' said Keith.

'Hatters?' (that was Luton Town's nickname) 'More like Shitters!' Dan concluded.

Some of the houses had already had their windows smashed and you could see neighbours talking heatedly with the Police and there were lots of heads shaking and gesticulation. The pace around us had picked up markedly now that the smell of horse shit, hot dogs and fried onions were in the air, but the Police were still making their presence felt and wouldn't let anyone out of their sight for a second. So Keith reported back once more.

'Loads of Luton up by their side-stand. Fuckin' tossers!'

As he spoke, he swung his clenched right hand about in the customary 'wanker' sign and the rest of the Chelsea fans about them followed suit. Again, 'We hate Luton!' rang out. It was so loud this time that the hairs rose up on the back of Adam's neck. Amazingly, just after it, they could hear a muffled, 'Luton!' 'Luton!' in response. They then followed that up with 'Shit! Shit! Shit!' and 'Come and have a go at the Chelsea A-G-G-R-O!'

Then before long everyone was shivering in the turnstile queue, but it at least gave Adam time to purchase a match day programme. Unfortunately, the queue wasn't moving very fast and there was only twenty minutes until kick off, so the crush started to worsen as the atmosphere cranked up dramatically. There was loads of singing and chanting now coming from inside the ground with 'Zigger Zagger' and 'Carefree' (about fronting it large in a hostile environment) getting their first airing of the new decade. Chelsea were quite clearly already making their presence felt in large numbers and Dan was missing out.

'Let us in you bastards!' he shouted.

'I wonder where Pete is?' Adam queried as fans berated the turnstile operators.

'Up the Luton end by now, I reckon', said Dan.

'You reckon?'

'Yeah....'

'What about all the Police?'

'So? They won't stop him'.

'How will he get in?'

'He'll just make out he's Luton'.

'Won't the Coppers know?'

'No, he's done it loads of times. Him and his mates'll probably wait till the kick-off and then steam in. Everyone'll be thinking there won't be trouble inside the ground. But there will....'

After finally negotiating the turnstiles, they then climbed up some concrete steps and found themselves by the main toilets, which was swimming in urine and after they had all increased the level of it - Keith dutifully pissing up the wall, they bought some teas and a burger and moved out on to the away terrace.

Chelsea had been given the whole end and it was already virtually filled to capacity. The players had recently been warming up out on the pitch, as the supporters already inside the ground had chanted out some of their names when Adam and company were queuing up, which would usually be followed by the player waving back in acknowledgment and the supporters then cheering in return: 'One - Tommy - Langley! There's only one Tommy Langley. One Tommy Langley!' If it was widely acknowledged that one of the Chelsea players was not too accomplished with the ball, everyone was more than relieved that there was, in fact, only one of them.

One of the first things Adam noticed apart from the tiny Stands and the crummy state of the terracing was the condition of the pitch. It was frozen solid. Adam hoped that the players had brought their skates, because they were going to be needing them. There was also a very serious chill factor, as the ground was badly exposed to all the elements. The away end was completely uncovered. They then began to move about the terracing to find the best vantage point and settled for half way down the left hand side. This was right next to the Luton side-stand where the braver home supporters had proliferated and already chanting was swinging back and forth between the two sets of supporters. Adam looked at his programme and noticed that the Luton Manager, David Pleat wanted to give the Blues a tough match, but hoped that the game would pass off trouble free, it being New Year. 'Fat chance', Adam reckoned. Unfortunately, there were too many people with reputations to maintain. Adam decided that the programme was a complete disappointment as well. Two of the main features, being about motoring and Rod Stewart, who they all hated.

'What the fuck has that twat got to do with football!?' declared Dan.

'Thinks he can play for Scotland', Adam added.

'Even my Grandad could play for them', mocked Keith.

On the singing front, the Chelsea fans were keeping their morale up with a bit of Dusty Springfield, to the tune of 'Those were the Days': 'We'll - see - you - all outside, we'll see you all outside! We'll see you all, we'll see you all outside!' From the information that Adam had already been given, the Luton fans weren't just going to be seen outside. They were going to be seen very close-up inside, as well. Then the Chelsea wound the locals up even more: 'Can you hear the Luton sing? No-oh, no-oh! Can you hear the Luton sing? No-oh, no-oh! Can you hear the Luton sing? I can't hear a fuckin' thing! Woho, woaho, oho!' Then everyone went 'Shhhhhh!' and it wasn't long before you could hear a pin drop in order that the Luton fans might be about to respond. If the match had been against Tottenham, any 'shushing' moment would have probably descended into a depraved taunting, as if it was the sound of the showers in the Nazi Gas chambers. Luckily, for the season of good will, it wasn't.

It was fast becoming ridiculous. Luton were supposed to be at home. Eventually they replied with the repetitive, 'We hate Chelsea!' This was then followed by laughter, jeers and wolf whistling by the massing away supporters and another song quickly followed, which was usually reserved for Liverpool supporters or anyone living north of Watford: 'In your Luton slums. You look in a dustbin for something to eat, you find a dead rat and you think it's a treat, in your Luton slums!' Just as the song reached its climax, the players appeared on the pitch to a great roar. The Chelsea team was largely at full strength and as they stretched and passed the ball around in the warm up down the visitors end, the atmosphere suddenly turned nasty. Up the Luton home terrace, everyone was looking about them as if at any moment, something was going to start up. The Chelsea fans had already noticed that Luton had fielded two black players, Brian Stein and Ricky Hill, and it wasn't long before whistling and sickening jeers started to be directed at them both and the odd banana skin sailed over.

Once the two teams had arranged themselves ready for the match the referee blew his whistle. The game kicked off and everybody waited for the trouble to start. But it didn't. Not yet, anyway. Maybe Pete and his mates couldn't get in? Maybe Icky wasn't about after all? Maybe there was going to be a New Year cease fire?

Despite the icy conditions, the game was a bit of a classic. It was end to end, nail biting stuff. Chelsea scored first, through Mike Fillery and this helped to lighten the mood because the supporters were too busy celebrating to worry about starting trouble. Shame it was only temporary, because Luton equalised soon after through Mal Donaghy and Chelsea heads turned once more to the terraces. It was at that moment that fighting flared. The home end started to almost fall apart. Different factions were whirling their fists around at each other and kicking insanely at anyone caught up in it. Soon, the Luton fans were running away across the terrace in different directions to get away. Kids down the front were even trying to get on the pitch. The Police moved in, but it was too little too late. There would be a moment of truce, to draw breath, then the fighting would start all over again.

While the battle raged, the football continued and Luton's Mike Saxby rubbed salt in the wound by scoring a second. He'd been ably assisted by Ricky Hill who had been berated with disgusting shouts of 'Fuckin' Nigger!' 'Get back to the jungle, you coon!' and a low rumbling chant of 'Oogh! Oogh! Oogh! Oogh!' whenever he got the ball, as if Ricky Hill was some sort of ape and not a gifted, footballing human being. This was the green light for vicious confrontations all around the ground, although it was now all becoming more of a massacre. Even in the Luton side-stand, what had previously been thought of as a safe haven. In the away end, for a bit of a laugh, fans were trying to get on the pitch to stop the match but were held back by a fence and Police reinforcements infiltrating the terracing. Suddenly, Dan turned to Adam almost pointing;

'It's Pete up the other end, with his mates. Over to the right! Look! See....by the pillar!'

Adam and Keith looked. They rubbed their eyes. Then rubbed them once more. At first they couldn't make him out at all because of the distance, but Luton's tiny stadium also had quite a small pitch so the other end wasn't as far away as it seemed at other grounds. Keith was there alright. His thickset demeanour and his red and blue shirt and bomber jacket were unmistakable. He was busy punching a Luton supporter to the ground and as the terrace parted, Pete waded in heavily with some ferocious kicking. He even cajoled the Luton to fight him, almost single handed, whenever he wasn't dishing it out. Others around him followed his lead. Adam stood there stunned. 'A friend of a friend of mine is a seriously dangerous hooligan', he thought to himself. He had naively presumed that all Pete's threats and banter were just for show. No, the pictures coming from the other end were clear. He was for real.

'Fuckin' do the cunts!' Someone shouted out for good measure. 'Stab 'em!'

As the game continued almost oblivious to the violence, Pete and the Chelsea mobs up the other end carried on extracting their petty revenges. Then, out of the blue, Ian Britton equalised which helped to calm things slightly, but it was a repellent roller coaster ride on the terraces at the best of times. When Luton went in front again, the Fascist contingent made themselves heard once more with 'We - are - Nazi's!' Adam turned around, as it was coming from just behind him and saw quite a large faction Seig Heiling.

The Luton fans, to their left, had pulled well back from the end of their stand that joined the away end for their own safety and they were beginning to look petrified. They were also getting pelted with some coins and Adam had heard that they were sometimes sharpened up before the match. A few had even been thrown on the pitch to try and put off Luton's forage's up field.

By now Adam had had more than enough. He felt sick. It was the naked, depravity of it all that he just couldn't stand. It was like watching a cancer. He slowly turned to Dan, who like Keith, was finding it difficult not to get carried away by it all.

'I'm not coming to matches any more…'

There was a pause for a moment as the noise of the crowd took over.

'What?' Dan replied amongst the din.

'I ain't coming to matches…'

'You're joking?'

'No. I don't need this fuckin' shit'.

'What you talking about?'

'I don't wanna go anymore!'

'Oh, come on - '

'I just wanna watch the fuckin' football!' Adam shouted.

Dan and Keith stared at him for a moment, finding it hard not to break into laughter. Then as they clocked each other for a moment, a burly supporter who had overheard everything turned to Adam with a grin;

'Fuckin' poof….'

Adam didn't return fire. The bloke was a lot bigger than him. The last thing he wanted was to be taken out by one of his fellow supporters. From then on, Adam just tried to watch the rest of the game in cold silence. He didn't want to sing anything anymore. He didn't want to chant anything. He didn't want to do anything. In future, Adam decided that he just wanted to watch 'Match of the Day'.

Then he saw something quite bizarre. Among the group of Seig Heiling Chelsea morons was a big black Skinhead who was looking as though he might be saluting along with his mates, who were busy spitting out vile hatred whenever Brian Stein or Ricky Hill got the ball. Adam just couldn't believe what he was seeing and hearing and he didn't know where to begin to comprehend how people could act like that. As all about, descended further into the pit, it even passed him by that Clive Walker, who Adam idolised, had equalised with fifteen minutes to go.

Unfortunately, Adam was in a complete daze for the rest of the game. Towards the end of the match, the Chelsea fans sang: 'We can see you, we can see you, we can see you sneaking out!' at all the Luton fans who were hurrying away from the ground before the final whistle. Trying to save themselves from a good kicking, even though the match was clearly heading for a draw.

The score had obviously been completely immaterial from the start, not that that ever condoned such behaviour. Whatever the motives, Adam really didn't care anymore. 'That's exactly what I wanna do', he thought. 'Sneak out and never come back'. He didn't have to wait much longer though, as the whistle blew and the match finished in a 3-3 stalemate.

After being held in the ground for what seemed like the best part of an hour, the long journey homeward began, herded once more like cattle back onto the train. Then there was the same absurd carry on all the way back to London.

It would be Adam's last Chelsea away game for some time. Dan, he would see less and less of, here and there, at the odd gig or occasional home match. Keith, Adam never saw again. Pete, he found out got arrested that day and ended up in Court. Icky? Adam never did hear what happened to him, or if he was even at the match. Though some years later Icky did end up in prison, doing a long stretch, after a lot of publicity.

Still, it wasn't all bad. It had been a happy New Year.

GUITARS

It was a complete fluke that Adam even started playing an instrument. Whenever Plug had vaguely mentioned getting a band together he had always fancied playing the electric guitar himself and Adam had only considered playing the Bass guitar because there were two less strings so it seemed as if it might be easier to learn. Also, the strings were much thicker so he would be less likely to miss them when doodling about the fret board. Neither of them really wanted to sing, but Adam was in the end marginally more inclined to give the vocal chords a try out even though he was still a little bit shy about it, because Plug had probably the world's worst singing voice. Even in school assemblies he had sounded flatter than anybody else and that was saying something.

One weekend, when Plug came up to London, they ventured down to the local High Street to loaf about, not really with any musical intention or ambition. As they got off the bus, right next to the stop was a little music shop called The Music Box, which was so small it looked as though it only had one or two musical instruments inside it, because there was just no room for anymore. They both decided that they would have a browse around to pass the time and there was a lot of musical paraphernalia; song books, sheet music and packets of strings behind the tiny counter. The shopkeeper slightly resembled the costume hire shop owner from Mr Benn, the popular children's television programme and when he came over and asked if they needed help, Plug replied.

'Er......we're looking for some guitars. We wanna start a band'.

'Well, I've got just the instruments you're looking for', said the shopkeeper, sensing an opportunity and even though he was weary of their appearance at first, he gave them the benefit of the doubt and pointed to the far wall where a lone red bass guitar was hanging. It looked like a cheap copy of the Rickenbacker bass that Bruce Foxton used in the Jam.

'How much is it?' said Plug.

'Forty pounds', was the reply and at that moment Adam sensed that Plug was suddenly contemplating becoming a bass player.

'Can I have a look at it?'

'Sure, have you ever played one before?'

'Er...no....never'.

'Right, well hang on a minute....'

And the man reached up and took the bass down from the wall. He then plugged it into a tiny practice amp which was sitting about. After a minute or so of crackle and hum and bashing the top of the amp to get a clear sound, the guitar was then handed over to Plug who didn't really have a clue what to do with it. After a plectrum was passed to him he tried to twang the open strings and then attempted to hold one of them down. The resulting noise was horrible and sounded totally tuneless. Plug then tried playing really fast and scraped the plectrum quickly on another string. The shopkeeper's hair almost stood on end.

'What about a guitar?' Adam probed, thinking that he might give one a go.

'I have a Kay - Les Paul copy - in the back of the shop, if you'd like to try it?'

'Yeah. How much is it?'

'It's forty-five pounds'.

'Oh, right. Can I try it?' Plug had some money on him, enough to maybe buy the bass. Or at least think about it. Adam unfortunately had none.

'Course....'

After Adam went through the same sort of approach as Plug, but with even less precision and rhythm, you could sense that the excruciating noise was about to make the shopkeeper run out of his store. It was a far worse racket than his violin lessons at school. With amplification there was just no escape. The guitar, although cheap, seemed reasonable enough and it's maple colour was quite fetching and although the wood was very light it looked similar in shape to the guitar Mick Ronson used on Ziggy Stardust, still one of Adam's favourite albums.

Once Plug had had a good look over his instrument and checked it for any scratches and knocks, he chirpily pulled out the required money and his impulsive purchase was then placed in a triangular shaped cardboard box. He also bought a cheap looking guitar strap and lead, even though he had nothing to connect it into when he got home. That didn't matter a bit though, because Plug now had a guitar. A real bass guitar.

Adam asked the shopkeeper if he could keep the guitar for him as he didn't have sufficient funds on him. Once he had picked it up within the week, that was it and he was going to spend the next six months or so annoying the neighbours and the rest of the family with his painful renditions of various punk anthems. Although that wouldn't last long as his parents were about to throw him out of the house. Likewise, Plug busied himself playing along to most of his record collection and after a couple of months he was beginning to have a breakthrough. He could play the monotonous bass riff to 'Public Image' by PiL. He could just about play the opening guitar section to the Pistols' 'God Save The Queen', that's only when the ends of his fingers weren't covered in painful blisters.

After some more weeks, their combined rehearsals began to take shape and once Adam began staying regularly at Plug's house, and began studying a chord book like a Yogi monk, he started to make a bit of progress. They had managed to rig up amplification by connecting their guitars to Plug's stereo and at least they could hear themselves. Plug had since purchased a little practice bass amp aswell and he was busy working it all out.

One band Adam particularly liked to play along to was the Skids. The guitarist Stuart Adamson had a crunching tone and his rapid riffing sounded excellent. He had recently been interviewed in Sounds magazine and Adam also thought that he had a terrific attitude, saying that he was proud to be a punk and proud to get up on stage and stick up two fingers to the likes of Led Zeppelin. Rather than bother getting to Number One, he wanted to write classic singles like 'Down In The Tube Station', 'White Man', 'Borstal Breakout', 'Shot By Both Sides', 'Here Comes The Summer', 'Boredom', 'Anarchy', 'Neat Neat Neat', like 'Alison'. Adamson was really glad to be part of it all and he reckoned it was the best time to be alive. And the more Adam and Plug practiced on their musical cricket bats the more they were beginning to feel the same.

MALCOLM OWEN

It was Summer 1980 and in between more serious guitar rehearsals, Adam finally moved out of home and began living with a new girlfriend, Carol, at her mother's place in Battersea. She fancied herself as a bit of a model, and her mother had already rubber-stamped their living together, as she was a little bit bohemian. Adam counted his good fortune again, as he had just bumped into her one night at a gig. There was plenty of coincidence in it all as Adam had only ventured out at the last minute, deciding to see one of his favourite bands, The Ruts, who were appearing at the Marquee Club in Wardour Street.

Earlier, that same evening, Adam had met up with an old friend of Alex's from school and they were going up to meet Dan and a few other mates inside the venue. As they left the tube station and turned the corner off Shaftesbury Avenue, they talked animatedly of the forthcoming concert and how great it was to be seeing such a top band.

As they turned once more and began to stroll up Wardour Street, Adam suddenly became aware of three Skinheads up ahead, looming towards them. 'Oh, Christ...' he said under his breath. The one in front was tall and looked hard. His two cohorts were shorter but stockier. One of them reminded Adam of a Bulldog, the other looked as if he'd been hit in the face with a steam shovel. All three had tattoos carved into their arms which stood out like railway tracks, advertising 'Skins' or the latest love of their lives.

Adam just tried to concentrate on what his companion was saying, to take his mind off the imminent danger, but as they brushed past their worst nightmares, the tall Skin picked him out, with some eye-balling and Adam knew that it wasn't because he fancied him and wanted to exchange telephone numbers. He gulped and thought 'Shit, my number's up!' but on the surface still tried to remain calm, knowing that any sign of weakness would play into their hands. So, Adam just carried on walking past with his friend seemingly regardless. Then the tall Skinhead piped up.

'Oi, mate! You got thirty pence?'

This was a common occurrence at the time while queuing up at gigs, because some people would always try their luck and get some extra money by force.

Adam thought for a moment. It felt like an age. 'What do I do? If I give them thirty pence then they'll think I'm a chicken and do me over and then help themselves to whatever I have left anyway', and he only had enough money for the Tube, the gig and a couple of pints of beer.

'No, sorry mate....' he replied foolishly and continued walking.

Maybe the Skin didn't like his dyed cropped hair and the bondage trousers were also an effrontery and once they fully clocked Adam's 'Bone Idol' jacket that was it. He was now their number one target. They certainly didn't have much of a sense of humour. They were now virtually stalking their prey and muttering to each other and it was becoming obvious, that there was going to be a further exchange or two.

'Oi, mate!' 'I said...have you got thirty pence?!'

Adam just bit his lip and carried on walking and told his nervous friend to do the same and to not look back, because the skins were closing fast, catching up with every step. However, they were fast approaching the Marquee and sanctuary and Adam prayed that they might just let it rest, and let them go on their way. But no such chance.

Next thing Adam knew, a searing pain was flashing through his body as the Skinhead giraffe connected one of his steel capped DM's up his backside. As Adam clutched himself and let out an audible groan, a second boot launched itself right into the pit of his stomach. This one, added to the impact of the first, really took the wind out of his lungs and he hit the deck. Adam's hands even scraped on the pavement as the Skin came round into view.

After witnessing Dave getting unanimously 'done-in' at the Sham concert, Adam reckoned that his best defence was definitely not going to be lying down, curled up in a ball, so he tried to scramble to his feet with the aid of the side of a parked car. But just as he was about to regain his posture the Skin had grabbed hold of him and was up close and personal, glaring right in his eyes. Adam reckoned he definitely wasn't in their best books.

'You've got thirty pence! You fucking liar!'

Just as the psycho spat out his bile right into Adam's face, he turned his head round to discover that his so-called friend had scarpered.

He peered up the road towards the Marquee. The 'friend' was nowhere to be seen. 'Maybe he's gone to get help?' Adam thought. 'He'll be back. With the Seventh Cavalry. He wouldn't leave me all on my own?

He's obviously gone to find reinforcements?' Like hell. He had melted away into the night. Then suddenly, Adam caught a glimpse of him right up the street looking back over his shoulder. He had 'guilt' written in big letters all over his face. So much so that he had even walked on way past the venue. Obviously he had decided that he was prepared to forfeit even The Ruts concert to save his own hide and let Adam handle the three stooges on his own. 'Cheers. Thanks a lot!' Adam thought and immediately wiped him off his Christmas card list.

'Look mate, I'm skint', he offered to baldie number one.

'Bollocks you are!'

'I am, honest....'

With that the tall one pulled his fist back and Adam watched in slow motion all the way as it connected with his nose. He was all but knocked out and as he fell down again, he hit his head hard on the pavement. All he could remember was lying dazed on the ground, for some time, trying to stem the blood from his nostrils, while the two smaller storm troopers stepped forward and leered down at him.

'That fuckin' showed you!' They chuckled.

That they certainly had, but what, Adam wasn't quite so sure. That three of them could beat him up showed a lot of skill and resourcefulness. Only trouble was it was pretty clear that the lanky leader was the only one doing the striking. The short arsed seconds had just been sitting watching in the posh seats. The other thing it showed was that whoever Adam thought was a friend might not necessarily want to stand by him when the dirt hit the fan.

Happily, seeing the state of Adam and his sorry demeanour, the Skinheads eased off their venom a little. They knew he wasn't going to retaliate. He was a pathetic punch bag, a sitting duck, and sooner or later they would become bored of hitting him. Or so Adam tried to reason. 'That's lucky', he thought, 'It could have been worse'.

Just as he was enjoying the reprieve, the goose stepper who looked as if he'd had the recent altercation with a shovel, landed a toe punt right between Adam's legs. Luckily, his tartan bondage trousers were quite loose at the time and the full force of the kick was also deflected by straps and pieces of material. Even so, the impact on his testicles still made his eyes water and had he spoken soon after he would probably have sounded like Donald Duck.

'We hate fuckin' Punks!' said public enemy number one.

'Surprise, surprise', Adam sighed. You'd think by now he'd got the message.

'And fuckin' Chelsea!'

Bollocks, so they had noticed the writing on top of his jacket as well. Great. Adam knew it would be foolish to try and explain to them that it was the Punk band and not the football team, because he was a Chelsea supporter anyway. It wouldn't have rung true with them, and besides they weren't the listening sort. They had never been brought up on 'Jackanory'.

As Adam slowly picked himself up once more and wiped his swollen face with his shirt sleeve, the appearance of his blooded nose made them all stand back like graet artists to admire their work. As they surveyed their victim, Adam felt his numb nasal passages.

'Shit, I think it's broken', he muttered, in almost a whisper and immediately he began to act like he was really hurt. He staggered around dramatically and pretended that he was not worth hitting anymore, and amazingly he found that it seemed to work. Adam's sad, Oscar nominated performance had the desired effect. He had completely bamboozled them. And after hurling a string of abuse that required virtually every word to be bleeped out, the Skinheads left him alone and moved on to some other lucky soul further down the street. Except of course for that one last passing kick.

Once Adam had recoiled his body and he was further away from them, he managed to make his way along to the Marquee, because whatever happened, he didn't want to miss The Ruts. He suddenly had a ridiculous vision of himself watching the band at the front of the auditorium whilst lying flat on a hospital bed, connected to tubes and covered in bandages. He decided that if he had gone to the Police they probably would have just spent the whole evening laughing in hysterics at the sight of him and the state of his clothes. And he was convinced that they weren't going to assign their best detectives to the case.

Eventually, Adam arrived outside his destination short of breath. In fact, it took about ten minutes just to gather himself. There was now no queue at all because the gig had already started and from inside you could hear the reggae support band, Misty, were on stage with their unmistakable throbbing bass lines, jingly guitar and keyboards.

Misty had played with many Punk bands during this period, including The Clash and Stiff Little Fingers, and there was always a strong link between Punk and Reggae music as they were both anti-establishment and instigated by creative individuals who felt outside of the mainstream: bands like Aswad, Steel Pulse and Black Slate all shared billings on major Punk tours. Three members of Misty - Pocky, Rocky and Bertie had even contributed to backing vocals on the single 'Jah War', which had been in the charts and was featured on The Ruts, 'The Crack' album. In fact, the first Ruts single 'In a Rut' was released on Misty's very own 'People Unite' cooperative label, which both bands were signed to.

The man at the box office was hardly concerned by Adam's manner and the blood clotting down his front, and once Adam had said that he was okay and that he had mates inside who would help him out, the man sat back, took the cash and allowed him in.

Adam entered the compact confines of the Marquee and looked for the rest of his mates. Once he had collared them and told them what had happened, which hardly needed explaining once they had caught sight of him, there was little surprise, because Skinheads had been harassing people all night. Even members of Misty had been confronted by them outside. Adam looked across at Dan, and even though he was looking sheepish, because he considered himself a Skinhead who just happened to like Punk music, he stood up and with the others bundled out of the club to have a look for the Skins, and perhaps obtain some revenge. But it was all too late. The Skinheads were long gone. It was a forlorn attempt at retribution but it did make Adam feel a little bit better. When they returned, they made sure Adam was alright, reckoning that his nose at least wasn't broken. Just knocked about a bit. Once Adam was in the toilets giving himself a good wash down, with a pint of water obtained from the bar, he soon found himself beginning to look forward to the headliners.

Misty's roots reggae had sounded excellent, but unfortunately Adam had missed most of their set, as he was still in the cramped, dingy toilets trying to clean himself up. As he wiped his face, and hummed along to Misty's last number, 'See Them A Come' the odd punk came in and dropped some amyl nitrate or a 'Speckled Blue', and judging by the loud groans, an amorous couple were starting to get it together in the cubicle.

In the gap between the bands, Adam tried to work through all the pints bought by his more than sympathetic friends. It felt satisfying to survive a beating by a group of Skins, and to be able to tell the tale, and that no one had thought he had 'bottled it'. Then Adam noticed this striking girl sat right next to Dan, and he realized that he had seen her occasionally at gigs before, but had no idea who she was. More importantly, the girl seemed quite concerned about his state, and from what he could tell it didn't seem as if she was going out with anybody. He hoped that she wasn't a friend of the bloke who had left him to fend for himself. Because whenever his name was mentioned, he was quickly chastised and a price was put out on his head. If he ever turned up in future, he was going to get jumped.

So with the problem solved, they then started to position themselves right down by the front of the stage. A good place to watch Malcolm Owen, the raucous Ruts lead singer right up close and also observe Paul Fox their excellent guitarist. Adam had already been using a friends little practice amp for a few months by now and he wanted to watch him closely to try and suss out that elusive galloping guitar riff from their hit single 'Babylon's Burning'. He was already becoming pretty obsessive about the instrument and rated Paul Fox one of his top guitar heroes because he effortlessly fused searing soloing with choppy orientated rhythm. He was unique, and topped off with Malcolm Owen's highly authentic vocals, 'Segs' hypnotic bass structures and Dave Ruffy's syncopated, thunderous drumming, they were a winning combination. 'Babylon's Burning' reached number seven in the UK charts the previous summer and it would be their highest climbing single, with a terrific appearance on Top of The Pops. The song was an absolute classic, graphically depicting the state of the nation and highlighting what was going on all around. After one year of Thatcherism, the future looked bleak: Riots in the inner cities, mass unemployment, racism, International terrorism, football violence, apathy, ignorance, drugs, police brutality, etc. You name it. There was a very long shopping list.

After waiting some time offstage to crank up the anticipation levels to the max, The Ruts suddenly bundled onto the stage. They looked pent up. Focussed. All pulling together. As a band they spouted some rhetoric but it was easily digestible, because they were genuine and at the end of the day none of them took themselves too seriously. 'What a formula', Adam thought. The Ruts instantly became the band that made Adam want to get up on stage himself, despite his anxiety with performing. Because Malcolm Owen wasn't a poser as some of the other's undoubtedly were, he almost made it a natural progression. He really cared what he was singing about and his lyrics were poignant because they were personal and sung with complete abandon. He was the real thing. His voice scraped like gravel in concrete and he didn't mess around with that trendy jacket or cultured haircut, he just got up on the stage in his braces and jeans and had a go.

The temperature in the Marquee was now so hot it wasn't long before Owen had dispensed with his customary Fred Perry shirt and began swaggering around in his braces. He reminded Adam a lot of Morgan Webster, the awesome lead singer of 'Menace' for his hundred and ten percent attitude on stage. You felt that every gig might possibly be his last so he took no prisoners. Yet, he seemed to have a winning way with an audience as well, with his cheeky comments and passionate delivery and the spectator's attention couldn't help but stay connected.

The Achilles heel for Owen however, was his fatal addiction to heroin. He wrote about it with a unique visceral power. One of the first songs that the Ruts played at the gig was called 'H-Eyes' and Adam remembered that the singer had once referred to it in NME saying that it was about a mate of Owen's and his own problems with heroin. He knew it wasn't good for him, but it was nice at the time, but the consequences were clear. It was going to kill him. Prophetic words indeed. After this gig, Malcolm Owen would be dead from the drug, inside a month. What a talent and what a waste. It reminded Adam of his oldest brothers seeing Jimi Hendrix and Jim Morrison live at the Isle of Wight Festival in 1970 and within a year, both were dead. And what a tragedy, that heroin was wiping out the punk ranks. Sid Vicious had already succumbed. You could bet your bottom dollar Johnny Thunders would follow suit. And even though people bickered about who was to blame for introducing it to the punks, the blame resting largely with the American rock stars, nevertheless it was about and thriving.

Adam felt that amyl nitrate and other drugs of that kind were not exactly harmless, but at least there was less chance of them killing you. He had taken the drug a couple of times before gigs and it just meant that he pogoed around more furiously and salivated more, which resulted in him launching a hail of phlegm at the headliners.

The only other drugs that he had taken were so accessible like ganja, that it hardly raised the eyebrows and it was debatably less harmful than cigarettes, and Speed. One Saturday afternoon, Adam swallowed a small, blue Speed tablet, given to him by Alex, and he then spent the rest of the day sitting on a Circle Line Tube train whizzing round and round. While he travelled on his circular roller coaster, he chatted to strangers animatedly about nothing in particular and then he was incredibly ill. But Heroin? That was a different game entirely and in a way the death of Malcolm Owen confirmed Adam's hate for that particular drug with a vengeance.

Everyone was becoming loosened up in the close, sweaty Marquee and Adam noticed even some eye contact from the girl, Carol. The songs were coming thick and fast now, and after a few wired up punks shouted out 'Savage Circle!' The Ruts duly obliged. This song was an early number on the Ruts debut album (the album reaching number 16 in the charts) and it was as potent as its name. This was quickly followed by the stunning Babylon's Burning, and the furious Human Punk. The pogoing was awesome, some of the most manic Adam had ever taken part in. He was surprised that the floor hadn't given way (at one gig featuring the UK Subs, the venues' carpet was the only thing stopping everyone from falling through into the basement below as some of the floorboards had given way. It didn't stop the pogoing though. As the carpet sagged sadly, everyone chanted 'C.I.D!' 'C.I.D!' and carried on jumping).

Malcolm Owen had this great way of mangling out the words as if he'd just made them up on the spot. He prowled centre stage, like an urban sniper - rigid as a rifle, twisting his face and spitting out the words. The music seemed to cut right through him and then he'd wrench out a verse and then a little bit more. Paul Fox meanwhile, wound up the tension with the searing guitar introduction to 'In a Rut', a classic football terrace anthem (another thing Adam loved about the band was that they usually went from one song to the next without much delay, except perhaps for some rousing banter from Owen, which really built a crescendo). One minute the audience was trying to touch the ceiling careering up and down, and then suddenly they would change the tempo and play a skanking reggae number like 'Jah War', about the assault of Clarence Baker (Misty's manager) by the SPG.

The Ruts were always one step ahead live and they fused Reggae and Punk, in Adam's opinion even more effectively than the Clash. For them it was organic. It was a reflection of the multicultural environment that they all shared. This made the adrenalin rush that much more intoxicating. After the swirling bass of 'Jah War', they then returned to the more orthodox rhythms of 'Something That I Said', another successful single and 'You're Justa'. With a little build up after a cool down they then went completely loopy to the crunching, 'Criminal Mind', 'Back Biter' and 'Out of Order'.

As Adam and his mates propelled themselves high into the Marquee vortex, he had now forgotten about the unfortunate episode outside the venue and sweated off what seemed about ten pounds in body weight. The songs were intelligent and uncompromising, 'Dope for Guns' and 'S.U.S' (about the Police's 'arrest on suspicion law' that had created much unrest in the inner cities) followed. Again the tempo changed and the band launched into the atmospheric 'It Was Cold', with a brilliantly poised guitar solo again from Paul Fox. This was a real crossover song, which suggested that the band, had they continued in their present guise, might have attained the heights.

The gig was reaching its storming climax and they played their present single 'Staring At The Rude Boys' as part of their encore. This song was fairly pertinent to what Adam had just experienced right outside the venue and his mate Dave had at Sham's Last Stand and as he jumped about, he sang along to the lyrics with extra gusto. It seemed as if The Ruts had taken on Sham 69's mantle as social realists but they were more experimental, combining both the aggression and inspiration of Punk, with the musicality and rhythm of Reggae.

When Adam heard about Malcolm Owen's death (he died in a bath like Jim Morrison) he felt crushed. He was without doubt one of the greatest live performers Adam had ever had the privilege to see and in the reggae song 'Give Youth A Chance', he spoke movingly for a lost generation. Trouble was, in the end, he was only human just like everyone else who came to watch the band. For Adam, it certainly felt like another huge stake right in the heart of Punk.

Owen's self penned, ironically titled reggae-dub song, 'Love In Vain' acts as a moving epitaph, with its poetic lyrics about his very real dilemma. Regrettably, he could never rid himself of his own tragic fixation with heroin.

5

UB40

Since the disastrous beginnings to Adam's career in the Supermarket, he had found it increasingly difficult to obtain any worthy kind of employment. School had at least sheltered him from the vagaries of the outside world and it's many hurdles, but his achievements in terms of qualifications were miniscule and it was then that he started to regret not putting his nose to the grindstone. He only had one 'O' level, which wouldn't really set him on the path to the Managers chair. He had long ago decided it was pointless to stay on for sixth form a further year, because it was patently obvious to any neutral observer that he wasn't achieving anything, and it would probably result in only one more 'O' level at best or a CSE in cookery. No, he had to face the sticks and stones of the employment ladder and so began his first battle with unemployment. At least he wasn't alone. At Thatcher's command, many distinguished trades and lifelong careers were feeling the inevitable squeeze.

Back at his last school, it hadn't been for lack of trying. The careers officer, who was a fussy lady with ridiculous glasses, took more than a passing interest in Adam's failure.

'So, have you considered a future career?'

'Er, no....not really'.

'I see'.

There was a long pause, that you could drive a huge juggernaut between.

'Well, there must be something that you would like to do?' said the flailing careers advisor.

'Er....don't think so', Adam stumped up, cagily.

'Some employment that you might like to pursue?' she tried again snootily, clutching at straws. 'Something to give you a sense of fulfilment - a sense of purpose?'

'Er....no'.

'Nothing?'

It took ages to shake his head. Partly because it looked like he might suddenly nod, but then he held his head still again and decided, that with it, he was just going to shake.

'Nothing at all?'

There was another black hole of a silence.

'Well....I've always wanted to play for Chelsea?' He admitted eventually.

'What, as a professional footballer?'

'Yeah'.

'Is there any likelihood of that?'

'Er...no...not really'.

'Right....well....'

At that moment she opened a large folder crammed full of super careers.

'Is there nothing else that you have ever considered?'

'I've always wanted to play in a band'.

'Oh, yes? What kind of band?'

'A punk band'.

She winced.

'I see....and you can play a musical instrument?'

'I played a bassoon once in 2nd orchestra. I liked it'.

Ms 'career opportunity' coughed and adjusted her glasses.

'Well, I'm afraid, music is a very precarious occupation. Only a very few can ever hope to make it. Being realistic, I'm afraid I really don't think that you have the necessary skills'.

Adam shuffled in his plastic chair, just as she turned the page in the folder to another wonderful future. Eventually, frustrated, she looked up, her glasses almost misting up.

'Have you ever thought about joining the armed forces?'

'Umm....no, I haven't. But I wanted to be an astronaut', he said with a hint of seriousness.

'Astronaut?!' She flinched. 'What, with just one or two O levels?'

'Yeah, why not?' He challenged, somewhat naively.

'Why not?'

Her expression would have been the same had she just trodden in shit.

'Why not?!' she repeated for full effect.

'Yeah, I'm keen'.

'Keen?'

'Yeah....'

'Look, I don't think keenness is really going to be quite enough to make you an astronaut. No, I think you're going to have to stay just that little bit closer to earth, don't you?'

Eventually, Adam had to sign-on in what looked like an old second world war aircraft hanger and the air was tense. He couldn't believe the amount of forms that had to be filled out. It was enough to give him writer's wrist. Once he was seen by the manically depressive signing-on pen pusher and had his details verified, which took so long he almost grew a beard in the time, he was then advised to look round the adjacent job centre for any suitable vacancies (in those days it was a pretty basic place, but there were a wide variety of jobs on offer).

As Adam checked out the jobs advertised on little white cards up on the boards, he instantly thought how ridiculous some of the vacancies were. Were they really being serious? He hoped not? Talk about taking it all with a pinch of salt.

Over the following years, whenever Adam couldn't obtain a suitable vacancy other than working in a supermarket or on a building site carrying bricks about in the summer, he found the task of looking in the job shop window a demoralising occupation. The feeling of being on a proverbial scrap heap was never ending. It wasn't the lack of employment, the variety advertised in the job centres never ceased to amaze him, the only problem was that a lot of the jobs weren't particularly enticing and if he was unlucky enough to get one of them, he'd probably live to regret it. Also, the wage packet for most of the jobs wouldn't get him very far even in the Third World and hardly made 'signing-off' a viable prospect. But he was supposed to feel useless if he wasn't in employment so the pressure was always on to take anything that came along. Even if that meant screwing tops on toothpaste tubes or landscape gardening in the Antarctic.

There were posters and notices and cards, all advertising various incredible opportunities. One job poster in particular caught his eye. It showed a happy young man dressed in shorts and sandals on a particularly sunny beach, holding a decorated Christmas tree in his arms. Above the man was the caption: 'LOOKING FOR A CHRISTMAS JOB?' And below him, 'IT'S NEVER TOO EARLY TO START!'

The only catch was the fact that when the poster was pasted up on the wall of the Job centre it was still only March.

What I'm sure Adam and many of his fellow jobseekers would have preferred was the prospect of some kind of job for Easter, considering that it was just around the corner. I mean what's wrong with Easter? Or failing that perhaps some kind of job for the summer, such a nice proposition especially with all that hot weather, or maybe even some kind of glittering new post obtained by the onset of autumn, with still not a Christmas tree in sight - although in the shops sometimes it was hard not to trip over festive decorations by the August Bank holiday.

Employment. Work. Anything. Was it too much to ask? Digging ditches. Managing children's parties. Cleaning the Houses of Parliament. Certainly a job for life was out of the question, but maybe it could be something that might at least pass the time. Even if it was only for a day or two. You know, like trying your hand at being a Ballroom dancing teacher for example. Or having a stab as an apprentice Beekeeper?

Mind you some jobs were hardly worthy of the name and those that were, weren't likely to set you on the path to a triumphant career. Well, not just yet anyway.

Here are just a few of the job vacancies that Adam saw advertised on those little white cards;

'LEAF CLEARER' required - no experience necessary.

'TEA PERSON AND HANDYMAN' - on the job instruction.

'GRAVEDIGGER' - experience necessary. Ability to work in all weathers.

'FISH ASSISTANT' - to serve and advise customers on their choice off fish. Should not be squeamish.

'STATIC SECURITY OFFICERS' - immediate start. (Were you allowed to move about, Adam wondered?)

'ICE CREAM SALESMAN' - van provided.

'SECURITY AGENT' required.(Contact with the CIA and MI5 a possibility? Failing that Adam might get to meet the Queen)

'TRAINEE ERECTORS' - will be trained by experienced erectors. (Scaffolding, Adam presumed)

'GATE OPERATIVES' - inspecting tickets whilst maintaining a safe environment for passengers. (Lots of responsibility)

'SANTA AND HIS HELPERS' - required for central shopping complex. (Adam wouldn't have been a very convincing Santa but he might have excelled as one of the pixies in the grotto. Shame the employment was so temporary)

'BELL PERSON' - to welcome guests in a congenial manner, arriving at hotel.

'DOOR PERSON' - helpful manner and good communication skills essential.

'YARD PERSON' - prepared to work on their own.

'TOWN CRIER' - part-time. Costume provided. (There were times Adam wanted to do a lot of crying all about town)

'TOILET ATTENDANT' - at busy metropolis. (A vacancy with real prospects)

'MOBILE CLEANER' - tools provided. (What, able to move about again? And what tools were they kindly providing, a mop and bucket?)

'LIFEGUARD' required. (In London?)

'MOWER OPERATOR' needed. (Adam always wanted to drive one of the big ones!)

'SANDWICH DELIVERY PERSON' - communication skills and tidiness an advantage. (Adam probably would have scoffed them all)

'HOUSEKEEPER' vacancy. (Preferably round Adam's house)

'DOG HANDLER' - experience of dogs necessary and owner of large dog preferred, if not, dog may be supplied. (So no luck if Adam was going to turn up to the interview with his beloved Poodle or prize Chihuahua)

'LIGHTHOUSE KEEPER' - able to be away from home for long periods. (Let's just say that Adam was the perfect person for the job. Shame that he was just a little bit too young)

'MILK AND CREAM PROCESSOR' - candidates must have knowledge of pasteurised milk and cream and knowledge of cream separation. (Adam would probably make a right old mess, but he'd certainly give it a go)

'SUNDAY DRIVERS' - HGV qualified applicants only need apply. (A great opportunity to take in the countryside)

'SILVER SERVICE STAFF' required. (Smaller cutlery on the inside or the outside? Also, napkin or serviette?)

'NAPPY CARE REPRESENTATIVE' - experience necessary. (Another potentially messy career)

'WATER SAMPLER' - visiting customers houses and taking samples. (No way was Adam doing that in London. The water tasted fucking horrible)

'FINE TURF OPERATIVE' - experience in maintaining cricket tables and bowling greens and experience in the use of fine turf equipment. (Wasn't this job better known as a Groundsman? Great summer job though)

'KNIFE THROWER'S ASSISTANT' - flexible hours. (Flexible knives?)

'HUMAN CANNONBALL!' for popular Circus. (A cynical attempt at reducing the unemployment figures perhaps?)

'UNDERWEAR FITTER' - man or woman. Apply within. (Adam reckoned this vacancy would be snapped up quickly)

Most of the jobs seemed ridiculous on paper. So what were they going to be like for real? Adam quickly decided that he would work extra hard at the band stuff, and make a real go of it, so that he could perhaps stave off the need to become a part-time Beefeater or a Lollypop Boy.

SWEET BITTER

The formation of a new band the 'Allies' was certainly a new adventure for female punk singer Honey Bane (Donna Boylan) who Adam reckoned that he could more than identify with. She was similar in age and had had some well documented childhood brushes with the Law and experienced an absent without leave home life, so there was some sort of connection. More importantly, Adam really liked her music, especially the classic song 'Violence Grows' from the Fatal Microbes EP and the by now, legendary vinyl collaboration 'You Can Be You' with the anarcho-punk band Crass. So much so, that back at school, Adam had penned a short poem in his dinner break about the singer's compelling 'Girl on the Run' song. He kept quiet about it though, as writing a poem at school wasn't a particularly wise move. As a result, it was pretty much his only creative moment.

Rushing through the corridors

Laughing, crying

Running from the routine

Living, flying

Dodging all the screeching

Rules and regulations

'Going to the city!'

'And never coming back!'

Racing through the crazy streets

Coloured sparks in hair

Words, dreams and uniforms

Ain't tucked in don't care

Thoughts and schemes like bullets

Spewing all about

Catch that number 13

Then scream and shout.

Bane was now even dropping her earlier made-up first name for the real and more mature - as Sounds magazine put it, "Donna" if you please'. Having by now realised that there was no point in exhausting further the various Fatal Microbes line ups, her fresh departure seemed to open up an exciting avenue, appearing with experienced, gig hardened musicians like the ex-UK Subs bassist, Paul Slack, and the rest of the Allies line up; the hard hitting 'Steve Jones' on drums (not the irrepressible Pistol) and the expressive Swift on guitar, who was certainly not just a closet bedroom musician.

The UK Subs, already considerable Punk legends, had been founded on their inexhaustible appetite for playing every type of venue, from the less than friendly Town Hall to that subterranean toilet the length and breadth of Britain and across Europe. Many venues which other bands would simply turn their noses up at, Charlie Harper and company would assault with relish. And with half of that rhythm section now in Donna Bane's new band, the signs were auspicious.

With so many positives about, Adam thought the group's hastily arranged debut gig at Clapham's 101 Club, supporting the new look UK Subs seemed appealing and one that his girlfriend Carol would definitely enjoy. Especially, as she had already started to become a little bit bored of the male orientated punk rock straight jacket. For her, bands with a front woman were a bit more of a spin on the old template. The added plus was that her mum's flat in Battersea was just around the corner.

The 'Allies' tight musical unit seemed to have potential and certainly a powerful stage presence, despite the hasty formation. And for Adam, making mental notes could perhaps influence the direction of his own band. He hoped that they would play the classic material, and maybe there were even more diverse dishes on the menu too, perhaps a bit of Reggae/Ska and even a rock tinge, what Donna called their 3-Tone Sound. Whatever the situation, when the cranked up herberts in the audience demanded a pogo, Adam reckoned the Allies would still be able to hold more than their own. Donna's following had always been loyal, despite being perpetually in search of that ever more sporadic Bane appearance. She could pop up just about anywhere. On stage with Killing Joke. In the studio with Jimmy Pursey. She had absolutely no fear. But performing was most likely going to be the least of the problem. Even the earlier outfits that Honey fronted, had themselves hinted at an intimidating undercurrent, which made for an electrifying but hazardous live experience. The many explosive gigs earlier that year where violence was never far away, being a prime example. But crucially, it was the hurdle of a similar vision or mindset amongst the new band members that would most likely scupper the prospects. One thing Adam already knew from being in a band, however elementary, was that at least he and Plug could completely trust each other.

Another difficulty would lie surely in the speed of it all, as Adam was beginning to find out. Everything was as hurried as an amphetamine; get the band together, rehearse it in, shape the music, write the lyrics, learns the songs, get the gig, do the date, drink the beer money, load the van up, that's if they had one, start again, keep the band together etc, etc. All this graft trying to retain that elusive punk ethic, the DIY code, while also trying to manoeuvre around the limited punk M25 of, 'You gotta be true to your punk roots', 'You're only allowed three chords', 'You gotta keep it loud' and 'You have to play fast!'

The recent interest from the Subs independent label Gem Records, was encouraging for Donna and resulted in about six songs being quickly recorded in demo form at a South London studio to begin chiselling out the up to scratch Bane sound. Top tracks from the demo were 'My Boy Fights' and 'Allies Anthem', a title busting rocker to give the band's following and Adam, perhaps even more of a sense of identity. The other numbers were more experimental musically, searching even, as if the quartet were short sighted buskers struggling to see if any elusive pennies had been dropped.

The gig was fly posted locally as a bit of a knees up, a celebration and even a 'barmy army manoeuvre'. When Adam and Carol arrived, the venue was packed to the rafters, with as many punters as could be squeezed at short notice into the luxuriant pub rock auditorium, with its Victorian purple curtain backdrop, whitewashed walls and decrepit electric wiring permitting. There were probably some reviewers waiting in the wings, and some fanzine junkies hovering, but in terms of a long line of rock critics, this being a Monday night and downtown Clapham, they were conspicuous by their absence.

However, Adam would later find out by reading the music press reviews that The Allies had had no last minute rehearsal, not even a moment's sound check and what's more they weren't even using their own gear, always a risky business and the PA certainly wasn't the best. Carol reckoned that due to the cutting feedback and distortion from the more than close up speakers, her hearing was never the same again.

Keen to break into their stride as soon as possible, the Allies piled onto the stage, the spectators staring back avidly, although perhaps in the back of their mind waiting for their maestro's Charlie Harper and Nicky Garrett. Paul Slack was sporting a pair of none too hip sunglasses. Donna looked more sedated in her dress choice than previously. Her hair now dark raven was more stabilised than elevated. Her stage clobber was all crisp white shirt and suit. Her make-up had a hint of Goth with most of the accent round the eyes and the lips. A kind of doll among thugs. Behind the veneer lurked the rest of the band in the obligatory black, who supported ably from the shadows, all the incredible angst and holler.

With no announcement but the drum click count, the first song began. The bouncing 'My Boy Fights' managed to force the crowd into some moving factions and early gobbing, partly due to the expectant shouts for Donna's previous material. But anything more rocking than an organ grinder would have had the devotees jumping. After another experimental number or two, Bane announced to resounding applause, that there would be a more advertised exposure, at the second wave punk sanctuary the Music Machine in Camden Town, which Adam was more than pleased about, it being one of his favourite venues. Most likely guesting again with the Subs, with more vinyl 45's certain to follow from all the busy demoing.

And, as if by magic, the haunting opening bars of Violence Grows chilled the venue, the cheering and clapping from her announcement having almost smothered the song's start. Bane's storytelling was so intense, alongside the spiralling, echoing riff, that it was as if she was holding up a long mirror, reflecting all the jagged attitude crowded right in front. As the loping bass and reverb finally diminished, Adam marvelled at how much contrast there was already in the brilliant set. The first Lesson had just ended. The only problem might be that it was almost too far ahead of it's time for its own good. 'How can you even try to categorise it' he considered. Adam almost tried there on the spot, but of course he couldn't. Carol couldn't either, as she just shrugged.

In the short hiatus before the next surprise, the requests started up again, the newly born 'Allies Anthem' more than achieved its objective, working up the audience again into another frenzy, especially when the band suddenly then careered into a potent 'Porno Grows' and then tailgated into a fast and furious 'Girl on the Run'. The song's thundering bass riff and drums almost seemed chopped up into great undigestable chunks by slicing, manic guitar. The treble managed to cut through pretty much in line with Adam's exacting specification's, as if the Crass band members from the original recording had entered the building. He also noticed that a cartoon-like 'slam dance' was beginning to break out in the crowd to the mid paced barnstormer. At the song's more than chaotic, but intentional climax, Adam turned to Carol.

'That's one of the best songs ever!'

'Definitely one of the loudest!' she replied half joking, with her hands almost covering her ears.

Wrapping up the lethal set was a brief punk medley of 'Boring Conversations', that then cleverly flowered into the reggae dub song 'Guilty'. The latter causing a swathe of spitting and dubbed down pogoing, and also the repeated grabbing of Donna's mike stand. Perhaps because of all the sweaty bedlam, and Carol fast becoming a fresh punk critic, she argued that sorting out the sound and all the levels could have helped the nerves.

'You're joking!' said Adam, adamant.

'She was nervous. You could tell!'

'Yeah, but who wouldn't be, with the Subs coming up!'

Adam had to admit the feedback and treble on the guitar alone cut through the lobes like a chainsaw, not that the already half deafened clientele were that bothered, and with the next edition of Sounds, the reviewers reckoned the cool punk diva had managed a 'sensual vocal' as Duncan Disorderly commented, which was certainly against the odds. No mean feat with some prototype Mohicans breathing down her neck.

Eventually, after a further swelling of the crowd through the eye of a needle, an emptying of the booze supplies and all the expectant banter, the new UK Subs came up and right according to plan ripped up the venue. The band were in unstoppable form despite the old certifiable hits being largely banished from their set. Harper didn't waste any time, dedicating the mind blowing 'You don't Belong' to the largely absent muso music reps and spat out the words like he always meant it. Again microphone stands were soon fought over as the new bassist Alvin Gibbs motored through the catalogue. The peroxide Garrett, all ammo belts and fatigues, made shapes with his guitar like a demented Chuck Berry. Suddenly after another flurry of caustic rock 'n' roll and an explosive encore the gig ended in a heap of writhing leather, boots, studs and audience fists raised in the hot air. Not because the group had run out of songs but because they couldn't carry on; the ever present axe hero Garrett deciding to smash up the drum kit (Not in itself an unusual occurrence as he had already recently used his Gibson SG as a warhead, puncturing the crumbling ceiling tiles down the Marquee during one frenetic final encore). If Paul Slack had regretted leaving such an incendiary band, as he watched tight lipped through the chaos, he probably wouldn't have shown it, while Donna would go home at the end of the night with not so much a milestone surpassed as another punk tattoo etched on her memory.

HANGING AROUND

Throughout the late 70's and early eighties, Adam spent a lot of time hanging around. So did a lot of other people. The punk band The Stranglers had written a brilliant song about it, called just that, Hanging Around. He used to play it repeatedly on his record player to everyone's annoyance. He knew it was one of the few things he was remarkably accomplished at. After leaving school and the supermarket he was even presented with a certificate. It was to come in handy. There was always a queue; a queue for a Tube ticket; a queue for the gig; a queue for the bar; a queue for the bog; a queue for the bus home; a queue for the bathroom; and probably a queue the next day at the local labour exchange.

Adam did a lot of queuing in those days: Sometimes he hung about, but couldn't get into the gig; and other times he couldn't get in, so he hung about. This always happened whenever he tried to see the band Crass. Of all the so-called 'Anarcho-Punk' bands, if you saw them live, you could give yourself a damn good slap on the back, a Blue Peter badge, and a hot cup of cocoa for having the courage to go and see them and return with a full set of dentures. Crass were top anarchists, and they had a flagrant disregard for religion, politics and family values. They were like the Sex Pistols on steriods - they had a habit of annoying people.

As a result, there used to be a lot of people not happy that Crass would be in the vicinity when they played a gig, as there had been with the Pistols. A lot of these people had Bachelor degrees in violence, and for some reason, the fixture - a Crass concert - always used to attract a large presence of Skinheads who were always ready to 'have a go' at the heavily anarchist Punks dressed head to foot in black. Crass' lead singer called himself, Steve Ignorant, and as an outfit they were totally uncompromising and the chanting of 'Jesus dying for his own sins, not theirs', was an original sentiment passed down from none other than Patti Smith.

It was clear. Crass were rubbing a lot of people up the wrong way and in Adam's opinion, and the Metropolitan Police, their first single 'Reality Asylum' remains unquestionably one of the most controversial Punk records ever released. Certainly, not to be played in a darkened room late at night on your own.

When Adam thought back on his attempts to try and see Crass, he always compared it to a highly dangerous Chelsea away match. Anything could happen and if you made it home afterwards you could count yourself lucky. If you managed to see Crass live it would prove to Adam's peers that he was a true punk and not a fraud. He had already seen the Dead Kennedy's twice and could consider that quite high up on the impress-ometer, but Crass was the band that he had to see. He wasn't even in a position to lie.

'I saw Crass last night....'

'Bollocks you did!'

It just wouldn't wash and if he had tried to explain exactly what had happened, one of his mates was bound to have known and would have asked him something like 'What was the exact number of Mohicans present?' or 'How much saliva rained down on the band?' 'How many Crass insignia's were on the backdrop?' Technical questions that would have surely found him out. And even then there was always someone called Sid or Spike, who was hanging about next to the pillar by the toilet, and,

'He didn't see you....'

So there Adam was, hanging around desperately trying not to, but he would always regret not seeing Crass, just like he always regretted not seeing Charlie Cooke the first time he went to Chelsea.

THICK AS THIEVES

Plug was staying round Carol's house for a couple of days while they did some rehearsing, although because her mum was about too much of the time, they had to play at a much lower volume, which meant that they could hardly hear themselves. Mind you that probably wasn't such a bad thing.

As it was a nice day and Plug had just received his wages in cash, from his new job in Basingstoke, they thought they'd go to the Wandsworth town centre and then perhaps the market, a proper lads day out, to look in the rare record shops and stalls. Plug also wanted to purchase a new bass guitar and he'd been saving up his wages hard. Adam always enjoyed record collecting with Plug, because he was such a knowledgeable accomplice and always had a keen eye for a rarity.

Anyway, they left the house and ventured to the bus stop just up the road. Adam was wearing his favourite 'Bone Idol' jacket as usual and some white bondage trousers with red straps so tight he could hardly walk in them, and attached to the back of his trousers was one of his flexible bum-flaps, which was really a 'Guinness' bar mat. He spiked his hair with the aid of some Vaseline, well past it's sell by date, and Plug was dressed militarily in his army fatigues, bomber jacket and large DM's.

After a short but measured stroll, they were finally about to reach the bus stop to sit down and wait an hour or so for that red box, when out of the corner of their eye a police car came careering into view. The panda car swerved close by and then stopped provocatively right in front of them. They jumped back. It was like an episode of The Sweeney, only even more dangerous. As they both prepared themselves for the worst and looked ironically at each other, two burly constables extricated themselves swiftly from the motor.

'Right lads. What are you doing?'

'Sorry?...' Adam eventually offered to the burlier of the two.

'What are you up to?'

'We're about to catch the bus', Plug countered confidently.

'No, I mean what are you doing here?'

'He just said....' Adam replied, trying to confuse the issue.

'There's been a break-in at a house in the next street and we have reason to believe that you were involved'.

'What?!' Adam and Plug answered in shocked unison.

'What exactly are you doing here?'

'We've told you!' Plug blurted out, panic stricken.

'Well?'

'We're catching the bus to go shopping', Adam said.

Plug nodded his head, but it was probably more in disbelief, suddenly realising that he had at least the equivalent of two weeks wages in his jacket pocket and it was all in brand spanking new notes. It was going to take some explaining back at the Station, especially if they got hold of their personal files and had even just a cursory glance.

'Shopping?' Constable two, chuckled.

'Yeah. For records'.

'Records?' The policemen clocked each other, amused. Then one turned back, 'What sort of records?'

'All sorts', Plug defused, cleverly.

'Punk?' the Number two simplified, scratching his head.

'Maybe....' Adam looked nervously to his comrade.

'Are you mates?'

'Yeah...'

'Why aren't you at work?'

'I haven't got a job', Adam countered, stupidly.

'I see. Well, stand against the car and turn out your pockets'.

'But - '

'Turn out your pockets!'

The situation was fast becoming ludicrous and Adam had certainly never experienced such a stressful shopping expedition. Also, between his bondage trousers and his leather jacket he had what seemed like at least fifty zips, so it was going to be a long day.

'That's right. Everything out of the pockets!'

Adam went first; unloading matches, cigarettes, a rubber band, a snotty handkerchief which both Constables ignored, a guitar plectrum, a door key, which raised eyebrows, a soggy ticket stub from a recent gig, an old Tube ticket, some fluff, a crumpled piece of paper with some phone numbers and addresses scrawled across it (by now the Coppers were both yawning, although when PC number two saw Adam's 'Support your local Police Force - Break the Law' badge on his jacket, his demeanour darkened further) and about twelve pounds in cash and small change, which soon descended into farce, because Adam kept finding penny bits all over his person and it took another eternity to extract them, even with the assistance of grumpy Policeman number one).

As the search for the Holy Grail was half completed, Plug was then frisked by number two, and eventually, after unloading a large rucksack's worth of stuff (Plug was a great hoarder), the crisp wodge of cash was exposed to the daylight which he had so carefully saved. There was at least two hundred quid in notes that had never gone into circulation before and the Policeman's faces lit up.

'Where did you get this?'

'From work', Plug stumbled.

'Work? But I thought you said you were unemployed?'

'No, that's my mate'.

'Yeah, his mate'. Adam interrupted.

'So you've got a job?' Constable two detected.

'Yeah. I got paid this week'.

'Then where's your wage slip?'

'I haven't got it with me'.

'I see. Why aren't you at work?'

'I'm on holiday'.

'Holiday?'

'Yep', said Plug with a hint of sarcasm.

'And what do you do?'

'I'm a cinema projectionist'.

The Plods looked at each other in amusement. At this point Adam wanted to ask the Constables what their favourite films were but decided against it. Shame, because Plug knew all the best releases and could reel off dialogue or a memorable scene at the drop of a hat.

'A cinema projectionist?'

'Yeah....'

'What, you show films?'

'That's right'.

'Where?'

'Basingstoke'.

'Basingstoke?!'

There was a pause.

'Well, what are you doing here then?'

Adam jumped in.

'Shopping - '

'Look!' and the chippy policeman was fixing his eyes on him. 'You better tell us what you're doing or you'll just have to come down to the Station'.

There was a long pause as the situation finally dawned in their craniums. They'd been 'Sussed' and the Police had the full weight of the Law behind them. They could do anything they liked. They could make them Morris dance at the side of the road if they really wanted or have them pogo up and down, backwards and forwards, along the white lines in the middle. Adam looked once more at the Plods. They were smug gits alright. They'd obviously done lots of overtime at the Academy and now they thought they had him and Plug in check mate. But it was nowhere near over yet.

'I live round the corner', Adam revealed to the boys in blue, as Plug looked at the floor trying to keep a straight face.

'You live round the corner?' Number One puffed, disbelievingly.

'Yeah, just down the road', Adam stumped up more confident now.

'Down the road?'

'Yeah....'

'And who do you live with?'

'My mother and sister'.

'Your mother and sister?'

'Yes'.

'And I suppose you live in a house?'

'Yes, I live in a house', he nodded. They were just like a tape recorder, repeating everything each other said.

'Right, then. In the car!'

After a brief squabble about who was going to get in first, Adam and Plug sat reluctantly in the back. The Policemen followed and once they were comfortable in the front, and had asked for both names and ages, the walkie-talkies were soon out and what sounded like a complicated order to the local take-away emanated with lots of crackling in response

(Adam felt that they were on their way to imprisonment for sure. He would have to write a final letter from his cell and ask for forgiveness for going shopping, yet he would say that he would be brave at the gallows and try not to choke too much over his last meal).

Just then 'Regan' turned round.

'Whereabouts is your house?'

'My house?'

'Yes, where you say you live'.

'Er, you go down the road and take the next right'.

'What's the name of the road?'

'Drax',

'Drax?' PC number two shuffled in his seat.

'Yeah, Drax Road' (this always made Adam and Plug chuckle because 'Drax' was the name of one of the baddies from James Bond).

'What number?'

'Twenty-three'.

Plug looked nervously at Adam as the panda sped off, but at least it meant that they wouldn't have to walk back to the house from the bus stop after their shopping trip. They were being taken expertly right to the front door.

'Is it this right?'

'No, just a bit further. Keep going'.

'This one?'

'No, the next one, that's a dead end'.

'I thought you said it was the next right?'

'I thought it was....'

PC one tutted loudly to PC two, who shook his head despairingly as he swore at the cracking up connection back to base.

'Is this it?'

'That's it, yeah'.

'Now where?'

'Er, you go along this road.....turn left at the end....then follow the road down the hill....and then go on a bit....round the corner....and you'll find the house on the left....'

The Constables clocked each other once more and Adam began to sense that they weren't really believing him, so much so that he soon had visions of them gleefully polishing their handcuffs. They probably thought he was a devious crook trying to save his own skin with a ridiculous flight of fancy. PC one, then put his foot down impatiently on the gas and they sped on to their destination:

'I can't see the numbers. Is this the house?' He probed.

'No, it's the next one'.

Policeman number one was now beginning to sound like a taxi driver. So much so, that he was even thinking of giving him a tip.

'This one?'

'Yeah, this is it....'

'Sure?'

'Yes'.

As the Peelers sighed, the panda car pulled up and they all got out except for corpulent Policeman number two, who sat snuggly in the close fitting passenger seat and watched as Adam and Plug were escorted to the door by Stirling Moss. After Stirling rang the bell, and twiddled his thumbs, confident in the outcome, Adam tried to put a brave face on the whole situation but however hard he tried, he just couldn't stop feeling like one of the Three Stooges, especially as he wasn't at all sure that anyone was even in.

The door eventually opened and Carol appeared with a great deal of surprise, almost stepping backwards. As she looked out on the situation, Adam tried to make light of everything with an inane grin. Plug tried hard not to look mortified. The Policeman suddenly put on his best airs and graces:

'What's happened?' Carol probed.

'It's nothing to worry about. We have been making various enquiries and I'd be grateful if you would be able to identify these two young men. One claims that he lives at this address and that he is your brother. The other that he is a friend'.

Carol glanced apprehensively at Adam and Plug, up and down, and round and about, checking them over almost as if she was worried that they might have gone out and shaved all their hair off since she last saw them or appeared on the doorstep showing off some new outrageous garment. Adam suddenly thought, 'if she wants to disown me, now is surely her moment'. Fortunately, after Adam had winked at her more than a few times to give Carol her cue, she soon recognised them. She continued unfazed as if acting oblivious, being relieved for the moment that at least they hadn't turned up again showing off Mohican haircuts or large tattoos. She turned back to the Policeman.

'Yes, Officer, that's right. This is my brother and his friend. Oh, dear, what have they been up to?' It was a faultless performance.

The Policeman's helmet almost deflated, especially as at just that moment, Carol's mum appeared also confirming the positive ID. The Sheriff then began to look as if he was munching on a considerably sized humble pie and as he swallowed it slowly, he tried to contain his truncheon. Officer two, back at the panda, who had been busy with a useless radio and was still trying to give a running commentary to the station, just sat there looking dejected. Yes. It was as clear as day. Even for Poirot and Co. And they both knew it. Adam and Plug had been telling the truth. They had been on their way to the shops, to do a bit of shopping.

PC One spluttered, 'Oh, don't worry madam. They've been up to nothing at all. There's been a break-in up the road and we found them near the scene so we had to verify their identities. You know, to discount them from our enquiries. Just procedure - you understand, nothing at all to worry about'.

'Yes, I see....well, thank you'.

'Not at all, madam. Sorry to trouble you'.

After the Officer had told Adam and Plug to be more careful in future, and bid them adieu, Carol turned and gave him daggers. 'But what had we done?' Adam thought. They'd been good honest citizens waiting at the bus stop, on their way to do a little shopping. They might have even picked up a bargain.

What Adam did know was that if the Metropolitan Police were coming down hard on him and his mate as if they were hardened criminals, then the real crooks must have been having a field day. The burglars who had broken-in up the road were probably already sunning themselves on a beach in Acapulco, at that very moment. Adam bet they were even laughing to each other.

'Good thing those two young punks came along, eh?!'

'Yeah! Not half. I reckon the one in the silly trousers couldn't have run far from the Old Bill neither!'

After a cup of tea and some further questions, there was a dressing down from Carol;

'Christ! What the hell did you do that for!?'

'What?' Adam responded, sheepishly.

'Saying what you did to the Police?!'

'Look, I dunno…'

'Why didn't you just say who we really were?'

'I dunno. I just panicked!'

'We could've all been arrested!'

'It was the first thing that came into my head!'

'Well, at least someone here's on the ball…'

And Carol had certainly been more than that.

Adam and Plug then considered whether going out again that day was a good idea. In the end, they decided that it probably wasn't, so they continued their practicing once more, albeit with the volume turned right down, but safe in the knowledge that they were well out of reach of the local constabulary's clutches.

BAND ON THE RUN

It was getting serious. What were they going to call the band? Their outfit. Even if there was still only the two of them and Adam had already asked Carol to join but she was having none of it. So, a two piece it frustratingly remained.

What on earth were they going to call themselves: The 'Rotten Fruits?' The 'Rancid Lumps?' It was a tough one alright. It would need all their creativity and imagination. After a particularly heavy rehearsal session where strings were broken and neighbours fretted, Adam and Plug sat down immediately and tried to solve the crisis.

'How about 'Chaos UK?'

'Mm.....no, too obvious'.

'Oh, there's a band called that anyway....'

'I know - the 'Revolving' Doors!'

'No....too American'.

After a brief pause they tried again.

'The Windows?'

'Too DIY....'

'Red Rage?'

'Too serious....'

'What about, 'The Cretins?'

'Too stupid. Even for us'.

'I've got it! 'The Stiffs'.

'Heh, that's good....'

The first song that Adam and Plug had written together was called 'I'm So Stiff', a simple tune about being exceptionally lazy. The words went something like: 'I'm so stiff, I'm so stiff, from the top of my head right down to my dick'. Another line went, 'But if you think I'm stiff, you oughta see me dad'.

The song had potential, but unfortunately the riff only had two notes, so it wasn't long before they had become bored of playing it. Shame, because it had Top of the Pops written all over it.

The difficult search for a moniker continued,

'Ummm.....The 'Little Stiffs?'

'No, hang on, it's too like Stiff Little Fingers'.

'Oh, yeah....shit'.

After scratching their heads together for a while they'd go back to the drawing board.

'The Revolvers?'

'Nah, too much like the Pistols'.

'I know - 'The Tossers'.

'No, too limiting'.

'Beelzebub?'

'Too hippy....'

'The Bollocks?'

'No. It's got 'The' in front of it'.

'Well - 'Bollocks' then!'

'No, it doesn't sound right....'

There was a noticeable pause again. The two of them stared out of the window looking desperately for inspiration. After what seemed like about five minutes, Plug trumped up.

'How about, 'Three Minute Warning?'

'What d'you mean?' Adam replied unsure.

'You know, the three minute Government warning you get before a nuclear strike'.

'What, like in that stupid 'Protect and Survive' manual?'

'Exactly'.

'Heh….that's brilliant!'

'Thanks', said Plug triumphantly.

So there it was. 'Three Minute Warning'. It fitted well with their punk protest credentials and had a nice ring to it. It also didn't have 'The' in front of it. Also, as Adam played both guitar and sang, that meant that even with a drummer they would be a 'three' piece. That was the clincher. As soon as Three Minute Warning was confirmed, they then thought about the design of the name - the logo.

'How about Three Minute Warning in blood red lettering?'

'No, too Heavy Metal'.

'Gothic writing then. Like on a tombstone'.

'Maybe…..no, that's too like that Damned album'.

'Large, ransom note lettering?'

'That's been done to death'.

'What about silly Seventies bubble writing'.

'No, too cheesy. Too Starsky and Hutch'.

'I know….big capitals like in the titling for The Professionals'.

'What Bodie and Doyle?'

There was a further pause as Plug shook his head.

'Yeah, I know what you mean....'

Again their craniums would get a good scratch once more, then they would return defiantly to the task in hand.

'Lettering like Italics?'

'Too simple....'

'Roman numerals?'

'What for, the 'Three?'

'Could be....'

'I've got it!' Plug jumped. 'Stark white lettering on a black background'.

'What like in a Government warning?'

'Yeah....'

'I can just see it. That's excellent!'

'Cheers...'

And before you could say 'Number One', Plug was off stencilling his Bass amplifier with the proud moniker:

'THREE MINUTE WARNING'

in stark white lettering, like in a Government warning.

RIGHT TO WORK

Adam and Plug had a few false dawns. Finding a drummer was the area that they had continuing problems with. This meant that whenever a gig was set up they usually couldn't do it because they didn't have any percussion. But they did have a manager though. Their mate, Dave. He even mentioned the fact that he was prepared to start learning the drums himself to solve once and for all the nagging problem. No drummer.

One gig had already been set up in Basingstoke, but their part-time sticksman who lived just over the road from Plug bottled out of performing at the last minute which put them in a tricky situation. His name was Mike, and because they weren't quite sure what his surname was, they decided to call him, 'Stand', as in, 'Mike Stand'. Shame really that he couldn't summon up the necessary courage to appear live, because his punk name was inspired.

So, it certainly wasn't Adam and Plug's fault. They were raring to go and they had the material. The hours spent at Plug's house and Carol's mum's had definitely paid off. They had become fairly accomplished musicians and had written some interesting numbers. They had an anti-Thatcherite song called, 'Public Cuts', in honour of their school mate Louie. The chorus was totally uncompromising:

One last cut, Maggie's throat!

Tow the Tories out to sea and sink the boat.

One last cut, Maggie's throat!

Don't be dumb, don't give 'em your vote.

Some of the verses weren't far short either.

Well Maggie Thatcher you can stick it up your arse

I'm sick of your preaching, smugness and your face

Your economic strategy is just a farce

Your Government's begun the end of the human race.

But they could even mix it up a bit with the more discerning Punk rockers too, with a galloping guitar and bass riff in their song 'Member of Parliament', which Carol reckoned reminded her of The Ruts'

'Babylon's Burning'.

Looking in the job shop window,

Nothing.

Only jobs for mental torture,

Mindless.

I don't wanna fight in Ulster,

Killing Children.

I won't train to be a killer,

Their death machine.

Member of Parliament,

You make me sick.

Sat on your arse all day

You're full of shit!

They could even be reflective, with a song called 'Killed in Action' about being a heroic soldier (which would fit in really well with the imminent outbreak of the Falklands War and the general mindless jingoism about to descend on their fair Isle). Plug had come up with some good lyrics as well as a powerful bass riff to fit Adam's edgy guitar part.

The warrior, he is so brave and true

Gun in hand, he's ready to die for you.

The warrior, fearless in dignity,

Gives his life, fighting for liberty.

It's a game, a military fantasy

He's a pawn, ignored by history

Killed in Action

He was a brave man.

Killed in Action

But do they give a damn?'

Writing the lyrics was a difficult process but it was one of the most fulfilling things they had ever done. When the words were eventually finished, after they had worked hard at getting the best out of themselves, they would try them out with the music usually written already. Mostly, the lyrics were about what it was like to be living in the paranoid early eighties, trying to survive under the Thatcher regime with the supposed nuclear threat from the Russians ever present.

It didn't help that the chemical weapons research establishment at Aldermaston and the nuclear bomber, Cruise missile base at Greenham Common were literally just a bike ride down the road from Basingstoke. If there was going to be a nuclear conflagration, which at that time seemed fairly likely, everyone in that area was going to get it in the neck. Even in a bunker a mile under the ground. It was a depressing fact of life. But there was an upside. It gave Adam and Plug lots of song-writing material.

Look at the Superpowers

Stockpiling their bombs waiting for the hour

They said deterrence would prevent world war

But now they tell us it's not true anymore.

The US thinks limited war can be won

In the European theatre get it over and done

In the United States you're an acceptable loss

If Europe's gotta go they don't give a toss!

We must Protest and Survive.

The band could be serious. But they could also be quite humorous in an Ian Dury and the Blockheads sort of manner. Dury was certainly a big influence. Along with The Sex Pistols and of course, Sham 69.

Plug wrote some brilliant lyrics with Adam about when he worked on the night shift in the local factory, for a catchy twelve bar blues riff that they had played over and over again when they were first starting to rehearse. Blues riffs were always a good starting point because they were simple and repetitive and if they wanted to, they could play them literally all day long.

I've got a new job, I'm doing fine

The money ain't bad with my overtime

I'm gonna get a car a house and a wife,

Guess I'll be working here the rest of my life

I'm working the night shift every night

Clock on when it's dark, clock out when it's light.

Only get a holiday twice a year

But it's a job, so I don't care.

I've got the night shift blues.

I start on the night shift at 10 pm

It's six in the morning when I get home again

We're making lots of money for the Boss

Cos he gets mad if we run at a loss.

Seen him after work in his big black car

If I work like him I can go far

That's what he tells me all the time

But is it just a trick to keep me in line?

I've got the night shift blues.

The boss man, he says, he says, 'Boy,

You and your union are making some noise

Take my advice if you wanna survive

Pick up your pension when you reach sixty five

Cos this is my factory you'll do things my way

Or you're out on your arse and you won't get no pay!'

I think it over and I say, 'So what!'

'I don't want what you're piss factory's got!'

I've got the dole queue Blues.

They would frequently try out new drummers when they could. They spent quite a lot of time and effort trying to recruit them from the music press.

'DRUMMER REQUIRED FOR PUNK BAND'

Influences: Sham, Pistols, Ruts.

If they were lucky and a drummer replied to an advert they would go to a rehearsal studio and record the results. Adam's brother Alan had some friends who knew some musicians and they tried out a couple of drummers through him too. One of their best ever demo tapes, although it was known as the dodgy demo because it was recorded straight onto a tape recorder, had most of their material on it at that time which was about seven songs and they recorded it as an open rehearsal at the 'Albert Haul' a small rehearsal studio in Putney, with a drummer called Roy Dodds. He was fantastic and helped make Adam and Plug sound like a serious unit for the first time. Unfortunately, he had too many commitments to join, so they had to hunt around once more. (Dodds would later drum for Fairground Attraction).

For the demo tape, Dave, who was still their manager, designed a little photocopied picture cover of a nuclear power station with missiles coming out of the top with some human skulls underneath. It was definitely eye catching - a sort of Monty Python montage. The typing on the tape's sleeve was also done by Dave, who thanked Roy Dodds for playing drums and also thanked his mate 'Soggy' for the use of his typewriter. Dave typed the revealing information, 'The above tracks were recorded on a portable cassette recorder therefore the quality is slightly bad'. This was an important admission when trying to sell copies of the tape in the Basingstoke shopping centre. Even though the tape wasn't of the best quality, it showed that there was some definite potential and remarkably, Dave managed to get them a gig on a major 'Right to Work' march, on the back of a lorry. 'Brilliant', Adam thought. He'd recently seen the Jam playing a gig on a lorry during a large CND march in central London and they had been terrific. Their hit single 'Going Underground', played within earshot of the Houses of Parliament perfectly summing up the paranoia of the time.

'Our first gig, on a lorry. But we still haven't got a drummer!' Adam said to Dave with a note of apprehension.

'Don't worry. We'll sort it…'

'How?' said Plug impatiently.

'I'm gonna get on the blower and call up some people'.

Adam and Plug looked at each other.

'What people?' Adam said.

Dave looked at them both for a second and then he was off again.

'Well, there's my mate Ricky Goldstein who used to be in Sham. He ain't doin' nothin' at the moment, so he might be available. If that's no good, Mark Laff from Generation X ain't doin' much either'.

'You reckon these people are gonna wanna play with the likes of us?' Plug challenged.

'Yeah, why not? It's a 'Right to Work' march. They'll look good playin' on it, and besides, it'll only need a couple of rehearsals to get it sorted'.

'A couple?' Adam questioned.

'Yeah, easy. You two have been doin' nothin' else for more than a year'.

'I s'pose….' Plug pondered.

'True', Adam admitted.

'I'm gonna get on the dog and bone'.

And he did. Dave rang up every contact he had, which was a long list of people he had bumped into at gigs or just in the street. He spoke to various people who were all busy playing or had other commitments. He even made out that he had rung Charlie Watts, the legendary drummer of the Rolling Stones, via his manager, but that Charlie was unavailable due to a heavy touring schedule abroad.

'Charlie Watts playing on a Right to Work march….didn't reckon on it somehow!' Plug teased.

'What are we gonna do? We'll have to cancel the gig', Adam moaned.

'No way! Not again', replied Dave. 'I've got one more idea'.

'Oh, yeah. What's that?' taunted Plug.

'Rab, from the Wall....'

There was a pause.

'Who?' Adam and Plug countered.

'Rab Fae Beith, of The Wall....'

'The Wall?'

'Oh, good band they are', Adam said.

'Yeah, they're alright', added Plug.

They all knew their stuff. The Wall were quite a heavy Punk outfit whos singles had done well in the Indie charts and they had the likes of Jimmy Pursey and Steve Jones of the Pistols producing them. Also, Adam had seen them at the Music Machine in Camden and rated them pretty highly.

It was Dave's last throw of the dice, but he didn't look concerned, because you could bet your bottom dollar he would have another trick up his sleeve if that one didn't work. It seemed like he was on the phone for ages. The longer Dave spoke, the more Adam and Plug were becoming quietly confident that they might finally have the vacancy filled, or at least have someone who looked half convincing holding a pair of sticks. This was confirmed when Dave smiled as he put down the phone.

'Bingo! We've got a drummer!

'What, Rab?'

'Yeah....'

'Excellent!

Adam and Plug were ecstatic. Their first gig and they would be playing with an experienced Punk drummer, who had recently toured the UK with Stiff Little Fingers.

'He's willin' to do the rehearsals for free and he'll just take a cut of the gig dosh, if there is any'.

'Nice one!' said Plug excitedly. 'When can we rehearse with him?'

'In the week. Twice before the gig Saturday. I'm gonna send him a demo tape so he can learn the songs on his own'.

True to his word, Rab turned up to the first rehearsal and it all went well. They found a cheap rehearsal studio through his contacts in south London and he turned out to be really helpful. He cut an imposing figure with his large, stocky frame and strong Scottish accent. His arms were covered in large tattoos all the way down to his wrists and he had very short cropped hair, which made him look authentically tough. On the Wall's picture sleeves, he was often to be found with a Mohican haircut, earrings and a ragged leather jacket covered in badges, studs and assorted Punk paraphernalia.

'He looks the business', said Dave after the first rehearsal, 'and he can double as a bouncer too'.

'Yeah, we won't get no trouble with him about', Plug concluded.

They were pleased. Rab beat an impressive rhythm on the drums, wellying the kit and keeping Adam and Plug's guitar and bass in check, especially if they got too carried away. He also seemed to like the songs. After the rehearsal, they went back to Rab's flat and chatted about music and listened to The Wall's second album that had just been released. Adam told him that he had practiced along to the Wall's first album, 'Personal Troubles and Public Issues', regularly when he was learning to play guitar. Rab seemed impressed and told them that he thought their main influences were The Ruts, because of some of Plug's reggae influenced bass riffs and Sham 69, due to their fast and furious protest songs. He also thought that Adam sang a little bit like The Wall's previous lead singer, Kelly, and Adam wasn't complaining. That was definitely a compliment.

The news of the imminent Right to Work gig on the lorry spread like wild fire among their friends. The news that they now had a well known and respected Punk musician on drums was even better. It gave them credibility. As Rab was some years older than them, he could also impart a lot of his knowledge and experience too. The Wall were signed to Polydor Records and the major label already represented The Jam and Siouxsie and the Banshees. Rab said that he knew Siouxsie Sioux and was also quite friendly with Paul Weller. He also knew The Jam's producer, Pete Wilson really well, having worked on a lot of The Wall stuff with him, so as far as Adam was concerned, Rab certainly knew some influential people. He certainly had his finger on the pulse.

At the second rehearsal, they even had a small audience, being the day before the gig and acting as that necessary all important warm up. And they could put the finishing touches to the set which now consisted of eight songs. If they ran out of material, as it would probably take ages to journey through the streets of north London down to the Houses of Parliament, they agreed to just keep playing the set over and over again. They had all their songs ready and had even considered doing a cover version of Chelsea's, classic song, Right to Work. They decided that it was a classic that was definitely an option when they had exhausted their own material.

After the rehearsal, all the last minute plans were finalised. Adam's brother John was going to be their roadie and driver for the day and he was ready to help out with the guitars, amplifiers and crucially Rab's drum kit.

That night Adam couldn't sleep a wink. He had never played a gig before and the butterflies were so bad he thought he was about to be sick. He wasn't sure if he was going to be able to deliver. Especially as he was not only singing all the songs and having to remember all the words, but he was playing all the guitar stuff as well. As the night drew on, Adam kept repeating the lyrics again and again in his head and he was in fear that he would forget them or the guitar parts or both. It wasn't looking good. The unpredictable nature of playing live on a lorry also didn't help, 'what if we drive over a sleeping Policeman on the way?' he contemplated, 'I'd be sure to hit a wrong note, or fall over. The gig would come to a grinding halt and we'll never live it down'. 'Oh, fuck it!' he decided, 'if that happens, I'll just do a load of manic jumping around and blast out a load of feedback!'

'Good. Now get some kip!' ordered Carol, knowing that she too needed the sleep just in case Adam pulled a sicky. Then she might be in line for an awkward promotion. From roadie two, to vocalist. It was highly unlikely but with her support at a hundred percent, if she had to she would certainly give it more than a go. She also happened to know the song lyrics just as well as anyone else.

In the morning, Adam rubbed his tired eyes and stuck out his tongue in front of the bathroom mirror and considered the feasibility of going into hospital with a nasty disease so he could get away from playing. As he struggled to put on his moth eaten Crisis T-shirt and worn out denims for the gig, he found that his nerves were now becoming unbearable. He wasn't even sure he could hold the guitar properly, let alone strum it.

Soon, Plug and Dave arrived, and it was action stations. They loaded up the cars with the equipment and then drove up to Rab's house to pick up his drum kit. When they arrived he seemed relaxed, and Adam could tell that it must have just felt to him like another gig, but it helped to give them all confidence. They then motored up to North London to rendezvous with the Right to Work march. After checking an A to Z, they finally reached the address in Islington, where the march would begin and there were hundreds of people milling around and the Police were starting to patrol by the route. Dave's contact wasn't back from organising, as they were early, so they all went off to a local greasy spoon to kill some time. Adam couldn't eat anything due to his nerves, so he slurped on some strong sugary coffee to try and keep himself awake. As they waited, Rab regaled them with some stories from The Wall's tour with Stiff Little Fingers and reckoned the best gig was at Glasgow Apollo, because they had a large local following that went mental when they played their classic single 'Ghetto'. Adam could well imagine the commotion, as it was a cracking song with a ton of echo and distortion.

It seemed as though they had been in the cafe for an age when they ventured back to meet their contact. Adam and Plug were now getting psyched up to do the gig and wanted to have a look at the lorry they were going to be playing on. Sure enough, by the house was the large truck, but there was little activity around it. They rang the doorbell to the organiser's house and were let through into the living room. They all bundled in and sat down. The woman had some bad news:

'The generator's blown up on the lorry, so I'm really sorry but you won't be able to play'.

Everyone looked around at each other surprised. Although it was a shock,

Adam was privately relieved that they weren't going to be appearing, but at least they had turned up with the intension of performing and had been denied the privilege at the last minute through no fault of their own:

'There's no way it can be fixed?' said Dave.

'No, I'm sorry. But don't worry, you'll still get paid'.

That was a relief. And the money for the day was good. Ironically, it would turn out to be their highest paying gig.

After a chat they reloaded the cars and headed home. They decided that it was difficult for them to even go on the march, as it meant leaving all the equipment about, so they bid the organisers farewell and returned on their way to south London with the payment burning a hole in their pockets.

The fact that they hadn't played on the march probably worked out as a blessing in disguise. Adam still didn't quite feel ready to perform in front of a large audience and he knew that Plug felt that way too. However, they had geared themselves up and next time they would have to deliver. One thing was certain, they now had a great contact in Rab, who was prepared to help them out as best he could. The only problem was that The Wall were touring again soon and that meant that he probably wouldn't be available to do many gigs in the future, so Dave had to make a decision: Whether he was going to play the drums in the band for real or not? In the end, when push came to shove, he decided that he was going to get down to some serious practise and become the permanent drummer.

TERMINAL JIVE

Would you believe it, after a couple of months, Dave was ready to play live. Even he wouldn't have admitted that he was the world's best drummer, but what he lacked in finesse, he more than made up for in his determination and he was fast modelling himself on Keith Moon in terms of his presentation, with lots of crashing drumming and spinning of drumsticks - even though he'd usually have to stop the beat every now and then to pick them up off the floor. The plus side was that they all knew each other well and Dave could continue to be their manager and try and hassle them some gigs.

Eventually, Dave obtained another gig in London at the Moonlight/ Starlight club in West Hampstead. They would be supporting Terminal Jive, a fairly well known new wave band from Basingstoke. Dave had a coach confirmed for the gig so they were at least going to be playing to an audience and not just one man and his canine. Because Plug and Dave were both from Basingstoke it automatically gave the Terminal Jive audience another local group to support. With fifty or so devotees and Punks from Basingstoke on the coach and the rest that they could get along themselves, Dave reckoned that they would easily have a hundred or so there. For Three Minute Warning's first official gig, that was certainly promising.

Dave's drumming was coming on pretty fast, although in terms of hours, he still had a lot of catching up to do. But soon they were starting to sound like a unit and Dave already knew the material, which was a huge advantage. Adam had also just written a new song called 'No Rules', that he was more than proud of.

There are rules for your schools,

There are rules for your home,

There are rules for your work,

There are rules for your church.

Rules all around you,

That try to deny you,

Your sanity,

Your humanity.

You think it's unfair,

But I just don't care,

Cos I got no rules, got no rules,

Got no rules, got no rules.

The song was fast and furious and Adam thought it had quite a catchy melody and sing along chorus. Plug and Dave liked it too and they quickly added the new tune into their set, which now meant that they had about eight songs.

The day of the gig at the Moonlight came round fast and luckily Adam's nerves weren't nearly as bad as they had been for the aborted Right To Work concert. They travelled up early to the pub in West Hampstead for their sound check. This time his brother Alan was their roadie for the day, and he drove with some of the gear; the odd guitar case and amplifiers, in the back of the car. Unfortunately, Carol was unable to make the bands first gig, a source of some annoyance, the consequence of her best friend's hen party conflicting massively in the diary. Anyway, as they motored through the grey landscape of London, Adam flicked through copies of the New Musical Express and Sounds for any mention of the gig with Terminal Jive. In NME there was nothing, not so much as a whiff of an imminent first performance, but to Adam's surprise, down the bottom of one of the gig pages in Sounds was a small advertisement that said.

THE MOONLIGHT/STARLIGHT CLUB

Thursday: TERMINAL JIVE + Three Minute Warning. Doors 8pm

He let out a loud yelp and his brother nearly careered the car into the side of the road.

'We're in the paper! Look!'

Even though it was only a small mention of the gig (which was regularly advertised by the venue anyway), he was still ecstatic. It felt fantastic to get a mention in the press however small and it helped to give a boost to his confidence, especially as he knew in the back of his mind that he still hadn't performed live. 'One cancelled gig on the back of a lorry certainly doesn't count', he reckoned.

When they reached the venue, Plug and Dave were already busy setting up for the sound check and because Dave didn't have his own drum kit, luckily they were able to use Terminal Jive's. As Dave chatted to the other band's drummer, Adam spoke to their lead singer. He'd only heard a little bit of their stuff before and it was very different. They had a sort of Indie/New Romantics feel to them, with swirling vocals and edgy guitar, whereas Three Minute Warning were more mainstream Punk with the occasional melodic moments.

Adam showed Plug and Dave the advert and they both looked really pleased. They hadn't been expecting it. But soon it was down to work and before long they were unloading the car and heaving the equipment into the venue and up a flight of steps to the first floor. The room had a long bar down the right hand side. It was quite a long space and everything was daubed in black paint. The stage was fairly small but at least it was raised up which helped to separate the bands from the audience, also it meant that Adam had a little bit more of a distance from them, which would help with the nerves situation:

'With a hundred in 'ere it'll look well full', Dave boasted.

'Yeah, it's not a bad little space', said Plug.

Soon the sound check was under way. Being the headlining act, Terminal Jive had already done theirs so it just left the support band to make sure that everything was okay. This was the first sound check Adam had ever experienced so he was really nervous, not knowing what to expect and as a result he had some trouble remembering the lyrics in a couple of the songs. To cover up he just made out he was chewing over the words in some sort of slouchy punk attitude. It didn't sound too great, but at least the band were loud.

After the sound check they had about two hours to kill before they were on stage, so they all went off to find some grub. Once located, after scouting up and down the high street, they sat down and devoured their burgers, chewing energetically over the evening's entertainment:

'We've gotta really go for it', said Dave.

'Yeah, I know', Adam agreed.

'Rab says he's comin' to the gig'.

'Great…' Adam said with a gulp, nearly choking.

'He wants to see us play live'.

'That's good....' Plug faltered as he tried to down a sliced tomato.

'Yeah', Adam added for effect.

Then he thought for a second. It was nerve racking enough playing to friends and family, but someone who they all looked up to and who they knew was an experienced musician, well that was a different matter entirely. As Adam instantly felt the butterflies increase he tried to convince himself that it didn't really matter. Besides, they had nothing to lose, being young, being novices, and they were only two or so years out of school, so they'd hopefully get support just for having the bottle to go up on the stage in the first place. Or so Adam thought. To try and ease the situation, he decided that he was going to sing and play as if he knew none of the audience. As if he had never seen any of them before in his life. But it wasn't easy. If he got so much as a broken guitar string it might all go belly up. Adam looked at his watch and then across at Plug, who looked nervous too:

'Fuck it!' Adam said to Dave. 'If they don't like us, there's nothing we can do about it. I'm just gonna try and enjoy it as much as possible'.

'Yeah, me too', said Plug, hesitantly.

After polishing off their fries, they sat about wasting as much time as possible with idle banter. And with the rest of the time they tried to complete the crossword in Sounds:

'One across is.... 'Ill fated singer of Love Will Tear Us Apart?' said Dave.

'That's a piece of piss - Ian Curtis!' Plug replied cockily.

'Yep....'

After Dave filled out Curtis' name with a leaky biro, he carried on to the next clue.

'Three down is....."Flares and....?"'

There was a pause.

'What?' Adam said.

'Flares and....?'

Dave raised his eyebrows.

'How many letters?' Adam probed.

'Eight'.

'Oh, that's Slippers! The Cockney Rejects single', Plug chirped.

'Nice one', said Dave.

'Yes!' said Plug, punching the air.

After a moment, Adam tried again.

'What's left?'

'Er, nine across....'Bassist with Rotten outfit?'

'Mmm....' Adam scratched his head.

There was another pause.

'Er....'

'The third letter is H....'

'Umm....'

'That'll be Jah Wobble of Public Image!' Plug butted in.

'Yeah, well done'.

'Yes!!' And Plug was punching the air once more in triumph.

It never took long to complete the crossword with him about.

When they finally returned to the venue the coach had arrived and they found the mini invasion from Basingstoke was at the bar laying in to the drink as if it was compulsory. The venue was filling up quickly and before long some of Adam's old school friends and Rab had arrived, and now his nerves were almost unbearable. Luckily, he had come up with a cunning plan for when he was on stage. He was going to wear a pair of sunglasses. The only problem was that they weren't the most trendy on the market (he had even considered wearing a pair of his dad's). But despite making him look silly, he thought they looked a little bit unconventional and gave him that little bit of extra detachment from the audience, because Adam couldn't see a thing in them. It was a risk wearing them on stage alright, because there was a good chance that he would probably fall off the stage if he got carried away, or failing that he would most likely trip over the drum kit or crash into Plug who was always totally engrossed in his complicated bass playing. But if it stopped him collapsing from heart failure during the set, then so be it.

The auditorium was becoming hot and smoky and before anyone could say, 'Ladies and Gentlemen, would you please give a warm and riotous welcome to those youthful punk legends 'Three Minute Warning!', Adam and Plug were strapping on their guitars and plugging in to their amps with lots of healthy feedback and whining of microphones. Dave meanwhile was trying to get comfortable on his drum stool and was nervously fiddling with his wrist bands. Eventually, Adam stood up to where he thought the microphone was, and luckily avoided banging his nose on it and took a gulp of air as the surprisingly loud clapping subsided, which seemed to drown out any chants of 'Get off!' or 'You're shit!'

In front of Adam, he could just make out the bobbing heads of the audience but he couldn't really make out anybody's face in particular. Not in detail anyway. So, the sunglasses had done their job.

'Alright?....' he said almost hesitantly after a pause, and there was another shout of 'Rubbish' and 'Get on with it!' in reply, but it didn't put him off. It was far too late for that. If anything, it spurred Adam on even more.

'We're 'Three Minute Warning', and when the time comes three minutes is about all you're gonna get!'

And with that declaration, they smashed straight into their first song called Fallout, which was all about the horrible consequences of a nuclear attack.

The bomb has dropped on London

A blinding flash lights up the sky

And beneath the rising mushroom cloud

The contaminated people die.

Fallout....

Forty miles from the crumbled city

The heat wave is frying them slow

Their skin is scorched and bloody

Their eyes just drip and their faces glow.

After the song tailed off with feedback and the sound from Adam's guitar plectrum grating down the strings which sounded like a missile falling, they got a shock because people seemed to like what they were doing. Even though they were an easily converted Basingstoke crowd, it helped to build the confidence, and it wasn't at all easy in the sunglasses doing Adam's unintentional Stevie Wonder impression.

Before the clapping subsided, to keep the pace going they launched into the next song, a bit of a terrace anthem called Nowhere To Go, which was all about the lack of opportunity for young people in early eighties Britain. It was a more conventional type of rock song with some thunderous drumming from Dave, a pulsing hypnotic bass pattern by Plug and it allowed Adam to show off a little with a guitar solo that wasn't a million miles from the one in the song, Into the Valley, by The Skids:

The test card's on the TV, so I go downtown,

But no money to spend, I just hang around,

I walk along the streets, but it's a wasteland there,

I can sense the boredom, I can taste the fear.

What is my identity

In this corrupt society

It has been taken away,

Nowhere for us to go today.

I can't get away from the mindless routine,

Of production line life and the social obscene.

I get abuse just for being young

I'm told it's a crime when I have some fun.

Unemployed hours tick my life away

Wasted time, hopes, dreams, decay

I'm a statistic without a say

Nowhere for us to go today.

I've had enough attitude from vacant heads

To them I don't exist, they've more concern for the dead.

Every day is like the last, nothing ever happens

All the time I'm just let down in this rotten heaven.

I'm stuck like a bullet in a gun

My mind's like a criminal on the run,

I'm the one they wanna throw away

Nowhere for us to go today.

With the next tune they decided to lighten things up a bit with a cover version of Hey Joe (Jimi Hendrix had done a classic cover of it already which they all loved). Towards the end of their version they increased the speed until they were playing it literally at a hundred miles an hour and because Adam was starting to relax a bit more on stage he started doing a bit of jumping up and down which he'd copied off Paul Weller of The Jam. Weller had this brilliant knack of twisting high up in mid air, which looked terrific, while he was still playing. Adam just had to be careful he didn't lose his footing on landing. Luckily, he managed to avoid propelling himself through Dave's bass drum or careering onto the dance floor and he found that they were now beginning to work up a head of steam. In the gap before the next song, Adam improvised an introduction.

'This one's for all those tossers in Number Ten!'

And they were off again into Member of Parliament, which at the time was a bit of a band favourite.

Soldier boys get told to line up

Obey,

Bureaucrats prepare for trouble,

Unrest,

Country's in a state of crisis,

Millions jobless,

Politicians have the answers,

So they tell us.

The Union Jack is slowly fading

Crumbling

This is Britain's final hour,

Dying

No way out there's no escaping,

We are sinking

MP's argue in confusion,

Doing nothing.

The gig seemed to be going well and although people didn't know the songs, they seemed to like the attitude and the odd punk looked as though he might break out into some crazed jumping around at any moment. Unfortunately, the rest of the set seemed to whiz by in a whirlwind of adrenalin and frenzy. Eventually, they played the newly penned No Rules which went down really positively and finished off with a couple more protest songs. One of them was the Ruts-like, Suffer in Silence, which was all about the turmoil in the inner cities.

People in the UK are becoming afraid

They're throwing petrol bombs and building barricades

Don't try and be clever don't make no fuss

When the Police arrest you with SUS

Cos they are always in the right

They can do with you what they bloody well like.

And you suffer in silence

Suffer in silence, suffer in silence

Cos the Magistrate will just ignore.

They didn't play an encore, even though the audience seemed as if they weren't averse to a little more entertainment. To be honest, Adam was just relieved to have got through their first gig without any major hitches: no guitar strings had broken: he'd managed to remember all the words to the songs, except on a couple of occasions when he just covered up in his best Tourette's syndrome: the bum notes that were played weren't too noticeable: Dave had held onto his drum sticks for dear life and had kept the rhythm most of the time: Adam hadn't fallen off stage despite the sunglasses and nothing had been thrown at them. Mind you if they had been gobbed at Adam probably would have looked upon it as the highest compliment, especially if it was launched by any of their mates. But 'never mind', Adam thought. It was a start. They were blooded: 'On their way', as they say. From now on he hoped that they wouldn't have so many hitches and no more frustrating gig cancellations or problems with drummers. It seemed as though their path was becoming clearer. Even if they were to disappear without trace in a year's time or less, they were certainly going to give it everything they had and have a bloody good laugh in the meantime.

After the set ended in a crashing display of noise and feedback, Adam thanked the audience for making the long trek and for giving them support. Then, after unbuckling his Aria Pro II guitar and quickly whisking off the dodgy shades, he helped move the equipment from the stage, all except for his 'Ohm' 60 Watt guitar amplifier which Terminal Jive's guitarist was using and their drum kit, which Dave had bashed about impressively, only moments before. Then, after getting the odd pat on the back and some words of encouragement from their mates, they all stood and watched the headlining band Terminal Jive put the PA system through its paces for a second time.

It wasn't long before more of the audience had gathered at the front and as quite a few of them knew the forthcoming material (Terminal Jive already had a couple of good quality demo tapes out, as opposed to TMW's dodgy demo, which sounded like a hydraulic lift recorded through an old sock) people shouted out requests as the band came on.

As soon as they launched into their first number, the fair haired lead singer span about and began to liven up the crowd with his banter and histrionics. Adam thought he had a lot of energy and it was clear that they had already done a few gigs because they seemed confident. The guitarist had some good moments too, echoing the brash vocals with atmospheric jangling sounds, and it was certainly cool to see someone on stage who could play, using Adam's very own amplifier.

Down the front, the Basingstoke residents started dancing and jumping to the music and although the venue wasn't completely packed out, there were certainly enough people there to create a good atmosphere. As Adam sipped his pint of lager and watched in a state of euphoria, pinching himself almost, having survived the ordeal, he felt a great sense of relief.

'We've done a gig!' he leaned over to Dave as the noise blared.

'Yeah, I know - '

'To a hundred people....what a buzz. I can't wait for the next one!'

'Nor me!'

Plug looked well pleased with himself too, especially as he'd been nervous as well.

'Well played, Plug', Dave beamed over.

'Yeah, and you mate....' replied Plug, lighting up one of his favoured Gauloises.

Terminal Jive completed their set in a final crescendo of sonic and the swaying rabble from Basingstoke seemed more than pleased with the gig. As they all downed another drink or two in further celebration at the bar, Adam's brother and friends from school were mostly full of compliments and Rab seemed impressed by the performances. Although he thought Adam's sunglasses were definitely a fashion mistake.

'The glasses made you look a right twat!' he said.

'Thanks....' Adam countered, trying to make the best of it.

As far as he was concerned though, looking a twat wasn't such a bad thing and he thought that his peroxided hair might have had something to do with it - clashing as it did with the specs. Anyway, when the Sex Pistols had first appeared on TV, everyone thought that they looked pretty twattish, but it certainly hadn't stopped them and there had been a queue of punks ready to look twattish in full cartoon-like technicolour: Captain Sensible and Poly Styrene for a start.

'Wait till we hit Basingstoke', said Plug confidently.

'Yeah, there must be some venues there we can play', Adam replied.

'We'll sell 'em out with this lot', Dave boasted.

'Yeah....and the girls aren't bad too', Adam added, swigging on the dregs of his beer, as he noticed two attractive punkettes at the bar.

'Not bad...' said Plug, turning round to look, as the girls posed and preened their spiky coloured hair.

'Well nice', added Dave, his eyes on stalks as if he had suddenly become a rock star by proxy.

'They're friends of Si's....'

(Si was a well known Mohican Punk from Basingstoke who was famed for racing majestically around the Kempshott streets like Mad Max, on his beloved Trike). Just after Dave had spoken, the very same Si sauntered over:

'Well done. That was fuckin' great for a first gig!'

'Cheers mate', Dave countered with one eye still on the girls.

'When's the next one?' the mohawk probed, his spikes as rigid as spears.

'Dunno yet....' Dave replied.

'Ah, it won't be long though', said Plug.

'No, I reckon it won't', Adam confirmed.

'We might even play a gig in Kempshott', Dave gleamed.

'Great. Yeah! If you do, I'll get all my mates along. You know - Septic, Sychic, Liz - all this mob!' Si then turned lazily to indicate his group of friends at the bar.

Unfortunately, before they could question him further on the girls, the sound guy told them that they had to start moving their gear out of the venue as quickly as possible. At least they weren't short of a helping hand. And before the coach returned on its magical mystery tour, lots of people helped with the final load up. Rab was more than useful, picking up the equipment like they were just a load of toys lying about. 'He's not just a drummer and bouncer....he's a weightlifter as well', Adam thought.

Of course there was the small matter of obtaining their dosh in the hand from the venue. Something that was always a minefield of problems. When it was eventually sorted out from the box office, it all had to be split up between the bands. Dave, being manager, had the responsibility of handing out the money, but they all got a shock when they realised that they weren't getting as much as they had for the Right To Work gig, that they had never even played. As they pocketed the money with some quizzical glances, the ten quid burning tiny holes in each of their pockets, Dave had a go at the venue:

'An' I bet they made fuckin' loads on the bar!'

'More than likely...' said Plug, well wised up to the situation.

'Oh, well....we did a good first gig. That's the main thing', Adam reasoned.

He wasn't that bothered. If they had done it for free, it still would have been worth it. Just for the buzz.

It was almost funny. The three of them had been so wrapped up in the gig and the occasion that they had forgotten about everything else. Even the chance of chatting up some of the punkettes. Adam put it down to nerves. Still, he reckoned that they had played their socks off, so with a bit of luck they'd be remembered, or at least their socks would.

As the coach headed off, with its cargo of pie-eyed youth, Dave and Plug began their journey back to Basingstoke, while Adam headed back to south west London with his brother. On the way they dropped off Rab in Clapham, who said that he would definitely be in touch. As he vacated the car his closing gambit was, 'One more thing....get rid of them fuckin' glasses!'

So, Three Minute Warning had turned up and played. They had completed their first gig, in the smoke, without any major mishaps, with a large responsive audience. Without too much of a fuss. What a relief. And what an adventure. And that was just the start. The band were on the map.

Adam reckoned that now they were going to be unstoppable. They were going to be a force to be reckoned with.

'We're gonna be legends....in our own lunchtimes', said Plug smiling.

'Yeah', Adam replied, laughing at the joke.

'And household names....well, we will be round my household'.

ROADIES

After the live debut with Terminal Jive, Dave managed to hassle another gig, in Harlesden, north west London, just down the road from where Adam and Plug had first seen The Clash at the old Roxy, which had now sadly been knocked down and replaced with residential homes.

The gig in Harlesden at the Town Hall was part of a festival of live music and although they had few of their followers (there was no coach from Basingstoke) it was a good experience and the three of them were becoming more accustomed to playing live.

Around this time, Rab phoned to say that The Wall needed an extra pair of hands at their forthcoming gig at the Marquee and would Adam like to come along and help carry some amplifiers. He'd get in free and meet everyone. He added that, Chelsea, one of Adam's favourite bands, were also playing with them, resulting in Adam replying that he might take some time to think about it.

'Like hell!'

He jumped in the air after putting the phone down, his head nearly going through the ceiling.

'The Wall and Chelsea at the Marquee....How good is that!' He blurted out to Dave when he next spoke to him, almost swallowing the phone.

'Fuckin' hell! Rab must've liked our gig'.

'Yeah, I reckon!'

'So you're one of their roadies at the Marquee?' Dave quizzed excitedly.

'All I've gotta do is help them lump some equipment about'.

'Brilliant'.

'There's no problem if you and Plug wanna be roadies too'.

'I don't know about Plug, but yeah, I'll come'.

'Great'.

Sure enough, two days later, Adam and Dave travelled up to the Marquee to meet The Wall. Fortunately, this time there were no Skinheads about down Wardour Street, so they arrived there in one piece. Plug's shift at the cinema in Basingstoke meant that he couldn't make it, but he was certainly there in spirit. 'An American Werewolf In London', was being re-shown at his picture house and even though Plug had seen it about three hundred times already, because it was such a favourite film of his, one more time most definitely wouldn't hurt. Not so much as a scratch.

After loitering about for a few minutes, they met up with Rab, next to the shady front windows of the Marquee. He had cropped his hair even shorter than when they had seen him at the gig, which seemed an almost impossible feat, and his worn black leather jacket was even more infested with badges and Adam noticed that he had 'The Wall' logo spray-painted like a stencil on his left arm.

'Alright, Rab....' the two grinned sheepishly.

'Aye, alright?' Rab growled back.

There was a pause as he then consulted someone in the box office. As he chatted away, the two of them glanced inside the Marquee window at the records, gig listings and posters. From the look of things the legendary Johnny Thunders was shortly about to be making another appearance. While Adam and Dave discussed whether they might catch his Chinese Rocks, eventually Rab came over.

'There's not much to do. You two might as well go down the pub'.

'Okay, then....'

So they did. Rab told them to come back in about an hour and all they had to do was tell the guy at the box office and he would let them in.

'Thanks', they said nervously.

'It's ok...'

'Free entry at the Marquee. Fuckin' hell!' Adam said to Dave under his breath as Rab strolled back inside.

'Yeah, I know....' replied Dave, nudging him.

Adam was like a kid who had been given his very own sweet shop and a large set of keys.

'I can't wait for the gig. Maybe we'll meet Gene October!'

(The enigmatic, showy front man of Chelsea who was always one to watch live, even though his stage banter was sometimes as long as the songs).

A pub called The Ship, was about fifty yards up the same side of the road so without further ado they entered in and Dave purchased some beers. (Adam didn't usually buy drinks in pubs, not because he was stingy, although sometimes due to lack of finances he could be a little bit frugal, but because there was a good chance of the landlord consulting him about his youth, challenging him to prove that he wasn't under age. Put it down to genes or what you will, but Adam still looked as though he might be sitting his 'O' levels at any minute).

As soon as they had sat down, Dave leaned over.

'Blimey....it's Ali McMordie!'

'No way...'

'Straight up!'

'Where?'

'Over there, with them birds!'

'Christ!' Adam said, looking over at the wrong table, where two elderly gents were busy reminiscing.

'Not them….Look. Over there!' Dave added with about as much subtlety as a brick.

'Oh yeah….shit', Adam whispered, finally clocking him.

(Ali McMordie was the cool bassist in Stiff Little Fingers and he reminded Adam a little of Paul Simonon of The Clash in terms of his stage charisma, even looking a bit like him as well).

'Let's go over'.

'You reckon?' Adam replied nervously.

'Yeah, why not?' said Dave, and he was off.

Before you could say, 'How do you do', Dave had introduced them both, and before anyone had any time to worry about the interruption, they'd sat down at the table, with Adam trying desperately not to spill his pint all over Ali's girlfriend.

Dave was fearless in these situations. Adam was usually tongue tied, partly in awe, especially as he had already seen SLF three times and he felt that they were by now bordering on legendary status. Luckily, Ali turned out to be really friendly and he seemed keen to talk. He was in the pub with some friends just killing time. Dave told him that they were roadies for the day and that they knew Rab, The Wall having recently toured with SLF, and that they were in their own band which Rab had even played in. Ali seemed pretty impressed, although it was probably more from their enthusiasm than their gigging portfolio (they hadn't yet appeared on Top of the Pops like Stiff Little Fingers, but by the way Dave sparred people would have thought that they already had had a Number One).

'Goldstein and Treganna from Sham are good mates of mine….'

'Really', said Ali, glancing across at his attractive girlfriend, who Adam was having trouble not becoming intently focused on.

'Treganna's now playin' with Stiv Bators in 'The Lord's of the New Church' of course', said Dave, name-dropping like no tomorrow.

'Course....' said Ali eventually.

'Goldstein's in the Bootleg Beatles'.

It was always entertaining to see Dave in full swing, flexing his networking muscles and anyway, it was his prerogative: Dave was still Adam and Plug's manager.

'Aye, a lot of the bands are changin'. Look at The Wall, they've had a few line ups', said Ali.

'Look at The Ruts since Malcolm Owen died - Paul Fox's now giggin' with Rat Scabies from The Damned'.

Dave was now in full flood. A rock'n'roll encyclopaedia with his phaser on stun and it was a while before anyone else could get a word in.

'So what do you play in the band?' Ali's girlfriend said, eventually turning to Adam, politely trying to bring someone else into the conversation.

'Oh, I sing and play guitar'.

'What's your band called again?'

'Three Minute Warning', Adam said proudly.

'It's a good name'.

'Yeah, it's alright....'

'Are you gigging?'

'We've just done some London dates and now we're hopin' to play Basingstoke', said Dave, his manager's hat back on.

After another beer, Ali wished them well for the future and made off to the door with his partner. As he left Dave told him that they'd see him from down the front of the auditorium at SLF's next London date.

As they finished off their beers and savoured the encounter, as if luck would have it, two New Romantic looking girls came over.

'Is anyone sitting here?' said the blonde, wearing a strange hat.

'No, no, course not. Help yourself', said Dave, and before you could even think of breaking out into 'Stand and Deliver' Dave was off, chatting them up.

The girls weren't especially into Punk, but this didn't put them off and anyway they were a good laugh and easy to get along with like a house on fire. The only snag was the fact that they had to catch a coach to take them back to Plymouth where they lived, so they didn't have much time. Luckily, it wasn't long before they had paired up, despite Adam's reservations concerning Carol, and Dave was soon busy kissing the brunette while Adam had his hands full, necking with the blonde.

But it soon dawned on Adam that they had to pull themselves together. They had a job to do. They were on a mission. They couldn't just spend the rest of the evening canoodling with two young ladies. How irresponsible. Were they not roadies? The girls had to hurry back to the west country as well, so Adam supposed it was fate getting in the way again, but he and Dave couldn't really complain, because fate had put them all together in the first place. They left the smoky pub, the four of them hastily trying to exchange telephone numbers, but Adam knew that it was to little purpose. Then there was one last fumbled snog and the girl's were gone.

When Adam and Dave finally returned to the Marquee, after rubbing off some bright lipstick marks, the burly bloke in the box office was as good as his word, and after checking diligently that their names were on his piece of paper, he allowed them in. As soon as they entered the Marquee's claustrophobic interior, they located Rab near the stage. The Wall had just finished their sound check and people were busily making ready for the gig. The barman was dusting down his pumps and the DJ was doing the finishing touches to his selections.

On the press releases it seemed as though both bands had equal billing, but for some reason or other, The Wall were going to be playing first.

'How was yer drink?' said Rab.

'Great', replied Dave, 'We met Ali McMordie in the boozer'.

'Oh, aye....I know him', said Rab completely unfazed.

Just at that moment, some of the other band members were hovering about. Rab introduced Andy Griffiths, the lead singer, the fairly recently recruited bassist Claire Bidwell and a wiry punk from Dundee known as 'Gumsie Elbow' who was the band's full time chief roadie.

'Heh, Gums, these two are here to help you with the gear', Rab shouted.

'Thanks lads', said Gumsie, grinning back.

'No sweat...' replied Dave confidently.

Adam later found out that The Wall had another couple of roadies, one called 'Beaver', but he was unable to help out anymore due to the commitments of his new job. And there was also a mohican called 'Jock the Noo', with his nickname tattooed on his skull, helping out as an on-off extra pair of hands, although now more off possibly as a result of one too many heavy sessions which had ended up on glue.

So there was Adam and Dave, plucky replacements, ready to hump some equipment about and even though they looked like they might actually be more of a hindrance than a help, they weren't complete plonkers and they certainly felt that they knew their onions when it came down to the musical bits and pieces. Anyone would have thought that they were about to go on a world tour, such was their youthful enthusiasm.

Soon the door had opened to the Marquee and various die hard punks and assorted new wave types started filtering through. Adam and Dave, having so far done absolutely nothing, apart from a lot of standing around thinking about eventually lifting something, they retired to the bar near the stage, where Adam suddenly clocked Gene October, the Chelsea vocalist, with the guitarist. They seemed to be gulping down beverages at a terrific rate and between guffaws of laughter, they chatted animatedly with each other. Adam turned to Dave.

'Look...Gene October'.

'Yeah, course it is', said Dave, like an impatient teacher. 'What did you expect?'

'I know, but....but he's the lead singer of Chelsea. One of my favourites'.

'Well, go and say hello to him'.

'But....what do I say?' Adam replied, his tongue stuck in his throat.

'I dunno....tell him how much you like their stuff'.

Adam stood there for what seemed like a lifetime, clenching his plastic pint of lager, sipping nervously as he weighed up his opening gambit:

Adam: Hi Gene! How's it going? Really liked your third single - Urban Kids. Great! Are you gonna play it tonight?

Gene: (Bluntly) What's it to you?

Adam: (Flustered) Er....I'm one of your fans. You know. Have been for some time - used to have 'Chelsea' written on the back of my jacket.... always used to get me into trouble....'

Gene: (Unimpressed) Yeah? Why?

Adam: (Floundering) Well, it's a long story, but..... (pause) Can I have your autograph?

Gene: No. Fuck off!

Adam: Oh, okay....

Or,

Adam: Hi Gene! I'm in a punk band too. We call ourselves Three Minute Warning. We nearly played this Right To Work march, but the generator blew up. We were gonna play your song Right To Work, but we couldn't play.

Gene: (Unimpressed) Yeah? So?

Adam: (Floundering) Well....you see, we were gonna play YOUR song.

Gene: (Bored) So what?

Adam: (Panicking) Us....'Three Minute Warning', WE were gonna play it!

Gene: (Turning away and laughing with the guitarist) Who?!

Adam: Three Minute Warning -

Gene: WHO THE FUCK ARE THEY??!!

Adam: Er....right.

You see it was always a tricky one, but just as Adam was plucking up all his courage to go over and introduce himself to the singer who seemed ready to rock at any moment in his extrovert stage clobber, Rab appeared out of nowhere and saved the day.

'What are you two drinkin'?'

'Pint a lager please', gabbled Dave.

'Same here, cheers', Adam said full of relief, knowing that an introduction from the tattooed drummer would definitely be more credible. Just as Adam was about to suggest it to Rab, the DJ dropped his stylus onto a loud punk offering by Discharge and they almost flinched as they tried to hear themselves amidst the noise.

'We're on soon!' Rab shouted as he strode off to the bar.

'Oh, right...' replied Adam, looking at Dave.

They were both like a couple of impressionable kids. Their attention would switch at the push of a button, so all thoughts of chatting to the Chelsea singer were quickly relegated to the back of their minds.

When Rab returned and passed out the refreshments, they then sauntered around to the front of the Marquee's stage. There were already a lot of people in the venue although it was by no means completely packed to the rafters, and as Adam and Dave positioned themselves down the front next to some hard looking punks, Rab asked if they could help Gumsie and move the amps once the Wall had finished their set. They said that they would and it felt great to have some responsibility for a change and not just be a member of the audience. They were roadies now, people with a purpose.

Eventually, The Wall came out on to the stage to cheers and requests from the quickly massing spectators. Loud requests for 'Ghetto!' and 'New Way!' quickly followed. While the band looked quite unusual. Andy the frontman, was now the heart of the band, having been there at its inception and he had survived all the frenetic line up changes, even switching from being the bass player to becoming the lead singer, which he might never have pulled off if he hadn't had such an expressive voice or the ability to write a good lyric.

Claire on bass had a lot of stage presence, dressed all in black and you could tell she was a highly experienced musician, concentrating intensely on her moody bass patterns. The guitarist, Baz, was an accomplished axeman alright and he moved around his guitar almost like a serious session musician. Rab of course was the band's engine room and he spent the next fifty minutes whacking his shiny Eddie Ryan kit like some atomic metronome. To say that the band could sound like a ton of bricks was an understatement, they reminded Adam of a large industrial generator, but they could also play and mix up the styles. It was classic, thoughtful punk.

They performed quite a few songs off their new album 'Dirges and Anthems' which Adam had only recently purchased, so some of the songs weren't that familiar, but they were catchy tunes with great themes: Walpurgis Night, English History, Money Whores, Chinese Whispers, Only Dreaming, etc.

But the gig really took off when the band played their older, more familiar songs and it wasn't long before pogoing started up, especially when they heard the distinctive opening chords of the bands first single, New Way written by Ian Lowery. A song that John Peel had championed, with its powerful cry about not fitting in to the machine, or working in tomorrow's dream. The song sounded terrific live, the chorus like a terrace anthem, the verse an inspired punk-reggae riff. After loud cheers from all around at the song's crescendo the band went straight into their second single, Exchange, which sounded almost like the Pistols at such loud volume. It certainly hit the spot, so much so that everyone was starting to push each other about - Adam and Dave included. As they jostled and jockeyed about in the audience, Adam spat out the memorable words, all about angst ridden youth. The audience were working up a sweat alright, even Dave had found himself jumping up and down, which was something that Adam rarely saw. He was usually more bothered with contacts and hustling and talking a good talk. But Adam reckoned even he, still a young upstart Maclaren, had to have a day off once in a while.

It wasn't long before The Wall were into their encore which included their barnstorming anthem, Ghetto, and the audience was immediately won over. This thunderous song was another of Adam's favourites. It seemed to be a lot of other people's aswell. A hundred percent attitude played at a hundred miles an hour. When The Wall left the stage everyone chanted for more, but it seemed as if they wouldn't be playing another song, due to time, and the fact that the evening was a double bill, so Adam and Dave perched themselves at the front of the stage, and wiped the sweat off their faces, ready at any moment if Gumsie needed help with the equipment.

They tried to make themselves look as though they might be useful, which was always a bit difficult, though they didn't overdo it as that would result in them lugging a load more amps and speakers about. But once Rab had disentangled himself from his large drum kit he nodded over, as if to say 'Well, what are you waiting for!' They then leaped up on to the stage and the amazing thing was, no one stopped them, no bouncers, no nothing. 'At last', Adam thought, 'I'm on the stage of the Marquee'. It felt superb to look out at the audience, although it was difficult making them out because of the bright lights. He felt as though he had just played the gig himself.

'Here! Can you help us with this?' said Gums.

'Sure mate', said Dave, as they took the other end of the large guitar amplifier.

Most of the stuff was placed out of the way at the back and side of the stage or in the Marquee dressing room which turned out to be a poky little cell, it's walls and ceiling completely covered in spray paint and scratchy graffiti, made by all the bands who had ever appeared there. Things like, 'SPIZZ WOZ 'ERE', 'C.I.D! C.I.D!' and 'IF YOU DON'T WANNA FUCK ME, BABY, BABY, BABY, FUCK OFF!' mostly in what seemed like a black marker pen, but also in crazy felt tip colours and jumbled up hieroglyphs.

'Fuckin' hell!' Adam said, turning to Dave. 'Look at this place'.

'I know....Oi, cop this - Pete Shelley's signature!'

'No way....' replied Adam staring at the unreadable Buzzcocks scrawl. 'It is as well!'

Just as Adam was trying to decipher a provocative yellowing gig advertisement next to the legendary Mancunian's autograph, some of the members of Chelsea huddled into the dressing room, like adrenalin fuelled rock stars, October among them.

'Who are you then?' said the guitarist.

'We're with The Wall', Adam blurted out all star struck.

'Yeah?!'

'We're helpin' out....you know, roadies', explained Dave with a swagger.

'Sorry lads, but we've gotta get ready', said Gene.

'Yeah, sure mate', replied Dave as if they had always been great friends.

'No problem....' added Adam who was trying desperately to stop making a fool of himself by going on about how great he thought Chelsea were, and eventually he managed to manoeuvre respectfully past the band and out of the door. Adam soon found himself back at the side of the stage where Gums and Rab were doing the finishing touches to the changeover.

'It's all done!' said Rab.

'Great', Adam replied, relieved that when it came to removals, Rab and Elbow certainly knew their stuff.

'We might as well watch Chelsea', said Dave who was now standing behind, exhaling a large cloud of cigarette smoke.

'Good idea'.

Once more, Adam and Dave were down the front, but this time so were Rab and Gums and the rest of the band. Chelsea eventually appeared after checking their hair and ego's and from the first song to the last they played some great amphetamine filled rock, with Gene October playing the part of the energetic swaggering punk poet, shooting as always from the hip. One minute he was cajoling the audience with a visceral clenched attitude, the next he was into himself, berating the world that had made him a loner.

Towards the end of their set they played Right to Work and Adam and Dave laughed, because it reminded them of the demonstration that they never got to play. Just like The Wall before them, Chelsea's classic tracks stuck out like a saw thumb. Adam stood there watching October closely as he hugged the microphone and ranted emotionally about 'Twelve Men' and the stinking state of the nation and thought to himself, 'I got into the gig free, I've roadied for the Wall, I've met Chelsea and Ali McMordie, I've been on the Marquee stage and been right inside the dressing room and met one of my favourite bands, and even if that wasn't Pete Shelley's signature right there on that wall, it certainly won't get much better than that'. But of course it did, because a few days after the gig, Rab rang up and asked Adam if he wanted to join The Wall on a temporary basis as they now didn't have a guitarist anymore. It took him about a millisecond to decide.

'Definitely!'

'Good. But you'll need to learn the songs'.

'No trouble', he replied, as if nothing could be simpler.

After putting the phone down, it suddenly began to sink in. 'I'm virtually straight out of school and I'm in a punk band with records out. Brilliant!' And before you could say, 'Session musician!' he was playing along to all The Wall records that he had. The first album didn't leave the turntable for about a month, the stylus jumping about repetitively in certain places which just meant that he played those particular bits over and over again. His copy of the Ghetto single ended up with scratches, coffee stains, fingerprints and the remnants of a jam sandwich on it. To say that the fingertips of his left hand were pitted and scarred from practising too much would be an understatement. His right hand was so stiff from strumming the guitar repeatedly, that he couldn't even play with himself for at least a week.

Alongside learning the material in anticipation of appearing live, he also thought it would be a good idea to get all their stuff and find out as much as he could about the band. Yes, it was back to being a detective again. Hardly difficult, when he opened his cupboard to find it stuffed full with old copies of Sounds and NME.

THE WALL

The band were formed in early 1978 in Sunderland. Their first line up consisted of Ian Lowery on vocals, John Hammond on guitar, Andy Griffiths on bass and Bruce Archibald on drums. Their first single was the 'New Way' EP for Small Wonder Records. It sold up to around 20,000 copies, John Peel playing it regularly on his popular Radio One show. It was a song that Adam heard many times on his radio and it was one of his favourite singles.

Due to the success of the first single, the band moved down to London where two new members: Nick Ward on guitar and Rab Fae Beith on drums, were taken on, (Rab had been in both Kirk Brandon's The Pack and the Patrick Fitzgerald Group and met The Wall when they toured the UK with Teardrop Explodes). They issued their second single, 'Exchange', again for Small Wonder, which reached number 26 in the first ever published Independent Chart. The single was produced by Steve Jones (the Wall being the first band to be produced by an ex member of the Sex Pistols).

After this single, The Wall's line up changed once more - Lowery left and was replaced by Ivan Kelly on vocals (ex of northern Irish band Ruefrex), who made his debut on a UK tour with the Angelic Upstarts (it was this very line up of The Wall that Adam had seen at the Music Machine in Camden, which was later to become Steve Strange's Camden Palace venue). Their next single 'Ghetto' was released on Fresh Records, in August 1980, and was produced by Jimmy Pursey of Sham 69. Pursey also brought along the producer Pete Wilson from Polydor to assist him in the studio. Wilson being notable for his tremendous Sham 69 and later Jam/Weller classic production values. However, things got out of control as Pursey seemed to be more interested in his young prodigy Honey Bane who he was taking under his wing and soon after signing to his record label Zonophone Records (a subsidiary of EMI). In fact things became so much out of control that Pete Wilson finally stepped in to work on the individual instrument overdubbing and mixing stages himself and ended up completing the mastering. Not surprisingly, he was to become a feature as the Wall's debut album 'Personal Troubles and Public Issues' credited Pete Wilson as the producer and for the 'Ghetto' single's addition on the LP, the specific production credit was added; * 'Produced by Pete Wilson with Jimmy Pursey'. The song was a gig DJ favourite and when Adam first heard it, his mates used to change the words of the chorus just for a laugh from 'Barbed wire, Ghetto!' to, 'Raspberry Gateaux!'

The results of the Pursey/Wilson recording sessions were encouraging for all parties. Another quality punk outing hit the official Indie chart with Pursey's name on it and 'Ghetto' spent more than three months in it, peaking well within the top twenty. The album soon after, reached number 15 in the Indie Chart and added another guitarist, Andy Forbes (ex of The Straps), to the lineup.

When Kelly and Nick Ward departed soon after, the band carried on as a three piece with Andy Griffiths now on lead vocals and bass. This line up was then immediately signed up by Polydor Records and their debut for the major label was the 'Remembrance' EP, again produced by Pete Wilson which was promoted by a UK tour with Stiff Little Fingers, better known as the 'Go For It' tour. Around the same time The Wall released the single 'Hobby For A Day' as their final single for Fresh Records which reached number 14 in the Indie Chart and was one of Gary Bushell's favourite releases around this time, when he was still writing for Sounds magazine.

A second Polydor single, 'Epitaph' was released soon after, towards the end of 1981 and it also saw the addition of Claire Bidwell (ex of The Passions, another Polydor outfit, who had a chart hit with their release 'I'm in Love with a German Film Star') on bass guitar. (The Epitaph single also demonstrated The Wall's diverse musicality with the song's Ska-reggae influences. Andy Griffiths even played saxophone on the record).

With Griffiths now well established as the band's lead vocalist, the band then released an album for Polydor in early 1982 called 'Dirges and Anthems', which came with a free 7" single, 'Plastic Smiles'. The band then embarked on another UK tour to promote it.

After a day or so, once Rab's phone call had finally sunk in, Adam decided to tell Plug and Dave.

'I'm in The Wall'.

'No way!'

'They've asked me to be their guitarist'.

'That's great! But what about us?' said Dave in cross examining mode.

'There won't be a problem. I'm gonna do both'.

'You reckon?'

'Why not? Most of their stuff I can play already and I'll just be like a session musician'.

'Well, I hope so cos we're goin' into the studio with Parsons'.

'What, Parsons of Sham?'

'Yeah, he's gonna produce our next demo', announced Dave, as if he had just lit himself a large Havana cigar.

'How did you get him?' Adam replied even more excited.

'Since Sham split, he's gone into producin' and my mate Treganna asked him'.

'Blimey!'

'It'll be good that you're in The Wall, cos they're with Polydor like Sham', said Dave.

'Can't hurt, can it?'

'Exactly'.

'Rab thinks I can do both, no problem'.

'Good'.

Then Adam told his parents one morning, on one of his irregular visits.

'I'm in The Wall', he said grinning from ear to ear as he crunched some Frosties.

'What?'

'I'm in The Wall. A punk band'.

'In the wall?!' Adam's dad looked around bemused.

'Yeah, a punk band'.

'You mean your friends, in a band?' said his mum trying to work it all out.

'No, another one....they're signed to a major'.

'Major?' his dad muttered unenthusiastically.

'Yeah, Polydor'.

'Polly who?!'

'Polydor. It's a record label. The Wall want me to play guitar for them'.

'Really....'

'You know, play some gigs and stuff'.

'Stuff?'

'Record with them'.

'What about looking for work?'

'Well, I'm doing this now....'

There was a long pause waiting for the penny to drop.

'I see....'

Adam's announcement went down like breaking wind in a lift, but it didn't bother him. There was no way he was going to let this opportunity escape. There was no way that he was going to live to regret anything.

After about a week a rehearsal was scheduled, at the bassist's house in Hammersmith, where they would begin work on the new songs for the next single (Rab had already mentioned that they were thinking of releasing an up tempo punk cover version of the Beatles 'Day Tripper' as an EP, also with a 12" release with ten tracks on it, so it was going to be like a mini album), then the band would go into the studio and finish recording a demo to choose the best material.

The rehearsals in the dingy basement of the terraced house, went really well and although Adam was nervous being relatively inexperienced, he was welcomed into the band. The good thing was he had done his homework and could play virtually every song as it sounded on record, although due to nerves, they sometimes had to tell him to slow down because he had a tendency to run away with himself. With the new songs, Adam was able to work on them with Rab, who had written most of the riffs with Andy. However, two songs, 'Castles' and 'Industrial Nightmare' were being worked on completely from scratch, so Adam could put some of his very own string bending towards the greater creative effort.

Things got even better when Rab lent him his very own flashy Gibson 'Flying V' (the guitar so-called due to its ostentatious 'V'- shaped cutaway) and 100 watt Marshall valve amp and 4" by 12" speaker cabinet. (The guitar factory production sound of Steve Jones of the Pistols had been continued since he worked with the band on their second single, and a little bit of early Slade's sonic was thrown in for good measure. It was no coincidence that one of the tracks on the forthcoming single was going to be a cover of Slade's, When I'm Dancing). Whatever, the sound was loud and furious and it wasn't long before Adam found himself in amplified heaven annoying all the neighbours and their pets.

Meanwhile, rehearsals for Three Minute Warning stepped up a gear. Through another of Dave's contacts they found themselves a great little rehearsal studio at 'Sychic's' house in the wild woodlands near Basingstoke. Sychic's dad was a funeral director, so it wasn't unusual for them to find gravestones with RIP or some uncompleted message from the bereaved lying around the rehearsal room next to the equipment. Sychic even had a headstone at the end of his bed. It didn't put them off though, and they regularly retired for a break in his mobile home to drink tea and smoke some large illegal substance that he and his blonde bombshell girlfriend, Suze, had somehow managed to roll inside some Rizla's. Sometimes due to their recreational habits, it was difficult returning to play because no-one could remember exactly where they were, but usually they were just about responsible enough to carry on for a few more ear splitting minutes. In reality, it was probably more like an eternity. After puffing some of Sychic's 'Moroccan' it could take Adam half an hour just to find the rehearsal room again and then another to put their guitar straps back on, that's if they hadn't already broken down in fits of hysterics along the way.

After a couple of weeks, Adam, Plug and Dave finally went into the Matinee Studio in Reading to record their long awaited demo. They eventually met up with Dave Parsons, who turned up all screeching tyres in his TR7. He looked unrecognisable. The short military hair cut worn for Sham had long since grown out and he was now experimenting with some bleached highlights and sunglasses. But whatever he'd done with his appearance the visage was unmistakable, shaped as it was by four albums and countless single picture sleeves.

It was strange. All those years they'd been following Sham 69 and here they were with the lead guitarist, helping them out. They were only recording two songs, Adam's recently penned No Rules and the 'day in the life' Night Shift Blues, but it was a brilliant feeling to work alongside a well known, respected musician, who'd been on TV and the Top of The Pops more than once.

With the borrowed 'Flying V', to use alongside Adam's own Aria, he could use two guitars to create a different sound, something Dave had already advised him about.

'Bring another guitar with you, it'll give us another sound'.

'No worries'.

Parsons brought his very own Gibson 'Les Paul' along to the recording which Adam couldn't take his eyes off. He didn't seem to have bothered with a case, he just pulled it out from the passenger seat of his motor. It had a lovely varnished look and a brilliant sound. To everyone's surprise Parsons even fancied playing guitar on the demo tape and there was no way that anybody was going to stop him. When it came to selling the demo in Basingstoke, at a more than affordable price, it would certainly help to shift some copies: 'ROLL UP!' 'ROLL UP!' 'GET YOUR LATEST THREE MINUTE WARNING!' 'HEAR YOUR LOCAL HEROES PLAY WITH SHAM LEGEND!' As people prepared for the market on a Saturday, Dave's sales tactics always worked a treat. Well, sold a couple more anyway.

The engineer in the studio was really helpful too, considering Adam didn't have a clue how it all worked. He knew about recording on to a tape recorder round Plug's or at a rehearsal studio, but a fully fledged recording studio was alien. It was the same for Plug aswell, though Dave had some experience already with other band's that he had managed.

They started out by playing the two songs just as a band, so that they had a basic track with which to use as a foundation. They would then play individually over the track to record the different instruments, over-dubs, vocals and backing vocals. The studio was fairly basic with an eight track recording desk, but the engineer was a whiz at bouncing tracks about and improvising, so they found that it was more than enough.

As they stormed through No Rules, headphones pinned to their ears like three manic Cybermen, Parsons sat in the control room and listened. When they neared the end of the song he put his thumbs up as if to say 'Well done'. They were relieved. No Rules had loads of youthful energy and they had managed to get through it all with no major cock ups. Dave was a little nervous about his drumming because he was still learning to coordinate the whole kit, but he was getting there. He certainly gave it everything he had. Plug's bass playing was as solid as a concrete house, so Adam was able to be a bit loose and manic over the top of it - the noisy icing on the cake.

Once they had the basic track recorded and were happy with it, they then put down Night Shift Blues, which took a lot longer because it was a more complicated song with a more complex feel and bluesy shuffle. It must have taken them at least five takes before Parsons reckoned it was perfect.

They then had a quick break to chat about what they had all been up to. Parsons was surprised to hear that all three of them had seen Sham's infamous 'Last Stand' concert at the Rainbow, though he wasn't that surprised to hear that Dave had been jumped by a large Skinhead.

'That gig was a nightmare. We just couldn't carry on. Loads of people were getting hurt and there was nothin' we could do about it. We'd had enough of all the trouble…'

'What are the rest of the band doing now?' probed Plug.

'Well, Jimmy's into producing like me, Kermit's in 'The Lords of the New Church' and Dodie's gone back to being a milkman….'

'Blimey', said Adam, surprised.

'So, no chance of you reforming?' questioned Plug, eagerly.

'No, I don't think so. Not now'.

'That's a shame....'

Then Parsons turned to Adam.

'Dave was telling me you're in The Wall?'

'Yeah, I'm filling in for them'.

'Nice one. Good band. They use Pete Wilson - the same producer we had. Didn't Jimmy produce one of their singles aswell?'

'Yeah, he did 'Ghetto' for them', interrupted Dave, filling them in while sipping his tea.

'Oh, yeah....I heard a story about that. He got pissed up or somethin' and didn't turn up!'

'Summat like that...' said Dave, chuckling to himself.

After the basic track had been put down, they then began re-recording the individual instruments, adding any drums, bass, and guitar that was needed before attempting the main vocals. After Adam put down the main guitar riff and chords, Parsons meanwhile had been sitting next to the engineer with his Les Paul, diligently working out a brilliant harmony for the chorus of No Rules.

'I've got this little run that'll fit in nice over your chords', he said to Adam as his fingers scuttled effortlessly down the fret board.

'Sounds brilliant', Adam replied in awe, feeling honoured that Parsons had thought their stuff at all worthy of his more than accomplished guitar skills.

As Parsons took a couple of minutes to perfect his part, almost made up on the spot, Adam looked across to Plug who seemed more than impressed. And Parsons' clever fret work not only fitted, it gave No Rules a quality hook, a really catchy melody.

'He's fuckin' amazing!' Adam said to Dave as they watched the maestro casually enter the sound booth to record his gem, which he was about to pick in one take.

'Yeah, I know....'

'He's even adding some cool stuff to my guitar break', Adam replied, more than pleased as Parsons bent his strings wildly up the neck.

'He says he wants to do backin' vocals on the songs an' all', countered Dave.

'You're joking?' said Plug nearly falling off his chair.

'No. I told you. He likes the stuff. He wouldn't be doin' it if he didn't'.

Adam looked at Plug again and it suddenly dawned on them. On many occasions before, in and out of school, they had both been reminded that they were both useless wastes of space, and that there was probably nothing that they could do or achieve that would have any benefit to anyone. Well, nothing of value anyway. It was as if they had been born only to find themselves in the wrong lifetime. The wrong time space. Because of the repetition, they had even begun to believe the blueprint. The bullshit. It was almost natural.

Thanks to Parsons and the likes of Rab and even Dave's irrepressible ambitions, they were beginning to acknowledge that buried down deep within them there might in fact be something. Something that was useful. As Parsons recorded his memorable riff, Adam suddenly thought of them at the Sham concert three years before and there and then dreaming of one day being in a band. And here they now were, recording with the guitarist.

After Adam completed the vocals, which he had already memorised down to the last word, him, Dave and Parsons then finished off by doing the backing vocals for both songs. Plug had declined, because even he admitted that he had butter fingers when it came to holding a note.

They put the finishing touches to the fairly simple backing vocals with Dave singing a loud 'Fuckin' bore!' during the final verse of No Rules which worked a treat. Parsons was more than used to doing extravagant backing vocals. On Sham's 'If The Kids Are United' it seemed like a whole army of football supporters had been recruited to do the backing vocals and hand clapping.

Once all the bits and pieces were completed it was then down to the engineer and Parsons to mix it all together. This seemed a frustrating part of the process because the songs were played over and over again, sometimes paired down to the bare minimum of vocals and drums via the various little controls on the recording desk, but it was exciting watching an experienced musician put everything together and the engineer was more than happy to find himself working with the Sham legend. While the fine tuning seemed to go on and on forever, they all took turns in making sugary cups of tea.

The end result? Well, for Adam, Dave and Plug, it was a baptism of fire alright, but it was a great experience and Parsons had certainly done them a big favour, at no cost, which was something that they knew they'd never forget. The music was nicely shaped too with the engineer baking it all in the oven at the optimum temperature to Parsons' particular specifications and when the final copy of the cassette tape was in their hands they just couldn't wait to play it.

When they eventually wandered outside to find the evening reluctantly drawing in, they said their goodbyes.

'We'll be in touch', Dave said.

'Yeah, let me know how it all goes....'

and before you could say, 'Hurry Up Harry', Parsons had whizzed off, all wheel spins and flying gravel.

'What a laugh....' Adam said to Plug, who was looking more than happy.

'Tops!' he answered, after he'd taken it all in.

Luckily, Dave had brought his camera to the recording as well, so they had a few instamatic memories of the event for future reference (including one cracking picture captured by the engineer of the four of them posing proudly in front of the studios modest recording facilities) and as they drove back to Basingstoke in Plug's Sunbeam Alpine, bantering excitedly all the way, the freshly born demo tape blared out repeatedly, at full volume.

WALKING DEAD

'So how d'ya fancy being in Melody Maker?'

'Yeah....great!' Adam gabbled to Rab, virtually speechless.

'We've got an article coming up so they want some photos'.

'Where are they taking them?'

'A pub in Clapham on Saturday morning.

'Excellent! Saturday....right'.

The next couple of days went in by in a flash as Adam tried to control his excitement. But it wasn't easy. He just couldn't believe it. He had only been involved with The Wall for a short period of time and he certainly hadn't considered having his picture taken for a major music magazine. Well, definitely not one as established as Melody Maker anyway. A lot of Adam's mates were sick with envy when they found out about it. But he couldn't understand it. They had been busying themselves since school with furthering their careers, and seemed happy enough with their lives, whereas all he ever wanted, was to play in a band or appear at Stamford Bridge in a blue and white shirt.

Plug and Dave however, seemed much more realistic about it all and they knew that any publicity was bound to be a good thing in the long run.

'Jammy git!' said Dave, crunching loudly on some crisps at the next rehearsal.

'Lucky sod...' added Plug, after devouring a piece of toast.

But Adam knew that they were right behind him really. They were just showing a healthy competitive spirit. Had it been either of them in his position, he was sure he would have reacted the same.

Finally, the day of the photo shoot came around. The Wall were going to have quite a large article in the magazine, with news about the next record and a tour to promote it. Also, Adam would get a mention as their guitarist (calling him Meanaxe, because once while playing in a rehearsal, Adam had said, 'That sounds like a right meanaxe', and after that the name had stuck).

Everyone was present for the shoot, except for the bassist, who was unavailable because of illness, so that day it seemed as if there were only three people in the band. Andy was in T-shirt and jeans, while Rab was in his familiar Punk regalia, all studded belt and zips over his shirt and tattoos, while Adam wore faded, turned up jeans, Doctor Martens and T-shirt, a sort of early Slade skinhead look. While they posed about in the beer garden of the pub by a large pillar, the photographer snapped away like some manic David Bailey, telling Adam all the time to relax and try and be as natural as possible.

When the article came out a couple of weeks later, Adam rushed down to the local newsagent, and once purchased, hurriedly turned to the relevant pages in the magazine and there in glorious black and white was the article. To his relief, not only did he get a mention in the interview, but the picture accompanying it seemed as if he was a really important member of the band, because he just happened to be heavily favoured in the picture, leaning up against the pillar with arms folded. Adam recalled thinking how nervous he was at the time but this had just served to give the photo a more aggressive edge.

'We're goin' into the studio in Chelsea next week to do the demos', said Rab next time Adam spoke to him.

'Great', Adam said again, trying to pinch himself (the studio was a large 24 track recording facility that the band had worked at before through their record label Polydor. It was a top location near the King's Road and bands like Ian Dury and The Blockheads had recently worked there).

'And we've got some gigs in London'.

'Where?'

'The Blue Boy - Skunx and Ronnie Scott's'.

'Ronnie Scott's?'

'Aye, upstairs, in three weeks time'.

'Three weeks? Shit!'

'We're gonna play the next single Day Tripper too'.

'Oh....right'.

Not only that but Adam was going to get paid for doing the gig and the work on the demo, which would then be used for the single. It wasn't going to be a huge amount, in other words, Adam wasn't going to be retiring to the Bahamas just yet, but at his age it was beginning to feel like all his Christmas' had just turned up all at once. Or, that three buses had just arrived after a particularly long wait and had virtually concertinaed themselves into each other. The real problem was going to be trying to fit everything in, because Adam was still doing all the band stuff with Dave and Plug and they still considered imminent world domination a realistic objective.

Dave had been more than busy as usual and had fixed up Three Minute Warning's first local gig in Newbury, which was just down the road from Basingstoke. They rehearsed as usual at Sychic's legendary establishment and soon all was set for their first crucial neighbourhood appearance. As Adam was now a qualified motorist, his brother's weren't press ganged into being roadies (he had managed to pass his driving test at the third attempt. At the second test he had the misfortune to have the same examiner that he had at his first who proceeded to fail him on exactly the same thing - reversing around a corner - and straight after he had informed Adam with relish that he had failed again he told him that it was very uncommon to get the same examiner a second time. Afterwards, Adam made a mental note not to put him in his best books).

His first mode of transport? He was the proud owner of a battered Fiat 126 'Bambino', the sort of car that had an engine the size of a hair dryer and could manoeuvre itself easily into spaces a push bike would have had trouble fitting into. Not for nothing was it soon nicknamed the 'comedy car' and its colour, a sort of sickly bright yellow, as if someone had just thrown up all over it, made sure that he would always be noticed wherever he went, even if heavily disguised in a large pair of sunglasses and a silly hat. Luckily, the tiny car had a sunroof, because it was often to be found with amplifiers, guitar cases and microphone stands protruding dangerously out of the top. But what it lacked in sophistication it more than made up for in character.

One time while hurtling along the motorway at its customary fifty miles an hour, the rain was lashing down so hard that the windscreen wipers failed, so Plug had to lean unselfishly out of the car to move the blades up and down so Adam could see out of the front to carry on driving. By the end, Plug was so soaked through to the skin that he more than resembled a drowned rat, but thankfully, they managed to reach their musical destination intact. Afterwards, Plug, who was a bit of a mechanic on the quiet, fixed the problem temporarily with a long piece of green garden twine that he had found knocking about. (To be honest, Plug was an ace with motors and could usually be found revving some old banger or other outside his parent's, that's of course if he wasn't rehearsing. Any job that he did on his mates automobiles came with a personal guarantee, what he called his 'end of the road warranty').

On another occasion, Adam's car's thin excuse for a fan belt snapped en route to a rehearsal, but he didn't need Plug's help this time, fortunately one of his long Doctor Marten boot laces came quickly to the rescue.

Adam used to drive about town a lot at that time, either going to rehearsals or recording sessions or gigs, but sometimes he'd just drive around London when there wasn't anything else to do. Sometimes he'd give a lift to Rab if he needed to visit the Polydor offices for something or pay a visit to some of the record shops that he would regularly exchange rarities with.

One time he not only chauffeured Rab but one of his mates, who wanted to come along on one of their excursions. He was really big, roughly weighing in at what looked around twenty stone. Mind you, there was Rab as well and he wasn't small.

So there they were, all crammed into Adam's tiny car - its wheels already buckling under the pressure - as it had already taken about fifteen minutes just to get comfortable. And off they went. Only trouble was, Adam had left the hand break on, without realising and they spent the next twenty minutes cruising at about five miles an hour along the high street. They were beeped at and taxi's flashed their lights and lorry drivers stuck their fingers up and swore at them as they held up all the traffic in south London.

'Can't you go no faster?' Rab demanded, while doing the V's out of the window in reply to one of the lorry drivers shouting at them and once the driver caught one look at Rab's imposing demeanour he was instantly all sweetness and light.

'Er....I don't think so', Adam replied, nervously trying to rev the

Bambino's exhausted engine, but to no avail.

'Jesus....it must be me mate in the back of yer motor!'

'It ain't me!' implored his friend who was doing a good job of filling the whole of the back seat.

'If this goes on much longer', Adam reckoned, 'we'll be doing one long wheelie soon'. As they continued at a snail's pace down the street.

'Oi, you in the back! You'll have to get out!'

'No chance! I'm comfy'.

'Yer too fuckin' fat!'

'Bollocks I am!'

'You gotta get out!'

'Well, I ain't!'

'Oh, Christ!'

'I ain't getting out!'

'Get out! '

'Hang on a minute! Hang on! Hang on!' Adam butted in.

There was a pause.

'Er....I've left the hand break on...' he announced, feeling a right idiot.

'Argh, you stupid tink!' shouted Rab.

'Told you it weren't me!' his mate leaned over, with a triumphant grin.

'Ok. Ok!' replied Rab.

Suddenly there was a jolt and they all shifted forward about a foot as Adam released the hand break. As their collective mass shifted at a terrific rate Adam thought they were all goners for sure. Rab's teeth nearly ended up on the dashboard. Adam was close to head butting the steering column. The back passenger was not far from crushing everything in his path. There was a sound of buckling metal and a clanking exhaust and at the end of it, the car was only going slightly faster. They were now managing only about ten miles an hour if that and traffic behind them continued to beep and flash at them.

'Oh, for fuck's sake! It is you in the back!'

'No it ain't!'

'It is!' implored Rab completely running out of patience.

'It ain't! It's the motor!'

'How many times! It's you!!'

'No, it's this car!'

And on and on it went. They soon decided to return to Rab's before the car exploded and after a ridiculously slow journey back, with lots of recriminations, the car gave out a great sigh of relief when its occupants finally got out.

Unfortunately for the rear seat passenger, that was the last time they came along and the car was never quite the same again, although it did have its moments. One night, Adam was driving around the King's Road, before dropping off Rab who needed to deliver some tapes for the forthcoming recording in the studio. As they careered along Gunter Grove, having turned off the Fulham Road, Rab filled him in on all the local punk nostalgia.

'See that house over there? That's where Johnny Rotten lived'.

'Blimey!' Adam said squinting out of the window.

'He's over in the States now. Used to have loads of parties there. Sid Vicious and Poly Styrene and loads of other people used to go'.

'Did you?'

'Did I fuck! I'd only just come down to London then'.

'Oh, right....'

After Rab got out, Adam then collected Dave who was meeting him at

Sloane Square Tube station. He obviously hadn't eaten for a while and he looked famished.

'Alright!' opened Dave. 'Oi, look, is there anywhere we can stop as I'm starvin''.

'Yeah, down the King's Road if you like'.

'Yeah, great, and I can get myself summink'.

So off Adam sped once more, back down the King's Road. About half way down they saw a late night shop which Dave reckoned would be ideal for munchies. After Adam had stopped at the side of the road, Dave got out and traipsed into the store. Adam waited patiently in the Fiat and before you could say 'Cash Till', Dave was racing back with a large pizza and a big bag of crisps in his arms.

'Get goin'! Get goin'! Quick! I've nicked a pizza!!'

As Dave scrambled frantically back into the car, his legs almost hanging out of the door, like it was the 'Dukes of Hazard' there was a loud noise from the direction of the shop. A right commotion.

'Shit!' Adam said, panicking. 'You nicked a pizza?!'

'Yeah, now get goin'! Move it!'

'Jesus! I don't fuckin' believe it!'

He revved the accelerator pedal as fast as he could and luckily the trusty 650 cc's barked into life and off they raced, which must have been quite comical. A Fiat 126 being used as a getaway car. Problem was at the next traffic lights Adam stalled the engine, so Dave was frantically looking out of the back of the car expecting his pursuers to catch up with him at any moment. Thankfully, the engine roared again to life and they escaped and although Adam was worried that someone might have taken the car's registration number it turned out to be a false alarm.

'Why the fuck did you nick a pizza?!' said Adam disbelievingly, the G Force from his racing driving contorting his face.

'It was the first thing I could get me hands on!' said Dave as if he was some great train robber.

'Fuckin' hell!!' added Adam, shaking his head as the yellow Fiat burnt up the tarmac and disappeared into the night.

Yes, stupid they might have been, but the pizza tasted good and the cheese and onion crisps were wolfed down sharpish. And the car (eventually nicknamed the 'Meanaxe Mobile') had again proved itself more than up to the task.

So there Adam was, scrambling out of his favourite patched up Latin racer, right in front of the Newbury venue, ready for their local appearance and lo and behold there was none other than Dave himself, pacing about on the pavement looking really nervous. Of course he had something urgent to say.

'We ain't called Three Minute Warning anymore'.

'What?' Adam replied, sensing a bomb about to explode.

'We ain't Three Minute Warning?'

'What d'you mean?'

'We've had to change our name'.

'Why?!'

'There was this thing in the NME last week about a band called Four Minute Warning. They've just brought a record out'.

'So?!'

'Well that means we've gotta change our name'.

'Change the name?'

'Yeah....'

'To what?' Adam probed, more than suspicious.

There was a pause as Dave removed a large lump from his throat.

'Er.....The Walking Dead'.

'What?!'

'The Walking...Dead....'

'The WALKING DEAD?!'

'Yeah. Good name ain't it'.

'But...'

'I knew you'd like it!'

'Like it?! Why call us the Walking Dead?'

'Well, it's a line from one of our songs'.

'But who the fuck are the Walking Dead?!'

'WE ARE!' said Dave, confidently.

'No we're not we're THREE MINUTE WARNING!!'

'Walking Dead....' parried Dave, somewhat negatively.

'You've gotta be having me on?!'

'No. Straight up. It's on the posters. Look....'

'Oh.....Fuck me!'

And there they were. Two large posters with lettering big enough to knock you out,

"WALKING DEAD" + Support

hastily pasted up by the entrance to the venue.

'I don't believe this!'

'There's nothin' we can do about it. The other Minute Warning are bigger than us. They've got a single out!'

'SO?!!'

'It's like we'd gone and nicked the name off them!'

'What?! We had the name first!'

'Well....'

'We did!'

'Fucker...ain't it'.

'Fu - Oh, fuckin' shit!'

'I've told Plug....'

'You what?!'

'I've told him'..

'Yeah? And what does he think of it?'

'What?'

'The Name?!'

'He's ain't too happy about it'.

'D'you blame him?!'

'No, but he knows we ain't got no choice'.

'Oh, fuckin' great....'

This was going to be an interesting evening alright. Then it suddenly dawned on Adam that their audience from Basingstoke would probably not even know that the three likely lads were going to be playing in the neighbourhood. Adam reckoned that if they were aware that they were appearing they certainly weren't going to be expecting a drastic change of identity, especially one that conjured up images of mad zombies devouring human flesh down the high street and frightening experiments initiated by some insane professor late one stormy night.

Then Plug showed up.

'It's a fuckin' shit name ain't it!'

'Complete and utter bollocks!'

'Fuckin' Christ....'

'Yeah., but I s'pose we'll still have to fuckin' play', Adam replied, trying to restore a crumb of comfort.

'And what else could we do?' countered Dave. 'We'd only have to change it later anyhow'.

'But why didn't you change it AFTER the gig?!'

'I thought about it, but I reckoned we had to change it quick. I did it the other day'.

'Well, what about telling us?!' Plug said, stating the obvious.

'I had to make a decision, there and then and I saw this title on a horror vid?'

'Horror vid?!'

'Yeah, it was some horror film with zombies and they looked like punks...'

There was a long silence as the dust settled with a loud thud.

'Oh, well....FUCK IT!' said Plug.

'And we've still got the bleedin' gig to do!'

'JESUS!'

'Yeah, you're right'...., mumbled Dave, beginning to sweat.

As predicted, the gig turned out to be a complete disaster. The noisy support band had quite a few watching them, well, about ten people, but as soon as they finished they all walked out after them, obviously to obtain autographs. Meanwhile, the Walking Dead were left to play to the sound guy, Carol, a moody girlfriend of Dave's and Plug's brother, who didn't even have a dog (probably because he was too embarrassed to hang around) and what was worse, was the fact that the venue was quite large and while they played reluctantly onstage (Adam and Plug trying hard not to smash up all the instruments) they tried to work out what the takings at the door might be. But you didn't need to be a whiz with figures. It was quite clear. The money from the gig would probably just about finance a very short trip to the local sweet shop.

After the gig, the debrief was heated.

'WALKING – FUCKIN' - DEAD! That name's gotta go!'

'You're fuckin' right it has!'

'Well, what d'you suggest then?!' said Dave, trying to dodge the bullets.

'How about….the Complete Prats!' started Adam.

'Yeah, or….the Wailing Wallies!' said Plug, grinning.

'What about the Tepid Tits?!'

'The Crazy Craps?!'

'Heh! How about the Fucking Farts?!'

'Or the STUPID CUN -

'YEAH….Alright, ALRIGHT!' said Dave impatiently. 'Whatever it is, we're gonna have to think long and hard about it….'

'Righto….' said Plug, looking deflated.

And so they did. And after a week or so of flying recriminations, half of Basingstoke saying, 'Gig? What gig?!' and mind-numbing thought, the new name was launched triumphantly to the world (Well, a small town in Hampshire).

'FOUR MINDS CRACK'

The obvious fact that there were only three of them in the band didn't really matter. The name was a little bit quirky and they all liked it. The title itself was taken from the lyrics of a brilliant song 'Action Time Vision' by the band, Alternative TV, who were an early influence: Adam and Plug had played their stuff over and over again in rehearsals, as their simple mix of punk and reggae-dub was irresistible (the lead singer, Mark Perry, had been the creator of the first Punk Fanzine 'Sniffin' Glue' and was a top lyricist as well).

So now they had their new name which they were all completely happy with (one that thankfully didn't warrant accompanying cackles as they walked along the street or didn't encourage witty references to schlock horror movies as they sipped a quiet pint in the local). It was beyond doubt. Even though the rails had definitely come off for a moment, they were now thankfully back on track. It was business as usual again. Admittedly, after one huge sigh of relief. And as the saying goes, 'throw a large enough brick into a pond and you're bound to get some ripples'.

They had literally returned from the dead. But this time they would be taking no prisoners. This time they were in full out attack, and never giving up. So just you watch out The Clash. Just you watch out Wembley Stadium. Yeah, just you watch out folks.

100 CLUB

Recording with The Wall went smoothly in the Chelsea studios and most of the tracks to be included on the 7" EP and 12" were put down on the demo. To work in such a large established studio environment (a stone's throw from the hallowed Stamford Bridge) was a real eye opener and Adam was definitely learning fast about the ins and outs and the dos and dont's. And although tweaking controls and watching the master tape spin round wasn't really his cup of tea, creating lots of audio commotion in the recording booth again and again definitely was.

Likewise, the gig upstairs at the legendary Ronnie Scott's in Soho, went off without so much as a hitch, which was a relief, because Adam had spent what seemed like most of the day between sound check and gig, sitting nervously with Rab in an American style diner off Frith street, killing time. He felt like a windup toy guitarist about to be let loose upon the West End.

'When you come on, don't go mad like a tink!'

'Ok...'

'Try to keep in time!' said Rab, side-tracked by a pre gig fry up.

'Don't worry. I'll keep it as tight as I can', Adam replied as convincingly as he could, his fork tapping out an anxious rhythm on a salt cellar while 'Party Fears Two' by the Associates, blared out from some distant radio.

'Good. Any trouble on stage, look over to me an' I'll sort it out'.

'Cheers....' Adam muttered, swallowing his butterflies.

As it turned out, playing the gig was a real buzz, not only because Adam found himself on stage alongside older, more experienced musicians but it felt great to belt out anthems that only six months before he had been quite content just to sing along to on his record player at home. One song in particular called 'Hobby For A Day' he played with extra relish as it was one of his all time favourites: a haunting and memorable riff. It was all about the consequences of joining the army, something that some of his friends from school had already recently done and no doubt due to the Falklands war, were now perhaps regretting. Especially Adam's mate, Alex's older brother. The once proud possessor of the Pistols back catalogue was now sadly a distant name on the memorial at Goose Green.

The record had started with the sound of a soldier respirating atmospherically through a gas mask, while drums and guitars punched and flailed about. Out of the intro emerged a memorable bass riff and solid drumming that dragged the song through the nightmare of war. The reality of the valiant soldier, his legs now amputated and his eyesight lost forever. Live, the song almost seemed to smash through the grubby walls of the venue with its intensity, Rab all the while trying to rein in Adam's youthful exuberance and his attempts to jump around, the bassist Claire, echoing Andy's passionate delivery with swift, ghostlike phrasing. The nerves were all the more immediate, as Adam's brothers were also attending the gig. Considering that they had played a very large part in developing his interest in music in the first place, it was only fair that he was now busy rearranging their hearing. The audience's attentions were now cranked up high as the band continued the fully focussed performance, strutting out the back catalogue; New Way, Exchange, Ghetto, Remembrance, etc, and songs off the recent second album, Dirges and Anthems. Meanwhile, dread-eyed punks filtered about and beyond, knocked clean out of their sweaty stupors.

Nearing the climax, the band launched into another terrace anthem, a popular first album track called Career Mother, which sounded like Slade on a bucket load of amphetamines. Once the audience was on the ropes, with little alternative but to shout out 'More!' The Wall powered into the frenetic new cover version of Day Tripper by The Beatles, the instantly recognisable intro riff unleashed from Adam's guitar. For a bleary-eyed youngster, who had only recently met his eighteenth birthday head on, Adam justifiably considered 'it wouldn't get much better than that' and if he never did anything music-wise ever again, he could at least feel that he had been some small part of a greater picture, however blurred the vision.

After the gig, his brothers patted him on the back and told him how surprised they were with the level of his fretwork, even if it was for no more than just getting up there and having a pop and as exiting punters dodged the spilt beer, rubbish and puke littering the dance floor, Adam savoured some celebratory pints of lager, bought for his noisy exertions. And then a few nights later it was repeated all over again, at The Blue Boy, Skunx.

After the exhilarating experience of the gigs, the adrenalin took about a week to fade back into Adam's blood stream as the breath of day to day living once more took hold. It seemed like there wasn't a dull moment anywhere to be found and it wasn't long before Dave was on the phone again, his head chock full of plans.

'I've picked up this old amp that geezer from Mud used to use!'

'You're joking?!'

'No. It's a battered, old hundred watt Laney with cab and it kicks like a mule!'

'Great....all I need now is a silly dress like the guitarist!'

'Yeah, and don't forget the dodgy earrings!'

Dave laughed loudly and after regaling Adam with a chorus of 'Tiger Feet!' it was back to more serious matters once again.

'Oh yeah, I forgot to tell you. Dave Parsons wants to sell his guitar'.

Adam had been looking for a more permanent replacement, as it was too difficult to borrow the Flying V all the time and his Aria wasn't quite up to the demanding task of axe grinding, and after pondering the proposition, he eventually found himself licking his lips in anticipation.

'Which one?' he said hopefully.

'His Gibson SG'.

'What, the purple one?'

'Yeah....'

'He's used it on the telly and that gig we saw and everything!'

'I know'.

'How much does he want for it?'

'A hundred and fifty quid'.

'A hundred and fifty?'

'Yep'.

Adam thought for a moment. For a guitar with such previous punk history it could hardly be bettered. Then he thought about his recent wallet-bulging wage packet from his adventures with The Wall.

'Well, I can use some of the gig and recording money'.

'Nice one, cos I told him we'd be round his to pick it up'.

'When?'

'Next week'.

'That means I'll have it in time for the 100 Club!'

'That's what I was thinkin....'

(Rab had sorted out a support slot for Four Minds Crack at the legendary Oxford Street venue, supporting the punk band The Straps who he knew well and needed a support act. One of the Wall's ex-guitarist's, Andy Forbes, had also played for them so there were strong links).

When Adam and Dave went round Parsons' house, set in a secluded Surrey village not far from Hersham, to pick up the guitar for sale,

Adam had a good look round at the guitarist's memorabilia - lots of framed discs and dramatic pictures from Sham's heyday and the inevitable rack of guitars. He looked at all the stuff in awe and when Parsons presented his Gibson SG, which he was so kindly parting from, pulled like magic from a plush lined flight case, he filled Adam in on the guitar's colourful past.

'It's great. Got a fantastic sound. I used it for years, till I got pissed off with all the agro. At the end of one of our last gigs - I think it was the Rainbow - I whacked it into my amp and the stage and snapped it. Look....you can see where the neck's been broken'.

'Yeah....right...' Adam mumbled, incapable of stringing a sentence together.

'But it's been fixed really good. No problems'.

As he poured wide-eyed over the guitar, Dave kept saying, 'Yeah, that's quality....' while he slurped his tea and dunked a biscuit. The fact that the guitar had been damaged live and then completely repaired just added to its aura. 'What a brilliant weapon to have in the band's musical armoury', Adam concluded, 'an instrument with real history and some story to tell'.

He passed over the readies to the Sham man without hesitation and told him that the guitar had definitely found the right new home. Adam was absolutely certain he wasn't going to be smashing it up on stage, he was more likely going to be relentlessly rubbing varnish into the wood, or conscientiously polishing the mother of pearl. But on the other hand, there was no way that he was going to be too scared to play it.

The following week Adam got his chance. The day of the gig at the 100 Club they all met up with Plug, outside his Basingstoke picture house. It was a handy central location and near the main shopping arcade. Si, the band's number one, hardcore Mohican fan, was there too, as he had volunteered to be their roadie for the gig and to help with the general order of play and crucial equipment carrying and if they met up with trouble, to give the impression that he wouldn't be running away from it (well not straightaway anyway). Also there was his off-on, on-off girlfriend Liz, who was a well spoken, gorgeous punkette from Poplar (none other than Elizabeth Hurley, the media magnet). Dave boasted that he had had a bit of a fling with Liz's sister, although as Plug succinctly put it.

'He probably just got a sticky finger....'

They finished loading up and soon realised that there was going to be absolutely no room for passengers, not even in the glove compartments. Decisions had to be made and fast. Liz had already seen the bands first gig, so she wasn't too bothered to leave Si on his own, wedged ridiculously between an amp and a drum stool. After a bit of dilly-dallying, they double checked that they had all the equipment, including a recently purchased second hand Vox AC15 valve amp and once everything was ticked off from their mental list, they began their precarious way towards the 'smoke'.

As they travelled up the motorway to the great metropolis, being vigilant that they didn't lose any important items on the tarmac along the way - like one of the band members for example - the storm clouds gathered ominously and it wasn't long before all hell let loose. As the driving wind and rain shook them about in their mini convoy of trusty rust buckets, Adam tried to go through the lyrics in his head to a new song called In The Night that he and Plug had recently penned. Adam fancied them playing it as part of their set at the 100 Club, because it was edgy and as catchy as you like.

The day is over the dusk draws in

You hurry home before the night sets in.

You reach your door as the darkness falls

See shadows dancing on the wall.

In the night

They're creeping up on you.

In the dark

You don't know what to do.

The grey wind howls

Along deserted streets.

The dead of night

The dead of night.

The TV flickers a cold blue light

A fluorescent image of another life.

The video figures won't hear your screams

When you wake up from their neon dreams.

Sat all alone again wishing the night away

Your anxiety lasts till the dawn of another day.

In your mind it's not just a fantasy

You dream your dreams and know no reality.

Adam felt a real buzz when they finally arrived in Oxford Street, 'This is where the first major punk festival with the Sex Pistols, The Clash, The Damned and the Buzzcocks took place', he thought to himself. And here they were following on in their own kind of way, albeit without any of the fame or the notoriety but still passing on the musical baton in their own individual manner.

After unloading and the cursory cigarette, they entered the venue, via a narrow but welcoming entrance way and a street sandwich board. They all got such a feeling of nostalgia, so much so that Adam nearly dropped his amplifier on Plug's foot. The 100 Club was the one punk venue that Adam hadn't yet been to and not only that, but it had also featured greatly in the sixties and early seventies with seminal films like Blow Up, where there was a great gig sequence with The Yardbirds. So it felt almost familiar, in a celluloid sort of way.

In fact, everything about the place jumped out at them. The nostalgia. The rock history. You could just imagine the Sex Pistols creating a right old commotion right there on that long narrow stage, or The Clash with their paint splattered clothing, crashing out some sheet metal riffing. You could picture Sid Vicious attempting to hit the drums during Siouxsie and the Banshees' shambolic debut, or the Buzzcocks, letting rip with their manic buzzsaw delivery, and even The Damned playing at a thousand miles an hour as if their lives depended on it.

Adam wasn't bothered that they were only playing in a support slot. The fact that they were there at all was enough for him. They had a long time to sit around, so they were able to watch the headline band The Straps, a well known south London outfit who had supported many well known bands like the Damned, going through their paces in the sound check. They sounded a bit like Crisis, and the guitarists Simon Werner (also from Kirk Brandon's The Pack) and Dave Reeves liked to play the theme tunes to both Camberwick Green and Trumpton as they messed around in the warm up between songs, which raised a few laughs from Adam and Plug. As The Straps continued to rehearse through their songs, Dave turned around.

'Shit! I've left my drum clips at home!'

'What?'

'My clips to hold the bass drum down. I ain't got 'em!'

'What does that mean?' Adam replied scratching his head.

'They hold the whole thing together on the stage so it don't move about'.

'Oh…great!' said Plug, who looked over to Rab who was starting to chuckle to himself.

'What the fuck are we gonna do?'

'Can't you borrow somebody else's?' Adam advised cleverly.

'No, they won't be no good. They've got a different kit'.

'Oh, fuckin' hell!' said Plug again and Rab was off in hysterics.

'Look it ain't my fault!' pleaded Dave, starting to panic.

'Yeah, it is!'

'No it ain't. I just forgot 'em that's all!'

'Ah, Jeez....you lot are useless!' said Rab cutting in, his solid, tattooed arms folded over each other.

'Have you got anythin' I can use Rab?' asked Dave, hopefully.

'Aye, I just happen to have some drum clips on me'.

'Yeah?!' said Dave wide-eyed.

'No, course not, yer tink!' and Rab was off in hysterics again.

'Rab, can't you help us out?'

There was a pause as Rab tried to contain his laughter.

'Help you out?...'

'Yeah....'

'Help you out?!'

'Oh, bleedin' henry....' said Dave almost throwing in the towel.

'Look, you'll be okay, just put something in front of the kit'.

'Like what?' replied Dave.

'Well, I dunno....' said Rab, trying to contain himself again.

'Look, let's just sort it out in the sound check', concluded Plug.

'Aye, good idea....'

So they did.

The sound check was spent watching Dave's drums sliding around the stage as they put some of the songs through their paces. It must have been like watching 'Punks on Ice'. The 100 Club stage was so narrow that Dave was in danger of ending up in the audience with the drum kit right on top of him, but you had to give it to him, it didn't stop him playing. Not for a moment. He'd stand up mid song like Keith Moon, and instead of smashing up all his equipment, he'd try and drag the bass drum back upstage a little while whacking the toms with one of his sticks. It reminded Adam of the beginning of The Monkees TV programme, where one of them is lying in a bed being pushed along down the high street. Adam could just picture Dave still playing for dear life as he glided past the shoppers along Oxford Street.

Then Si, their trusty roadie, came up with a brainwave.

'Why don't I crouch on the edge of the stage in front of the kit and stop it from moving about?'

'Heh, good one....' said Plug

'Yeah, that'll do it', Adam added, turning to Dave who was looking exhausted.

'See, it won't move about then'.

'Aye, try it out...' said Rab who was now sat in the auditorium.

Si did just that, and you know what? It worked. Only thing was it looked completely ridiculous. Instead of standing in front of the kit, Si somehow put his head right inside the bass drum and his arms out to the side outstretched, while the rest of his body sort of hunched over and around, his Mohican spikes resting against the cymbals. It looked a right picture. Sort of Performance Art - punk style. But they didn't have much choice. Dave wanted to use his own drums and was adamant about it. Perhaps he felt that he wouldn't be able to play so well on somebody else's kit, especially as fellow drummers like Rab, would be present at the gig.

After the sound check they sauntered off and got a beer, still chatting about the consequences of Dave's mobile kit. The stage was so narrow that Dave's drums were right at the front with Adam and Plug stood either side, and that was all in front of the main bands' equipment. The second support band used the Straps kit and they were a really heavy punk outfit, a bit like the band Discharge, who played one chord at a million miles an hour for what seemed like twenty seconds and then they'd begin another. Their singer, who looked like a gangly serial killer, ranted and raved about the state of the nation with lots of swearing thrown in. Adam thought their name sounded like 'Asylum' but he couldn't be too certain, as it seemed almost as if they had just started up and were only just getting their anarchy together.

As Adam watched them, he suddenly wondered how Four Minds Crack would go down because he knew they weren't a traditional million miles an hour, one chord, twenty second song sort of band. They were trying to do their own thing. Well, as much as they could, because it was becoming nigh on impossible to be unique. You had to follow the leader to a certain extent because if you had a guitar, bass and drums there was no way that you were going to be sounding like a classical orchestra for example. Mind you that was half the fun of it. Keeping it simple and hopefully keeping it real.

After the sound checking was finished the doors opened and a right motley bunch of punters plodded through the venues doors. There were some doomy looking leather studded punks who had probably come to see the support band. Some of Four Minds Crack's Basingstoke contingent, mainly Si's mates, who were obviously coming along to catch their very own Mohican buddy cavort in front of Dave. And there were some other assorted punks and new wave types who had turned up en masse to watch The Straps.

'What are you wearing for the gig?' Plug asked Dave during a quieter moment.

'Er, this....' said Dave revealing a freshly washed white T-shirt under a tatty sweater. The shirt had a cheesy picture of the band 'Sweet' on the front and their name in lurid gold writing leapt right out.

'You're joking?' challenged Plug, his eyes almost popping out of his head.

'No. Why?!'

'The SWEET?!!'

'Yeah, what's wrong with that?'

'What's wrong with that?! Just that they're a silly band from the 70's. That's what!'

'Nah. They're great! I love 'em. "Ballroom Blitz!" "Ballroom Blitz!"

'But this is a punk night?!' replied Plug trying to cut in.

'Yeah, so?'

'They'll fuckin' murder us when they see your shirt!'

'Nah, they won't'.

'Yeah, they will!'

'Won't'.

'Will. Just look at their dodgy barnets?'

'So what! It's the music. "It's, it's a Ballroom Blitz!" "It's, it's a Ballroom Blitz!"'

'But they look right states!' sighed Plug, beginning to give up.

'Complete plonkers….' Adam added, shaking his head (even though he had to admit he had loved their stuff. But that was in the mid 70's).

'No, they ain't….'

There was a pause as Dave launched himself into the air guitar intro to Teenage Rampage.

'What's the problem lads?' Rab chipped in reluctantly.

'It's Dave. He wants to wear his dodgy 'Sweet' T-shirt on stage!' said Plug.

'No one's goin' to see him anyhow. You've got that Mohican bloke in the way remember!'

Rab had a point, but Adam and Plug weren't convinced. Sweet were definitely not punk and anyway, Dave was usually the one who was the most fashion conscious, so it seemed an even more strange choice of stage wear. And Adam and Plug remembered all too well the consequences of Dave wearing the wrong T-shirt at the Sham gig, but it made no difference. He was unmovable.

'This'll be interesting', Adam said to Plug, 'a mobile drummer, wearing a Sweet T-shirt, playing behind a punk performance artist'.

'Yeah....they won't have seen that before', Plug chuckled reluctantly.

Before long they found themselves up on stage. Because of all the problems before the gig, Adam's nerves weren't as bad as he had expected. But once he got up there he was still bricking it. This was the 100 Club after all. Before the first song he managed to get a bit of applause for Si, their very own human drum-clip. It worked a treat because as soon as they stormed into No Rules, Si tried to start jumping around which just looked silly, but some of the punks in the audience lapped it up and started to pogo along with them.

'Are you gonna be fuckin' off then!' muttered one punk to Adam at the side of the stage, sneeringly trying to put him off.

'No, I reckon we'll be sticking around for a bit!' he replied instinctively.

'Fuckin' SWEET?!' the heckler replied ironically.

'Brilliant', Adam thought. 'Si's hilarious leaping about obviously wasn't working after all'.

'Yeah, it is fuckin' sweet!' Adam added as they piled into another tune.

That seemed to do the trick and by the end of the gig, the rude punk seemed to be enjoying the set and Adam even caught him jumping up and down, during their last couple of songs. That was certainly compliment enough.

Dave, even in his Sweet T-shirt, hit the kit with awesome venom, and Adam and Plug sat on the top of the din with a solid crunch. They finished off the set with their recently written 'In the Night' and it received a loud cheer from the Basingstoke contingent, who although not accustomed to it, gave it the thumbs up and by the end were even singing along to the chorus.

After their set, all three of them sat back exhausted, but relieved, to watch the headliners, The Straps. As their potent Punk musing got underway, Dave admiring open mouthed the bands expert drummer (none other than Jim Walker, the original drummer of Public Image), who was helped greatly by the fact that his kit remained largely stationary. They cranked through their catchy set with a lot of appreciation from their hardcore following with brilliant renditions of their early singles like 'Brixton', the rhythm guitarist again borrowing Adam's amplifier, because his had blown up at the end of the sound check. While the lead singer Jock Strap, worked up the crowd masterfully, mates of Si's championed the irrepressible roadie.

'Oi, Si! How's your head, mate?!'

'It's alright....'

'Fuckin' ell! I've never seen that before. Jumpin' about in front of the drum kit!'

'We might even add it in again at the next gig just for a laugh!' Si chuckled.

'You'll end up deaf!'

'....What?!...' muttered Si, daftly.

There was a momentary pause.

'Oh, for fuck's sake....'

You see Si was not only a roadie, he was also a comedian.

Reports of the support gig were definitely positive. There was even a rumour that one of the large white noughts from the 100 Club stage backdrop had fallen off during Four Minds Crack's set. Dave was adamant.

'Nah, it never!'

'How would you know? You were too busy twattin' the drums!' said Rab.

'A zero fell on your head!' laughed Plug. 'I saw it!'

'Aye, it did. Didn't you notice?!' said Rab pulling Dave's leg further.

'Yeah, the sound guy stuck it back up half way through!' Adam added.

'Your havin' us on?!'

'No we ain't....' teased Plug.

'No way that happened!' said Dave, his head beginning to spin around.

'Yeah....it did. I could see it from where I was standing', Carol testified.

'Look, you're all havin' us on! No way that nought fell off?!'

Everyone nodded in unison.

'IT DID!!'

There was a pause as Dave squirmed.

'Oh, no....'

It was confirmed. Dave was sometimes even more gullible than Adam, although thinking about it, between the two of them, it probably would have been a photo finish.

Despite all the theatrics there was much to take from the event. They had played well, despite the portable percussion. In fact they had created a little bit of a commotion. More than ten Punks had pogoed up the front while they were on and they were only the support. Even better was the news from the management. The woman running the bookings for the 100 Club had given them the seal of approval.

'I like you lot. You can play your instruments'.

Adam reckoned that had she seen them only a year before, she probably would have called the Police to escort them immediately off the premises.

'We need some supports and you'll fit the bill perfectly'.

When Dave reported back to Adam and Plug, they were made up.

'Great! Now we can build a London following'.

'That's after we've cracked Basingstoke!' Reminded Dave.

'Yeah, and Basingstoke must be cracked!' said Plug wittily.

Soon after, Rab worked with them again, producing for them in an eight track studio in Basingstoke. They put some more of their old songs down on tape and called their demo 'Nervous Breakdown', because the songs were full of angst and youthful energy and hinted too at the third world war that might just be coming around the corner.

They even created the 'Hooligan Nights choir', named after one of The Wall's songs, which consisted of them all performing football terrace style backing vocals to the song 'Nowhere To Go'. For even more authenticity, they shouted out a loud 'Piss Off!' at the end of the song. No one was exactly sure who they were aiming it towards, but it sounded like they meant it and coupled with one of Dave's manic drum rolls, it certainly stood out.

Alongside their burgeoning efforts, The Wall's 'Day Tripper' EP and 12" LP were finally completed at Southern Studios, a large 24 track studio in North London, renowned as the studio run by the anarchist punk band, Crass, and where they recorded their records. It was another great studio to gain the experience of playing guitar in and Adam enjoyed helping out with Rab again on some raucous backing vocals as part of the Hooligan Nights choir once more and he was able to tinker about with the odd extra guitar run. It was all about putting the finishing touches to the record before the final mastering process. When the single was finally released, Adam read the press response in the music press avidly, which commented on the record's frenetic and noisy credentials. The lively Slade cover was also highlighted. He even watched excitedly as Day Tripper crept up the Indie charts.

Unfortunately, behind the scenes, all was not well. Bands like The Wall were starting to throw in the towel. Even Adam, Plug and Dave had begun to question the merits of continuing to jump about in their worn and repetitive clothing. A great support slot in Andover with the anti-nuclear band, The Subhumans, went begging when they pulled out at the last minute. It was partly due to Plug having the flu and also to their contradictory lack of ambition. It seemed as if they were more prepared to be brilliant at being failures, than being mediocre at being successes. Adam was certain it was a great opportunity missed. The Subhumans were a well followed band and were regularly in all the music papers. They were intelligent and melodic and played stirringly at a hundred miles an hour. Perhaps if Four Minds Crack had played, they could have converted some of their colourful tribe, but it was becoming clear: At the very moment that it seemed to be getting somewhere, the fickle hand of fate was tugging the tartan punk rug from under their feet. They had even been offered a recording contract in New Zealand of all places for a compilation punk album. Only problem was the fact that none of them could afford the expensive air fare over.

'What the hell are we gonna do now?' Adam said to Dave with a bee in his bonnet.

'We've just gotta get on with it…'

'Like how?'

'Well, we've got the gig at the '5-1-0 Centre'.

'Could be our last', said Plug, as if he was almost staring into a crystal ball.

'I hope we get a good crowd'.

'Should do, it's down the Harrow Road. It's old Clash territory…'

'They won't mind you wearing your T-shirt then', said Plug with a raised eyebrow.

'Nah…' replied Dave, acknowledging the leg pull.

Plug was proved right. It was pretty much Four Minds Crack's last gig. They did one further demo session at the studios in Reading which they produced themselves but as far as playing live was concerned, it was their last major live appearance. But it least it was the best. The venue was packed and they played for well over an hour, with two encores, all for the benefit of both the Right to Work and CND, a combined campaign. They even picked up a following of local kids who promised to make it to their very next performance. Shame it didn't look like there was going to be one.

SPLITTING UP

Everyone seemed to want to move on. Start up another chapter. Do something different. Or just get the hell out. The old yell and shout of punk had given way to a new sparkling era. The one chord wonders were now commercially synthesized. Grubby misfits were now trying to be synchronised outfits. New Romanticism had already kicked in big time and death knell acts like 'Wham' were fast coming round the corner. Yes, it was clear. The eighties were taking hold. Grasping everything into its sugary, floury pulp.

Bands were splitting up, going west, never to be heard of again. Others were going east and doing the same. Punk and it's more commercial offshoot, New Wave, were now regimented vaudeville acts and the 'Oi' movement was a predictable bootboy racket at best. Even Ska had become scarred. It was meltdown. One great musical 'No Entry' sign.

On the personal front, Carol had decided that a life of rock n roll, or as she sometimes put it, 'a life on the dole', wasn't really for her. Adam couldn't believe it, although he had sensed it coming for some time. The cracks couldn't be ignored, and he suddenly realised that he had been more concerned about music and where it was all going and the monthly purchasing of guitar strings and plectrums, than his girlfriend. Perhaps he only had himself to blame.

'But the band… That last gig. We had a sell out!'

'I know…but there's no money in it. It's not going anywhere'.

'Well, we'll get on a tour with other bands, you'll see!'

'I wanna go back to college..'

'College?!' said Adam, almost choking.

'You know, get some more qualifications…'

'Well, what about us?'

'What about it?'

'What are we gonna do?!'

'I dunno….' Carol then slowly turned her head and looked away, and Adam found himself in a corny scene from a movie.

'Right….' Adam sighed, as he took in the bombshell.

They were moving apart, and fast. Even Carol's mum wasn't the same, she had even stopped asking him how everything was all going. The result was clear. For Adam, living with Carol wasn't an option anymore. He would have to bite the bullet, return home and despite all the difficulties, start all over again.

Down at Stamford Bridge, Chelsea had avoided a potentially calamitous relegation to the Third Division (the lowest point in their illustrious history) by the skin of their teeth, thanks to a last gasp goal from Clive Walker against none other than Bolton Wanderers. Off the pitch, there was a combustible new chairman in the shape of Ken Bates, who had bought the ailing club for just £1 (shame Adam hadn't heard about his hasty intervention earlier, because he certainly had more than a pound in his rusty old 'Cash for Chelsea' tin). But whatever, it was clearly all change and so the great and unending rebuilding of the club began.

Inevitably, all this upheaval would have an effect on Adam. As far as The Wall were concerned that was all out of his hands, because he had no say in the decision making and as it transpired, the lead singer wanted, like Carol, to jack it all in and return to art college up north. The bassist meanwhile wanted out and Rab had his mind made up to set up his own production company, so that band's future was now written. It didn't have one.

Adam toyed with the idea of playing for other bands, even considering a guitar vacancy in the UK Subs which he had been told about, but he just couldn't get enthusiastic playing other peoples stuff, however good it was. And everyone was sounding just like a broken record. Maybe it really all was just an impossible dream. Punk's image had kissed the mirror and the reflection had long since shattered. As a result, by the grand old age of nineteen, Adam was feeling burnt out.

With Four Minds Crack, Dave had begun to voice 'artistic differences'.

'Punk's goin' nowhere. It's had it. Let's do somethin' else'.

'Like what?' Adam replied, almost shrugging.

'I dunno. How about Psychobilly - like the Meteors or King Kurt?'

'I thought you said guitar based music was finished?'

'Yeah, I did....well, I meant - 'cept for that'.

'On stage they just chuck baked beans over each other or jump in the crowd'.

'Yeah, I know. They're a good laugh!'

Once Dave had said his piece, they would spend the next hour or so trying to think of an alternative avenue for their musical ambitions, even if it meant contemplating quiffing up their hair and becoming second division Rockabilly's, or an alarming Alarm. But it was no use. There was no way that Adam was suddenly going to become an irascible Shakin' Stevens or a shady Showaddywaddy when the sonic junk of punk cluttered up his blood stream. It would be like moving from one empty test tube to another with no guarantee of success (ironically for Dave, his Punk ambitions would be far from over as he would later go on to drum for the UK Subs, the Angelic Upstarts and the Sex Gang Children).

Plug had already confirmed that he had completely lost the desire to play live.

'I just don't enjoy it anymore, mate...'

'What d'you mean?' Adam countered, trying not to look too concerned.

'You know, playing in front of a live audience'.

'Why?'

'Dunno....just don't fancy it, that's all'.

'I see....'

'Sorry mate...' Plug said, almost to himself.

It was a major setback, as Plug was fast becoming more than an accomplished musician, and setting the sonic for the band (at least in later years he too would find his niche with his own recording facility and some tasty session playing).

The band's sound which had rubber stamped their individuality, also turned out to be a noose around their neck. They never really wanted to fit into any category or pigeon hole that people put in their way - 'You can play your instruments so how can you call yourselves punks?' - and now wasn't the time to start.

But another thing was clear. If Adam could get it together and play guitar in a band and sing the songs at the same time in front of the occasional large crowd of people, who would sometimes show their displeasure by throwing things, and if they showed appreciation it would be with spitting, or jumping up and down, it meant only one thing: Adam had the bottle to get up on stage and give it a go.

'Punk is long dead. All over', he thought. 'But what about doing something else? Something other than music? But what?'

He didn't really know. He hadn't really ever thought about it much before. He never seemed to have the time. And time was moving on.

Adam paused for a moment, to take stock, and looked out of his bedroom window. In the distance he could just make out an aeroplane dashing through the clear sky, its long tracer tapering away like someone's memory. Eventually it disappeared from view and then he turned back and surveyed his bedroom. Posters, graffiti and Chelsea emblems covered the walls. Musical equipment and power leads lay all about. Ashtrays and cold cups of tea sat around as a portable black and white telly flickered in the corner. On the screen was some pompous Politician talking about 'youth opportunity'. Adam stared at the image for a moment and thought to himself, 'I bet he doesn't mean opportunity of the "Do-It-Yourself" kind'.

When he had finally taken the whole thing in and chuckled at the sight, with a steady hand he slowly placed his trusty Gibson SG back in its battered old case and ritually closed and locked up the lid.

Lightning Source UK Ltd.
Milton Keynes UK
30 March 2011

170121UK00002B/12/P

9 781452 001524